D1290863

Death of a Doll

HILDA LAWRENCE

PENGUIN BOOKS

Penguin Books Ltd, Harmondsworth,
Middlesex, England
Penguin Books, 625 Madison Avenue,
New York, New York 10022, U.S.A.
Penguin Books Australia Ltd, Ringwood,
Victoria, Australia
Penguin Books Canada Limited, 2801 John Street,
Markham, Ontario, Canada L3R 1B4
Penguin Books (N.Z.) Ltd, 182–190 Wairau Road,
Auckland 10, New Zealand

First published in the United States of America by
Simon & Schuster, Inc., 1947
First published in Great Britain by
Chapman & Hall 1948
Published in Penguin Books in Great Britain 1954
Published in Penguin Books in the
United States of America 1982

LIBRARY OF CONGRESS CATALOGING IN PUBLICATION DATA
Lawrence, Hilda.
Death of a doll.
Reprint. Originally published: New York:
Simon and Schuster, 1947 (An Inner sanctum mystery).
I. Title.   II. Series.
[PS3523.A9295D4   1982]   813'.52   82-5200
ISBN 0 14 00.6307 2   AACR2

Printed in the United States of America by
Offset Paperback Mfrs., Inc., Dallas, Pennsylvania
Set in Caledonia

To
L. W.

DEATH OF A DOLL

1

Angeline Small stepped out of the elevator at five o'clock and nodded to Kitty Brice behind the switchboard.

"Cold!" she said with a bright grimace. "Have they lighted the fire in the lounge?"

"Yes, Miss Small."

"Good," Miss Small said. But she walked briskly across the square lobby and checked for herself. There was only one girl in the lounge, a night worker in a Western Union office who went off to her job when the other girls came home. Miss Small found this routine confusing. When she went to her own bed at midnight, after coffee and gossip with Monny, she wanted to know that all of her seventy girls were safe and sound in their seventy good, though narrow, cots, sleeping correctly and dreamlessly because they were properly nourished and had no ugly little troubles that they hadn't confessed.

Miss Small switched on more lights, approved the fire and the bowls of fresh chrysanthemums, and spoke to the girl who was huddled in a deep chair with her eyes closed.

"Good evening, Lillian. Or should it be good morning?"

The girl looked up with a long, insolent stare and closed her eyes again.

Time for a little heart-to-heart talk with this one, Miss Small decided. Mustn't have sulks and surliness, such a bad example for the others. Perhaps a tiny note in her mailbox, an invitation to a nice cup of tea in my room. These poor, love-starved babies, I must do all I can.

"Isn't that a new coat, dear?" she asked.

The girl got up and brushed by the outstretched hand. "Excuse me," she said. "I forgot something."

Miss Small watched her cross the lobby with an arrogant stride and enter the elevator. I'll win her over, she promised herself, but I won't say anything to Monny. Poor Monny. She worries so when she knows I've been hurt. . . . She looked at the wrist watch Monny had given her the Christmas before and admired the winking diamonds. Five after five. Monny would be winding up her conference with Mrs. Fister and the meals would be better for about three days. Then they'd have coffee jelly again. I do wish she'd let me talk to Mrs. Fister, she fretted. I know how to handle people.

She returned to the lobby and entered the railed enclosure that was the office. A broad, flat desk faced the street entrance and behind it was the switchboard. A panel of push bells covered the wall behind the board. The bells rang in the rooms at seven in the morning and six in the evening. That was when the dining room opened. They also rang to announce visitors, phone calls, and emergencies. In the five years of its existence Hope House, a Home for Girls, had met and vanquished one emergency—a fire in a wastebasket. At right angles to the desk stood an orderly hive of glass-covered mailboxes, too often empty.

Miss Small glanced at her own box and spoke reprovingly.

"Kitty!"

Kitty gathered herself together and rose in sections. She was a tall, thin girl with poor skin and lips that were faintly blue.

"There's something in my box, Kitty, and you didn't give it to me."

"Headache," Kitty murmured. "I'm sorry, Miss Small, but you went by so fast before, and it's only a note Miss Brady put in."

"Miss Brady? Hand it to me at once, please." Miss Small tried to keep the pleasure out of her voice. Darling ola Monny, she told herself, she's thought of something nice for us to do later on. Maybe the theater, or a really good movie, or a little supper at that new French place. She opened the envelope carelessly under Kitty's curious gaze.

ANGEL [Monny wrote], Fister was frightful, wept all over the place and I'm exhausted. But we've got to keep the old fool happy, so I'm taking her out to tea because—this is what I tell her—because she needs to get out more, and what would we do without her! After that I've got to see Marshall-Gill about the party, she phoned. Angel, you'll have to take over the desk for me until Plummer goes on at eight. There's a new girl coming in, Ruth Miller, I'm afraid I forgot to tell you. Forgive? She's to go in with April Hooper. Explain to her about April, will you? That's something else I forgot, but you'll do it so much better than I would! I'll come to your room at the usual. Yours, M.

Miss Small tucked the note in her blouse and sat at the desk, smiling at the daily report that was fastened to the blotter. Monica Brady's sprawling hand had okayed a suspicion of mice on the second floor, uncovered a flaw in the addition of a plumber's bill, and questioned room 304's explanation of why she had stayed out all night. Under 304's explanation, which was a new one, she found the new girl's registration card. Ruth Miller, age twenty-nine, saleswoman at Blackman's, no family or known relatives. Then came the confidential information in the staff code. Middle class, some refinement, shy, not a mixer, underweight, poor vision and teeth. Probably tonsils. Recommended by M. Smith and M. Smith.

Miss Small frowned. That meant three girls from Blackman's. It wasn't wise to have more than two from the same place. Two could be friends, three could be troublesome.

The front door swung open, admitting a raw, damp wind and a chattering pair who called "Good evening,

Miss Small," as they hurried to the elevator. The evening had begun.

From the rear of the lobby a clatter of china and silver began in a low key and steadily rose, the silent switchboard came to life with a series of staccato buzzes, and the front door opened and shut at frequent intervals. In a short time the institutional smell of large-scale cooking and thick, damp clothing had routed the fragrance of burning logs and chrysanthemums. The Hope House girls had lived through another day and were coming home.

At five o'clock Mrs. Nicholas Sutton approached her favorite clerk in Blackman's toilet-goods department on the main floor. The clerk was Ruth Miller. Young Mrs. Sutton, snug and warm in her new birthday sables, slid a shopping list across the counter and made an honest apology.

"I ought to be shot for coming in so late," she said. "You've got all your adding up to do."

Ruth Miller took the list and smiled. In the year she had worked at Blackman's Mrs. Sutton was the only woman customer who had regarded the counter between them as a bridge, not a barrier. In consequence, she gave Mrs. Sutton the same devotion she had once given a star on top of a Christmas tree; they were both remote yet intimate; untouchable but hers.

She read the list rapidly, frowning because she needed glasses and also because she couldn't decide whether or not to tell Mrs. Sutton about her wonderful luck.

"They use too much soap at your house," she scolded gently. "You had three dozen two weeks ago. I expect it's the servants, they're all alike, you've got to be firm, Mrs. Sutton."

"I know, I know." Mrs. Sutton slumped into momentary dejection and showed every year of her age, which was twenty. "But have you ever tried being firm with a sixty-year-old woman who wakes you up every morning with a cup of tea because she once kept house for a

4

duke? Hell's bells. Well, charge and send, and I'll put them all on the dole." She smiled at the plain, pleasant girl and wondered for the third or fourth time why she didn't take her away from that counter and put her in the Sutton nursery. She'd be wonderful with baby. "How've you been, Miss Miller? And why aren't you wearing your glasses? That's crazy, you know."

"They're broken," Ruth Miller said. "But I'm getting new ones."

"I should certainly hope so! Crazy to put off things like that. But otherwise you look very chipper."

Ruth Miller's pale cheeks flushed. "I'm just fine," she said. She'd tell Mrs. Sutton why she was fine, too. Some people might think it was silly, but Mrs. Sutton would understand. Mrs. Sutton always surprised you that way. All the money in the world herself but she understood about not having any. "I've got a new place to live," she said breathlessly, and her calm, plain face was almost pretty. "No more subways and furnished rooms with not enough heat and eating any which way! And only six blocks from here, a lovely place, you can't imagine! It's a kind of club, a hotel for girls, with breakfast and dinner, and they even have a room in the basement where you can do your own laundry. It's lovely, and so cheap, and all the hot water you want. I think that's what got me. No hot water is awful."

"No hot water is the devil," Mrs. Sutton agreed. "Are you sure the place is respectable?"

"There's a church group behind it."

"Yah!" Mrs. Sutton jeered. "They're after your soul, you poor thing. Don't give them an inch. How'd you ever find it?"

"Two girls in our stockroom live there. I knew they made less than I do, but they always looked better somehow. You know—nice coats and gloves, and permanents, and all that. So I asked them how they managed and they told me. And then I went over there and talked to the Head, a Miss Monica Brady, and she said she could give me a room with another girl. Eight dollars a week, can you imagine, with the food and all

5

those privileges! I move in tonight and——" She stopped because Mrs. Sutton was staring straight ahead and her eyes were as wide as a child's. She turned her own head to investigate, and her heart gave a sickening lurch. On the rear wall, above the elevators, a small red light blinked steadily and evenly. One-two-three, one-two; one-two-three, one-two. The light was little more than a crimson blur, but she could read its silent message too well.

"I know what that's for," Mrs. Sutton said softly. "Old man Blackman is a friend of my father's. But what's the dope? I mean what does the blinkety-blink say?"

Ruth Miller looked down at her hands and saw that they were trembling. She tried to fill in the sales slip, but it was useless. I'm a fool, she told herself; I've got to stop acting like this. She didn't look up when she answered. "One-two-three, one-two means the main aisle, hosiery. . . . It's a woman."

"The idiot," Mrs. Sutton observed cheerfully. "Pulling a thing like that when the store's almost empty. She deserves to be caught. Idiot, she must be crazy. . . . Hey, maybe it's not a professional, maybe it's a kleptomaniac. For heaven's sake, maybe it's somebody I know! I'm going over!"

Ruth Miller's hands gripped the edge of the counter. "No," she said. "No. Don't do it, don't go. It's not fair, it's awful; don't go, Mrs. Sutton, please."

Mrs. Sutton gave her a quick, surprised look. "Okay," she said carelessly. "You're a nice girl, Miss Miller, and I'm a no-account lug. Well, so long. We're going down to Pinehurst tomorrow, be gone until after Thanksgiving. See you when I get back." She turned up the collar of her sable coat. "Be good," she smiled.

Ruth Miller watched the slim, straight figure as it walked without hesitation to the side-street exit. Mrs. Sutton was avoiding the main aisle where a high voice was raised in tearful expostulation.

It was then five-fifteen. In another fifteen minutes she would begin a new life. She filled Mrs. Sutton's order and sent it down the chute, and tallied her sales-book. When that was done, there were only five minutes left.

Down in the toilet-goods stockroom Moke and Poke, self-styled because they were both named Mary Smith, managed between them to spill a few drops of "Chinese Lily" perfume. They apologized profusely to each other for such carelessness and removed the evidence with fingers that flew swiftly and accurately to ear lobes and neck hollows. It was a crying shame, they said. Five dollars an ounce and ten drops gone. The buyer would have a fit if she knew, and they wouldn't blame her. A little old ten-drop fit. "Chinese Lily." Funny how "Chinese Lily" was the one to spill when "English Rose," twelve dollars an ounce, was standing right next to it. They exchanged long looks and rubbed their elbows in the remains.

"By the way," Moke said, "do you happen to remember by any chance where we happen to be going tonight?"

Poke furrowed her brow. "Are we going anywhere?"

This was repartee of a high and secret order. They leaned against the stock table and shook with silent laughter. They pushed each other about like puppies. They had spoken volumes and said nothing. They were going to dinner with two boys from haberdashery. In Chinatown.

Moke wiped her face with a scented palm. "No kidding, Poke, we did forget something. That Miss Miller's moving in tonight, and we didn't tell her yet that we can't walk home with her."

"Should we have told her?"

"Sure. She may be counting on us. First night and all. And the poor old thing don't know anybody there but us. . . . Whoa! Too late now."

Out in the corridor the closing bell clanged. Upstairs the closing bell was a carillon that dropped sweet notes from vaulted ceiling to marble floor and echoed chastely in crystal chandeliers. But down in the basement it was a gong that screamed against concrete and steel, renewed its strength, and screamed again. Moke and Poke were inured.

"Too late," Moke shrilled above the clamor. "She don't really expect us anyway. Put your money in your shoe, don't ever let a fellow know you got any. Come on." They left the stockroom and elbowed through the crowd that streamed toward the lockers, working busily all the while with pocket mirror and comb.

Ruth walked slowly down the last block. Other people were coming home to shabby brownstone tenements and rooming houses, stopping on the way to buy food at the corner delicatessen, collecting the week's laundry from the Chinaman whose basement window was beaded with steam. She watched them from the secure heights of one who was bound for a warm dinner, a bed with a cretonne cover, and a writing desk of her own. There was a shoe-repair shop in the middle of the block and next to it a dry cleaner's. Very handy, she told herself, especially the cleaner's. For when I get my blue.

The blue was a suit that every woman in New York was trying to wear that fall. It was a bright, electric blue that dulled the eyes and hair of all but the very young, and consequently drew the middle-aged and sallow like a magnet.

Ruth dwelt on the blue. Seventy-five dollars in stores like Blackman's, sixteen-fifty on Fourteenth Street. She had eleven dollars saved up and her week's salary was untouched. She asked herself what she was waiting for. Take out eight for board, she figured rapidly, no carfares, and lunch in the cafeteria is twenty cents. I can do it and maybe a hat to match. And who's to tell me not to? Nobody. This is a new life and I want to look nice. I can do the glasses next month. Who's to tell me the glasses come first? Well, maybe Mrs. Sutton, but——
She put Mrs. Sutton out of her mind. I want the blue, I need it. There's nothing like a touch of color after black all day. . . . That Miss Brady said dinner was from six to eight. I'll eat right away and get down to Fourteenth Street. Saturday night, they'll be open late.

I'll wear it to the dining room tomorrow. There's nothing like a good first impression, and you never know when you may meet somebody. Some of the girls may have relatives in New York and Sunday's when they'd come to call. And have dinner, maybe. Sunday dinners are always special. . . . She saw herself entering the dining room, alone and poised, sitting at one of the small tables, saying something pleasant to the maid who served her. Wearing the blue.

The house was straight ahead. She went up the steps.

Miss Small raised her head when the door opened. This was a stranger with a suitcase, therefore the new girl. She consulted the card quickly, verifying the name. Miller, Ruth. It was important to get a name right, to make a girl feel as if she were expected and wanted. She stood up.

"Well, Ruth," she said, holding out a hand.

Ruth advanced, blinking in the light of a powerful lamp that a previous social worker had installed for a purpose. It was trained to shine directly in the shifting eyes of board-payers who had spent their money for new clothes and claimed their pockets had been picked again, and in the calm, wide eyes of supplicants for week-end passes to visit what they called married sisters.

Ruth narrowed her eyes and saw a young woman with fair hair and a bright smile. She was disappointed. It wasn't Miss Brady. Miss Brady was dark and thin and her voice was loud and comical. Who was this? Then she remembered. This must be Angel, Miss Angeline Small, the social worker who was Miss Brady's assistant. Moke and Poke had described her. Miss Small does a lot of good, they'd said; she keeps you from making a mistake that'll ruin your whole life for a minute's pleasure.

She smiled at Miss Small when she took her hand. All around her were girls, coming and going, laughing and talking.

Miss Small adjusted the light. "There," she said, "that's better, isn't it?"

It was better, much better. She had almost been

blinded by the glare, and now she looked eagerly about her. She could see the other girls clearly.

She saw the dark blue curtains at the dining-room door, the elevator and its uniformed attendant, the telephone switchboard and its operator, the girl with red hair who slouched against the office railing and whistled under her breath. There was a single yellow rose on the desk and an open money box filled with bills and silver. Miss Small had light blue eyes and a rosebud mouth.

"Kitty Brice and Lillian Harris," Miss Small's voice was saying, "this is the new girl, Ruth Miller. She'll be in 706 with April Hooper. Lillian, I'm afraid you'll be late for work, dear. Are you waiting for something?"

The red-haired girl drawled, "Not any more." She removed her felt hat, cuffed it into new angles, and sauntered to the door.

"Seven-o-six," she said over her shoulder, "I'm in 606. Drop down sometime."

Miss Small went on. "Lillian is rather abrupt, but you mustn't mind. And now, my dear, let's talk about you. Do you want your dinner at once or would you rather go to your room first?" It was a stock question and the answer was always the same. Room first. To primp. A faraway look came into Miss Small's eyes. She had made that answer herself three years ago, when she stood where Ruth was standing now, and Monny had smiled across the desk.

A chattering procession passed on its way to the dining room. One girl stopped at the desk and asked for a tray check.

"Who's it for, dear?" Miss Small wanted to know. "Not Minnie May again?"

"Yes, Miss Small. Miss Small, I'd ask you to find me another roommate, I really would, except that I'd have Minnie May on my conscience. I think she needs my influence, I really do, and because of that I'm willing to put up with a lot. But it's hard on me."

"I'll have a little talk with Minnie May later. Didn't I see her just a minute ago?"

"Yes, Miss Small. She came down with me, but she went right up again. She says the whole place smells of last night's fish. She's—well, she's in a state, and it isn't last night's fish, either."

When the girl went away, Miss Small suddenly realized that Ruth Miller hadn't answered her question. She examined her sharply and closely for the first time and was disturbed by what she saw. Why, she's frightened, she told herself. Or is that shyness? No, it's fright. She looks as if she were cornered, or caught, or something dreadful like that. She looks terrified. For a brief moment Miss Small felt the contagion of panic, but she quickly recovered. She rapidly scanned the lobby, but there was nothing unusual that she could see.

The invisible diners chattered behind the blue curtains, as harmless as a cageful of sparrows. Mrs. Fister, the housekeeper, stood by the dining-room door calmly collecting the tray and guest checks. Jewel lounged beside the elevator, waiting for the after-dinner rush. At the switchboard, Kitty's bony hands darted from plug to plug, and her monotonous voice droned on without a break.

Miss Small's eyes met Ruth Miller's for an instant and the girl looked away. She made a quick decision.

"I know what we'll do," she said briskly. "Here's your key, your room is at the rear. Now you run along and look things over, and when you're ready, come down to room 506. That's mine. I have a nice little suite all to myself. We'll have our dinners sent up there, and I'll tell you all about our little rules and so on. Fun? And you'll want to know about your roommate, too. She's just gone in to dinner, but she'll be around later."

"I have to go out," Ruth said. They were the first words she had spoken and they were thick and strangled.

Miss Small nodded agreeably, but she left the office enclosure and followed the shabby figure to the front door. "Some other time then," she said. "But do take your key; slip it in your purse, dear. There, now you're really one of us!" She pretended not to see the shaking, fumbling hands and went on brightly. "And let me have your suitcase. I'll send it up to the room, and you'll find it ready and waiting when you come back."

She carried the suitcase to the desk and shook her head reprovingly when Kitty Brice laughed.

"Didn't want to give it up, did she?" Kitty said. "Hung on like a drowning man. Would you say she peddled diamonds or dope?"

Miss Small smiled wryly. "Another odd one, I'm afraid." She sighed, and returned to her work.

The November night grew older slowly. Outside the cold increased and the street gradually emptied. The front windows of the tenements and rooming houses were thriftily dark; only the lights of Hope House burned through the murky fog.

At ten o'clock the lobby was deserted except for Kitty, nodding at the quiet board, and Miss Ethel Plummer, an elderly spinster who took over the desk at night because it meant free room and meals and didn't interfere with her regular job. Her regular job was piecework which she did at home, fine embroidery executed with sequins, tiny beads, and metallic thread. She sat behind the desk, a shaded light trained on the strip of sea-green gauze that lay across her sheet-covered lap, her steel-rimmed spectacles reinforced with rubber bands to keep them from slipping. Round wooden hoops protected and framed the pearl-and-silver rose that grew under her stubby fingers.

There was one other light, over by the door. The elevator was closed and silent, and the indicator showed it stationary at the seventh floor.

Been up there for the past fifteen minutes, Miss Plummer said to herself. And Jewel doesn't live on seventh, she's calling on somebody. She ought to leave the car down here when she does that, so people can take themselves up without waiting. Having coffee and doughnuts with April, I guess. I couldn't enjoy that myself, sitting there and watching the child fill cups and spoon out sugar. I'll never complain about my life again, I'm really blessed. . . . Thinking about cups made Miss Plummer thirsty.

"Any of that tea left, Kitty?"

"Sure." Kitty crept over with a thermos jug. "You finish it, I've had enough. . . . That's pretty, Miss Plummer. What's it going to be?"

"Front panel of a bride's mother's dress. Big house on Fifth Avenue three weeks from today, if I don't go blind first. Anything happen before I came on?"

Kitty shrugged. "We got a new girl and our social standing remains the same. Kind of cuckoo, but she won't bother me any. This place is getting terrible. Old maids, fresh kids, and people with something the matter with them. If a good-looking girl walked in here, I'd drop dead. So would she, in five minutes."

Miss Plummer snipped a thread. "Now Kitty, you could be pretty yourself if you'd only take a little interest."

"Zilch. I know what I look like." Kitty came closer and lowered her voice. "What's the big idea, Monny taking your sister out to tea? What's Monny got up her well-cut sleeve? Come on; you know. Give."

"I must say you're not very respectful. And it's none of your business, although I don't mind telling you. It's the meals. Miss Brady thinks they could be better."

"If they were better, they'd raise the prices. Let Brady eat out, she can afford it." Kitty hunched her shoulders and peered at the clock. "Nearly ten-thirty, hour and a half to go."

"You've had a long day, dear, and I know you're tired." When she thought of it, Miss Plummer tried to talk like Miss Small. "Poor dear," she added.

"I'm cracking up," Kitty said hopefully. "I'm caving in."

"Then run along, dear, and get a good night's rest. I'll take over the board."

Kitty's gratitude expressed itself in halfhearted objections. "You'll forget to switch it over to Angel's room when you lock up."

Miss Plummer used Miss Small's firm smile. "I won't forget."

"And the new girl went out. She's not in yet. I don't think she knows about self-service when Jewel goes off. Maybe she'll try to walk up. She looks like that kind."

"I'll tell her, dear; I'll take her up myself if she's timid."

Kitty sighed. "Thanks. I'll pull bastings for you tomorrow." She crept through the swinging gate and over to the stairs beside the elevator. The elevator's absence made no difference. She lived on the second floor with the maids and minor staff members, and they were asked to walk.

Her room was cold because she had left a window open. She closed it with a slam and sat beside the radiator. There were coffee parties in other rooms, and probably more than coffee in Minnie May's, but she didn't feel like prowling up and down halls and sniffing at closed doors. Tonight she had a pain around her heart and she hated her life. She thought of the years behind her and those ahead. Once she got up and started for the door. She'd go up to April's, she'd say she'd come to get warm. But she didn't go. She stayed where she was, hugging the radiator until even it grew cold.

Miss Small's suite, like Miss Brady's, was not furnished with the regulation maple, but she had done very well with the money she could afford to spend. Miss Brady had antiques from her own New England home, old Persians and heirloom silver, and Miss Small had walked warily in her steps with walnut, hooked rugs, and pewter. The Wallace Nuttings that she bought when she first came had been supplanted by Currier & Ives. Because Miss Brady had laughed at the Nuttings.

Miss Brady wasn't laughing now. She was stretched full length on the low couch, her untidy black head resting on pillows, and Miss Small sat at her feet. Within easy reach was a small table holding a spirit lamp and china. It was the hour for hot chocolate, small cakes, and confidences.

"Light me a cigarette, Angel," Miss Brady said. "Miss me?"

Miss Small complied. "Monny! You know!"

Miss Brady looked pleased. "You've got rings under your eyes. You do too much, you let these kids run you ragged. Look at me. I've been doing this stuff for years, and not a nerve in my body. . . . For God's sake, are you putting marshmallow in your chocolate? Disgusting."

"Sorry." Miss Small spooned the single marshmallow out of her cup and all marshmallows out of her life. "You were so late, Monny. I was afraid you were having more trouble with Fister."

"No. Fister is eating out of my hand. We had rum in the tea and that reminded her of her late husband. So I won on all points. Tapioca, coffee jelly and grape-nuts ice cream are out. Fruit and cheese in. I said I'd pay the difference out of my own pocket."

"Lucky Monny to have her own pocket."

"Stop that. Lucky Monny, period." Miss Brady reached for her chocolate and took a deep swallow. She stretched out again, her long, ugly face relaxed, her eyes smiling. "This is the best part of the day. . . . Marshall-Gill is the one who made me late. Talk, talk, talk, all about nothing. She swore she'd sent the stuff over for the party costumes. Did she?"

"She did. All cut out and sewed, only the masks to do."

"Cool!" Miss Brady said. "She'll be on hand for tea tomorrow, as usual, and sees no reason why we shouldn't do the masks then, Sunday or not. What do you say?"

"Whatever you say, Monny."

Miss Brady's eyes clouded. "What's wrong, Angel? You're miles away, you've got something on your mind. Don't you know you can't hide things from me?"

Miss Small hesitated. Then, "I'm worried," she said simply.

Miss Brady sat up and scowled. "Has some little tramp——"

"No, no, Monny. Everything's all right. I mean, don't

look like that! Nothing's happened at all. Only one sick tray, Minnie May, hangover, and only two week-end passes and I know they're legitimate."

"Then what——"

"The new girl, Monny. She came."

Miss Brady was openly puzzled. "Well? What's wrong about that? Isn't she all right? She looked all right to me."

"I don't know, but I have the most awful feeling. As if she were going to—bring us trouble. I'm afraid she's one of the quiet ones that—blow up. You remember that dementia praecox they had at the Primrose Club?"

Miss Brady shuddered. "Out the window, hanging to the ledge by her fingers. That woman down there, Motley, told me it was months before she stopped seeing that girl in her dreams. She had to go to a rest home to get over it. . . . What are you trying to do, scare me to death?"

Miss Small explained. She described the sudden transformation at the desk, the fear that took over eyes and hands, the averted face. "She was natural enough when she came in, exactly as you said on the card. Shy, quite ordinary in a nice, quiet way. Then all at once something happened. She changed, right before my eyes, and it frightened me. Somehow I got the idea that she saw something, or heard something, but I can't imagine what."

"Who was near the desk?"

"I thought of that, too. Just the usual crowd going to the dining room, stopping for mail, nobody that stood out. Wait a minute. Dot came for a tray check for Minnie May."

"Dotty, the girl evangelist! Who else?"

"Jewel at the elevator, Kitty at the board. Kitty noticed it, too; I imagine they all did. It seems ridiculous when I tell it like this. Kitty, Jewel, all of them as drab as Ruth Miller herself. . . . Oh!"

"Got something?"

"Lillian Harris was hanging around. She said something flippant, I forget what it was. Then she went off

16

to her job. The Miller girl went out, too, a few minutes later. . . . She didn't have dinner."

Miss Brady looked thoughtful. "Harris," she said.

Miss Small said quietly, "Lillian doesn't like me."

"I don't know what you mean by that, and I don't see how it fits in here," Miss Brady answered. "Lillian Harris was well recommended, but if she hurts you in any way, out she goes."

Miss Small raised puzzled eyes. "What do you mean when you say she was well recommended? She came here after that rule about references was thrown out."

Miss Brady grinned when Miss Small recalled the rule. They had drafted it themselves and fought for its adoption. They'd argued that a girl's past was her own private business and insisted on her right to live it down if she wanted to. The Board had fought back, prophesied scandal, and lost. From that time on, no one was asked for a reference. The rule was three years old and so successful that Miss Brady sometimes forgot its origin.

"I mean I knew about Harris," Miss Brady explained. "She used to have a friend here, used to visit the friend before she moved in herself." She ran a hand through her hair. "Suddenly I am very, very sick and tired of this job," she said. "There's nothing to it any more, I don't know why I stay. If I had half the sense I was presumably born with, I'd chuck the whole works and take you with me."

"Monny, darling! You're thinking about Europe again!"

"I am, and why not? Don't look at me like that; you know it's been on my mind for weeks. Listen. I get my grandmother's money next month, so why don't we resign? Reasons of health, and that's no lie, you look a wreck; and we'll grab the first boat and stay for a year. Two years, five years, forever. . . . Angel, you look about ten when you smile like that. How old are you anyway? I've never known."

"Thirty-three."

"I'm forty-five and don't tell me I don't look it. . . .

17

Paris, Angel, and Bavaria if they'll let us in, and I'll buy you a little blue hunting jacket and cut your hair in a bang. Look at that clock, after twelve and I meant to go to bed early. Oh well, if you're cheered up it's worth it. Feel better now?"

"Much!"

"That panic about Miller was probably your nerves. You're exhausted and I don't wonder. All these messy brats pouring out their beastly little troubles. Did you tell Miller about April Hooper?"

"Monny! I forgot!"

Miss Brady flushed. "That's too bad," she said. "You knew I hadn't time to do it myself, you knew I was counting on you. It was a very little thing to ask and I should think you'd want to remember——"

"Monny, I'm heartbroken! But honestly, she went away so quickly, she almost ran, and I didn't see her again. Monny, I can't follow a girl around, I have other things to do, you know that! I'll go up there now, I'll go at once——"

"Too late." Miss Brady's voice was cool. "I counted on you and you failed me."

Miss Small said nothing. She winked back sudden tears and turned away. They sat without speaking.

After a while Miss Brady spoke gruffly. "I'm tired too. Have I time for another cigarette?"

"Of course." Miss Small offered the box as if Miss Brady were a stranger.

"I didn't mean anything," Miss Brady said. "Forget it. I'll talk to the girl myself tomorrow."

"No, I will! I want to!" Miss Small seized the matches and struck one. They both laughed.

"We mustn't do that again," Miss Brady said.

"No, Monny."

"We nearly quarreled."

"I know. It was my fault."

"No dear, mine."

As things turned out, no one told Ruth Miller anything. She returned at eleven-thirty with the once-

18

coveted blue in a paper box. She had forced herself to buy it. It was all she had left of the new life she had planned.

A few hours before, when she had confidently walked into the future, she had come face to face with the past. Run, she had said to herself, run; you still have a chance. But she had been running for years, from city to city, from job to job, putting time and distance between herself and a screaming promise, and her route had been a circle. Above the chatter in the lobby she had heard one voice. In a sea of strange faces one face was not strange. It's a scheme, she'd said, it's a destiny. I'm lost.

But she had run again, out into the night, pleading with herself to be calm. She'd thought of Mrs. Sutton, maybe Mrs. Sutton would take her in and ask no questions. Maybe she'd listen and advise. But then she'd remembered that Mrs. Sutton was leaving town. And she'd told herself that Mrs. Sutton was too young, it wouldn't be fair to frighten her.

She'd begun to cry, standing on a corner and turning slowly and steadily as if she were surrounded. The fog was thick and the passers-by were dim and shapeless. She could follow me and I wouldn't know it, she wept; I wouldn't see her. My eyes——

That was when she'd remembered the eye doctor. The only man she knew except Mr. Benz. And his office wasn't far away, an office and apartment combined. She'd talk to him and he'd tell her what to do. He'd been, well—friendly. He'd been, well—interested.

She'd climbed the stairs to his office, but no one had answered her ring. She'd slipped a note under the door, asking him to call her at Hope House. "Leave a message if I'm not there," she'd written, "and tell me where I can reach you. I need some advice. It's important to me." She couldn't tell him how important. She couldn't write a word like death. It would look hysterical.

She'd left the doctor's building and walked to Fourteenth Street, telling herself to buy the blue because he would see her in it. But the scheme took care of that.

Ten minutes after she left the building a cleaning woman swept the note into the hall, down the single flight of stairs, and out into the gutter. Later on the rain washed the words away.

Outside the shopwindow she had looked at the blue and talked to herself again. Talked and argued and planned. Talked about the economy of spending money, argued about the possibility of mistaken identity, planned what she'd say to the doctor when he called. Maybe I made a mistake, she'd said. Lots of people look alike, you're always hearing of cases. There was even a man who looked like the President. And she didn't act queer when she saw me, she acted like she'd never seen me before. So I could be wrong. . . . But she saw her own shaking hands and knew in her heart that there was no mistake.

But I'll go back there tonight, she'd said. I've got to. There's my suitcase and the telephone call. Nothing can happen if I go straight to my room tonight and lock the door. A big houseful of people, I'll be safe for one night. That's all I'll need, one night. He'll call tonight or tomorrow and he'll tell me what to do. Maybe I'll laugh about this in a day or so. I bet I laugh, I bet I do. . . . She'd tried to laugh then but it had sounded wrong.

If I stay in my room, she'd said, I'll be safe. They can put the message under the door. No matter what, I'll keep out of sight until he calls. They have trays, I'll ask my roommate to bring me a tray. I'll tell her I have a headache. If I keep out of sight and don't let her see me again——

Buy the blue, she'd said, buy the blue and then you'll always have it.

Miss Plummer looked up from her embroidery when Ruth came in. "I've been waiting for you," she said kindly.

"Has a telephone call come for me?"

"No dear. You had me worried, staying out so late all by yourself. We lock up at midnight, except in the case of a special pass, and I wondered if you understood. Been buying something pretty?"

20

"I bought a suit."

"That's nice. My name's Plummer, Ethel Plummer. My sister's the housekeeper here and if you're hungry I think I can get you a little something."

"No thank you, Miss Plummer. I'd rather go to bed."

"You're a sensible girl, I can see that. I've no patience with late hours, although goodness knows I keep them! Your suitcase is in your room, dear, and you can run yourself up in the elevator, that is if you're not timid about machinery."

"I guess I am a little. I don't think I've ever tried to run an elevator."

"Well, never you mind, I used to be afraid myself, but you'll get over it the same as I did. I'll take you up this time and you'll see how easy it is."

On the seventh floor Miss Plummer pointed down a bare, dim hall lined on one side with closed doors. "You see that big door straight ahead? That's the fire door. You go right on through to the other side. There's a short hall back there, with the bath, the telephone, and your own room. It's the only room at that end and it's nice and quiet, almost like a little house set off to itself."

"Miss Plummer?" Her voice broke and she tried again. "Miss Plummer, do outside calls come in on that phone?"

"Oh yes. When that happens we ring a bell in your room." Miss Plummer smiled a good night, and the elevator closed.

Her room was dark. She could hear nothing but she knew someone was there. The unknown roommate, already in bed and asleep. It had to be the roommate, it couldn't be anyone else. She waited in the cool darkness, listening.

A voice spoke, a thin, sweet voice like a child's. "Turn on the light," it said. "There beside the door. It won't bother me."

She found the switch and turned it. In one of the two beds a small girl sat up in a welter of blankets, rubbing her short, fair curls and yawning. Her cheeks were flushed, and she looked like an animated doll.

21

"Hello," she said. "I had to go back to work after dinner, did you?"

"No, I went shopping." Ruth hesitated. "I'm sorry, but they didn't tell me your name. I'm Ruth Miller."

The small girl laughed. "I knew that. There's not much I miss! I'm April Hooper. That sounds silly, the April part, but my mother was English and she always said there was nothing prettier than an English April. So she called me that. You see, she was always homesick. Are your father and mother dead?"

"Yes." Her suitcase was lying on the other bed and she went over to it.

"Are your grandparents dead, too?"

"Yes." This was an odd conversation. She stared at the little creature smiling and nodding among the blankets.

"So are mine," April ran on. "All of my people are dead. I was born in this block, right on this very spot. They tore down three tenements to make this house, and then my grandmother died and I moved in here. I work around the corner, in the drugstore. Where do you work?"

She prattles like a little kid, Ruth thought. She can't be more than sixteen if she's that. She untied the string on the suit box. "I work at Blackman's."

"Like Moke and Poke. They were born in this neighborhood like me. You'll die laughing, but they have the same name and they're not even related. Mary Smith. But I guess you knew that. That's why they call themselves Moke and Poke. That's cute, isn't it? Have you known them very long? You do know them, don't you?"

"They sent me here." She held up the suit and shook out the folds. She was tired, and April's chatter was too shrill. But she knew she had to be polite. She needed April. April would bring her the trays. "Look, April," she said. She held up the suit.

But April had no eyes for clothing. She rattled on. "Moke and Poke are nice. Some people think they're fresh, but I don't. When the weather's bad and there's ice on the pavement, they call for me. Even when they

22

have dates, they call for me. They take the time. That's nice, isn't it?"

"It surely is." She hung the suit in the closet and closed the door. Chatterbox, she thought wearily. She could have made some comment, she could have said something. I'd have said something in her place.

"I think they're pretty, too," April said. "Their hair is so soft, and they take good care of their skin. It's like velvet. I like to touch their faces and they don't mind. It isn't often that you find a nice person who's pretty too. . . . What do you look like, Ruth?"

Ruth looked aghast at the small figure huddled in the middle of the bed. Why, the child's feeble-minded, she told herself with horror. Why didn't they tell me about her. Feeble-minded. And even Moke and Poke didn't say anything. I can't bear it, I can't, it's too much. She backed away from the clear gaze that was as innocent and candid as the voice.

A cloud came over April's face. "Oh," she said. "I'm sorry, Ruth. That's a shame, that's what it is. Nobody told you about me and I've scared you. But you're not to feel bad about me because I don't mind at all. I'm blind."

Ruth went slowly to the tumbled bed. Her hands automatically smoothed the covers and rearranged the pillow. April's hand found one of hers and held it fast.

"You're not to feel bad, do you hear?" she insisted. "When you're born that way, it doesn't make any difference. But there's one thing you've got to remember, please. You've got to make me turn the lights on. I've got the habit of not doing it because what's the use, but just the same I ought to. That's why I asked for a roommate, to make me remember. It scares the other girls to find me in the dark, like taking a bath and things. So you make me turn the lights on every time, even when you're going out on a date and I'm staying here. . . . I think the room looks nicer that way, too."

"They're on now. . . . Wait." Ruth went to the lamps on the two small desks. "Now everything's on. And you're right, it does look nicer."

23

She let April talk. April sold cigarettes and magazines at the drugstore. She knew where each kind was. She could ring up sales and make change without a mistake. She was worried about getting old and having to use rouge. She was afraid she'd put on too much.

When the lights were finally out, Ruth lay awake for a long time. She had promised to breakfast with April, in the dining room. There was no help for it. She had no choice. She went back to the first day she had gone to work at Blackman's, to the first time she had talked to Moke and Poke, to all the little things that had fallen into their allotted places in the scheme that led to Hope House. Whose scheme? She covered her face.

2

Moke and Poke screamed across the crowded dining room: "Hey kids, come over here!"

April led Ruth proudly, a paradox that brought smiles to many faces.

"We fixed it," Moke said. "You're going to eat at our table. One big happy family. Hey, Clara, two more breakfasts."

"Miss Brady's looking for you, Ruth," Poke said. "She wants to tell you about this afternoon, at least that's what she said."

"As if we couldn't tell you just as good," Moke jeered, "and no fancy lies thrown in. It's about the tea. We have a tea every Sunday, but this one's different. And worse. We got to make masks for the costume party. . . . What's the matter with you? You got a stiff neck or something?"

April answered importantly. "She has a sore throat and a headache and she talked in her sleep all night. She didn't want to come down but I made her."

"Next time make her gargle," Poke advised. "Salt water. Shut up, let me tell it. So we've got to make masks for the party tomorrow night. House birthday party. House is five years old."

"Got all our teeth and can we bite," Moke said. "Let me tell it, let me. Now get this. Mrs. Marshall-Gill, head of the Board, dreamed up a costume party, everybody dressed alike, rag dolls with the same old false face so nobody knows who anybody is. Rag dolls, I'm not kidding, with rag faces and holes to see and breathe through. She's even got a prize for the girl who guesses the most other girls. So we're going to make the masks

25

this afternoon, in the lounge. It'll be a scream. With bought refreshments."

The breakfasts came on two trays. Ruth pushed hers aside. Nine o'clock and he hadn't called. Nine o'clock. The lobby had been full of people when she and April went through. She had walked with her eyes lowered. People had crowded about them, jostling. She couldn't do that again.

"I can't go," she said suddenly and sharply.

Even April looked surprised.

"I can't go," Ruth repeated, but she spoke softly. "I'm expecting a call, I may have to go out." She put her elbows on the table and shielded her face with her hands.

Moke frowned and her shrewd young eyes moved about the room. Girls coming and going, House girls, the regular gang. Nothing to make a person turn white and hide her face. She looked at Ruth again. Not eating, either. Sick and no fooling. Sick or something. "Okay," she said lightly, "but you got to come for a minute anyway. It's a——what do I want to say, Poke?"

"A obligation."

"Right. Miss Poke here bought a dictionary for three dollars, and every night she learns a long word so her college-educated kids won't be ashamed of her. Next month she's going to buy the ring." Moke waited for a laugh, but none came.

Moke grew uneasy. She felt responsible and helpless. Maybe Ruth really was sick. We got her in here, she argued silently, and it's up to us to see she's okay. She fell back on her own never-failing panacea. "Listen, Ruth, why don't you go back to bed? Poke and I always do on Sunday. Go on, it'll do you good."

Ruth left the table hurriedly. But not until she knew there was no one between her and the door. When she had gone, Poke tapped a finger against her temple and wagged her head.

"No," Moke said.

April touched Moke's sleeve. "Is Ruth pretty?" she asked.

"Pretty? Honey, she's out of this world!"

Poke leaned over and tapped Moke's temple.

It was Miss Brady who knocked on her door at four o'clock. There had been one other knock, but it had come without footsteps and without a voice. She'd stood close to the door and whispered. "Who's there?" And no one had answered. But this time was different. She had no excuse. This time the caller announced herself at once.

"Ruth," Miss Brady shouted. "Open up!"

The door was locked. She'd locked it when April went down to dinner at one o'clock. Now she turned the key with a muttered apology. "I'm sorry, Miss Brady. I was asleep."

Miss Brady strolled about the room, unobtrusively taking in the red-rimmed eyes, the strained, tight features. Downright ugly, she noted. Homesick. Or maybe just sick. Or maybe Angel's right, the fool girl could be frightened about something. We could be harboring two halves of a nasty piece of unfinished business. A nice outlook, a sweet outlook, and it should happen to me when I'm ready to quit.

Miss Brady dug into her well-trained but curiously innocent mind and brought up her pet anathema. Some man, she thought savagely. Some pipsqueak. Miller had him and somebody else got him. No. Somebody else had him and Miller got him. These quiet pale ones fool you. Miller got him, and got something else with him, and somebody in the House knows it. Sure, the pale quiet ones fool you. Look at that girl last year with the baby, right under my eye. . . . She sat on April's bed and wondered if she could keep the distaste she felt out of her face and voice. So help me, she promised herself, if this one drinks iodine in the middle of the night, I'll break her back in six places.

"Ruth," she said mildly, "we missed you at dinner. You mustn't skip meals, you know. And Miss Small is worried about you. She thinks you need building up."

"I had coffee, April brought me coffee, that was all I wanted."

"Not enough. Now comb your hair and wash your face like a good girl and come on down with me. We're sewing in the lounge and Mrs. Marshall-Gill is serving tea. She's our most important patron, and she likes to know all the new girls."

"I don't think I——"

"You must," Miss Brady said firmly. "You needn't stay long but you really must make an appearance. Unwritten law, Mrs. Marshall-Gill's. Everybody shows up or else."

Everybody, more than seventy people. She could sit in a corner, off to herself, safe for a little while because of more than seventy witnesses. Safe for the rest of her life if she could prove she was mistaken. If she could study that face again, if she could listen to the voice, if she could prove to herself that she was wrong. . . . But that would be too good, too wonderful, she didn't have that kind of luck. Going downstairs to the tea was another part of the scheme, another small thing falling into place, lining up behind her, pushing her forward to meet the end. But I've got to know, she said; I've got to finish it. I can't go on like this. I can't wait for him to call, I can't wait. I've got to do something myself.

"Will you wait for me while I change my dress?" she asked.

Good God, Miss Brady marveled silently, vain too. "Go right ahead," she said.

Ruth dressed carefully in the blue suit. But how will I know if I've made a mistake? she wondered. How can I be sure? She knew the answer to that at once. If one pair of eyes followed her with a certain look, if one head turned in her direction then turned away, too quickly, she'd know. Not only know that she wasn't wrong but also that she'd been recognized. Then there would be no time to lose, not even a minute. She'd go to the doctor's office and sit on the steps until he came home. He'd find her a place for the night, he might even know of a job. She'd have to leave Blackman's. Miss Brady had

28

written Blackman's on her card, and anybody could read that card. And Moke and Poke——

"I'm ready now," she said to Miss Brady.

The elevator girl looked surprised when they got in together.

"Jewel," Miss Brady said, "this is Ruth Miller." Jewel nodded.

She knew a little about Jewel. She'd asked April when they'd walked down to breakfast. April had accepted the walk without question. April had said that Jewel's real name was Annie. . . .

They had never told her the other one's name, and they'd kept hers a secret too. They'd said she'd be better off if she didn't know. They'd kept it all a secret, it wasn't even in the papers. . . .

At the fifth floor three girls crowded into the small cage. Miss Brady introduced them briskly, but Ruth hardly heard. They had names like Betty and Peggy and Janie. They meant nothing, they looked exactly alike. Sometimes people do look alike, she reminded herself without hope. When the door slid open at the first floor, sound poured out from the lounge and filled the lobby.

Miss Brady swept her forward, like a dead leaf in the wind. She saw lighted lamps, trays of food, flowers, and a fire.

There was a vacant chair in a corner by the fire. Its back was to the wall, and she took it. No one spoke to her. She tried to make herself small and inconspicuous, but that was a wasted effort and she knew it. The bright blue suit betrayed her against the cream walls. She braced herself for whatever the next hour held and deliberately turned her face to the nearest lamp, inviting recognition. After a while, when still no one had come to her side, she began to breathe easier and dared to look at her neighbors.

Mrs. Marshall-Gill dominated the room. She looked like a charge customer, the kind who tapped her foot and called the clerks "my girl." She was calling somebody "my girl" now, a thin and brightly smiling woman who ran obediently from group to group with a dish of bonbons, who ran back for fresh supplies from a box on Mrs. Marshall-Gill's lap and ran off again. The woman looked like a paid companion and her lips moved in a constant chant, indistinct across the room. When she offered the dish to Ruth, the chant was, "Compliments of Mrs. Marshall-Gill."

A girl put a piece of heavy muslin in Ruth's lap and went away without speaking. She held it stupidly, wondering what to do. It was shaped like a small flour sack, and a crude face was penciled on one surface. When she found the needle and colored wool inside, she knew what it was. This was her party mask, and she was to make it herself. I'll never wear it, she thought, but they don't know that.

In a few minutes the girl came back. She said her name was Minnie May Handy, and she offered to help. Together they made the scrolls of yellow hair, the red buttonhole mouth, the long black lashes that fringed the cut-out eyes. If Minnie May noticed her trembling fingers she chose to ignore them.

Minnie May had a fretful and dubious Southern accent. She said, "My roommate says that every stitch you sew on Sunday you have to take out in Hell. With your nose. My roommate's terrible. When did you move in? Haven't I seen you before?"

"No," Ruth said. "You've never seen me before. . . . I came last night."

"It's terrible. No place to entertain, I mean what I call entertain. So what are you going to do? Well, you do it, and everybody waits up for you to come in and tries to smell your breath." She exhaled the disputed breath and filled the vicinity with clove. "I'm sick and tired of chaperons. I want an apartment."

Here was an opening, a safe opening even if someone overheard. She and Minnie May were temporarily isolated. The crowd had moved to the other end of the long room and overflowed into the lobby. Only Mrs. Marshall-Gill remained within earshot and she was counting costumes audibly.

"I can understand about wanting an apartment," Ruth said carefully. "I suppose you've lived here a long time." She was surprised at her own craft. Her voice was even and natural, the question was natural, too.

"Two years."

Two. That was more than she'd hoped for. Three would have been better but two was close enough to figure on. She'd have to hurry. The crowd was shifting again, coming their way. But she mustn't sound as if she were hurrying. She must sound as if she had all the time in the world.

"I suppose everybody here is from out of town," she went on. "New Yorkers would have families to live with, wouldn't they?"

Minnie May didn't answer. That meant she'd have to be more definite. She'd have to make Minnie May talk. "I suppose every state in the union is represented here," she said with quiet intensity. "Everybody from a different place. Even the servants." That was a good touch about the servants. That was natural and good.

Minnie May rolled her eyes. "What's eating you?"

She smiled gaily. "Maybe I'm lonely! I guess that's it. I'm just wondering if anybody comes from the same part I do. I mean it would be nice to find somebody that knew a mutual friend. You're Southern, aren't you?"

Minnie May gave her a long look. "Sort of," she said. She yawned and stood up. "Got to go. Got to make a phone call. See you some more." She strolled across the room, bowed demurely to Mrs. Marshall-Gill, and ducked through the door.

Two more people came in, Lillian Harris and the girl who had asked for a tray the night before. Then three more, then five. They all looked as if they didn't see her.

No one approached her chair. She sat erect, her fingers locked over the mask. She saw Moke and Poke over by the piano, Kitty Brice in a corner talking to a square, heavy woman in black with keys hanging from her belt. The housekeeper, Miss Plummer's sister. She looked for Miss Plummer but she wasn't there. Taking the board so Kitty could come to the party, that would be it. Miss

31

Plummer knew how to work the board. If the doctor's call came, Miss Plummer would tell her. Miss Plummer was reliable. April in the far corner, sitting on Miss Brady's lap, being petted and fed from a full plate like a little dog. Jewel in the doorway, slouched and sullen.

Mrs. Marshall-Gill spied Jewel and raised an imperious hand. The paid companion ran forward and was waved back. "Annie!" Mrs. Marshall-Gill's voice filled the room. "Annie, come here, I want a few words with you." Everybody watched and listened. The girl at the piano stopped playing, and even April twisted around on Miss Brady's lap. Miss Small hurried in from the lobby as if she had been summoned. She looked apprehensive.

"I want you to stop calling yourself by that silly name, Annie," Mrs. Marshall-Gill said clearly. "It's inappropriate and ridiculous and I don't like it. It may even be dishonest, I don't know. At any rate, you're to stop it at once. I looked up your registration, and your name is Annie, a solid, Christian name. You'll do well to abide by it."

"I don't like Annie," Jewel said.

"It suits your face," Mrs. Marshall-Gill said. A titter ran around the listening room. Jewel drew back. Dark red stained her thick, sallow skin. Even her neck was red.

"I don't like Annie," she repeated. "I like to call myself Jewel."

"That will be all, Annie. You may join the others for your tea."

Jewel turned, hesitated, and went to the door. She closed it gently behind her, but not before Mrs. Marshall-Gill explained her stand.

"Jewel doesn't match Schwab," she said.

Someone held out a cup of tea. It was Miss Small. Ruth took it in both hands but the hot liquid, thick with cream, spilled into her lap.

"What a shame," Miss Small grieved, "and it's a new suit, isn't it? But you mustn't worry, it'll clean." She talked easily, quietly. "Too bad about poor little Jewel.

That's an old feud. But she really is very trying. This is the fifth time she's changed her name, poor child. Now tell me how you're making out. If there's anything you don't understand, you must ask me. That's what I'm here for."

"I'm all right," Ruth said.

"You don't look it," Miss Small insisted gently. "Does April worry you? I'm so sorry I didn't warn you about that."

"Oh no."

"I'm glad. April's a dear, but I'm afraid we spoil her dreadfully. You really must meet some of the others. Why don't we walk around a bit? There may be a very lovely friend waiting for you in this very room, someone who will change your whole life. Shall we try it?"

Ruth brushed her lips with a handkerchief and averted her head. After a pause, Miss Small tried again.

"You know," she said, "I'm paid a very good salary for the work I do here, and if my girls don't bring me their little problems I'm very unhappy. I tell myself that I've failed somewhere. You understand, don't you?"

Ruth nodded. At the other end of the room Moke and Poke left the piano and walked slowly toward her, stopping at other groups on the way. Hurry, she begged silently, hurry, don't stop again. I'm afraid I'll say something, I'm afraid I'll give myself away.

Miss Small's soft voice went on. "We've had all sorts of girls here, from all sorts of homes, and we've managed to make them happy. Not at first, perhaps, but always in the end. Confidence is the thing that does it." Miss Small's voice dropped to a whisper. "I'm like a doctor, Ruth, you can talk to me and I never tell the things I hear, never. I want you to think about that. Think about it tonight." Her hand touched Ruth's lightly. "People are looking at us, but we don't mind that, do we? Now I must run off and talk to our patron. But I'll be thinking about you and worrying."

Ruth sat with bent head, staring at the dark stain on the blue, hardly remembering how it had come there, not caring. I didn't give myself away, she said over and

33

over; I didn't tell her anything. She wanted me to talk, but I didn't. It isn't safe to talk, not even one word, not even a lie. . . . Moke and Poke came up and sat on the arms of her chair.

"Listen," Moke said, "we dreamed up some funny business. You'll die. You know there's a prize for the girl that guesses the most other girls, a double strand of pink pearls——"

"Simulated," said Poke.

"Phony," agreed Moke, "but pink. Listen. If you embroider a little mole beside your left eye, then I'll know you. You can use the same stuff you used for the hair. What do you say?"

"I don't mind," she said softly. It wouldn't do Moke any good but she couldn't tell her that.

"You don't sound as if you meant it," Moke objected. "Do it now where I can see you. No, lemme. You look like you might be honest." She took Ruth's mask and went to work. "Poke's got one black eyebrow and one brown. Show her, Poke. Cute?"

They rattled on, repeating House gossip, giving priceless information, innocently pointing the way to escape. Sunday night supper was always cold stuff and cocoa, put on the table and no service. Sunday nights Monny and Angel always ate at Marshall-Gill's. At last year's party Minnie May had spiked the punch, and Fister was going to guard the table this time. At last year's party they had dressed as fairies because the people Plummer worked for had a lot of old gauze and busted sequins they were throwing out. Somebody jilted Plummer when she was eighteen and she still wore a locket with his picture in it. Plummer was okay, though, if you wanted to come in after midnight without telling the world. She'd slip the latch if she liked you. Last year a girl on the third took poison but Monny brought it up with mustard water. The girl had been sneaking down the fire escape after hours and sneaking back again and nobody ever knew it. Monny had paid for the baby and nobody was supposed to know that either. Monny was all right in her way but she had a temper and threw

34

things. Angel was all right, too, if you soft-soaped her and gave presents. She was working on Harris now, and it wouldn't be long. Harris was tough but Angel always got her girl. Angel knew what she wanted. Used to be a boarder herself until Monny promoted her. Minnie May's roommate, Dotty, had religion. Some people said she'd been in jail and got it there. Everybody had a past if you believed all you heard.

"You got a past, Ruth?" Moke grinned.

Ruth smiled. "Well, yes. Yes, that's right, that's what I've got."

It was after six when she finally reached her room. She wasn't hungry and she wasn't even tired. Her mind was clear and orderly because she knew what she had to do. She knew she had been right. She knew she had been recognized. She had seen the following eyes.

If one girl could use the fire escape without detection, so could she. The lobby wasn't safe. And it would have to be at a certain time, not when people were dressing to go out or undressing to go to bed. She might be seen through the windows.

She went to the closet and collected her clothes. Pack first, while April was still downstairs. Hide the suitcase on the fire escape outside the bathroom window. When April came she'd tell her she was going for a walk. No, that wouldn't do. April might want to come. Or she might even wait up. She'd tell April she was spending the night with an old friend, and later, much later, she'd write her a little note.

She went to the bathroom and looked out of the window. There was a fence dividing the courtyard from the building next door. A white cat sat motionless on the fence. She saw it clearly in the light from the street. Where the fence met the street there was a gate between the two buildings. It was open.

She returned to her room and finished packing. It's a relief to know the truth, she told herself; now I know where I stand, I know what I have to do. I lost my head last night, I didn't think straight. After all these years I didn't want to believe what I saw. . . . The doll mask was on the bed, together with the long, shapeless costume. I knew I'd never wear it, she said, I knew it. She touched the ridiculous mole that would have marked her from the others and hoped that Moke would win the pearls.

She went back to the night before, to the afternoon that was just over. She retraced every step. I don't think she knew me at first, she decided. Because of my glasses. I was wearing glasses before. But she knew me this afternoon. Maybe I have a special way of turning my head or using my hands. . . . She looked at her hands and saw they were clenched. Maybe I did that this afternoon. Maybe I did that the other time.

She went back to the other time. She saw an office, richly furnished, saw two hatted men with hard eyes, saw another man, hatless, sitting in a leather chair behind an ornate desk. She saw the other girl, her face twisted with fury. She heard the voice again, low and quiet at first, then screaming: 'I'll kill you for this. Some day we'll meet and I'll kill you with my bare hands.'

They'd told her not to worry, but she knew they were worried themselves. They'd given her some money and told her to leave town for a little while. They'd said it would all blow over. But she'd heard them whispering among themselves. They were as worried as she was. Five years ago they'd sent her away, but now she was caught.

She sat on the bed because her knees were shaking. April's alarm clock said seven-thirty. She noticed for the first time that it had no crystal. April read with her fingers. . . . I'll take a bath, she said, and then I'll be ready. And April will be back by then. She locked the suitcase and took it with her to the bathroom, first making sure there was no one in the hall. She studied the hall, wondering about emergency exits. Beyond her room, at the far end, were the packrooms, enormous cupboards holding trunks and old furniture. The fire door was at the front end, then the bath, the telephone, and her own room. I won't call him up, she said. They'll keep a record of the number. She could see it, she could see it in a minute and maybe follow me.

At eight she was ready and the suitcase was on the fire escape. She sat on the bed again and waited for time to pass.

At eight-thirty a bell rang shrilly over her head. She began to tremble. He had come home, he had found her note, she was safe. She saw Kitty's long, thin hands inserting the right plug, she saw Kitty swivel around in her chair and press the right bell. Her bell. He was calling at last. She'd tell him to come for her there. She wouldn't risk the dim halls and the stairs. She'd wait in her room until he was announced.

She didn't know the voice at first. But it wasn't his. It was level and toneless.

"Miss Miller?"

"Yes," she said.

"This is Mrs. Fister, the housekeeper. I'd like to see you in my room, please."

She answered calmly. "I have a headache, Mrs. Fister. Won't tomorrow do?"

Mrs. Fister was sorry. "I'm afraid it won't. I wouldn't ask you if it wasn't important, Miss Miller. Room 202."

She heard the receiver click.

Room 202. Second floor. She'd have to go. She would walk, stopping on each landing to look up and down, ready for flight if she met a figure coming toward her on the dim stairs. She'd have to go. It would look suspicious if she didn't. She mustn't do anything that looked odd or suspicious. She must pretend she didn't know.

There was no one on the stairs. The elevator hummed in its shaft, and the stairs wound down beside it. When the elevator stopped at a floor, she waited on the landing until it went on. It was better not to take chances.

Mrs. Fister's door was open, and she hesitated on the threshold.

"Come in," Mrs. Fister said, "and close the door. I asked you to come here because I'm having a little trouble and I think you're the one who can help me." She pointed to a rocking chair. The room was filled with rocking chairs, taborets, jardinieres, and a big bed, relics of a home-owning past. "My sister has the room next to this one, and we usually leave the communicating door open. That one." She pointed to a door. It was closed.

"Yes, Mrs. Fister," she said.

Mrs. Fister went on slowly. "April's in there. She's in bed, sick. She's been eating too many sweets."

She wanted to scream. Was this the thing that couldn't wait until tomorrow?

"I've put her to bed, my sister can sleep with me, you see I brought my own bed with me when I came." The level, toneless voice droned on. "April needs attention, not much, but she needs to be watched. I can't do it myself because I've got to go out tonight. On private business. There's nobody to watch her while I'm gone, that's why I called you. I was sure you wouldn't be going anywhere, and I didn't think you'd mind giving a little time to an afflicted girl."

She forced herself to say, "How long?"

"How long will I be gone?" Mrs. Fister was donning coat and hat, taking down a small satchel from the closet shelf. "Not too long, not long enough to make any difference to you. This is as good a place to sit as any. Say about two hours, maybe more, maybe less. You weren't planning anything, were you?"

"No."

"She won't wake up for a while, perhaps not till I get back. Don't go in there unless she calls, and don't give her anything but water." Mrs. Fister walked heavily to the door and turned. "The time will go faster down here," she said.

When the hall door closed she crossed to the communicating door, almost convinced that she would find an empty room. She turned the knob. April was there, lying in the middle of another big bed, covered with an eiderdown. Only the top of her head showed, like a doll's wig on the pillow. She left the door open and went back to the rocking chair. She watched the clock.

Mrs. Fister's clock was a parlor piece, of china and hand-painted roses. The gilt circumference was latticed, and threaded with red silk ribbon. The hands stood at nine.

Nothing can make me stay, she said over and over; nothing that anyone can do. Not even death can make me. I don't know why I'm here, but I had to come. Everything I've done since yesterday I've had to do. But nothing can make me stay. In two hours it will be eleven. From eleven to twelve it won't be safe. But after twelve——

She rocked and listened for sounds in the other room. There were none. She'll sleep until morning, she said, and I'll never see her again. Maybe next year——

She dozed in the chair and jerked herself awake. That was bad, she couldn't afford to sleep, not yet. She smoothed the blue with careful hands that lingered over the stain. It'll clean, she reminded herself.

Nine-thirty. Someone came down the hall and passed the door, singing softly. It was an elderly voice and the song was a hymn. Two more went by, walking heavily on stout shoes. The maids, she decided, back from the movies, the early show. The first one hadn't made any noise walking. That would be bedroom slippers, going to the bath. . . . She went to the communicating door, but April hadn't moved.

Ten o'clock. She was beginning to feel cold, although the room was stuffy. Ten o'clock was getting on, but still it wasn't late. She got up and stood by the hall door. When Mrs. Fister returned she wanted to hear her coming. She wanted to be standing by the door, ready to run.

At ten-fifteen she heard the steps she'd been waiting for. She had the door open before Mrs. Fister reached it.

"There was no trouble?" Mrs. Fister asked.

"Oh no," she said, edging forward.

Mrs. Fister tried to take her arm. "If you'll wait, I'd like to give you——"

"No, thank you. Good night." She never did know what Mrs. Fister wanted to give her.

Back in her own room she locked the door and turned

on every light. The ceiling light, the desk lamps, the lamp between the two beds. They would shine from the window down into the courtyard, articulate in the night. They'd tell a watcher in another window that she was there. But she wouldn't be; she'd be gone.

She put on her hat and coat and went to the bathroom, groping to the window in the dark. There she stopped. The window was open as she had left it, but it might as well have been barred. Rain fell steadily, striking the narrow, iron platform, rebounding from the glistening skeleton steps. She couldn't believe it, and put out her hand to touch the dripping rails. Her hand slipped as if she had touched grease. I can't do it, she said; I'd break my neck. Why didn't I notice the rain before? Then she remembered how Mrs. Fister's window had been heavily curtained. And she hadn't gone near her own. She looked at the brick walls facing the court. There were too many squares of uncurtained light. She could see into some of the rooms, and even name their occupants. The fire escape coiled against the wall like a black serpent, beautiful with treachery.

She retrieved her wet suitcase and went back to her room. Although her door was less than three yards away, she ran. By this time she was frantic, and she walked the floor until she was calm enough to plan again. The fire escape had been a bad idea in the first place. Dangerous. The main entrance was still hopeless; at ten-thirty the lobby and the lounge would be occupied. They were good places to sit if you were watching and waiting for somebody.

Maybe later, just before midnight, she could try it. They said Miss Plummer sometimes helped the girls. She could ask Miss Plummer to let her out because she had to mail an important letter. It meant leaving her suitcase behind, but that was a small price to pay. Am I making too much of this? she asked herself. And she answered quietly, No, you're not. No, you're not, and you know he won't call now.

Ten-forty. Still too early. What will I do, she wondered, if Miss Plummer refuses? She might. And she might have to put my name on a list, like a time sheet, and when I don't come back it might make trouble for her. But I can't help that, not now. If she says yes, I'll go. But if she says no?

If she says no, I'll go early in the morning, as early as six. I'll put the blue in my suitcase, and if anybody says anything I'll say I'm taking it to the cleaner's. They all saw me spill the tea. Then I'll go to Blackman's for one day only, so if anybody checks on me I'll be there, and it'll look natural. As if I meant to come back here tomorrow night. I won't go back to the store again, ever, and I'll lose a day's pay, but what's a day's pay.

At eleven o'clock she was thirsty, so thirsty that thinking about the cold water in the bathroom was almost unbearable. Shining nickel taps, beaded with cold moisture. Was it safe to go out in the hall at eleven? She wet her dry lips and figured her chances in the hall. She was in a blind alley, a dead end. Packrooms to the right, fire door to the left. Beyond the fire door, the stairs and elevator. If someone came down the hall on the other side of the door, would she hear the steps in time? Then, as she visualized the hall and saw the door, the bath, and the packrooms, she saw something else. The telephone. Black, shining, beautiful. The telephone!

She was not cut off from the world, the city, or people. She was not dependent on the call that hadn't come. She had only to lift her hand and speak and girls she didn't even know would give her voice safe-conduct.

I don't care if they do keep a record, she told herself, I've got to have help; and it's Miss Plummer on the board now, Miss Plummer is all right.

The police? No, she knew the police. They would talk to her nicely. They might even send a radio car and talk to her in the lobby. They'd talk to other people, too, and smile among themselves, and tell her to get a good night's rest. They might advise a sedative. A sedative, a good night's rest in her room alone, and no morning to wake to.

She stumbled over to the door. Call somebody, call anybody, call him. Pocket your pride, pride isn't anything. She held the door open with one hand and reached for the receiver. If Mrs. Sutton hadn't gone away, if Mrs. Sutton had waited another day—— It almost made her laugh to think of that. It was the scheme again, pushing her on. The destiny. But she didn't laugh, because, if she did, she knew she'd never stop.

There were millions of people at the other end of the telephone. The whole world was at the other end. Paris, London, New York, San Francisco, Chicago.

She gasped. Chicago! She threw a triumphant look about her. The fire door showed a bland, unmoving surface. In the other direction the sliding doors of the packrooms were in shadow, but they were still. Chicago!

Miss Plummer's voice was sleepy, but she didn't sound surprised.

"Miss Plummer," she whispered, "Miss Plummer, this is Ruth Miller. I've got to make a very important call. It's long distance, Miss Plummer, but do I have to pay for it right away?"

Miss Plummer said the call could be charged, and there was a new interest in her voice. "Go right ahead, dear," she said.

"It's to a Mr. Norman Crawford, person to person, please. In Chicago. I don't know the number or the address, but he's very prominent in Chicago and I know you can find him. A Mr. Norman Crawford in Chicago, the one who used to know a Ruth Miller."

Miss Plummer said, "I'll try, dear. But you'll have to speak up louder than that."

She leaned against the wall, one hand still on the door. Mr. Crawford would know what to do. He was the one who'd given her the money and told her to go away. He'd remember. He'd realize how bad it was. He'd call a lawyer or a friend in New York, he'd call at once and in no time at all it would be over.

She heard Miss Plummer speak to the operator and then Miss Plummer said, "We're trying, dear, but it may take a little while." She pressed the receiver close to her ear and listened to the distant voices. Far away someone spoke a number. She let go of the door while she wrote the number on the telephone pad. It would be a good thing to have, she might need it again. She slipped the paper into her pocket and listened eagerly. Voices came and went, a voice that was New York, a voice that was Chicago. Behind them was a sound of humming. She called it singing, she called it a singing wire. It was like music. Everything was working for her, looking for Mr. Crawford who was halfway across the United States of America.

A new sound joined the others, a low grinding sound like a metal wheel turning. She had begun to wonder about it when Miss Plummer spoke again.

"I think we're ready, dear," Miss Plummer said. "Just a second, dear. Hello, Chicago."

The low grinding sound grew. There's interference on the line, she thought. It's got to stop or I won't be able to hear. I've got to hear. "Miss Plummer?" she said. "There's something on the line." Then she remembered how clear Miss Plummer's voice had been, even while the grinding sound went on.

That meant the sound was outside the telephone.

She fought paralysis and turned her head. The heavy fire door was opening slowly, inching open as she watched. Then it stopped. She flung herself into her room and locked the door.

All night she sat in a chair before the door, watching the knob. She talked aloud in a gay, clear voice, and answered herself in a lower key.

"I'm awfully glad you're spending the night with me," she said to the door. "It's lonely without April."

She murmured a reply, and went on with her bright chatter. She kept it up. Hope House was lovely, everybody was so kind, she wished she'd known about it before.

The bell rang and she let it ring. "We won't answer that," she declared. "We're having such fun we don't want anyone else!"

Miss Plummer would think she had given up. She talked on.

Downstairs in the lobby Miss Plummer put the board in order for the night. She had made a note of the Chicago number, and now she looked at it curiously. There's no use in me trying again, she thought, she's gone to bed or changed her mind. All that excitement for nothing, and she wouldn't even answer the bell. Maybe it's just as well, though, seeing as the gentleman's down with the flu and can't talk. Old beau, sure's you're born, had a quarrel and felt sorry for herself. Wanted to tell him so and then thought better of it. . . . Miss Plummer fingered the locket at her throat. She folded the call slip and put it under Kitty's blotter, in case it should be wanted.

Upstairs the doorknob turned. Ruth laughed gaily. "Oh, I've never been anywhere," she said clearly. "I'm a native of Philadelphia. I lived there all my life until I came here last year."

3

Moke and Poke sauntered to the section manager's desk and checked in. Ruth was behind her counter, dusting stock and making requisitions.

"Good morning, Mrs. Blackman," Moke said. "I see you spent the night in the store."

"Oh I felt like getting up early," Ruth said. "It's such a nice day."

"It's such a nice day if you got fish blood. . . . What's the matter? You still sick?"

"Not me! I'm on top of the world!"

She watched their shining heads disappear as they clattered down a flight of stairs at the end of the counter.

The day moved as slowly as the night. She scanned the faces of the shopping crowds and they were all strange. That was good. At noon she ate in the cafeteria and bought a sandwich to take out in her handbag. The way things are, she thought, I can't really count on dinner.

Only one person had been in the lobby when she left at six-thirty, an elderly maid who was using a vacuum cleaner and who hadn't even looked up. That was good too. But at four o'clock she began to worry. Suppose Moke and Poke waited for her at the employees' door? What excuse could she give for not walking home? Suppose someone else was waiting too?

She closed her aching eyes. I'll try the doctor again, she decided. I'll put my pride in my pocket. And if he isn't there I'll go to the Travelers' Aid. They helped me once before and I paid them back. I'll ask Mr. Benz for an early pass and tell him about seeing the doctor. He

45

knows about my eyes, so I won't have to argue. I'll tell him I have an appointment for five o'clock. That will give me a good start.

Mr. Benz was sympathetic. He told her he was glad she was doing something about her eyes. "You run right along," he said, writing out the pass. "Do you want somebody to go with you? He may use drops, you know, and sometimes it's hard to see with those drops."

She thanked him and said she'd be all right. He was nice, they all were. She tried not to think of the next day and what he would say when she didn't come back. I'll write him, too, she promised herself, later, when I write to April and Moke and Poke.

Down in the locker room she collected her coat, hat, and good umbrella. Better leave the work shoes and old umbrella. It would look more natural if Moke and Poke came to find her. She got her suitcase from the parcel room, checked out with the doorman, and climbed the stairs to the street.

There was only one pedestrian on the street, a woman under a large umbrella, walking toward her. She started out, struggling with the suitcase and fighting the wind and rain. The woman ran into her and stopped to apologize.

"I'm so sorry——why, Ruth!"

It was Miss Brady.

"What are you doing out so early?" Miss Brady asked.

"I'm going to the doctor's, about my eyes. It's very important, so they let me off." She tried to move on.

"I'll go with you," Miss Brady said. "Silly to go alone when you can have company. Where is this doctor? Near here?"

"Yes, Miss Brady, he's quite near. I can go alone, I don't mind."

"I mind." Miss Brady looked at the suitcase. "What's that for?"

"I took my suit to the cleaner's," she said evenly. "My blue. I upset my tea, everybody saw me do it." A cab cruised by and she raised her hand. It wouldn't cost much for a block or two, she needn't go all the way. "Taxi, please! I'll see you later, Miss Brady." She opened the door and pushed her suitcase in. "Over to Sixth," she said.

Miss Brady got in with her.

"I think we'll skip the doctor," Miss Brady said. "This doesn't strike me as the right time for it. You didn't have an appointment, did you?"

She didn't answer. Be careful, she told herself; let her think anything she wants to. Don't give his address, you could be traced through that.

"No appointment," Miss Brady agreed. "So if he doesn't know you planned to come, you won't be missed." She gave the Hope House number to the driver, and leaned back. "That was quick thinking, that one about the doctor. Spur of the moment, or did you use it in the store to get away?"

"I don't know what you mean, Miss Brady."

"Well, we won't bother with that now." She locked Ruth's arm in hers.

The bell in the ceiling rang for dinner. This time she would eat. She used the stairs again, walking slowly, rearranging the hours ahead, dividing the night into minutes.

Miss Small had been at the desk when she and Miss Brady came in. Only Miss Small at the desk and Kitty behind the switchboard. It was still too early for the others. Miss Small had said something about the weather and told her the dining room would close at seven because of the party. She had looked at the suitcase and then at Miss Brady, raising her eyebrows.

I can be out of the dining room by six-thirty, she figured. Talk to April until seven, if April is around. My wool dress under the costume, no coat, no hat, no suitcase. This time, the police. . . . Maybe the police would lock her up. No hat, no coat, in the driving rain, of course they'd lock her up. The costume thrown in a gutter somewhere, and she'd hate to do that. The long-sleeved, shapeless garment was going to save her life.

47

It was her only ally. Dozens of girls, all alike, all with identical faces; white sacks to cover telltale hair, thick white gloves to hide familiar hands. Rag dolls crowding and pushing, disguising their own voices, imitating each other. Out the front door, down the street, money pinned in her dress pocket.

She was the first girl in the dining room, and for some minutes she was alone. When her food came she ate quickly. The room was filling rapidly when she left. She walked upstairs and found April having milk toast on a tray.

"Mrs. Fister brought it up herself," April said. "She thinks I'm well enough to come back here. I was awfully sick but she says I can go to the party if I sleep first. So I'm going to sleep." She put the tray on the floor and got under the covers. "Wake me up when it's time to dress, will you, Ruthie?"

She sat by the window and watched the lights go on in the court rooms. Other girls had begun to dress. She could see them running back and forth, laughing.

At seven-thirty she woke April. April was noisy with excitement, clowning like a little monkey; she tried on Ruth's mask and her own. "Now I look like everybody else," she boasted. They rode down together in the crowded elevator, with four other dolls who posed and postured silently and threatened to fall.

The lobby was already filled. Someone had started the phonograph in the lounge and the dancing had begun. Miss Brady and Miss Small were wearing gray sharkskin suits, exactly alike. Miss Brady stood halfway up the stairs and watched the milling figures with a smile. Miss Small moved from doll to doll, making wrong guesses and leaving a trail of laughter when she moved on. Miss Plummer, railed in at desk and switchboard, looked harassed and pleased in wrinkled chartreuse satin. Mrs. Marshall-Gill, in purple velvet with matching orchids, sat in a chair by the lounge door and bowed right and left, happily unaware of snubs. Dolls everywhere, leaning against each other, flopping, falling.

Dolls like herself, cut from the same pattern, identical. Someone brushed by and whispered, "Get a load of Fister guarding the punch." Moke or Poke. They know me, she thought in a panic, but then she remembered Moke's provident mole. Outside the dining-room door Mrs. Fister loomed over the table that held the punch.

Someone's arms went around her and she was dancing across the lobby and back again. That was a lucky break, she was one of the others, mingling with the crowd. She didn't know her partner, but she wasn't afraid. The girl was short, much shorter than she was. She peered at the lobby clock. It was eight, it was early, there was plenty of time. Maybe two hours before the unmasking, two hours to reach a door that was only a few yards away. She tried to lead her partner to the door, to prove to herself that it could be done, but other people blocked the way. Still, she knew she could do it if she were alone.

Another doll dragged her partner away, and she was left standing in the middle of the lobby, surrounded and hemmed in by chattering duplicates of herself. It was the best thing that could have happened. Now she could begin.

She held her head high and turned it right and left, as if she were looking for a special friend. The maids were helping Mrs. Fister now, handing out punch with one hand and defending the bowl with the other. She moved in that direction. She called it a clever move because it was misleading. A few precious minutes thrown away, but that was the way to do it.

As she drew near the punch bowl, someone in a white kitchen apron ran out of the dining room, a woman with a bright smear of blood on her bib. Her hand flew to her mouth in terror. The crowd fell back and surged forward again, leaving her alone on the outskirts. She saw Miss Small speak to Mrs. Fister and then go over to the desk. Mrs. Fister led the woman away, shrugging her massive shoulders. Someone said, "The chef cut his hand, that's all."

Apparently it wasn't serious. The maids went on as if nothing had happened. One of them carried a cup of punch to Mrs. Marshall-Gill. Miss Small went upstairs. Miss Brady said something to Mrs. Marshall-Gill and she too disappeared, in the direction of the kitchen.

She was desperate now. This was her chance, she'd never have a better one, but Mrs. Marshall-Gill was too near the entrance. She forced herself to circle the lobby again. Miss Plummer was at the switchboard, looking distracted, trying to get a number, and making futile little dabs at passing dolls while she pleaded, "Please, operator, try again; oh, somebody help me, one of you girls, please——"

Another circle around the lobby, and she saw Mrs. Marshall-Gill leave her chair and cross to the elevator. There was almost a clear path to the front door, not clear enough to make her conspicuous but exactly right. She gave the crowd a last survey and planned the final move. She would walk along the office railing and examine the mailboxes; then a short, diagonal cut to the lounge door; then another short cut to the street door. Slowly, easily, not more than five minutes at the most.

She was between the dining room and the office when she started. Once she thought someone pressed too closely from behind, but when she turned there was no one near. Only a doll in rubber sneakers who was looking the other way. A long line of dolls, noisily cracking the whip, came screaming down the center of the floor, and the doll in sneakers dragged her out of the way. She was flung against the office railing.

An arm in chartreuse satin reached out and clutched her shoulder. "You," Miss Plummer said, "you're not doing anything, are you? I've got to have help and everybody's so selfish. Chef cut himself and they want first aid and how am I to get it when everybody runs away! Slip up to Mrs. Fister's room like a good girl and get me the iodine and bandages, bedroom closet, top shelf, all marked. If the door's locked, you go right on up to Miss Brady's, there's an extra supply there. In the bathroom, and her door's bound to be open. Never locked. Hurry, that's a good girl."

"Miss Brady's room?" she repeated dully. "I don't know where it is."

Miss Plummer gave her a sharp look. "Don't know where Miss Brady's——oh, I see. Well, naturally you wouldn't know. Eighth floor, room 806. Mrs. Fister is 202. Please, dear, there's no time to lose."

No time to lose, she said to herself, no time to lose, no time to lose.

Mrs. Fister's door was locked. She tried Miss Plummer's door. Locked too. She turned in despair and ran for the stairs. No elevator now, even to save time; no elevator now at any price. Get there and get back before Miss Plummer complained about Ruth Miller's being slow, before Miss Plummer said Ruth Miller had gone upstairs. She'd given herself away to Miss Plummer.

She climbed, breathless, trembling, holding on to the railing, looking ahead as she always did, forgetting to look back. Behind her another doll climbed, slowly, without effort, sometimes looking down over her shoulder but never looking up. Two dolls on the dim stairway, climbing in the same direction, the first pausing for breath on the landings, the second pausing to fold her arms on the railing and watch the way she had come. The second doll wore sneakers. Ruth climbed on.

In Miss Small's suite, Mrs. Marshall-Gill adjusted her hat, which had been knocked askew too often, pinned back her straying hair, and washed her hands. That done, she sat at Miss Small's desk and wrote what she called a little note and a little check. "In appreciation," she wrote, "of the extra time and trouble you have taken and of your unflagging interest in our good work." The check was for one hundred dollars. She placed both note and check under Miss Small's paper knife. Nothing for Brady, she said with satisfaction. Not a penny, not a word. Sharp tongue and more money than I have.

Miss Brady's door was unlocked. Ruth went through the living room and bedroom to the bath beyond. The iodine and bandages were in the medicine chest. She collected them hurriedly and started back. She was hot

51

and her face was wet, and she pushed up the cotton mask. Twin lamps burned on Miss Brady's dressing table, shedding their light on gold and ivory, tortoise and enamel. Shedding their light on gold and ivory, tortoise and an enamel powder box. Her free hand went to her throat in a gesture that repulsed and acknowledged what she saw. She knew the box, she knew it had a bronze base, she knew the color and shape of the importer's mark on the under side, she knew the tune it would play if she raised the lid. Proof, proof, if she ever needed it. Sudden triumph shook her from head to foot and all caution fled. She raised the lid, and the room was filled with tinkling sound. *Believe me if all those endearing young charms that I gaze on so fondly today.* She repeated the words under her breath.

The music drifted out into the living room; it was entrance music for the second doll. The second doll moved slowly, lazily, silently across the floor to the bedroom door and leaned against it. For a while the only sound was the music. Then came a low chuckle.

Ruth turned. The iodine and bandage dropped from her stiff, gloved fingers. She backed to the wall with arms outstretched, her stiff, gloved hands beseeching.

"Nobody knows," she pleaded, "nobody ever will know, ever, ever. I was going away, I want to go, let me go." Her mask slipped to the floor.

The other doll advanced. "Nobody," Ruth pleaded. "Nobody. I've forgotten everything already. I forgot it years ago. I didn't come here on purpose. It was an accident. I'm going away tonight, I'm all ready to go. I found another place to live, I found another place to live far away——"

She could hear the musical box, but she could see nothing because a thick white hand covered her face. It wasn't her own hand. Something struck the side of her head.

Mrs. Marshall-Gill gave a final fillip to her hat, left Miss Small's room, and proceeded to the end of the hall where she rang for the elevator. She heard the preliminary buzz and waited for the active purr. Nothing happened. She rang again and again, and after the third ring the car came, empty except for the operator. She got in, affronted. This, she said to herself, is what comes of letting the masses act like other people. "The party is no excuse, Annie," she said. "You knew I was there and don't tell me you didn't. I rang three times—three. I call that deliberate insubordination. . . . Well, say something!"

The masked head turned slowly to face her. No words came from the red, buttonhole mouth, nothing showed behind the round, black-fringed eyes. The car sank gently downward.

"Annie?" Mrs. Marshall-Gill's voice broke in an unexpected falter. This is ridiculous, she told herself. An ill-bred, common little chit. I will not be routed. "I'm speaking to you, Annie!"

The thick white hand held the lever carelessly, the silent figure slouched against the cage. The face behind the mask still watched, Mrs. Marshall-Gill could feel it watching.

She discovered that her throat was dry and her knees unstable. Something like a cold wind was filling the small cage, wrapping its fingers around her heart, emanating from Annie. She backed into a corner, fighting for decorum.

"Annie," she began, but her voice was no more than a whisper, she could hardly hear it herself. She tried again. "I don't care what you call yourself, Annie," she quavered. "You may call yourself anything you like. I've been thinking it over and Annie isn't much of a name for a young girl. Jewel is better. Jewel, how would you like some calling cards engraved with your name? You'd like that, wouldn't you? You could give them to people and then they'd know, do you see? Annie, Jewel, aren't we going too fast? You're not watching the indicator, Annie, Jewel! Jewel——"

The car lurched to a stop. Mrs. Marshall-Gill got out and went to her chair. When she was able to raise her glazed eyes, the car had gone up again. She watched the dial, four, five, six, seven, eight. It stopped at eight.

Days went by, and Dr. Kloppel came too many times to Hope House. Too many nights he went down the halls preceded by Mrs. Fister's warning voice, "Man coming, man coming." There was an epidemic of hysteria that took a long time dying. In the rooms facing the courtyard three girls often crowded into one bed and talked all night, staring at the window.

Thanksgiving came, and Mrs. Marshall-Gill sent a large pumpkin for the Hope House pies, with instructions to save the seed for her country garden. It was, she said, a superior strain. She discontinued the Sunday teas.

Lillian Harris asked for day work at her office, and got it. She also asked to room with April Hooper. This pleased Miss Small, who saw in these moves a tangible result of her little talks. Lillian was a changed girl. She was cordial when she met Miss Brady and Miss Small in elevator and hall, and rose politely when they entered a room. Sometimes she even knocked on Miss Small's door to offer inexpensive gifts of flowers and candy.

There was no change in the evening routine for Miss Brady and Miss Small, except that they met more often in Miss Brady's suite. They had more privacy there, and that was an advantage. Girls with stomach aches, broken hearts, and doubts about the value of maintaining virtue didn't come to Miss Brady when they couldn't sleep.

"I don't see how you stand it, Angel," Miss Brady said. "The ratty little exhibitionists, they know you're soft and they weep down your neck for the kick they get out of it. One night a month is enough. You've simply got to set aside one night and issue tickets. You'll break down if you don't."

"It's my work," Miss Small reminded her. "And look at the success I've had with Lillian! Darling, you must admit that Lillian is almost human."

"I liked her better when she wasn't. That meeching,

mooching smile. And I don't like the way she keeps bringing you presents. She can't afford it."

"You bring me presents, Monny. I mean, don't we both?"

"That's different," Miss Brady said gruffly. "Look, I've got one for you now." She rooted about in the untidy drawer of an almost priceless desk and brought out two envelopes. "Came today and I got them before anybody saw them. Passports."

"Monny!"

"French Line, I think, maybe the first of the year. I'll see to it. We won't say a word until we hand in our resignations, bang. Can you see Marshall-Gill's face?" Miss Brady reproduced a reasonable facsimile.

"Darling!" Miss Small's eyes filled. "I can't believe it, it can't be happening to me! I've never been anywhere, done anything, seen anything, and now—this! Monny, when I think of the day I first walked into this place, not knowing, not dreaming——"

"Little navy blue suit with a frilled blouse and a white hat. All wrong, of course, but very cute. I remember."

"And you looked so stern! I was scared to death. And don't think you're the only one with a good memory. Dark red wool, I wish you'd kept it."

"Silly."

"Monny? Some of the girls came to my room after dinner. They said they were a delegation. They've been collecting for a marker for Ruth Miller's grave. I don't know what to do about it, I don't want to seem heartless. But we do frown on collections of any sort, don't we?"

"Send them to me. We can't have it. They're simply dragging the thing out, and that's no good. Time it was forgotten."

That was on a Sunday night in December.

On the following morning young Mrs. Sutton, back from Pinehurst, welcomed two elderly guests from upstate.

When Roberta Beacham Sutton invited Bessy Petty and Beulah Pond to New York, Beulah accepted for both of them. Bessy thought, reasonably enough, that she'd accepted for herself. She wrote Roberta according to her own formula and gave the letter to Beulah to mail. Beulah tore it up because it was six pages long, with a double row of kisses under the signature and a written injunction to the postman on the back of the envelope. "Postman, postman, do your duty, take this to a New York beauty."

At the bottom of her own letter Beulah penned a simple postscript: "My friend will be with me." It made Bessy sound like a charity case about to be given a treat, and that was a pleasing thought. Roberta knew Bessy wasn't, but Roberta's servants didn't.

Beulah had qualms about Roberta's servants. They were said to be British and uppity. So before she left Crestwood she practiced facial expression and posture. She also drilled Bessy in what she told her was a genteel carriage, but Bessy's pink and white fat was uncooperative. They stopped speaking for two days, and Beulah concentrated on herself. By the time they took the train, she had four expressions denoting elegance and couldn't make up her mind which to keep. A run-through rehearsal in the Pullman washroom, with an audience of one mother and two infant children, gave the vote to the world-weary one. She added a slow, dragging walk, indicative of thin, aristocratic blood. And she told herself it ought to take care of Bessy, too.

The Misses Pond and Petty, both in their late sixties, were not strangers to travel or anything. They loved life and had a passionate interest in death. Other peoples'. Along with their contemporaries they read the obituary page daily, but where the contemporaries accepted the printed fact, Bessy and Beulah challenged it. They didn't believe that natural death was as common as doctors and coroners made it out to be.

In appearance, Bessy resembled an aging Cupid and Beulah a rejuvenated hawk. When Roberta Sutton met their train and walked between them to her car, she

56

looked as if she were being preyed upon. But they were only loving her.

After breakfast Roberta offered a shopping trip, to be followed by lunch with Mark East. This was accepted with little cries of pleasure, and they started out. Under the eyes of maroon-and-gold attendants, Beulah insinuated herself across the apartment-house lobby and watched Bessy forgetting all the things she'd taught her.

Two hours off the train and Bessy trotted and rolled. She stopped to examine the soil of the lobby's plants and cried for water, which she almost got; she called a poodle in a monogrammed blanket the same things she called her egg man's unblanketed rat terrier.

"I adore Miss Bessy," Roberta whispered to Beulah.

"Wait," Beulah prophesied.

Roberta grinned. "We'll go to Blackman's first, if you don't mind. I need soap. Then lunch. Then anywhere you like. What do you want to see?"

Bessy said, "The Little Church around the Corner, the Little Bar at the Ritz, and Grant's Tomb."

They drove to Blackman's and Roberta made straight for the toilet goods, beginning to smile before she reached the counter. But Miss Miller wasn't there. A strange clerk with bleached hair was rearranging Miss Miller's stock. Roberta compared her watch with Blackman's big clock; it was only half past eleven, and Miss Miller never went to lunch before one. She spoke briskly to the strange clerk.

"Will Miss Miller be back shortly?"

The clerk looked blank. "Who?" Then she appraised Roberta's coat, hat, gloves, handbag, and all that could be seen of her blouse. This wasn't a personal, this was a customer. "I'm new in the department," she said formally. "Would you like me to inquire, madam?"

"Yes, I would, please." Roberta wanted Miss Miller to meet Bessy and Beulah. Miss Miller would enjoy that. "Perhaps, if she's been transferred——"

"If madam will wait," the clerk said, "I'll ask our section manager." She pressed a button under the counter and a tall young man glided to Roberta's side. His smile wrung from Bessy an instant, "How do you do?"

"Madam is inquiring for a Miss Miller," the clerk explained. "This is our Mr. Benz, madam."

Mr. Benz replied with an equal mixture of pleasure and regret. "Miss Miller is no longer with us, but I'm sure Miss Collins will do as well."

"I'm sure Miss Collins will do very well," Roberta agreed, "but I want to see Miss Miller just the same. Can you tell me where she is?"

Mr. Benz also appraised Roberta, and he hesitated before he spoke again.

Roberta saw the hesitation. She gave Miss Collins her shopping list. "Charge and send, please." And she added her name and address.

Mr. Benz was a young man with practical dreams of a little business of his own someday, and in preparation he had made a careful study of Blackman's carriage trade. He riffled through the list of Suttons he kept in his head and placed Roberta instantly. Born Beacham, oil; married Sutton, copper. Tycoon blood. Don't stall. When he spoke it was in a discreet whisper.

"If I may speak to you privately, Mrs. Sutton. The situation is somewhat unusual."

Roberta gathered up her bag. If they had fired Miss Miller, she was going to do something about it. She'd make her father speak to old man Blackman. Miss Miller might be a little slow, but she was careful. And she didn't madam you all over the place. "Thank you," she said to Miss Collins, letting her eyes say what she thought of bleached hair. "Come along, you two."

Bessy and Beulah followed her down the aisle, Bessy plainly agog and Beulah in the same state but not showing it. Mr. Benz was waiting for them at the main door. He indicated that his information was private, and he and Roberta moved out of earshot.

"In deference to the elderly ladies," he explained. "A regrettable situation. Miss Miller is unfortunately dead."

A slow pain took possession of Roberta's heart. Dead, she thought, and I never did any of the things I meant to do. That poor girl, alone in that dreadful place she was moving to. "When?" she asked.

"I believe, let me see, several weeks ago, before Thanksgiving. We were not informed directly, I mean there was no family involved. But we have other employees residing at the same address, and they told us. They wanted permission to open her locker and remove such possessions as were left, the shoes for wearing behind the counter, the extra umbrella, and the like. We valued Miss Miller highly and were sorry to—to lose her." Mr. Benz hoped Mrs. Sutton would let him stop with that, but he hadn't forgotten her tycoon connections and wasn't surprised when she went directly to the point he wanted to avoid.

"Before Thanksgiving? Then I must have talked to her just before she died. She wasn't sick then, she looked even better than usual. What happened?"

Mr. Benz knew there was no help for it. You had to tell these people the truth. They didn't want anything else.

"She killed herself, Mrs. Sutton."

Roberta heard her own reply, and it sounded senseless. "I was out of town. I just got back. I don't believe it."

"I'm sorry, Mrs. Sutton. Our own social service investigated, and that's the answer."

"Thank you," Roberta said. "It's Mr. Benz, isn't it? Thank you, Mr. Benz."

Mr. Benz bowed. Tycoons always had good manners. It paid.

Roberta said nothing when she herded Bessy and Beulah out to the car, and they asked nothing. They knew it wasn't necessary. Mark would take one look at Roberta's white face and she'd tell him everything.

Mark sat at his own table at the Lafayette and his own waiter hovered. The waiter knew Mark as a species of cop whose work permitted him to eat, dress, and kill time like a gentleman. At the moment, the gentleman was smiling at his own thoughts, which undoubtedly had something to do with one of the three ladies who were joining him for lunch. The waiter flicked his napkin and tried to guess which thought. He was wrong.

Mark was wondering what a pernod would do to Bessy if he told her it was only licorice water. But when they finally arrived and he saw Roberta, he decided to postpone the pernod. Roberta looked as if she couldn't cope. He embraced them all in Gallic fashion and compromised on vermouth cassis.

After the first drink, he said: "What are you concealing so imperfectly, Roberta?"

"Nothing," she answered. "Can't you forget your work for an hour?"

"Not when you look like this. What happened between the time you talked to me this morning and now?"

"The girl at the soap counter isn't there," Bessy said.

"Her name is Miller, and there's something nasty about it," Beulah added.

"Miller." Mark closed his eyes for an instant. "Miller. Wait. . . . Is that the girl who jumped from a window?"

There was silence before Roberta said, "I don't know. . . . Is that what she did?"

Mark said, "If her first name was Ruth, it is."

Then she told him all she knew, ignoring the food he had ordered until Beulah put a fork in her hand and Bessy buttered pieces of bread. Ruth Miller wasn't anybody, she told them; just a pale, quiet girl with a gentle sort of way. She'd been happy about moving to a girls' club, or something like that, because there was plenty of hot water and what she called privileges. The privilege of doing your own laundry was one and food that you didn't cook yourself was another. That was all. . . . "Mark, did you say—window?"

Mark spoke softly and persuasively. He knew, with more reason than Mr. Benz, that Roberta was not the kind of girl you hid things from. She was a weight-loser and a dreamer of bad dreams when she was kept in the dark. But there was more than one way to tell a story, all detectives knew that.

"I can be wrong," he said. "I dimly remember reading something or other. I always read those things, you never can tell, you know, but this one looked straight enough. Poor health, maybe insomnia, and there was another contributing factor, let me think. Oh sure, they were having a party and some of the people there said she seemed depressed."

"Depressed? I don't believe it. It was probably the first party she'd had in years. All right about the poor health and insomnia, but I won't go the rest of the way, I won't believe the rest of it. My Miss Miller was preparing to live, not die."

"I take a New York paper, but it wasn't in it," Bessy regretted.

Beulah turned with a soft snarl. "You take the *Times*. I told you to take the *Daily News* but no, you take the *Times*."

"My father always took the *Times*."

"And your father died. I'm not saying what did it."

"Hush," Mark said. "That's loose talk. What are you doing this afternoon, Roberta?"

"A church, a bar, and a tomb. . . . Mark, I don't understand about Miss Miller."

Bessy returned a half-eaten macaroon to the tray of sweets. "Shop girls," she explained. "Turpitude. When I was young it was nurses." She selected a meringue.

"I hope that explodes in your face," Beulah said. "See? Serves you right."

Mark added his napkin to the pool and waited for Bessy to emerge. "Skip the church and the tomb and stay with the bar," he whispered to Roberta. "It'll shorten your day in the end, if you know what I mean."

"Okay. Dinner tomorrow night, Mark?"

"Got it on my calendar. How's Nick?"

"Fine."

"How's the baby?"

"Fat. . . . Listen Mark, couldn't she have fallen? You know, overheated, opened the window—— You hear about those things all the time."

"Are you going to mope about this?"

"Certainly not! I simply like things straight, that's all. And I don't feel as if——I don't believe this one is!"

"Neither do I," Beulah said. "On general principles."

"Listen, you," Mark said to Beulah. "This is a big city. It has a police force. When somebody dies violently they take the place apart. And if they say suicide, that's what it is. This isn't Crestwood, this is New York."

"New York," Beulah repeated. "Isn't that the place where they sent a man to Sing Sing because he looked like somebody else?"

There was no answer to that. His neck had been out and Beulah's aim was legendary. He studied her disagreeable old face and was afraid he knew what she was planning. She and Bessy were in New York at his suggestion. He'd told the Suttons it would be a generous gesture, ending in happy hearts and peace on earth. It would, he decided, end in bloodshed, and twenty-four hours would tell whose.

"The country around here is beautiful," he said earnestly. "We must go for long, long drives every day and come back home exhausted. Sleep, sleep, sleep."

"That gives me an idea," Beulah admitted. "I think Bessy will go to bed early tonight." Her brooding eyes met his without recognition and told him plainly that Bessy was as good as tucked up and locked in. And they told him what she'd do it with. Nick Sutton's port. He listened spellbound.

"I may even go to bed early myself," Beulah said gently. "Young people don't want two old country ladies underfoot. After dinner we'll have a nice little talk with dear Nick, and then we'll leave you to your own devices. . . . How high up is your apartment, Roberta?"

"Twenty-eighth floor."

"That's too high. I don't wonder you're nervous. I wouldn't look out of the window tonight if I were you. I know I shan't. I'm beginning to feel psychic again. Mark, how high did you say that poor girl's—oh, excuse me. Social occasion."

Mark asked for the check. He had to ask twice, because there were other words in his mouth begging for precedence. When he finally stood hatless and alone on the sidewalk, waving Roberta's plum-colored Rolls out of sight, he condemned himself for not staying with it. He owed that much to the Suttons. He was probably going to owe them more. Then, being a man, he went back to the Lafayette and condemned himself again, over a cognac. The waiter looked as if he understood.

Psychic, he repeated. So she was going to be like that, was she? Mincing up and down the sidewalks of New York, making loud guesses about the bulges in peoples' pockets, seeing human hands behind the fall of every sparrow. Fall. Fall. Now wait, he told himself, wait. Where Beulah goes, crime doesn't necessarily follow. Wait.

She said she wouldn't look out of the window tonight. Why? An act. Trying to keep that suicide alive, because it was a nice change from wringing chickens' necks in Crestwood. And she wanted to know how high that girl's room was. Why again? Same reason as before. Making something out of nothing. That poor girl was one of the unfortunate ones. A girl who sold soap behind a department-store counter. A girl who—what had Roberta said? A girl who thought hot water was a privilege.

He was saying something Elizabethan to himself when the waiter brought the second cognac.

The waiter said, "*Vraiment.*"

4

In deference to their guests, who normally dined at six, the Suttons dined at seven. Their regular hour was eight. They preferred seven themselves because they were very young and always hungry, but Mrs. Hawks, the housekeeper, said the Duke preferred eight. Seven made his evenings too long. The Duke might be dead, she said, and he certainly was, but she tried to keep his time.

"She's wonderful," Roberta said to Nick while they were dressing. Dressing was another thing the Duke preferred. "I bet he paid her a pound a month and borrowed it back. We pay a fortune and throw in a couple of coats, and she makes us eat sardines for dessert."

"Get rid of her," Nick said.

"I don't want to. She gives me prestige. I went to the pastry shop because I felt like picking out my own tea-cake, and you should have seen the service I didn't get until I gave my name. I'm the lady Mrs. Hawks lives with." She laughed. "Hawks. For weeks I called her Ox because she did. Then she wrote me a note and there it was—Hawks."

"Note?"

"About soap. We were out of it." Her voice trailed off.

"What," asked Nick, "is there about no soap that makes you look like that?"

"Nothing. Come on. The old girls are waiting."

Cocktails preceded dinner, and coffee and brandy were scheduled to follow, but when they left the table and went back to the library Beulah murmured, "Nothing more."

"What!" Nick said.

"We're exhausted. It's been a long day and we've been on the go every minute. Poor Bessy is falling asleep standing up." This was spoken in a loud, compelling voice. Bessy got to her feet at once and swayed with closed eyes.

"Bed," Beulah went on, "for both of us. At home we never stay up after eight." A bald lie, but the Suttons didn't know it. Sometimes they sat up all night, quarreling. She waited for Bessy's protest, and when none came she was momentarily touched. I'll do something nice for her, she promised herself. But not tonight, tomorrow. "Come along, dear," she said. "Say pleasant dreams to Nick and Roberta."

Roberta walked with them to their room, saw them started on the way to bed, and left them. When she returned to the library, her coffee was cold but she drank it. Nick limped over to her side and sat down.

"You're deep in something," he said. "You hate cold coffee. Did those two wear you out?"

"No. They're nice."

"Is the thin one crazier than the fat one? I can't see any difference but there ought to be one."

"The Duke wouldn't talk like that. . . . Nick, why don't we go out? I feel like going somewhere. They won't care, they won't even know. And don't tell me you had a hard day at the office, you haven't got an office."

"Go where?"

"Some noisy place. You know, junky. Some place we'd get the devil for going to if we weren't married."

"But won't the Duke's lady friend——"

"She won't know either. She's going to the cinema with a daughter of a hundred earls. Come on, what are we all dressed up for?"

The attendant behind the desk at the library said, "Somebody's got those numbers. Do you want to wait?"

65

Mark said, "Yes." He took a chair at one of the long tables and relaxed. It was a pleasant though fusty place, smelling of old, printed pages and the fresh gardenia on a girl's coat. He wasn't surprised when his thoughts took a little jaunt into the past, even when they moved in a rhythm that was almost like waltz time.

He looked about him at the old, nodding heads and the young, undaunted ones. It was the young ones that made him feel the way he did. They made him remember that he hadn't been inside a public library for fifteen years. The girl he'd been in love with then had been trying to prove that Joan of Arc wasn't burned at the stake. He'd helped her. They'd proved it, too, he remembered with awe. At least she got some sort of pat on the back from Smith College. He wondered what she was doing now. Probably a literary agent.

He watched the new crop doing the same thing, bending over faded pages, making notes in little books, slipping other notes across the table with unmistakable looks. He knew all about those looks, too, and that made him feel good. He thought, for every life too unhappy to live, there's a new one being born in somebody's eyes. That brought him back to the present with a jolt, and his mind obediently fell into the old lock step. He went over to the desk.

"Here you are," the attendant said. "Just turned in."

He carried his newspapers back to the table and found what he wanted.

Late last night the body of a young woman in fancy dress was discovered in the courtyard adjoining the premises of 415 West —— Street. The pedestrian who made the discovery notified the police. The deceased was later identified as Ruth Miller, resident of a club adjacent to the courtyard. According to the police, she jumped from a window on the seventh floor. She was known to have been in poor health.

It told him exactly nothing. He opened a second paper.

66

Ruth Miller, age 29, was instantly killed last night when she fell from a seventh-floor window in a midtown hotel. Police list the death as suicide.

Overwritten, garrulous, saccharine. Mark suppressed a snort. No doctor? No background? No native of such-and-such, daughter of so-and-so? He opened a third paper. Nothing. A fourth. It looked better.

The body of Ruth Miller, a resident of Hope House, was discovered in the hotel courtyard shortly after midnight last night by a woman walking her dog. The position and condition of the body indicated that Miss Miller had jumped to her death earlier in the evening when there was still considerable rain. According to Dr. M. L. Kloppel, of 310 West —— Street, and Dr. Paul Myers, Medical Examiner, Miss Miller had been dead approximately three hours. She had been in ill health for some time and had attended a social function in the hotel against the advice of her friends. When found, Miss Miller was still wearing the rag-doll costume in which she had danced a few hours before. The verdict was suicide.

Well, well, he marveled, somebody slipped, somebody let a few facts in by mistake. Hope House. Dr. Kloppel, whose initials were M. L. When Dr. Kloppel was born his father had tiptoed into his mother's bedroom and said, Mama, we will call him Martin Luther. . . . When found, Miss Miller was still wearing the rag-doll costume in which she had danced a few hours before. Rag doll. Limp, flat, lying in the rain.

He copied names and addresses, returned the papers, and left the building. It was only nine-thirty; the night was cold and clear and made for walking. He stood on the curbstone and examined the stars. Couples moved along the sidewalk, arm in arm. Other couples came down the library steps, heads together, whispering. I should have married that girl, he thought. Then I'd be sitting home with a couple of dog books, proving that Hector never was a pup. Home.

Home to Ruth Miller was Hope House. Hope. "All hope abandon, ye who enter here." Dante. Hell. Canto three, line nine. . . . She'd wanted to live there, she'd been happy about it, she'd told Roberta so. Then a day or two later she'd danced in a rag-doll costume and jumped from a window.

He walked east, turned abruptly, and walked west. 415 West —— Street. Run-down neighborhood but respectable; rooming houses and railroad flats; third generation Germans, second generation Irish, first generation Greeks.

Hope House was in the middle of the block, an eight-story brick building with chintz curtains at the ground-floor windows and Venetian blinds above. The drawn blinds, discreetly barred with light, told him nothing except that the occupants of the front rooms could read the signs in the windows across the street. Gentlemen Only. The wide, glass door leading in from the street showed a small lobby, a desk, and a woman with gray hair who was sewing. He didn't go in. He didn't want to. There was, he decided, no point. He was there only because he didn't feel like going home.

At one end of the building a wooden gate opened into a courtyard. The gate was ajar. He touched it gently, and it swung inward. Well, he thought, why not? No harm done.

The small, square court was dark, and it smelled as if it were also clean. He stood with his back to the next-door fence and smoked a cigarette. Hope House, viewed from the rear, had a pleasing, dormitory aspect. Its walls formed a three-sided square and were spotted with lighted windows. Court rooms were cheaper than front rooms and clearly drew a less inhibited clientele. Most of the windows were open. Odds and ends of laundry hung from makeshift lines, drying handkerchiefs plastered several panes, and a burst of laughter, happily raucous, came from the second floor. The second floor was lively.

Mark looked up to the seventh. Only one lighted window there, on the right-hand wall. . . . So she left the party in her rag-doll dress, went to her own room, raised the window, and jumped. Did she hesitate at first, looking down at the windows of her friends? Those windows would have been dark and silent because her friends were dancing downstairs. They were dancing, they were having a party, and they hadn't wanted her to come. They said she was ill, but they hadn't worried. They hadn't missed her. Wasn't there one girl, even one, to notice that she'd gone? One girl would have been enough, even though she reached the seventh floor too late. She could have shortened that long wait in the rain.

Mark ground out his cigarette. I don't get it, he told himself. It doesn't add up. Suicide, yes, in spite of Roberta. That could happen and too often does. But something else had to happen before that, something that at least one person would know about. Every woman who lives in a place like Hope House has one special friend who shares her life; who won't go in to dinner until she comes, who worries if she is late, who is protective, jealous, and acutely conscious of her presence in any part of a room. And of her absence. No, it didn't add up.

Wait, he told himself. She'd only lived there a day or two, perhaps she had no real friends. But he ruled that out at once. Roberta had mentioned other girls from Blackman's.

He left the courtyard and walked east. Maybe he'd check on the friend angle tomorrow. But only to satisfy Roberta. He hailed a cab at the corner and rode uptown. He was out of sight when Beulah turned into the Hope House block from the other end.

Beulah walked with an affected limp because, she told herself, people with infirmities always look honest. She moved heavily, but her heart was as light as a feather. She thought she would have made a good general.

Lifting a bottle of port from an unlocked closet had

been child's play. Putting Bessy to bed with the bottle had been easier still. That was an old routine that played itself. The Suttons' front door had been a momentary problem because the Suttons had locked it when they went out, but in no time at all she'd located a keyboard. Hanging beside the hall telephone, asking for trouble. Somebody ought to tell the insurance people, but not right away.

She had found the library where four policemen had told her it would be, and the young man in charge of the newspaper files had courteously declined her tip. At that point she'd reached a psychic peak and Hope House had sent out waves. Whoppers. Cold.

She'd told herself that it was early, that Bessy was safe, that she had four hundred dollars pinned in the crown of her hat in case of trouble. And she'd walked in what she thought was the right direction for Hope House. It wasn't, but it was interesting. So many other women walked alone. Three blocks from Hope House she'd begun to limp.

The gray-haired woman at the desk gave her a look of combined sympathy and surprise.

"Good evening," Beulah said. "What a lovely place. Are you in charge of rooms?"

"Well, no, I'm not, but I'm afraid we haven't——"

"My name is Pond," Beulah said quickly. "Miss Pond. I have a niece, a very sweet girl, who's looking for a room in this neighborhood, and we both wondered if you——"

"I'm very sorry, Miss Pond, but——"

"What is your name, my dear? I'm a tired old woman and I like to know peoples' names."

"I'm Miss Plummer." Miss Plummer laid aside the square of tulle she was working on. "I'm very sorry, Miss Pond, but we haven't a single bed available." She remembered Miss Brady's warning about inquiries. There'd been too many, and Miss Brady thought it was curiosity. "Find out who sent them," she'd instructed. "Ten to one they're sob sisters." This one didn't look like a sob sister. And she was lame, too.

70

"Won't you take a chair, Miss Pond? I'm very sorry, but it's like I said. We're full up. But would you mind telling me how you heard about us?"

"Word of mouth," said Beulah, sagging into a chair. "I heard about you somewhere and looked you up in the telephone book. So cozy, so homelike, and an elevator, too."

The elevator had arrived with two girls who crossed the lobby and entered the lounge. She saw them take her measure, and there was nothing friendly in their sidelong looks. They were young girls, but their eyes were oddly apprehensive. She watched the lounge door close quietly and firmly as if it were shutting something out, or in.

She felt a warning chill, unpleasant but corroborating. The Hope House waves were coming fast, and she bobbed to the surface and rode them in. I was right to come here, she told herself; there's something going on. I'm an old woman, outwardly inoffensive, and asking for a room for a niece, and those children are afraid of me. She rambled on vaguely to Miss Plummer, who looked as if she might be a fool, while her eyes nailed the elevator girl to the door of the car and took her apart.

"My niece is a quiet girl who likes a refined atmosphere," she said. "No excitement, no strain, no emotional upsets." That girl is listening, she noted with satisfaction, and I'm purposely keeping my voice down. Not ordinary listening, either, not just killing time. Now she's coming over to look in the mailbox. "My niece hasn't been happy," she confided in a hoarse whisper. "I'm afraid it's a man. Do you have much of that here?"

Miss Plummer was startled by her own reaction and didn't reply at once. A man! That was the answer to the Miller business, a man. A man of course. That was the natural explanation, it was the only one that made sense. The phone call, late at night. Plain as the nose on your face. She'd try to find the number, she'd get in touch with the boy and tell him what had happened. But what a pity, what a waste. If the dear girl had only confided in her.

71

She fingered the locket at her throat and smiled at Miss Pond. "I guess we all have that trouble when we're young," she said. She wondered if Miss Pond's niece was a hope-chest case, a dozen of everything, all monogrammed. That kind of thing ought to bring out the best in people, it ought to make for kindness and consideration for others, none of this window jumping. She wished desperately for a vacant bed or even a folding cot.

"Let me think," Miss Plummer begged. "I certainly do wish——let me think."

Beulah nodded graciously. Miss Plummer's preoccupation was timely, because in addition to the girl behind the mailbox she had spotted another girl behind the switchboard. She smiled at the switchboard girl.

"Good evening," she said. "What interesting things you must hear."

The girl said, "I don't know what you're talking about." Her tone shocked Miss Plummer back into the conversation.

"Careful, Kitty," Miss Plummer warned. "Miss Pond meant that kindly. I don't know what's getting into you girls, acting as if everybody was a—— Jewel, is that you?"

Good, Beulah said to herself. She's caught her. Jewel, Kitty, silly.

"The mail was delivered at six o'clock as usual, Jewel," Miss Plummer said. She waited until Jewel returned to her stand by the elevator. "I apologize, Miss Pond. We've had some bad days here, and the girls are not themselves. None of us are. Now, I haven't even got a cot, let alone a bed, but I'm so interested in your niece, I can't help feeling I'd enjoy knowing her. You really ought to come back and see Miss Brady or Miss Small, they're the Heads. You can see them from eleven to twelve on Mondays, or by appointment. I don't say anything will come of it, but you might try. We've turned dozens away in the past weeks, not needing a bed any more than you and I, plain curiosity. Miss Brady and Miss Small have had to make a rule against

talking to strangers for that very reason. Not that I
consider you a stranger, Miss Pond. I know a lady when
I see one."

"Thank you," Beulah said. "I feel the same way, Miss
Plummer. But I don't think I understand——"

"It's on account of the—you know." Miss Plummer
lowered her voice. "I guess you didn't see it in the papers?"

"What?" breathed Beulah.

"Suicide."

"Why?" Instantly she regretted that single, sharp
word. Miss Plummer had winced as if she'd been struck.

Not so fast, she told herself. Try again. Her next
words were vague and sugared.

"I mean why in such a homelike place? I mean how
sad for all of you. Was it one of your girls?"

"Yes," Miss Plummer whispered. "She was poorly.
Best let it go at that."

"Of course," Beulah agreed softly. Then something
happened, and she smoothed her coat with a noncha-
lance she didn't feel. The quiet lobby suddenly filled
with the sound of running, invisible feet. Someone had
been standing on the dim stairway, listening. Someone
was running up the uncarpeted stairs, out of sight, leaving a trail of clattering, diminishing sound. The lobby
itself seemed darker than before; she thought she could
see it darken, but she told herself that couldn't be. I'm
a fool, she decided, I'm working myself up. It's only
ten-thirty and this is a big city and I've got four hundred
dollars in the crown of my hat. She tried to sound casual.

"Do I imagine it's darker in here?" she asked. "Aren't
some of the lights——"

The girl at the switchboard answered. "I turned them
off. We always do at this time." Kitty. Her name was
Kitty. She left her chair and came to stand beside Miss
Plummer. Miss Plummer took up her embroidery and
Kitty watched.

Beulah stood up and looked over her shoulder. The
elevator girl had stepped back into the cage and her

73

hand was on the lever. She was watching Miss Plummer, too.

"I don't suppose I could go upstairs to see the rooms?" Beulah asked. "I'd like to tell my niece about them. Just in case, you know."

Miss Plummer raised her eyes with a look that begged for an end to the conversation. Beulah met the look and gambled. She said, "Poor Ruth."

She heard the elevator door close and heard the whine of machinery in motion. She saw and heard Miss Plummer's scissors drop to the floor. She felt, rather than heard, a long sigh. She thought it came from behind her, but she didn't turn. It could have been her own.

"Why are you frightened, Miss Plummer?" she asked.

"I'm not," Miss Plummer said. Her mouth was stiff. "What in the world would I be frightened about?"

"I don't know. But when I mentioned my niece's name you looked as if I had hurt you."

A faint color returned to Miss Plummer's face. "I'm sorry," she murmured. "We have no rooms, Miss Pond, not for anybody. I'm sorry. And I'll have to ask you to excuse me. I must get on with my work."

Beulah reached across the desk for Miss Plummer's resisting hand. "I'll keep in touch with you in one way or another," she said. She remembered to limp when she went to the door and let herself out.

The street was filled with a bitter wind heavy with ocean salt. It cut through her clothes and made her want to walk faster than she dared. It gave her some comfort to blame her haste on the wind. She chose the same direction as Mark, but her thoughts were not along the same lines. She had no unselfish plans for soothing Roberta. She wanted, very simply, to be where she wasn't, and at once. Anywhere would do.

There's something wrong with that place, she told herself. I could feel people thinking one thing and saying another. And those two girls, looking at me like that when I'd hardly opened my mouth. Miss Plummer's face when I said Ruth——

She looked behind her, but the shabby, well-lit street, the small shops, and the hurrying pedestrians were so openly commonplace that she laughed boldly. But when she saw a cab half a block away, she forgot her limp and ran.

Miss Plummer folded her work and sat with her hands in her lap. She asked herself miserably if she'd said anything out of place. Anything against Miss Brady's instructions. . . . Ruth. Poor Ruth. It could be a coincidence, except for one thing. Elderly ladies with moleskin coats and what appeared to be real diamonds didn't come to places like Hope House to find rooms for nieces. They found small apartments near Columbia University or near one of the big churches. Pond. Miss Pond.

"Kitty?" Miss Plummer said quietly. "What did you make of that lady who was here?"

There was no answer, and she looked over her shoulder. Gone, gone off without so much as by your leave. Slipped away like the rest of them, like Jewel and the girls in the lounge and whoever that was on the stairs. Gone up to lights and company and leaving her alone.

She tried to remember if there'd ever been any Ponds on the Board. It could be that the Board was investigating. Somebody on the Board or related to the Board, somebody that wasn't known; talking to people like herself that weren't important, talking to the girls one by one, asking little questions about things. Maybe they'd decide to close the House. Mismanagement, carelessness. That was what Miss Brady and Miss Small were afraid of. You could tell.

Miss Brady had spoken very plainly at the House meeting right after. It was easy to see she was upset. Ruth Miller was an unfortunate type, she'd said, and as little or nothing was known about her she mustn't be judged or talked about. Ruth Miller had brought trouble and worry, but what was done was done and best forgotten. Something like that she'd said. And then there was the sign Miss Small put on the Bulletin Board.

STAFF AND RESIDENTS: Talk to no one, reporters, business associates, friends. Hope House has always had a splendid reputation and it's up to us to keep it so. This is Our Home.

Poor Ruth. Miss Plummer got up heavily and went to the switchboard. She looked vainly for the slip with the Chicago number. She turned over other slips, went back in the records, shook out the blotter. It wasn't there. Thrown out, she decided. Kitty wouldn't keep it because it wasn't a completed call. Kitty couldn't be expected to know it meant anything. And it was old, too, over a month old.

In April's room, April was doing the thing she enjoyed most. She was giving a party. She had boiled water on an electric plate and was pouring powdered coffee into cups, spooning out sugar, and cutting a bakery cake. The coffee table was stainless and crumbless. Her guests were Lillian Harris and Dot Mainwaring.

"I asked Moke and Poke," April said, "but they had a date. Lillian, have we got enough light?"

Lillian said all the lights were on. She was stretched out on her own bed, watching the other guest. "How long have you lived here, Mainwaring?"

"Two years. And I wish you'd call me Dot. All my friends do."

"Is Mainwaring your real name?"

"It is. And exactly what are you trying to insinuate, please?"

"Not a thing." Lillian took the coffee April offered. "I think I'll move out of the place soon."

April gave a little cry. "No, Lillian, no!"

"Oh, I won't go for a while, baby. Not until I can get you another roommate like Miller."

"Well, really!" Dot was horrified. "Of all the tactless remarks! April's trying to forget, we all are!"

Lillian yawned. "Didn't anybody ever die here before, naturally or unnaturally? I'm asking, I want to know."

"Nobody," April said in a small voice. "We never had

any trouble before. But a girl had pneumonia once and nearly died."

Dot's thin face flushed with importance, and she put a warning finger to her lips. That would tell Lillian Harris that April didn't know everything, and it would also tell her that strange things had happened before. . . . Lillian Harris didn't know about the others. That was because she didn't care to mix with people and hadn't been around very long, either. She'd tell her later, when April went to brush her teeth. It might do Miss Lillian Harris some good to know that God was in Hope House caring for His own and smiting the wicked. Maybe the wicked didn't always die, but they felt His Hand. Lillian Harris looked like a week-ender with that red hair and the way her clothes fitted.

Dot crumbled cake into her saucer with tense fingers. There'd never been any open talk about Lillian Harris, but it was odd the way she never had any callers, not even other girls. And when she went out, even on rainy days, she dressed as if she expected to meet somebody. It would be awful if Lillian Harris threw her life away. . . . Lillian Harris smiled at April as if April could see, and talked nonsense. She always talked nonsense, and when she smiled she looked as if she had a secret or was making fun of good people. There was only one kind of secret people like Lillian had, and it couldn't be kept forever. Somebody ought to tell her about the others, how they'd been found out and asked to move away from this wonderful Home. And how they'd never been heard of again. One day you saw them in the dining room, laughing too loud, and the next day they were gone, swallowed up by the city streets. And you couldn't help but wonder when you read about an unidentified girl down at the morgue. Sometimes you wanted to go down there yourself, to look, but you never did. Death was terrible even when it was right.

Dot looked at the long, exciting body on the bed. If Lillian Harris would only tell her things, she might be able to help her. If she'd be frank and not hold anything back, it would be good for her.

77

Lillian turned over and smiled at Dot. "You ought to know about this," she said. "What did they do with her clothes?"

Dot looked disappointed. "Do with whose clothes?"

"I know," April said. "She means Ruth. Miss Brady came in here and took them away. They were in a suitcase, all packed. Miss Brady told me afterward."

"I saw that happen myself, baby. I was here. I mean does anybody know where they are now?"

"In the packroom," Dot said eagerly. "I could have told you that all along if you'd asked me. Nobody claimed them. She didn't save any letters, and nobody's written to her since. It's very sad, really."

"So it is," Lillian said. "And where do you get the inside information?"

"I'm personal friends with Miss Small."

"Me too." Lillian shook her head. "But she holds out on me. . . . Why don't you wash your hair sometime, Mainwaring?"

Dot got up. "I'm leaving, this minute! It's nothing to do with you, April, I want you to understand that, but I'm not the type to take insults. And if I may say so, I'm sorry for you, Lillian Harris, I really am."

April waited until the door closed. "Lillian, you're bad! Did you have to hurt her feelings like that?"

"Sure. She was getting ready to reform me."

"You're awful. . . . Does her hair need washing, honest?"

"Sure." She smoothed April's soft curls. "You're sweet, baby, but you're too democratic. Next time you have a party, invite Minnie May. Gin smells clean."

April put her cheek against Lillian's. "S-sh," she whispered. "She's coming back, I can hear her. S-sh."

Someone knocked. "Come in," April called.

Lillian said, "It's Jewel. She looks like she's running away from a wolf. Come on in and shut the door."

Jewel closed the door behind her and leaned against it. "Can't stay, I'm still on duty. Listen, something funny happened downstairs."

"Well?" Lillian waited.

"An old lady came in looking for a room. She made out like it was for a niece. It was funny."

"How?"

"She made out like she was lame, but she wasn't lame. She was putting it on. She got her legs mixed up. First lame on one, then lame on the other. I was watching."

"Who'd she see?"

"Plummer, the dope. Plummer fell all over the place, lah-di-dah, make you sick. Then she whispered something to the old lady, I couldn't hear it all but I heard suicide. Then the old lady said something like 'Poor Ruth.'"

"I'm crazy about this," Lillian said. "Then what?"

"Then Plummer got cold feet and the old lady knew it. She made out like her niece's name was Ruth. And she asked to see the rooms even when Plummer told her we didn't have any."

"So." Lillian leaned against her pillow. "Where was Kitty?"

"She was there. Kitty told me the last part. I wasn't there then. I had to——I had to run up for a minute. When I got back the old lady was gone and Plummer looked scared. What do you make of it?"

Lillian laughed, softly. "I wouldn't even try to make anything. Get along, Jewel, you're scaring April to death. Some old busybody, that's all, maybe a reporter dressed for the part. What do you care, anyway."

"Care!" Jewel sent a long look across the room. "I don't care. I've got nothing on my conscience!"

"Nobody said you had."

"Nobody better. I'm only telling you. You said to tell you if I ever heard of anybody asking for Ruth Miller."

"This one didn't ask outright, did she?"

"No, but that's what she was getting at. It was plain as day. Even Plummer, the dope, caught on."

"Well, keep it to yourself. Who's still out?"

"Moke and Poke, Minnie May, and a couple of others. Jane, Gloria, I forget who else. Nobody much."

"Cake, or do you have to run?"

"I can eat it in the car."

Lillian took the cake over to the door. "Good night," she said, "and thanks."

April sat on her bed and waited for Lillian to come back. "What are you doing, Lillian?"

"Walking around, stretching my legs."

"Why did Jewel talk like that? I didn't see anything funny in it."

"Jewel has a bird brain. You know what a bird brain is? Teeny-weeny. And don't forget she was the first one out in that courtyard. She's still rocky."

"I never did understand how she——"

"Nothing to worry about, nothing to understand. Take off that bathrobe and get in bed."

"My teeth——"

"Skip them tonight. It's cold in the hall. Cover up."

"Maybe I will. . . . Lillian, what are you doing in Ruth's closet?"

"I like that! It's mine now, don't forget that!"

"I didn't mean anything, I just keep forgetting. Are you going to open the window?"

"When you cover up. I'll undress in the bathroom. Ready? Here we go."

April pulled the blankets to her chin. "Lillian?"

"What now?"

"What are you doing at the window?"

"Looking at the stars."

"Are they bright?"

"So-so. I've seen better. Turn over and go to sleep. I'll be back soon."

Lillian's voice was mild and soothing and her movements made no sound. She leaned out of the window and looked up, not at the stars but at the window directly above. It was lighted. She drew back and stood where she was, rubbing a finger along the white-painted sill. She did that every night and sometimes in the morning. No one ever saw her do it, and no one ever saw the curl of her mouth.

Miss Small told Miss Brady it was time to be thinking about their Christmas tree. "We might have our own little tree up here," she said. "I know we've always had it in my room, but with the girls running in and out at all hours it doesn't seem as personal as it should. And I know they look at my things when I'm not there."

"I told you to lock your door, Angel."

"You don't lock yours! But honestly, you know how it is, Monny. Mrs. Marshall-Gill thinks the girls should feel free to come to me whenever they like. . . . Do you mind having our tree here?"

"G'wan. I love it. . . . April entertained tonight."

"Who, dear?"

"Harris, of course, and Mainwaring. Funny combination."

"Oh, I don't know. April's lonely, in spite of Lillian, and she has to take what she can get. . . . What do you want for Christmas, Monny?"

"From you, not a thing. You spend too much, you go crazy. Don't look like that, I know what things cost."

"But, darling——"

"Woolworth's. I know, you can buy the ornaments, the tinsel, and stuff. And the tree. That's your share, and that's all. Now where'll we put it? Might as well settle everything now. Not much time left. Be here before we know it."

Miss Small's eyes wandered happily. "Lovely, lovely room. I feel so relaxed in here. All your beautiful, wonderful things. Well, let me see. What about that table in the corner? Is it very valuable?"

"Not if you want to use it. Angel, you're nothing but a kid. I didn't give a damn about Christmas until you came here. Tree on table. That's that. Now what do you want me to give you?"

Miss Small hesitated. "Monny, if you really do want to know——"

"What do you think I'm doing, making conversation? Do you think I like to hear myself talk?"

"Well, I've been thinking——I mean I haven't any—— I mean if we're going to Europe——"

"Come on. What are you dreaming about?"

"Pigskin luggage!"

Miss Brady collapsed against her pillows and roared.

"Does anybody in the whole world have one half as much fun as we do?" Miss Small marveled. "Darling, you're sitting on your cigarettes."

"Hand me another pack. No, nobody. . . . What's the matter?"

Miss Small had reached for the cigarettes, but her hand had stopped in mid-air. "Somebody coming down the hall, and I'm afraid it's for me. Oh dear, I simply can't bear another tale of woe."

"Might be for me, for a change," Miss Brady boasted. "Whoever it is, I'll get rid of her."

Together they listened to the slow, unhurried steps and waited for the knock. When it came, it had an almost human personality. It was light and measured, tempered with caution and certain of result.

"Come in," Miss Brady called.

Lillian Harris, wearing a crimson bathrobe and looking sleepy, edged into the room. "I'm terribly sorry, Miss Brady," she apologized, "but I didn't like to disturb Mrs. Fister. She's usually asleep by now. And I hate to interrupt you and Miss Small——"

"You're not interrupting," Miss Brady said. "What's wrong? April sick again?"

"No, not April." Lillian kept her place by the open door.

"Well, come on in and close that door. There's a draft. What's your trouble? You girls haven't been frightening each other, have you?"

"Oh, no, Miss Brady, April and I never did that. It's just that I've got a headache and nobody on our floor has any aspirin. I thought you might be awake and——"

"Certainly. There's headache stuff in the bathroom, all sorts. Go in and help yourself."

"I'll get it," Miss Small said. "Sit down, Lillian. We're very glad we can help." She left the room quietly.

"Coffee?" Miss Brady asked. "Although you probably shouldn't have it."

"I guess not," Lillian agreed. She drooped over the back of a chair. "We had some up in our room. Just Dot and the two of us."

Something in her voice sharpened Miss Brady's scrutiny. "You look as if you had things on your mind, Lillian."

Lillian raised sleepy, candid eyes. "Oh, no, Miss Brady. I don't feel well, that's all. And April—you know it's queer rooming with a girl like April. I know I wanted to do it, and I still do, but it makes me, well, nervous."

Miss Small returned with aspirin. "I understand," she said. "I've been wondering if it wasn't a bad idea in the first place. I've even been wondering if we ought to close that room up, temporarily. Although I don't know what we'd do for additional space. But no matter what we do, Lillian, you must try not to think of what happened. It was a dreadful thing, but you must try to think of it impersonally."

"That's it," Miss Brady agreed. "It isn't as if we'd really known the poor wretch. I suppose that sounds heartless, doesn't it?"

"No, Miss Brady."

The telephone beside Miss Brady rang once. She let it ring again before she picked it up. "Plummer's midnight report," she shrugged. "Mouse, cockroach, or centipede crossed the lobby floor at eleven-forty-five, heading south. Minnie May drunk again. . . . Well, Ethel?"

Miss Plummer's voice was audible but not distinct. Miss Brady listened with caricatured boredom, and Miss Small turned the pages of a magazine. Lillian Harris looked at the ceiling.

Finally Miss Brady said sharply, "Take it easy, Ethel. Start all over again."

Miss Small raised surprised eyes, and Lillian Harris looked sleepily interested.

Miss Brady didn't like what she was hearing. Her mouth looked as if she were tapping her feet, but she was as still as marble. Even her lips were still and stiff. She finally said, "Forget it and go to bed," and hung up. "The woman's a fool. She was born that way. I'll be glad when we——well never mind that! Lillian, what do you know about this?"

"About what, Miss Brady?"

"Tonight's caller. You don't miss much around here, so come on and talk."

"I don't know what you mean, Miss Brady. The only caller we had was Mainwaring."

Miss Brady tried again. "Been down in the lobby tonight?"

"No, Miss Brady. Why?"

"Some woman inquired about a room hours ago, and Plummer has suddenly made up her mind to have a fit about it. One of those midnight decisions, the old witching hour. She thinks it was the police. Know anything?"

"No, Miss Brady. But Jewel did say something about an odd-looking woman. Very odd, she said. But you know Jewel. I hardly listened."

"Well, take your aspirin and get along. Good night."

The two women waited until her footsteps died away.

"Monny! What did Ethel really say?" Miss Small's voice was frightened. "Don't tell me we're going to have trouble! Not now, not when we're almost ready to go!"

"Why should we have trouble? A fool girl chucks herself out of a window, so what? Too bad, but nothing to do with us."

"Monny, tell me what Ethel said!"

"Some old woman wanted a room for her niece. A niece named Ruth. If you know Plummer, you can guess what happened. She got pally with the old girl and talked too much. Now she's remembering, and she's worried. Police, she says. Or a reporter."

"Reporter?"

"Dead girls boost circulation. Don't think about it."

"But the police?"

"Don't think about it, I tell you. We've had all the police we're going to have. Plummer's a fool."

"I don't know. . . . Monny, I hate all this! All your wonderful work here, ending in a mess! All our plans. Monny, can't we go away now, can't we have a breakdown or something and resign tomorrow? I don't like things the way they are."

"I wonder. . . . We'll see. Maybe right after Christmas. We'll see. . . . Heat up that coffee, will you? I'm freezing for no good reason."

Miss Small absently heated the coffee. "I don't think Lillian had a headache. She's disappointing me again. She's gone back to that queer, secret manner. I'm ashamed of myself, I really am, but I keep thinking that Lillian may have known Ruth before; you know, known her somewhere else. Lillian was in the lobby when Ruth came, and Ruth was frightened, I told you that——"

"Shut up, darling," Miss Brady said. "Use your imagination for something pretty. Picture me on a camel."

Miss Small tried and tried.

They talked for another hour, building and wrecking plans, phrasing and rephrasing resignations, composing farewell speeches to Mrs. Marshall-Gill. One was for public delivery, one for the ship's concert.

At the end, Miss Small said, "Monny, that woman who came for a room, did she leave her name?"

"Pond. I told you not to think about that."

"I won't," Miss Small said. "I never heard of her."

5

Dr. Kloppel had washed only half the leaves of his rubber plant and wanted to finish the job. He clung to his white enamel basin and petulantly soaked and squeezed his sponge.

"If you want to know the kind of doctor I am," he said, "stop any man, woman, or child on this street."

"I'm afraid you misunderstand," Mark said. "I'm perfectly confident——"

"I'm an old man and I have all the money I need. I don't need Hope House. I go there once a week because those women neglect themselves and I believe in charity. I charge fifty cents a call and sometimes give the medicine away. I live alone except for a housekeeper who's gone around the corner to find me a chop for lunch. Now if you still question my integrity or diagnosis——"

"But I don't," Mark insisted. "I'm simply trying to trace the girl's origin. I thought you could help me."

"I can't. I never saw her before that night. I never saw her alive. She was dead on arrival."

"So I understand. Was there a post-mortem?"

"There was a broken neck. It seemed sufficient." Dr. Kloppel put his basin on the mantel and sighed. "Who told you to come here?"

"Nobody. I read about the case in the papers and got the idea she might be the friend of a friend of mine."

Dr. Kloppel raised one bushy white eyebrow. "I haven't got the time or inclination to argue that, but you needn't think I believe it. Now you listen to me, young feller. Hope House is what they call a hostel in some places but I never liked the word. It's cheap, good, and endowed, and it helps a lot of girls and women who'd have to live in hall bedrooms otherwise. It's managed by a rich and well-connected lady named Brady and backed by some fancy New York names. It draws all kinds of girls and all kinds of behavior. Give you an example. Couple of years ago one girl drank a little bottle of iodine because she'd got herself in the customary natural state. That turned her into a heroine. I told the neighborhood drugstores not to sell iodine for a week or so. Get me? I'm not dumb. Now when I'm called up at midnight and asked to look at a body lying in the courtyard and I'm told the young lady was anti-social, a liar, and sickly to boot, I don't have to read my books. I don't even need the open window to tell me what happened. Very sad but very clear. The young lady had an attack of remorse or melancholia. All I had to do was watch for a repetition or a half-hearted try. I watched, but everybody over there was scared silly. Only one girl developed an unusual interest in windows, and all she did was look out of them too much. I had a talk with her and figured she was showing off. Now go away and leave me to my washing."

"Dr. Kloppel, perhaps if you'll let me explain——"

"I don't think you're a reporter, because you're too late getting around and there's nothing to report anyway. You look to me like a natural-born snooper with money. Maybe you're all right; I don't know or care. If you still want to play, go to the rooming house next door and ask for Mrs. Cashman. She found the body, or her dog did. But keep away from Hope House. I want to play poker tonight."

Mark found himself on the sidewalk, grinning at the doctor's neat brass plate. Martin Luther Kloppel, M.D. Roberta would like the doctor. But what was that description of Ruth Miller? Anti-social and a liar. He wondered who had come to that conclusion after only two days' residence. Anti-social and a liar. Nice, hard words that didn't match Roberta's soft distress.

He looked at the house next door. A card in the clean,

fern-filled window said "Vacancies." While he stood there, trying to make up his mind, a small, neat woman with a white poodle came down the street and started up the steps.

"Mrs. Cashman?"

She nodded, and her round eyes glistened.

"I've just come from Dr. Kloppel's. He thinks you and I might have a little talk." He wondered why Mrs. Cashman braced herself before she spoke, but he didn't wonder long. No one, not even Mrs. Cashman herself, could hear her voice without an involuntary cringe. It belonged to a weeping giant.

"Sure we'll talk," Mrs. Cashman said. "If Kloppel says so, we will. I own my house and he owns his and all his friends are mine. What do you want to know?"

He told her in a whisper, hoping to coax her voice to the level of his, but the poor woman had been born that way. Her sobbing tones filled the street and in any other neighborhood would have brought heads to windows.

"This is the very dog," Mrs. Cashman caterwauled, inching the animal forward with a tiny, immaculate shoe. "It was raining pitchforks but Brother and I take our walk regardless. We're like the postman, neither snow nor rain nor heat, you know that piece on the Post Office wall. And we wanted a bottle of ale before the delicatessen closed. Well, around the corner by Hope House, Brother got away and I thought he was after garbage. Big garbage at Hope House on account of so many eating, and he sometimes finds a bone. Well, sir——say, you never told me your name and that's not fair."

"Mark East. And I only want to know if the Miss Miller who died is the same Miss Miller a friend of mine used to know."

Mrs. Cashman was not confused. "For your friend's sake I hope not," she said. "I didn't see her face because she had that mask on but I'm told it was pulp. Mr. East, I like to died. There was this bundle of rags I thought it was, lying in a puddle, and there was Brother

88

acting up. I might have known he didn't have no bone. So I got down to look. Terrible, huh? You should have heard me scream. And poor Brother let himself go. He's only a dog. You should have been there. Must have been close to one hundred present, and somebody started a rumor about the condition I was in and I heard it and I know who said it and I fixed her. Well, the poor girl was dead all right."

"You're a very brave woman, Mrs. Cashman," Mark whispered.

"Why, thanks!" Mrs. Cashman howled. "You'd be too, there's really nothing to it. Do you think it was your friend's friend?"

"I don't know. I haven't much to go on, but when I heard that a girl named——"

"Ruth Miller. She wasn't very popular; you'll have to excuse that, but truth's truth. While I was waiting for the police—I had to wait, I know the law—I was talking to one of the Hope House girls. She was the first to reach the scene, after me. And we kept each other company. Well, she didn't know who it was on account of the mask, and she kept saying to herself 'It's nobody I know, it's nobody I know,' like that. Then everybody else came and they had a terrible time deciding who it was. Awful, huh? And Kloppel cut the mask off and still they didn't know. But they found out somehow when the police got there, they've got ways of telling, and that's when I heard the talk. No, she wasn't popular. She was mental, poor soul, and didn't care to live. I'm sorry for you and your friend." Mrs. Cashman offered a small, immaculate handkerchief.

He declined it gravely. "I think I must be on the wrong track," he said. "I'm pretty sure this wasn't my friend's friend. But I wonder if you could tell me the name of the girl you talked to, just for the record?"

"Jewel. Jewel Schwab. She works there. I'd take you around myself but Brother won't go near the place. We have to go two blocks out of our way to get the ale now. Tell Jewel I said it was all right to talk to you. Any friend of Kloppel's——"

He moved off while she was talking, bowing over his shoulder to soften the appearance of bad manners. When he reached the corner he could hear her urging Brother up the steps.

There was work waiting for him at his office, but he turned into the Hope House block for a final survey. That night at dinner he'd tell Roberta he'd checked every angle and persuade her to forget the whole business. She's never quite recovered from Mary Cassidy, he decided, and that makes her edgy. Then, to his surprise, he discovered something about himself. He had never quite recovered from Mary Cassidy, either. Even in the bright, winter sunlight she came back to him and made him think of death. Not easeful death. The other kind.

He had identified many bodies in the past ten years, bodies abandoned to gutters, lying on good beds under linen sheets, waiting on marble slabs for once familiar eyes to look down and remember. The eternal patience of the latter had always hurt. He had taught himself to touch cold cheeks with a steady hand because there was no one else to say good-by, and had sometimes followed the old ones out to Potter's Field because they had come a longer way and rated company. The old ones were hard to take. Not that the young ones were easy, he told himself, but before that final decision they must have had one crowded, crashing hour of life that still echoed. But the old ones' hour had been too long ago, with too much time to forget in. . . . He turned his eyes inward and regarded himself. Why don't you raise canaries, he snarled, and blubber when you crack an egg?

A few doors from Hope House he slowed down and watched two women descend the steps and get into a waiting cab. Not the hostel type, he decided. Board members, with fancy New York names, looking for dust and waste in the kitchen. They were fairly young, smartly dressed, and something had happened to make them laugh. He didn't go in until the cab drove off.

A pale girl came from behind the switchboard and asked his business.

"Miss Schwab?"

"She's out. Do you want to leave a message?"

"No, thank you, it isn't that important. I've been talking to Mrs. Cashman and she mentioned——" He stopped because he recognized the look she gave him. The good-natured curiosity slipped from her face and emptiness took its place. She was remembering to forget.

"Do you know Mrs. Cashman?" he asked.

"She lives somewhere around here, that's all I know." Her eyes flicked over his shoulder, and he turned to see who was behind him. There was no one. An empty elevator stood open, that was all.

"You'll have to excuse me," she went on. "I'm busy. But if you want to leave your name, I'll see that Jewel gets it."

"No name, I'll call again. That will be all right, won't it?"

"Employees are not permitted to receive callers except at stated hours," she said formally.

"And what are the stated hours?"

"Regular times off." The formality vanished. "I don't know when Jewel's off. It changes every day. She's off now, but I don't know when she'll be back. It won't do you any good to come back, you'd better write." She was racing, trying to get away from him, ahead of him, out of sight. "Miss Brady has to make rules about employees or nothing would ever get done. And Miss Brady likes to see the people who call, too. She has to make a rule about that in case of—well, trouble. I mean people come in here and talk, I mean Mrs. Cashman has no business to——"

He saw her dismay when she spoke Mrs. Cashman's name. Her mouth opened and closed as if she wanted to take the name back and swallow it.

"Never mind," he said easily. "I know how you feel. Mrs. Cashman talks too much, doesn't she?"

It didn't work. "I don't really know her," the girl said. She stood behind the desk, her hands firmly planted on the blotter. "You'll have to excuse me," she said again. The hands on the blotter could have been pushing him out.

When he went down the steps to the street he told himself that at least one cliché had a firm foundation in fact. Eyes were boring holes in his back. He walked to his office, wondering how far a suicide could demoralize a houseful of women. Pretty far, according to Martin Luther Kloppel, who admitted he was not dumb. Women without men, Kloppel. Men without women, Hemingway. And also East, definitely East. East without Cashman.

After dinner Nick Sutton limped over to the fireplace and admired the color of his brandy in the light of the glowing logs. Mark watched him with deep affection. Nick Sutton and Roberta Beacham had come a long way from lemon sodas.

Roberta knitted thoughtfully in a chair by the fire, and Bessy and Beulah shared a love seat in name only. The atmosphere had a thin coating of felicity that no one in his right mind would touch with a ten-foot pole. It took Mrs. Hawks to crack it. She appeared in the doorway, garnished with jet, and announced her departure for the cinema with the daughter of a hundred earls who, poor thing, had brought herself to accept employment in Bloomingdale's basement and required a bit of fun.

"She's in straits, you might say," Mrs. Hawks said angrily. "When I think of what that girl was born to!"

When she had gone, Nick spoke dreamily. "One of these days I'm going to throw that woman out of here. She cows Roberta."

"No," Beulah corrected. "Not Mrs. Hawks. Ruth Miller."

Mark leaned back in his chair. Here we go, he thought. I don't know why I wonder about anything. She's done something. Every line in her face says so at the top of its lungs. "Well?" he asked coldly.

"Tell them what you did, dear," Bessy said. "All by

yourself, too, because I had one of my headaches and couldn't go with you."

Roberta looked from Bessy to Beulah with dawning intelligence. "No!" she implored.

"Yes," Mark said. "I don't know what it is, but yes. They're carriers, you know, like Typhoid Mary, only they pack a grislier burden. Look at them, if you can bear it. Gentlewomen, they're called. I wouldn't be caught dead with either of them, but I will. They'll wash up on Long Island at three o'clock in the morning in a blizzard."

Nick limped over and sat beside his wife. "Tell the old man, he never got beyond Princeton."

Beulah gave Nick her warmest leer. "Want to gamble on a sure thing, Nick? It won't cost you much, just taxi fares and shoe leather. And if you won't, I will."

"I will," Nick said reverently.

"Mark," she asked, "what does miasma mean?"

"Just what you think it means. Stink."

"Well, Hope House does."

"I know."

"What? You too? When?"

"Last night and this morning."

"Only last night for me," she said regretfully. "This morning I did the headwork."

"If somebody doesn't say something," Nick said, "I'll——"

"I can't talk with a dry throat," Beulah explained.

"Both of us can't," Bessy said.

When Mrs. Hawks returned from her belted pleasure, they were still talking. She made coffee and sandwiches, although such work was beneath her and no one had asked her to stoop, and served them with her own hands. But she couldn't understand the conversation. They were sitting around the big table with paper and pencils and it sounded like a new game. An American parlor game, having to do with crime, such as the one called "Murder." But no lights extinguished. The madam was in a rare state, too.

She lingered at the table and tried to read the writing on Miss Pond's paper. Miss Pond might give herself the airs of a duchess, but she had a schoolboy's fist.

"Mrs. Hawks?" The master's voice. "That will be all, thank you."

When she had gone, by the longest route, Nick looked pleased with himself. "That was only a modest warm-up," he said. "Next time I'll have her naturalized." He went on seriously. "Mark, I don't like what we've been talking about. I'm sold on the tragedy and the Hope House nerves, but if the police are satisfied I don't see——"

"Cop-lover," said his wife.

"I don't see where we come in," Nick finished. "But I wish you'd look into this thing quietly, just to shut Roberta up."

"I've been thinking," Mark said.

"So have I," said Beulah, "but I don't expect any credit for it. I'll get my reward in heaven, I always do. But rather than see Roberta grow thinner and whiter day by day, I'll swallow my pride and go back to Hope House and——"

"Beulah! You can't go back to Hope House!" Pond and Cashman, born affinities, coming together and playing with matches. "We haven't got a thing on those people, unless we count Roberta's hunch and your own wishful smelling. This calls for walking on little cat feet. We start at Blackman's, and I do it."

Roberta looked as if she saw stars. "Why Blackman's?"

"Everybody leaves a trace of his passing, said the poet. Blackman's personnel department may have some ideas about Miss Miller's character. They have records. The professional shoppers' reports for one thing, her time sheet that tells how often she was late and absent and why, her record with the store physician, her personal charge account. Twenty-five percent off for clothing to wear in the store, ten percent for things to wear outside. What did she buy to wear outside? See?"

"Yes," Roberta said. "It's terrible but it's wonderful."

"And they'll have her references. If what I dig up at Blackman's disagrees enough with what we read in the papers and heard from Kloppel and Cashman, then we'll move in."

"How?"

"I'll present myself to the lady Head and say I've been retained by a woman who had arranged to employ Miss Miller as a nurse to her child and who, consequently, wants to know what gives."

"And that's no lie," Roberta said. "I'd honestly thought of that."

"That makes it legal. So I'll say all that and tell them who you are and your name will open all doors. I'll have to use your name, do you mind, Nick?"

"Go ahead. And you'll have an out if we're wrong. Hysterical matron, stuff like that."

"Right. Now where are we? Blackman's."

"Mr. Benz is the floorwalker," Bessy said. "A young man who would look well on the stage. I don't mind going along with you and pointing him out. We exchanged glances."

"Mr. Benz, thank you, and I'll find him myself. That gives me Benz and I already had Brady. I also have a Jewel Schwab of Hope House, who can be seen by appointment only, and a clerk or something at the Hope House desk."

"Miss Plummer," Beulah said. "Oldish, gray hair, does beautiful handwork."

"No. This was a tall girl, pale, spotted face."

"Telephone girl. I saw her, too. She scared me."

"She's scared stiff herself. That's the thing that gets me, the only thing. It's all out in the open, clean as a whistle on the surface, but the people who lived with Ruth Miller have goose flesh."

"You should see my back this minute," Bessy said.

Roberta rose quickly. "You show me, Miss Bessy. We'll all go to bed now and let the men drink themselves into doing something." Her eyes were ringed with anxiety, but she led her guests from the room like a veteran hostess.

Nick watched her proudly. "Growing up. . . . Can you iron this out, Mark?"

"Sure. She won't like it, though. I'm afraid it's straight. Unpleasant, but correct in most details."

"Fix it up, that's all I ask. Spend money and so on." Nick tried to look old and cynical. "I don't care what you find out, but find something. I bet on a man in the bottom of the basket."

"I don't know," Mark said carefully. "If she was ill——"

"But Roberta can spot illness. She fooled around a hospital during the war. She was good, too. You wouldn't think it to look at her, she's so damned cute. And she liked this Miller girl. If it was corpuscles or anything like that, Roberta would have counted them through her skin and sent her eggs and cream and stuff. I know Roberta. . . . I'm afraid she's got something this time."

"Want the truth? I'm afraid so, too, but keep it dark. Beulah's miasma is the McCoy. I stood in the courtyard of that place, and it smelled even there, if you know what I mean. There were some pretty, normal scenes of girls getting ready for bed, but I don't know. I didn't feel good."

"Like the art guys who see a picture for the first time and know it's a phony?"

"Exactly like that. Like your grandfather knows a mine is salted when he meets the guy who owns it. Hope House is salted."

Nick poured another drink. "Nightcap. Blackman's tomorrow?"

"Yes. I don't expect much there for all the fancy talking I did, but the word may get back to Hope House that somebody's asking questions."

Mr. Benz had little to add to his previous story but he said that little well. It was easy to see how Bessy had marked him for the stage. He agreed that people like young Mrs. Sutton did a great deal of good in the world, and confessed that he, personally, would hate to see anything happen to the capitalistic class. He pinned a mental price tag on Mark's hand-woven tie, one of a gift dozen from Roberta's capitalistic father, and led him to the rear elevators.

"You'll find the personnel department on the twelfth floor," he told Mark. "Miss Libby. And may I be kept informed, or is that too much to ask?"

Mark assured him that nothing was too much, shook hands, and rode up. The twelfth floor had a cafeteria for employees, a glass-covered sun deck for the same, and the personnel office. He crossed the sun deck to reach Miss Libby. Two charwomen, reclining in steamer chairs, stopped heckling each other long enough to speculate about his business.

"He want a job?"

"Him? Naw. Can't you see he's rolling? . . . Now like I was telling you, I been offered twenty-five dollars for my hand-painted lamp. That's the kind of things I got!"

Miss Libby's office was designed to put the fear of God in salespeople who had Monday morning hangovers and cash registers that didn't tally. It was filled with a cold north light, a highly polished desk, and two chairs. One of the latter was occupied by Miss Libby. At first glance she looked too soft for her job, with mild blue eyes and a baby skin; at second glance she still looked soft but there was something about her red hair and her mouth.

"Sit down, Mr. East," she said promptly. "I've got all the time in the world, but I'm afraid you're wasting yours. Benz had me on the phone and told me what you wanted. What are you trying to do, grab yourself a fee and give us the kind of publicity we don't need? That Miller case is closed. There's nothing for you in it."

"You've said it all," he agreed. "Maybe I'd better see Blackman."

"Don't be childish, he won't know what you're talking about. He doesn't know Ruth Miller existed."

"Do you?"

"Look." Miss Libby flipped the pages of a folder. "I

97

have the dope right here. I don't know what you're looking for, but if it's trouble you won't find it. Here's the story, plain facts and no color. She was a good saleswoman, no more than that. Not executive material, not even hard enough for head of stock, which isn't as big a job as it sounds. She bought almost nothing in the store, shoes and stockings, that's all. She had no store pals, was never late or absent, and came to the dispensary only once."

"Why did she come then?"

Miss Libby read silently. "Damn," she said under her breath. "But that happens all the time."

"Did you say something, Miss Libby?" He liked the way she blushed when she was caught.

"She came because she was hysterical. A customer accused her of giving wrong change and took the place. That time the customer was wrong, and we proved it on the spot, but the girl went to pieces. You can't make anything out of that, it happens all the time. Almost always with the Saturday afternoon crowd. That's when you get the office workers, very superior because they have a half holiday. They go grande dame and devil the clerks, and along about five o'clock some girl cracks up."

"I see. This fine pretty world. . . . Where did Miss Miller come from?"

"Come from?" Miss Libby's eyes traveled down a page, and the baby skin colored again.

"Sure," Mark pressed. "The job before this one, references—you know what I mean."

"Now Mr. East, you needn't——"

"Come, come, Miss Libby. Where did she work before she came here? Even a dish-washer has references."

Miss Libby ground her nice white teeth. "No record," she moaned. "You've got me. But I can explain! You know what last year was like. Normally sane workers going crazy, yelling for higher wages, quitting jobs, cashing those compulsory bonds, acting like customers themselves, nobody to wait on anybody. We took what we could get. Miller was self-effacing and looked as if

98

she needed a job. We took her on. It says here 'never before employed.' I remember now that I didn't believe it after her first week's record came up. She knew how to sell, and she didn't make mistakes. So——"

"So?"

"So maybe you've got something after all," Miss Libby said grudgingly.

"Don't look like that. I'm not going to sue." He leaned across Miss Libby's immaculate desk. "So she lied about never having worked before, she didn't make friends, and she went to pieces when a Saturday afternoon lady accused her of short changing. . . . Girls like you major in psychology or something, don't you?"

"Yes," Miss Libby admitted. "And I'm supposed to be good."

"Well, be good now. What do you make of all this?"

"Trouble in the past. Maybe a brush with the law. On the verge of being found out and couldn't face it. Hell, Mr. East—sorry, excuse it, but I feel awful. But what can we do? It's too late."

"Maybe it isn't. Have you got the Smith girls handy?"

"They're outside now, trying not to look terrified. Come in," she called.

Moke and Poke filed in and lined themselves against the wall.

"You're not going to be shot," Miss Libby said kindly. "This is Mr. East. Did Benz tell you what he's here for?"

"Yes'm," Moke said.

"Then answer his questions, that's all." She tossed the next move to Mark with open relief and relaxed on the end of her spine.

"This is going to be easy," Mark said. "I hope you don't mind if I call you Moke and Poke. Now, did you girls know Ruth Miller very well?"

They answered simultaneously, affirmatively and negatively, and burst into tears.

"I know how you feel," he said. "That's the way Mrs. Sutton feels too. Do you know Mrs. Sutton?"

Moke recovered first. "We've seen her. She's cute.

We think she's lovely to take an interest, but we don't know what for."

"I'll tell her you said that, and I'll tell you why she takes an interest. She's afraid Ruth was in some sort of trouble, and it upsets her to think she wasn't here to help. So even though Ruth is dead, she wants to straighten things out if she can. You might call it a sort of memorial, see?"

"That's lovely," Moke said.

"Sure. And between us, we're going to help. All you have to do is answer my questions. Now. Hope House is full of girls. I wonder if there's any one girl you don't like?"

"We don't like nobody," Moke said. "It don't pay."

"I see. . . . Who is Jewel Schwab?"

"Annie Schwab, but she don't care for Annie. She runs the elevator."

"Nice girl?"

"Kind of grumpy, wouldn't you say, Poke?"

"Inhibited. She can't get a fellow."

"That's fine, that's the stuff. Now, I want to see Jewel tonight, but I understand a Miss Brady looks over all callers. Right?"

"She tries to. So does Miss Small. Who told you that?"

"A tall girl with spots on her face."

"Kitty Brice. She's the telephone operator and helps at the desk." The corners of Moke's mouth said she didn't care for Kitty.

"And who's Miss Small?"

"Miss Brady's assistant. Brady's the Head, Small's the second Head. They're educated, you could talk to them, Mr. East. The rest of us got orders nobody was to talk, but they'd talk to you. You tell them about Mrs. Sutton and they'll understand. You see, it's like this. There's a lot of swells behind Hope House, and Miss Brady and Miss Small have got to keep scandal out or it's bad for their reputation as Heads."

Mark nodded. "They're right. Scandal would be very bad. But suicide doesn't necessarily mean disgrace. It

100

could mean something sad, like heartbreak. Do you suppose that was Ruth's trouble?"

"No, sir!" Moke was positive. "Maybe we didn't know her so very well, but we know it wasn't anything like that. You notice a thing like that. It shows. . . . But I've been thinking about something. When she moved to the House she sort of changed. She moved on the Saturday and on the Monday she died. But I don't know——"

"Sure you know, Moke. Go on."

"Well, I don't think she ate all the meals, and that's funny because the meals are good. She said it was because she was sick, but she looked like she was in a trance or something. That was on the Sunday."

"Never looked like that in the store?"

"No, sir. . . . I wish we'd paid her more attention now." Moke's eyes filled again, but Mark went on as if he didn't see.

"Tell me about the Sunday. You, the other one, Poke. It's your turn now."

Poke watched his face while she talked, looking for a sign that said they were making up for that regretted lack of attention. She found it.

"We saw her on Sunday morning," Poke said. "We didn't see her on Saturday because we had a date. We had her to our table for breakfast, but she wouldn't eat. And Sunday was the tea day. The big tea, with bought refreshments, and sewing for the party." Poke covered the tea from start to finish; Mrs. Marshall-Gill, the costumes and the masks that made everybody look the same, the mole, and the simulated pearls, pink. And Ruth in a corner by herself.

Moke concurred soberly, bobbing her head. "Yeah, yeah, that's right. That's the way it was. And then she spilled tea on her new suit she'd saved up for." A sudden look of surprise crossed her face. "That's funny. The suit. That's funny."

"Funny?" Mark turned from Moke to Poke to Miss Libby. They were frowning at each other with complete understanding. "Funny?" he repeated.

101

"Yeah," Moke said. "When you save up for a new suit and get it, you don't jump out of a window."

He addressed himself to Miss Libby. "That is the kind of reasoning that drives a man crazy and cracks a case. . . . Now what about the party? Did Ruth look as if she were having a good time?"

They couldn't say. They'd seen her once or twice, because of the mole, but they hadn't talked to her much. Everybody was dancing and carrying on and hanging around the punch bowl. To see if Minnie May would slip in gin. But Minnie May didn't have a chance. Mrs. Fister never left the bowl but once and that was when the chef hurt his hand. And the maids ganged up while she was gone. The guessing started at ten o'clock and then they took off the masks. And the pink pearls were won by Dot Mainwaring, who was very religious and not very clean.

"Ten o'clock," Mark repeated. "According to Dr. Kloppel, Ruth had been dead an hour then." He made his voice as gentle as possible. "Didn't you wonder where she was? Didn't you miss her at all?"

"We knew she wasn't there," Moke said thickly. "But we thought she'd gone to bed. We knew she got permission from Mr. Benz to go to the doctor on account of her eyes, so we thought she had a headache. That's what we thought. The party was almost over and we were going up to her room to see if we could get her something when that dog——"

Miss Libby spoke for the first time. "Mr. East! Come to the point if you have one," she said sharply.

"Sorry," he said. "Sorry, and I mean it. But I've got to know about those eyes."

"We don't mind," Moke said. "We understand you got to know. It was about new glasses. She was talking about getting some. The others broke. So she got off early and went to the doctor's."

"Do you know his name?"

"No, sir."

"You're a hard man," Miss Libby insinuated. "What's the matter with your own eyes?"

He looked at Moke and Poke carefully. They still stood straight against the wall, but their cheeks were too white around the edges of the rouge they had salvaged from the last stockroom disaster. It was time to stop.

"Run along," he said, "and thanks." It sounded thin, but what else could he say to girls like Moke and Poke. "I may drop in at your place tonight," he added, "but don't tell anybody."

That wasn't enough and he knew it. He'd taken too much and given nothing in return, nothing that could be carried away and later used for comfort. "You mustn't worry about this," he said, "or think too much about it. Very often things happen because they're meant to. I know that sounds cruel and it bothers me too, but I usually find a good reason in the end. When and if I find the reason for this, I'll explain it to you, and you'll see how it had to happen the way it did."

They were entirely satisfied.

"Applause," Miss Libby said when they left. "But you do know your business. When and if you find a reason for this, will you explain it to me, too?"

"You'll be seeing me," he promised.

He went back to his office and worked on a profitable case involving a young man whose family didn't want him to marry the daughter of a longshoreman. He'd met the daughter and her father and the young man and his family, and thought they all deserved what they would inevitably get.

He called the longshoreman's daughter on the phone, told her to go ahead with the wedding and advised a prenuptial settlement. Then he called the young man's family and suggested that, in the end, a husky wife would be cheaper than the present succession of trained nurses and lawsuits. After that he wanted to bathe in an icy mountain stream, so he took Bessy and Beulah to the St. Regis for cocktails.

It was a wise and fruitful move. Bessy sketched the women's hats on the backs of all the envelopes he had in his pocket, using a pencil borrowed from the head barman. She borrowed it herself, without warning, and came back to the table with a single glass of cherry brandy paid for out of a child's clasp purse. The St. Regis customers loved her.

"She'll do it every time," Beulah sneered. "It's a trick to shame another round out of whoever she's with. I hope nobody in this place knows you."

"I hope somebody does," he said. "There's something distinguished about Bessy."

"There certainly is. Wait till her eyes turn pink. That's when we leave, in a hurry. Now, what do you know that I don't."

He told her, but not until he'd ordered the round. There was something distinguished about Beulah, too.

"Find the eye doctor," she said. "Maybe he wasn't an eye doctor, maybe he was something else altogether. Find him."

"Do you mind telling me how?"

"You live here, I don't. If you don't know the medical men in your own town, then you're not living right. You can put an ad in the paper, can't you?"

"Yes, I could." He thought it over. "Yes, that might turn something up."

"Of course it will. You're making too much of that shyness and the business of keeping to herself. How do you know she wasn't incurable, maybe a leper? How do you know she wasn't as blind as a bat, too? If she went to see a doctor just before the party, and he told her——"

"I'm almost glad you're here," he admitted, "although there have been moments. . . . I'll take care of it tonight."

Bessy entered the conversation with a squeal. "Look, Beulah! That fur hat with the rose is exactly like the one I sent away for the day Papa died and I knew I had the money. And I know where I can lay my hands on it this minute." She dampened the barman's pencil in cherry brandy. "I heard what you two were saying. If you put an ad in the paper, the doctor won't answer it."

"Why?" Beulah demanded, adding bitterly, "dear."

"Because he gave her the wrong medicine and knew it as soon as he checked his poison cupboard. So he knows it's the same as m-u-r-d-e-r. Always spell because you never know who's listening."

"Time," Beulah warned, shrugging into her coat. "Practically red."

Mark returned the pencil himself and put his guests into a cab. He directed the driver in clear tones. "This address and no other," he said firmly, "no matter what you're offered." Then he returned to the hotel and telephoned an ad for insertion in a morning Personal Column. It read: "The doctor who was recently consulted by Miss Ruth Miller is asked to communicate with the undersigned." He added his initials and home address.

It would have an ugly and suggestive look in type, wedged in between the deserted beds and boards and refusals to pay the little woman's bills, and it would be lingered over by speculative eyes. It would also, he feared, put joy in the hearts of the cranks.

He began to think of himself as henpecked, and ordered another drink. He counted the hens: Roberta, Bessy, and Beulah, the cool Miss Libby who might not be that at all, Moke and Poke, La Cashman, and a lady who was waiting for him in the immediate future, calling herself Jewel Schwab. . . . He knew what Roberta was afraid of, and several times he had been afraid himself, but tonight the lights and voices around him did not spell m-u-r-d-e-r. He thought of the dinner he could have with a clear conscience, and of the play that could follow, if he were in the canary-breeding business.

So he did what he knew he must do; he turned his back on the lights and warmth and struck out for Hope House. As he walked he wondered if the longshoreman's daughter had gone straight to Hattie Carnegie's. Naturally. And then to Elizabeth Arden's. And then, and only then, to a good lawyer. She was a normal, grasping woman, and he understood her down to the ground. He told himself he liked that kind. He didn't like shy

105

department-store clerks who were self-effacing to the point of rubbing themselves out.

When he reached Hope House, the lobby was filled with girls and women of all ages, streaming in and out of the dining room and lining up at the elevator. He saw the impression he made and began to feel better. The stream swerved and the mailboxes replaced the elevator as a vantage ground. He went up to the desk and spoke to the woman in charge. She was one of the two he had seen getting into the cab and laughing.

"Miss Brady?" she repeated. She was plainly surprised. "Why, yes, I believe she's in. May I have your name?"

"Mark East. Tell her, please, that I'm investigating Ruth Miller's death." He heard the rustle of sighs all around him. The woman at the desk, obviously Miss Small, looked as if she didn't believe him.

"Investigating?"

"Yes. At the request of one of Miss Miller's friends. It's a formality, that's all, and quite usual. People always want to reassure themselves when a thing like this happens."

"But I didn't know——" She was perplexed and annoyed. "I'm Angeline Small, Miss Brady's assistant. Won't I do as well? I don't want to trouble Miss Brady unless it's absolutely necessary. She hasn't fully recovered from the shock."

She was recovered yesterday, he told himself, if she is your dark-haired friend. Not only recovered, but laughing out loud.

"I understand your solicitude, Miss Small, but for the record I'd better see Miss Brady. I won't detain her."

Miss Small hesitated again. "You say you represent a friend of Ruth's? She gave us the impression that she had no friends, had no one at all. That's why Miss Brady was eager to take her in."

"Her friend," Mark said easily, "is Mrs. Nicholas Sutton. I suppose Miss Miller thought that claiming Mrs. Sutton, or talking about her, might sound like putting on the dog." He waited, looking over Miss Small's head to the girl behind the switchboard. Kitty Brice. "Hello," he said. "I couldn't stay away."

Miss Small left the desk and crossed to the lounge, asking him to follow. "Will you wait in here, please? Miss Brady will see you."

The lounge was empty and likely to remain so, for Miss Small firmly closed the door when she left him. He examined the good, simple furniture; the careful, correct prints; the bright, inexpensive rug. Very nice, he decided; a little too neat and institutional but probably heaven to the boarders. . . . I've got that woman's back up and I don't blame her. According to Kloppel, she's due to spend the night handing out aromatic spirits of ammonia. Brady won't like me, either. I'll go easy. He sniffed the air. No miasmas, nothing but burning logs.

The door opened and Miss Brady entered alone. She was the dark one, all right, and there was nothing institutional about her clothes and poise. And not in Small's class, although Small was good enough. This one was from another world entirely.

"Let's get to the point," Miss Brady said at once. She looked as if she hadn't laughed for years. "Are you a detective, and if you are, exactly what do you think you're looking for? And where does Mrs. Sutton come into this?"

He told her, and she listened attentively. "You work with girls, Miss Brady," he added. "You know how their minds behave. Well, it's even worse with a girl like Mrs. Sutton, who is younger than most of your charges and much, much less sophisticated. She was shocked and confused by Miss Miller's death, and her husband asked me to straighten things out. This is the only way I can do it." He smiled.

Miss Brady returned a cold stare. "I understand you were here yesterday, asking for Jewel Schwab. And you told the girl on duty that you'd talked to Mrs. Cashman. I don't like that, and I think I'll have to stop it. And don't think I can't. Well?"

It took five minutes of persuasive talk to win her over, and even then he wasn't confident. "I only want one fact," he said, "one statement from you that I can use. I don't care what it is, I don't even know what it ought to be. But I've got to reassure Mrs. Sutton. It isn't all business with me, she's a very dear friend. She insists that Ruth Miller wouldn't kill herself. I can't argue that. But I have wondered why the verdict was suicide instead of accidental death. Of course, I can go to the police, but you don't want that any more than I do. So you tell me. Why was it? Why didn't somebody say she fell? Wasn't that possible?"

Miss Brady was slightly mollified. "I suppose it was possible. But there were other things—her attitude, for instance——"

"That's it, that's what I want. Her attitude. I can't get the girl straight in my mind. Mrs. Sutton says she was quiet and kind. Dr. Kloppel says she was anti-social and a liar. How well did Kloppel know her?" He knew Kloppel hadn't known her at all.

Miss Brady colored. "He probably got that from me. Listen, Mr. East, my job here is just about as spiritual as yours. Every year and sometimes twice a year we have trouble about—things disappearing. In a place like this—well, it happens. And I have to keep watch like a jailer." Miss Brady paused, as if she were collecting facts and putting them in proper sequence. "On the afternoon of the day she died, I met Ruth Miller on the street. She should have been at work, and that in itself was odd enough to make me wonder. But there was something else I liked even less. She was carrying a suitcase. When I asked her what she was doing, she told me a vague story about a doctor's appointment. I didn't like the way she looked, and, frankly, I didn't believe her. So I said I'd go along. At that point she was either unwilling or unable to tell me the doctor's name. There was only one thing for me to do then and I did it. I brought her back here. I didn't believe the doctor story and I still don't, and I was interested in the suitcase. We've had the suitcase business before. Full of linen, silver, other girls' clothes, and jewelry. I tried to watch her during the evening, but you know about the costume party. They all looked alike. And I planned to have a talk with her later that night. I never had a chance. I've talked to several girls who think they talked to her, and they all say the same thing—that her behavior was decidedly peculiar. That's all."

"What happened to the suitcase?"

"I opened it, naturally. Nothing but clothing, her own. She was evidently planning to run away. Why, where to, or what have you, I don't know. I can only guess that she was in a jam of some sort, saw something closing in, and tried to skip."

"Maybe," he said, "it actually did close in."

"Here? In this place? Impossible." Miss Brady's strong face was faintly amused.

He tried to look amused, too. "What about Jewel Schwab? I'd like to talk to her. I understand she was the first person from the house to reach the body."

"She was indeed. That's our Jewel. Two years ago a man in the next block was knifed by his lady, and Jewel showed up before the blood. No, you can't talk to her. You can't talk to anybody. I won't have that mess all over again. Hysterics, enough to drive you mad. You tell Mrs. Sutton I know my rights. If you ask me, Mrs. Sutton has too much money and too much time and she ought to go back to school." Miss Brady stood up and walked to the door. He followed.

"Miss Brady," he asked finally, "are you and Miss Small satisfied to let things stand as they are?"

"Certainly. As far as we're concerned, the situation is clear, unfortunate, and finished." They were in the lobby, and she went directly to the street door and held it open. "Good night." She added, "My compliments to Mrs. Sutton."

He walked to the corner, framing a story for Roberta. Brady is no fool, he told himself. She knows her stuff. But he didn't want to talk to Roberta at once, he wanted time to rearrange his own ideas and soften Miss Brady's facts. The next day would be soon enough.

He had the kind of dinner he liked and saw a play, then went home to bed. At two in the morning he was called by a client in Washington who needed him at once for a delicate piece of identification. It was too late to call Roberta, so he wrote her a note and dropped it in the mail chute. At seven he was on a plane.

6

The elderly maid, Agnes, closed Mrs. Fister's door behind her and went to the second-floor closet where the mops and brooms were kept. She hung her dustcloth neatly on a hook and shuffled down the hall to the packroom where she had a little private business of her own.

Agnes often told herself she had the best job in the House. She looked after the public rooms downstairs and the staff rooms. She got tips and gifts of used clothing and was able to pass the latter along to the other maids, which made her feel like a staff member herself. She also got pieces of fruit and candy. Her apron pocket was even then bulging with a pear. From Mrs. Fister, who had a plateful on her center table, just like a real home.

The private business in the packroom had to do with Clara's low blood pressure and an old sweater that Agnes didn't need herself. Clara worked in the kitchen, which was always cold. The sweater would help. Agnes glowed with generosity and wrestled with the packroom latch.

The old straw suitcase, in which she kept her odds and ends for giving, was not where it should have been. She always kept it well to the front, but she hadn't looked at it for more than a month, and now somebody had pushed it to the back. She saw its familiar outlines behind a pile of wicker hampers, canvas telescopes, and hatboxes. She pulled it forward, dislodging a rusty bird cage that had no business there and upsetting hatboxes. Nothing was as it should be. She'd speak to Mrs. Fister.

There was something behind the suitcase that looked like a pile of rags. Probably oiled rags, probably explosive, everybody burned to a crisp one of these nights; she'd certainly speak to Mrs. Fister. She reached into the dark corner with distaste.

For a long time she knelt on the bare floor looking at what she held in her hand. The black-fringed, empty eyes looked back, the rosebud mouth curled in a crooked smile, the bright wool hair was covered with dust and cobwebs. Now what in the world, she asked herself. Now what in the living world——

She reached into the corner again and found the dress. It was wadded in a ball, and she shook it out, muttering. "Supposed to be turned in with the others to be stored away proper in case of future need, although I doubt if anybody'd want to put one on again." She upbraided the late wearer. "Not even folded, not even wrapped up, pushed back in the corner like it wasn't meant to be found. All that stuff piled in front; if it hadn't been for Clara needing a sweater, it could stay there till spring and I'd never know. I'll give that one a talking to when I find out who she is, boarder or no boarder." She smoothed the mask and folded it, and began on the dress. Sleeves turned in, doubled over at the waist, hem——

She carried the dress over to the light. There was a spot on the hem—at least, there had been a spot once. Now there was a blistered, brownish stain that somebody had tried to wash out. Like coffee. Agnes was enraged. "Rank carelessness," she fumed. "Prancing around with a cup of coffee, acting up, no respect to the Board that's kind enough to give parties at no additional cost." She paused. "But they didn't have coffee, they had punch; and sure's you're born that's coffee. Must have been one of those that keeps food in her room, attracting mice."

She took the mask and dress to her own room and hid them in the bottom of a drawer. "I'll fix her," she told her reflection in the mirror. "I'll find out and fix her. Not half washed out, either, as if there wasn't any soap to be had or in too big a hurry to get somewhere else. Somebody from another floor, trying to place the blame——"

She paused and studied her reflection in the mirror. It looked back with strange intensity and told her, without words, that she had paused because her thoughts were uneasy. "Humph!" she said defiantly, tossing her head. "I say that's coffee and it is coffee." But she locked the drawer before she left and put the key in her pocket.

At the same hour, in Roberta's dining room, Beulah neatly chipped the top from her breakfast egg and watched Bessy try to do it, too. Because Bessy had been perfect in rehearsal, the present performance was sheer obstinacy, so she was kicked for it.

"Well I'll be!" Roberta said.

Wrong leg, Beulah decided. Better act as if I had pins and needles.

"Letter from Mark," Roberta went on. "He's gone away, urgent business. And he says we're to forget Ruth Miller until he comes back and talks to us. He went down to that place and saw the woman who runs it, and he seems satisfied. He says you two are to relax and remember this is a holiday, but not necessarily Roman. He'll be back in a day or two. Sends love. That gives me a big pain."

"Well!" Beulah abandoned the pins and needles. It must have been Bessy's leg after all. "Satisfied, is he? He's been wrong before."

"I don't know." Roberta frowned. "He sounds awfully certain, and he's underscored a lot. Words like 'forget' and 'relax' and 'Roman.'" She put the letter in her sweater pocket. "What do you want to do this morning?"

"I'd like to visit the Cloisters," Bessy said.

"You aren't appropriate," Beulah assured her. There was egg yolk on Bessy's forehead. She looked like a yokel; yolk, yokel. Beulah applauded herself with a peal of light laughter. "Why don't we go to the zoo?"

"That's the thing," Roberta agreed. "And we'll take the baby if we can get him away from Miss Bassingworthy."

"I wouldn't put up with a nurse who called herself Miss Bassingworthy. What's happened to the Lizzies and the Delias? Make the woman tell you her Christian name and call her by it."

Roberta said, "It's Guinevere." When Beulah's face began to mottle, she hurried on. "But I think we can shake her. She's forever yapping about changing her English upper plate for an American model, and Nick said she could have it. Hands across the sea with teeth in them. So why don't I send her to the dentist?"

"Let me tell her," Beulah said. "I know how. I may live in the backwoods, but I've read Galsworthy." She got up briskly. "The nursery door is the one with the pandas running up and down, isn't it? Why not Teddy bears? The whole house is un-American."

When the door closed, Bessy removed the egg from her forehead and smiled at Roberta. "I knew it was there all the time, but Beulah has so little pleasure. And you mustn't be upset when I'm afraid of the lions. It won't mean anything. Is that the morning paper, dear?"

Roberta handed it over. "Nothing in it. You're a cute one, Miss Bessy."

"Thank you," Bessy said, scrambling the paper and dropping sheets to the floor. "Mark's ad should be in this unless he changed his mind before he did it. You know what I mean, don't you?"

"Sure. But what are you steamed up about? I thought you said an ad would be useless?"

"I said that because I wanted him to do it. That's the way I get things done."

"Bless my soul," Roberta said. "Go on."

"When I was against it, they were for it," Bessy beamed. "It always happens that way. . . . Wait a minute, I've lost the page. Of course I wanted Mark to advertise. Just think how that person is going to feel, even if there never was a doctor."

"What person?"

"The one who gave her a shove."

"Miss Bessy!"

"Somebody sitting at breakfast this morning, just like us, opening the paper just like me, saying there's nothing in it, just like you. And then finding——yes, here it is." She read the lines with relish.

Roberta leaned over her shoulder. "Miss Bessy, you think Mark's wrong about this, don't you?"

"I don't know, dear. I'm not very reliable about natural death and suicide. We'll wait and see."

"What good will waiting do? He's out of town and we're helpless."

"Not helpless. There may be replies and we can call for them."

Roberta read the ad a second time. "That's his apartment number. It isn't far from here. He can't expect anything or he'd have asked us to check."

"I don't expect anything, myself," Bessy admitted. "Not in the mail."

"Huh?"

Bessy was saved from an explanation. An infantile wail cut through the paneled door as if it were made of paper, and two adult voices rose and fell in accusation and denial.

"The Forsyte Saga," Roberta said as she charged out of the room.

Bessy was glad to be alone. She collected bits of egg and shell from the cloth, the center bowl of fruit, and the floor, and wondered why an egg that barely filled a cup on one occasion could cover a room on another. The voices outside the door were augmented by Roberta's. Something about teeth. Well, it was to be expected. Beulah had probably made comparisons.

She wanted no part of it, because she was already on Miss Bassingworthy's side, so she left the dining room by a side door and found her way to a small room Nick called his den. It held a battered desk, a telephone, and a leather couch for napping. Bessy sat at the desk and inserted a finger in the dial. It spun nicely. She liked it.

Mark had said relax. He'd said this was a holiday, not necessarily Roman. A Roman holiday. Make a Roman holiday. Butcher. Butchered to make a Roman holiday.

There now, she told herself happily. I live in the back-woods, too, and listen to me!

Butcher, she went on. Butcher, blood. Blood, murder. Murder. . . . In another minute she had an idea, practical, cheap, and all her own. She wouldn't tell a soul. Not a single soul except one. And it was every bit as good as anything Beulah had ever done. She gloated quietly and found a small flaw. It was a pity, but she'd never know which soul it was.

She picked up the phone book and turned the pages. Such a big book, so many names, and she had time for only one. Well, maybe later on—— Her fat finger traveled slowly down a page and up again. Hope. Hope House. She dialed carefully. It can't do any harm, she told herself, and it makes me feel useful.

A voice said, "Hope House."

Bessy glared into the mouthpiece and growled: "Murder will out!"

The scream exceeded her expectations. She sat back and tried to guess. Miss Plummer? Miss Brady? Miss Small? The one named Jewel? The one with the spotted face? One of those people she'd heard about and would never really know.

She had almost decided on the one with the spotted face when Beulah shouted from the dining room. She joined her, carelessly humming off key.

"What were you yelling about before?" she asked Beulah.

"Don't try to turn my attention to myself," Beulah answered. "What were you doing in there? Reading Nick's mail?"

"Beulah!"

"Never mind." There wasn't anything important in Nick's mail and she knew it. "The zoo is off. That woman——"

"Did you tell her what kind of teeth to get?"

"We never got around to her teeth. It was the baby's. He got a new one himself this morning and bit me with it. But it had a silver lining. That woman thinks he shouldn't go out, so I told Roberta you and I had some Christmas shopping to do. Go put your things on."

"But we haven't any Christmas——"

Beulah hissed. "Do you want to know what happened to Ruth Miller or not?"

Miss Plummer sat behind the desk, sipping a cup of tea and worrying.

At nine-thirty Miss Brady had come to her room and asked her to take the desk as a special favor. Her face had looked like thunder and her voice was hard. She'd apologized, though, and said it was an emergency. She and Miss Small had to see Mrs. Marshall-Gill, she'd said. That was odd, because they'd seen Mrs. Marshall-Gill the night before and come home late, looking like rags.

And now it was noon and the lounge was full of girls who had no business to be there in the middle of the day. Home from work in the middle of the day when there was no food served except to staff. And Kitty had brought the tea without being asked. Something was going on that she didn't know about, and nobody would tell her anything. When she'd asked Kitty, that one had slipped off as usual. In the lounge now, with the others, and the door shut.

Miss Plummer asked herself what it meant. Mrs. Marshall-Gill twice in twenty-four hours. And a man last night, according to her sister who'd refused to say anything else and was keeping out of sight. And that old woman several nights ago. It all added up to something, and it meant trouble. She'd been feeling trouble in the air for days.

Some of the girls had felt trouble, too. She'd seen it in the way they acted, short and snappy when there was no reason to be. And she'd heard whispers, ugly, troublemaking whispers. She looked at the lounge door and wondered what would happen if she walked in and asked for an explanation. Even Jewel was in there, and she had no business to be. Twelve to one she was on duty. Suppose somebody wanted to go to the top floor? . . . Miss Plummer thought that over. No one had

117

used the elevator for more than an hour. Everybody who came in went directly to the lounge.

She watched the front door open again. Dot Mainwaring and Minnie May Handy. She called to them, but they pretended not to hear. She saw Minnie May slip a piece of paper in her handbag. Newspaper. "Hello," she called again. This time they waved, but they didn't stop. They went in the lounge, too. Come to think of it, Miss Plummer remembered, Jewel had a newspaper this morning. She went out and bought it, I saw her. And I think Kitty——

She began to wish she took a paper herself. She never had because she tried to save her eyes, and another paper was a needless waste of money. Mrs. Fister took a picture paper and always told her if anyone had died or been divorced. And Miss Brady and Miss Small took the *Times* and the *Herald Tribune,* and the chef took a Polish-language paper. Four papers in the House every morning, and she was sure she'd seen at least a dozen clippings.

She thought of Mrs. Fister, but asking her would be useless. Mrs. Fister didn't believe in talk. Maybe somebody will tell me, she hoped. Kitty or Jewel, they ought to; we work here side by side, and what's news to them is news to me. Or Miss Brady or Miss Small. She remembered Miss Brady's face. We're in trouble, all right, she decided. There's something in the paper that puts us in a bad light. The House—— She pushed the cold tea aside and took up her work. She was afraid it was doubly important now.

At one o'clock Kitty and Jewel came hurriedly out of the lounge and tried to look as if they had never left their posts. The reason was immediately obvious. Miss Brady and Miss Small had been spotted from the lounge windows.

They came in with bright smiles and went directly to the elevator. "No lunch for us, Ethel," Miss Brady said over her shoulder. "We treated ourselves."

"Not so much as a thank-you for the extra time I'm putting in," Miss Plummer said when they had gone.

"Kitty, you come here, I want to talk to you. I can't keep quiet any longer."

Kitty crept over to the desk. "I know what you want," she said. "I was going to tell you when the gang cleared off. Look." Kitty placed a clipping on the blotter. "From today's *Times*. The personnel department at Blackman's showed it to Moke and Poke, and they bought one for themselves and beat it over here on lunch hour to see what went on. And they had plenty of company. Some of the kids saw the paper at their offices. Half the House knows it by now, and the rest will know it tonight. Nice little place we've got here, lady."

"Oh dear, oh dear," Miss Plummer wailed softly. "I never heard of anybody named M. E. Who——"

"That's the fellow I talked to, I told you. He was asking for Jewel."

"But what has Jewel——I don't understand why Jewel——"

"She was the first to reach the body, except Cashman. If you'll stop groaning, I'll tell you everything I know. I want to get it straight, anyhow, in case. Kloppel called Monny up at the crack of dawn, and I listened in. He was sore about a doctor being in the ad, he thought he was being insulted. Monny told him it meant a doctor Miller was supposed to have seen the day she died. That's mystery number one, and it's how I first got wise to what was going on. Now we come to number two. I was down in the kitchen having myself some coffee a little after nine when a call came in and Jewel took it. Whoever it was yelled 'You murderer!' and hung up. Jewel went crazy, and Angel had to give her more aromatic on top of the quart she had last night. Now number three. Around nine-thirty Marshall-Gill called Monny and said what goes on. She also said everything was very distasteful and please to give her an explanation at once. Monny was wild, I could tell, but she put on a good act. Cool as a cucumber. She told Marshall-Gill there was going to be an investigation, and she was trying to stop it. She said there was a society woman behind it."

"Society! Ruth Miller!" Miss Plummer's head reeled. That Miss Pond. That was it. "I knew it!" she wailed. "I knew it, Kitty! That old lady who came here, remember? She could be society! I felt it! What in heaven's name will happen to us?"

"Nothing will happen to us. Bunch of busybodies with more money than brains. That's what Monny told Marshall-Gill. But you'd better stop looking like that, or they'll think you did it."

"Did what?"

"Killed Miller."

"Killed!" Miss Plummer fell back in her chair. "Kitty?" she whispered. "Kitty?"

The switchboard buzzed like a scolding monitor. Kitty thumbed her nose, but her voice when she took the call was alert, sympathetic, and efficient. "Yes, Miss Brady?"

Miss Plummer held her breath.

"Yes, Miss Brady," Kitty said smoothly, "yes, I understand. No, Miss Brady, there's nobody here but Miss Plummer and me. . . . Yes, Miss Brady, I'll do it right away. Yes, Miss Brady."

"What?" Miss Plummer whispered when Kitty disconnected.

"What are you whispering for?" Kitty grinned. "I'm harmless. She's written a notice for the bulletin board; fast work, huh? Jewel's bringing it down."

They both turned to the elevator and watched the dial. The arrow was stationary at eight. Then it moved to seven and stopped. Then six, five, stop at five. Then four, three, two, stop at two. Kitty went over and stood waiting.

The bulletin said little, but it left no room for misunderstanding. When Jewel handed it over she also gave instructions. "You're to take everything else off," she said. "This is to go up there by itself. You got that straight?"

"I speak and read English," Kitty said.

"Well that's what they told me to tell you. Everything else off and this here alone. What's it say?"

Kitty looked aghast. "Do you mean to say you haven't read it?"

"I didn't get a chance. Miss Small rode down from Miss Brady's as far as five, and Harris got on at seven and rode to second. You see I didn't get a chance. Harris made out like she was reading a newspaper all the time, but I could see her watching me."

Kitty thumbed the last tack into place. "Well, you've got a chance now. Read."

Jewel and Miss Plummer crowded each other for position. Miss Plummer's lips moved silently but Jewel read with a lacquered fingernail.

Residents and employees will disregard the notice appearing in today's *Times* and refrain from discussion. It is the work of a practical joker.

> MONICA BRADY
> ANGELINE SMALL
> *For the Board*

Jewel's jaw dropped.

"Shut your mouth," Kitty advised. "It says so here." She returned to the switchboard and ostentatiously took up a magazine.

Miss Plummer watched her from the corner of an eye. Clearly it would do no good to talk. Kitty had decided to obey rules. That wasn't like Kitty.

Miss Plummer sat on, neglecting her embroidery, twisting her fingers in her lap, watching the hands of the clock. The day would never be done. She'd have to wait until midnight when she could talk to her sister behind a locked door, and she didn't want to wait. She wasn't even sure that waiting was safe. She wanted to talk to someone now, to tell someone about her sudden fears. Although, she reminded herself, there was nothing sudden about them. They'd been in the back of her mind for weeks, ever since the night of the party. Deep in the back of her mind, like something buried, but they turned themselves over like leaves when she was tired. If she could only talk to someone her own age, someone settled and not flighty, someone who might remember the things she was remembering and tell her she was wrong.

When Agnes came down to get a late lunch, she tried to signal her. But Agnes walked by with a bent head, as if she didn't want to see anybody. Not even a friend. That wasn't like Agnes.

She searched desperately in the past and tried to fit things together. There was that Miss Pond, for instance. She'd always wondered about Miss Pond. If she could see Miss Pond again, she'd ask her point blank if she had a niece named Ruth. . . . Miss Plummer massaged her knuckles and studied her shiny serge lap. She felt like crying and didn't know why.

At that same moment Bessy and Beulah stood in the middle of Fifth Avenue and Forty-second Street, lying steadily to the traffic officer. They told him they were from California and didn't know which way to turn. They referred to a mental confusion, but the officer, thick in the pre-Christmas rush, had his own interpretation. Time, temper, and traffic frayed and broke while they straightened each other out.

They were not lost, they told him above the screaming horns; they knew exactly where they were, but they couldn't find what they were looking for. An eye doctor whose name and address they had forgotten. Their niece's doctor, a lovely girl threatened with blindness who wouldn't have anyone else, lying in a dark room at the Commodore waiting for drops. They'd called on seven eye doctors and two prescription opticians between Fifty-seventh and Forty-second, and it had taken all morning because everybody made them wait. They were sure the man they wanted was somewhere near by. Not far from Blackman's, within walking distance. They could remember that much. Maybe north a little way, maybe south. Or maybe east or west. Did the officer know an eye doctor in the neighborhood?

They talked fast and quivered their lips.

The officer gathered them both in one huge arm and

released traffic with the other while he blessed their hearts. He gave them the address of a medical building, a list of drugstores that might be able to think of something, and indicated a famous firm of opticians several blocks away. Then he led them to the curb, patted their basely shaking hands, and turned them in the right direction for the optician.

They moved off with tremulous thanks. Out of hearing, Beulah said, "We've been doing this the wrong way. All that time wasted in reception rooms. They'd see us right away if we didn't look so healthy. Put your finger in your eye."

"No, Beulah, no!"

"So you won't co-operate?"

"No, Beulah, no! Why can't it be your eye?"

"Because I've done my share, that's why. Didn't I go lame for you?"

"Lame," wailed Bessy, "but not for me. I want to go home."

Beulah wanted to go home too. "Very well," she snarled, "we'll go. And I hope you remember it was your suggestion. Remember to your dying day, and if you don't, I'll remind you. Come along. Taxi!"

"No," Bessy said. "I've changed my mind."

The firm of opticians gave them another list, and they covered four widely scattered offices without result. By three o'clock they were six blocks from Blackman's, blue with cold, and sagging with weariness. A malignant wind swept around the corner and bit into their bones. Their noses twitched. The wind was spicy with the smell of oranges, hot coffee, hot dogs, and mustard.

"Where are we?" Bessy asked faintly. They were leaning against the partition of an orange-drink stand.

They bought and devoured two of everything, and, because it was the slack hour, the girl who waited on them put her elbows on the counter and listened.

"You'll have to pardon me butting in like this," the girl said finally, "but I can't help hearing. Did you ladies say eyes?"

There was little heart left in Beulah, but she still had the remnants of a voice. And by that time she was geared like a juke box. Eyes, yes. Her niece. A lovely girl, a missing doctor, total blindness or sure to be. . . . The coffee was hot and sweet, and some of its warmth crept into the lifeless words and dusted them with sugar. Beulah felt the change, heard it, and built sturdily. The girl hung on every syllable.

"My," the girl breathed. "Just like a story in a magazine. Just like those true-life stories on the radio." The fragrance of unrequited love fought with the oranges and mustard and won. Moonlight and honeysuckle filled the small enclosure.

"I don't know if what I'm thinking is any good," the girl said, "but the world is a small place. You hear that everywhere. There's a eye doctor in this building, I seen him myself lots of times, and he's a young fellow, too. Wouldn't that be something if it turned out to be him? You could try anyways. The door is right around the corner, and you walk up a flight. I don't know his name, he don't talk much, but he has coffee here sometimes."

Beulah thanked her warmly.

"Leave me know how it comes out, will you?" the girl begged.

"I certainly will," Beulah promised.

But when she and Bessy staggered around the corner against the wind and saw the flight of dingy wooden steps leading up into shadows, they looked at each other doubtfully.

"I don't think . . ." Bessy wavered. "I don't like——"

A hatless young man clattered down the steps and brushed by them with a muttered apology. They didn't see his sharp, appraising stare.

"No," Beulah said. "It can't be this. It smells funny. Now stop teasing me to go home. We're going."

Assisted by four male pedestrians, they hailed a cab and went back to Roberta's.

When they entered the library, Roberta was sitting by the fire with her head in her hands.

"I'm dead," Roberta said, "and I can prove it. I stuck a pin in my arm and couldn't feel a thing. Bassingworthy went to the dentist out of pure hellishness and left me with the baby. He's pink and white, and I'm black and blue. Did you have any luck?"

"No, we didn't," Bessy said promptly.

"Yes, we did," Beulah said. "We didn't buy anything, but we covered a lot of ground, and it was what you might call interesting. Maybe we'll go out again tomorrow. Now what about Mark? Have you heard anything, dear?"

"No. My hearing has been impaired by an alphabet block. An X, in case you ever wondered what an X was good for."

"I'm afraid you don't love your little baby," grieved Bessy. "I hope and pray you aren't one of these girls who put babies in bottom drawers and——"

"Look straight through her," advised Beulah. "Pretend she was never even born. Now if I were you I'd call Mark's apartment. Don't you know the girl who takes care of his messages?"

"Sure I know her. Name of Henning. You know, that's not a bad idea." Roberta inched herself and chair over to the telephone. "I can't walk. I can't even stand up. I have ten more bones in my body than the book says." She moaned softly as she dialed. "And they're all in my back, low down. I've been a horsie, giddap, giddap. . . . Hello, Miss Henning?"

They heard Miss Henning plunge into narrative. It was clear that she had news of some sort. Roberta's face told nothing, and neither did her cryptic responses.

"You don't say," Roberta drawled. "You don't tell me."

Miss Henning's voice crackled on. When the end was reached, Beulah helped Roberta with the receiver.

"Well?" Beulah barked. "What?"

"Henning had fun," Roberta said enviously. "Miss Brady swore at her."

Miss Henning had reported two calls for Mark, one from Miss Brady at two-thirty and another, anonymous, at two forty-five. Miss Brady had identified herself at once.

"With cuss words," Roberta said. "Henning liked her. Brady was sore about the ad. She said Mark was no gentleman because he'd promised to lay off and hadn't. She said she wanted to see him right away. When Henning told her he was out of town she sounded surprised. Really surprised. Then quiet. Henning says you could have heard a pin drop. Then she tried to find out if anybody else had called about the ad. Henning said dozens. A big, black lie, of course, but Henning wanted to hear Brady swear again. She did. And that's all of that. Brady swore, but gently, and hung up."

"What about the other call? The anonymous one?"

"I'm coming to that. Look, Miss Beulah. See that piece of fancywork hanging on the wall over there? Give it a pull, will you, and tell whoever answers that we want a lot of sherry. I can't move, but I can still swallow."

Beulah pulled the bell and waited at the door for Mrs. Hawks. When the sherry came she closed the door firmly in Mrs. Hawks' face. "Here," she said, easing the tray onto a low table. "I'll pour. Now what about that call?"

"That one was a girl, low voice full of excitement. Almost whispering. Henning got the impression she was getting away with murder, like calling up on the sly or putting something over on somebody. Because of that, Henning tried to get her name. No luck, although the girl admitted she was interested in the ad. When Henning told her Mark was out of town, she sort of gasped. Henning asked her for her name again—she says she had a feeling something was really wrong—but the girl said names didn't matter. And she said Mark would hear from her again. She hung up on that and Henning tried to trace the call. Of course she couldn't."

Beulah frowned. "That could be a Hope House girl."

"Could be a crank, too. I asked Henning about the cranks, but they haven't been heard from. Guess they're working on that kidnap case in Jersey."

Beulah twisted in her chair, saw Bessy reaching for the decanter, and slapped her wrist absently. "You mentioned rope," she said to Roberta. "When you were talking to Miss Henning. Rope. What was that for?"

Roberta flushed. "Small talk," she said. "Chit-chat. Henning says if you give people enough rope they'll do it every time."

What Miss Henning had said was: "Mr. East told me not to give you his address unless you sounded as if you'd reached the end of your rope. Have you?" And she had answered: "Any day now."

"What do you want to do?" she asked contritely. "It's a long time till dinner."

"Nothing," Beulah said. "We'll simply sit, if you don't mind."

They drew their chairs closer to the fire and sat without talking. They were still there when Nick came home. After dinner they played bridge for an hour and went to bed before eleven.

Twice during the night Roberta got up and looked out of her window. She looked up at the sky and down to the street far below. The taxicabs were like toys and the people were no larger than dolls.

April went to bed early because she was tired but she woke at eleven when she heard someone in the room.

"Lillian?"

"Sure," Lillian said. "Sorry, baby, but I thought I was being quiet."

"You didn't make any noise. I guess I've been restless. . . . Lillian, are the lights on?"

There was a pause before Lillian answered. "Sure. I wish you'd stop talking about lights. What difference do they make? Sure they're on. Put your hand on the bulb if you don't believe me."

April had heard the soft click, but she didn't say so. "You're cross tonight," she said mildly. "Of course I believe you, Lillian, and I won't speak of them again. . . . I guess you're tired. I'm tired, too. It was awful in the store today, I didn't have a minute to myself. The boss had my lunch sent over from the Greek's, roast lamb, and he paid for it himself. And he brought me home, too."

"He's all right. You stick with him."

"I'm going to. He says I can always stay. His other girl used to rob the till. . . . Are you reading, Lillian?"

"No."

"I heard paper, that's why I asked. That's all. I'm just talking."

"I'm not reading now. I was, but I've finished."

"I'm glad you're home, Lillian. When you aren't here, I always wait for you. I like to lie here and wait for you to come down the hall. I don't care when you're late, because I always know you'll come sometime."

"Okay. . . . What did you do tonight? Have fun?"

"No. I haven't seen anybody. I went out in the hall and tried a few doors, but nobody answered. And there wasn't anybody in the lobby when I came in. Only Miss Plummer, and she said her head ached. She didn't feel like talking."

"It's a quiet night. I noticed it myself."

April's face followed the other girl from closet door to window. "You aren't undressing, Lillian. It's late. You ought to come to bed."

"Oh, it's not as late as all that. I think I'll go down to see Plummer."

"Why?"

"Oh, business. Maybe I can talk her into making me some Christmas presents. Sachet bags, stuff like that. She can run them up in an hour or so."

"That'll be nice. She can use the extra money, too. I heard Mrs. Fister say she makes less every year. It's her eyes. I'm sorry for people like that."

"Me too. I'm heartbroken about Plummer! What kind of sachet do you like, baby?"

"Carnation."

"You've got it. . . . Listen. I'm leaving you now, but you're not to stay awake. It's very nice to know that somebody's waiting for you, but I don't want to think of you lying there by yourself, listening to the clock.

This time I may be a little late, so you go to sleep. Hear me? I mean it. And I'm turning off the lights so nobody'll bother you."

April slid down beneath the covers. "All right," she said. "I'm asleep already." She heard Lillian's laugh and counted the footsteps that crossed to the door. She heard the door open and close. There was another sound, too, the same sound she had noticed before. The faint rustle of paper. She decided that Lillian was taking Miss Plummer a sachet pattern.

She was warm and happy in the endless dark, thinking how nice Lillian and Miss Plummer would look bending over the pattern in the lamplight, choosing pretty colors and designs.

At midnight Mrs. Cashman discovered that her icebox held cheese but no ale. She trotted into the hall, took her things from the hatrack, and whistled for Brother.

"Walkie-palkie," she said when he waddled to her side. But when she opened the front door, she instantly fell back. The wind had died down and a quiet, devastating cold had taken its place. She hesitated between the hall and the warm kitchen, arguing silently. Maybe I don't need ale, she told herself; on a night like this maybe I need hot cocoa. Hot cocoa, she repeated. Hot cocoa—what am I talking about? In God's good name, I haven't touched the stuff since I was fourteen, and it made me sick even then. I need ale.

She changed her hat for a knitted shawl and told Brother to stay where he was. "You don't need to go," she reminded him. "You went at nine and don't say you didn't because I know better. And if I take you now we'll have to go the long way on account of your nerves and it's too cold. Shut up, I always come back, don't I?"

She walked briskly up the street, which was the short way, and rounded the corner. The front of Hope House was dark, as it should be, and farther on the lights of the delicatessen glowed. "Sam's," they spelled in warm, red letters. Good old Sam. Been there almost as long as she had.

Sam said he had just about given her up. "I figured on dropping by your place," he said. "I figured you was running low, and when you didn't come around I thought you had a stroke. How many?"

"Three large, I got my carryall. What do you know, Sam?"

"Nothing. You?"

"The same. No news is good news, as the saying goes."

"And keep smiling," Sam added. "Sardines?"

"Why not? Six. Brother can eat a box by himself. Seen Kloppel lately?"

"No. He don't come in here. That woman does. She's a close buyer. It don't surprise me he's thin. Pickle?"

"Dill. Maybe I'll have him over tonight. He's an owl, like me. Nobody's business when we go to bed or how. Jewish rye, Sam, and that'll be all."

Out in the street she cradled the shopping bag in both arms, like a baby, and walked slowly. She was thinking of her kitchen, of Kloppel, of her red checked tablecloth and the good food in the bag. When she came to the gate that opened on the Hope House court, she stopped. She told herself it was a funny thing to do. She'd avoided the gate ever since the night of Brother's discovery.

There was no one on the street and she thought quickly. It wouldn't hurt anybody if she stepped inside the court for a little minute. It wouldn't hurt and it would be something to tell Kloppel. A topic of conversation. The gate opened on oiled hinges and she entered.

One, two, three windows lighted. Second floor, fourth floor, and seventh. Seventh was the floor the girl jumped from. She counted the windows from the end, because Kloppel and the internes had told her which one it was. No, that one was dark. The blind girl lived there, so of course it was dark. Such a terrible affliction. She closed her eyes for an instant, to see what it felt like, and opened them in a panic. I'm addled, she told herself.

She counted the seventh-floor windows again, and laughed as heartily as she dared. I sure am addled, she repeated. That seventh-floor light's in a bathroom, and who should know better than me who saw the plumbing go up like a piano; late bather, using all the hot water and wasting electricity. Fun, fun, fun, if you don't have to pay the bill. . . . As she turned to go, the light went out. She was as pleased as if she'd turned it off herself.

Later, when Dr. Kloppel stood at the stove warming his ale, and Brother sat in his own little chair eating his sardines, she told him about her visit to the courtyard.

Dr. Kloppel grunted and came back to the table. "Keep your voice down." He nodded to the stout wall that separated the Cashman kitchen from his own. "She doesn't know I'm here. I mean she thinks I am, but she can't prove it. I left quietly. . . . You keep away from that place. I don't like it any more. I'm thinking of resigning."

"It should have happened years ago. Fifty cents here, fifty cents there, and having to hold their hands, too. Did somebody insult you?"

"If I read your mind correctly, it would be a compliment. No. . . . By the way, did a young fellow come to see you about that suicide?"

"He did. I sent him over to talk to Jewel. He's what I call a nice young man. Broke my heart the way he talked. Going to all that trouble for somebody else's girl."

"That what he told you?"

"After all these years of living side by side, you're not going to call me a liar, I hope?"

"No, no. I couldn't make him out, that's all I meant. What's this?"

"Sardines. Take a couple. Well, I made him out fine. He's a Christian."

"I'm not going to argue religion. . . . Did you happen to see the *Times* this morning?"

"I told you to take a couple, they're little fellows. No, I take the *News*. Why?"

"Somebody's advertising for the doctor who treated Ruth Miller. Not me, because I never did and everybody knows that. I don't mind saying I'm worried."

"If you're worried that means you're hiding something from me, and if you're hiding something from me you'll live to regret it. If Cashman were alive he'd tell you the same. What is it?"

"That young man, he said his name was Mark East. The ad in the *Times* was signed M. E. I remember he asked me about an autopsy. They didn't do one, not my fault and none of my business, that's for the police department. But no medical man likes to have an autopsy rammed down his throat."

"Nasty things, contents of the stomach, I never saw one and hope I never will. There goes my telephone, I bet that woman knows you're here."

"Tell her I'm not."

Mrs. Cashman opened the kitchen door and went into the hall. The phone was on the wall. "Hello," she howled. "What do you want?" After a pause she said, "Sure he's here, sure."

Dr. Kloppel joined her, sandwich in hand.

Mrs. Cashman clung to the phone. "You don't tell me! I don't believe it. Sure he's coming, right away." She hung up.

"You could have lied," Dr. Kloppel said.

"I could not. Right off the bat she hollered murder. Put me at a disadvantage. Hope House wants you. I think I'll go, too."

"No you won't. Do you think I want to be talked about?"

"You're going to be anyway, and not because of me. Don't you want to know what happened? It's terrible."

"Mrs. Cashman, if you're withholding——"

"Don't look at me like that, you didn't give me time. They found a girl in a bathroom with her head bashed in. Kloppel, don't you shove me!"

7

Miss Libby's call came a few minutes after nine. Roberta knew that Bessy and Beulah were still asleep, and that was the only good thing about the cold, dark morning. She turned to Nick who was only half awake himself. "This is the end of a rope, if you know what I mean," she said.

"No, but I'm a good listener."

"Then listen while I call that girl at Mark's house." She dialed the bedroom phone. "I can't tell this twice. Just snuggle in your pillows like somebody waiting to win the last battle while somebody else does the preliminary fighting. . . . Hello, Miss Henning, please."

Her mouth was trembling and Nick sat up hastily.

"Hello. This is Roberta Sutton. I want Mr. East's address, telephone number, and anything else you've got. Rope's end."

There was a pause while she jotted numbers on a pad. Then—"Anybody call you? . . . Yes, she called me, too, that's what's the matter with me. Don't give that number to anybody else, Miss Henning. Thanks."

She disconnected, and dialed long distance. Nick watched.

"Better make it person to person," he advised.

"I am. Don't talk to me. And listen hard. I'm closing in."

Mark was as calm as Nick. "Take it easy," he said. "Nobody's going to cut you off. Go ahead." He let her talk without interruption.

She babbled. It was Miss Libby, Miss Libby at Blackman's. She was raving mad because the Smith kids had come to work in hysterics and had to be sent home. Moke and Poke. The Smith kids. There'd been an accident at Hope House and they were hysterical and Miss Libby didn't like it and thought somebody ought to look into it.

"And you've got to, Mark," Roberta said. "It sounds awful. Last night somewhere around one o'clock a girl went into the bathroom to get a drink. The blind girl, the one who roomed with Ruth Miller. Of course she didn't turn on the light because she never did that. She didn't need it. She went straight to a basin beside the window and got a drink and that was when her foot touched something soft. She thought it was laundry, a bag of laundry that somebody had left, but when she tried to pick it up her hand got wet and sticky. She knew it wasn't water. She was blind, but she knew that. So she screamed. And because it was dark in there nobody knew where she was. They heard her screaming, but they couldn't see her. Not at all. It must have been awful. And when they did find her, she was sitting on the floor with the girl's head in her lap. She was saying the girl's name and running her hand over the girl's face, because that's how she could tell who it was. I hate it!"

"Where's Nick?" Mark asked.

"Right here, the lug," Roberta said. "Well, so they got the doctor, and he fixed up the girl's face and head, or whatever it was, and she's alive but only just. Miss Libby says everybody in the place is terrified. They traced the blood on the floor, at least the doctor did, and they think she fell in the shower and tried to reach the window for air, or the door, and got mixed up. Concussion. Miss Libby says it looks on the up-and-up, but she's afraid Moke and Poke don't agree. They didn't want to go home, but she made them. Now you say something. Are you coming back here or not?"

"I'm coming right away," Mark said. "By plane. Is that all you know?"

"That's enough, isn't it? That poor blind girl!"

"Don't go into that again. I got it the first time. Listen, Roberta. Take Bessy and Beulah to a matinee and have dinner in one of those places with two loud bands. Tell them nothing and keep them occupied. I'll get in touch with you when I can. And by the way, what's the girl's name? Not the blind one, the other."

"Lillian Harris."

"Room alone or with someone?"

"I don't know. What difference does that make?"

"Probably none. Hang up, I'm on my way."

She dropped the receiver and Nick replaced it for her.

"Do you remember the last time you were up to your neck in somebody else's trouble?" he asked.

"You know I remember. Two summers ago. We fell in love as a side line."

"Then let me remind you that the situation is unchanged. . . . Robbie, keep out of this. You have a family now."

"We could go in and tickle him if Miss Bassingworthy would let us," she said wistfully. He arranged it with Miss Bassingworthy.

Too many Hope House girls stayed home that day. They drifted up- and downstairs and in and out of each other's rooms, collected in lounge and lobby, and looked over their shoulders when they were alone. Miss Plummer, again pressed into day service, abandoned her embroidery and stood guard at the desk. Miss Brady issued the usual orders. There were to be no interviews.

"I'm counting on you, Ethel," Miss Brady said. "People have been falling in bathrooms for years. I've said that until I'm hoarse, and now I'm handing it on to you. We've got to keep out of the papers. Mrs. Marshall-Gill says she is ravaged. Of all the——well, never mind. Just break up any group that starts whispering and be firm. No callers allowed, I don't care who they say they are or what they look like."

"Is Lillian——"

"She's all right. Unconscious, but nothing to worry about. Mrs. Fister's up there, and she's entirely capable."

Miss Plummer looked distressed. "I know my sister is a wonderful nurse, and she likes doing for sick people, but I can't help feeling that a hospital——"

"Why?"

"Well, I can't help feeling that having her in the House will keep reminding the girls——"

Miss Brady looked through Miss Plummer before she answered. "You're tired, Ethel, and I'm sorry. Try thinking of something else."

Miss Plummer tried, but it was no use. "April," she blurted. "Poor little April in the same room!"

"It's what April wants. She likes to feel useful, and she is." Miss Brady's voice was wearing thin. "Now carry on like a good girl. Miss Small and I are lunching with Mrs. Marshall-Gill. Got to. And for heaven's sake, smile!"

Miss Brady ran the elevator up to the eighth floor herself. Jewel was sleeping off a double dose of sedative. In the middle of the night's upheaval, Dr. Kloppel had gone from room to room looking for rolling eyes and closing them with capsules. Miss Plummer had kept out of his way. She was afraid of pills that put people to sleep. Sometimes they slept too well, and couldn't hear. Now, groggy with weariness and her own thoughts, she struggled with desk and switchboard and tried not to weep.

Mrs. Cashman called at noon. She presented a bunch of frozen chrysanthemums, bought for ten cents from a street vendor who wanted to go home where it was warm. The flowers were for the invalid, she said.

"The Harris girl," she told Miss Plummer. "That's the name Kloppel gave me. I can't say that I really know her, but a knock on the head is an introduction. My compliments, and tell her I say she's a lucky one."

Miss Plummer smiled, according to instructions. She didn't care for Mrs. Cashman. Her sister said Mrs. Cashman was common. "I'm sure I don't know what you mean by lucky," she said.

"Lives in the same room as the other one, doesn't she? And the other one's dead. Very coincidental, as I said to Kloppel, but he drowned me out. You want to know something?" Mrs. Cashman lowered her voice by ducking her head. "I think I saw it happen. Or nearly saw it happen. I'm trying to figure it out but it don't make sense. She wouldn't take a shower in the dark, would she?"

Miss Plummer folded her hands on the desk. She'd been waiting for someone to say that. "Oh I don't know," she said. "Young girls are funny. . . . What do you mean about—seeing it happen?"

"That bathroom light. I was walking by the courtyard along around midnight and I saw it. It was on. And I saw it go out. Now from what I could wring out of Kloppel, that was about the time she hurt herself. Along around midnight, he can tell. And he figures she laid there about an hour before they found her."

"Well?" Miss Plummer said mechanically.

"Well, you see what I mean about the light? It's over by the door, I know it like my own. So I ask myself questions. Like this. Would she fall in the shower, get up, walk to the door, turn out the light, walk back to the window, and fall down all over again? Or would she wash in the dark, which I don't believe for a minute. Funny, you say? Funny, funny, funny."

"Mrs. Cashman——"

Mrs. Cashman crowed. "See? It's getting you, too! I tell you it don't make sense. Nobody washes in the dark but April. And nobody walks around turning off lights with a broken head. Scares you, don't it? You look green."

Miss Plummer saw with horror that the elevator was returning from the eighth floor. "Mrs. Cashman," she whispered, "we don't want any discussion of this. I've had my orders. The Heads are very strict about it, and Mrs. Marshall-Gill——"

"Who's discussing?" Mrs. Cashman's howl was haughty. "I'm only saying what I saw. The Heads ought to be grateful. It's a good thing for them I get around the way I do. I saw the other one, didn't I, laying in the rain? She'd still be there for all of them. And as for this one, I'm only sorry I didn't hang around a little longer, I might have seen something really good. Put that in your pipe and smoke it."

"Mrs. Cashman, the Heads and Mrs. Marshall-Gill——"

"You tell the Heads and Mrs. Marshall-Gill that I wouldn't live in this place if they paid me! You tell them the neighbors are talking! You tell them——"

The elevator door opened, and Miss Brady and Miss Small stepped into the lobby. Mrs. Cashman underwent a short convulsion and indicated her flowers.

"A little tribute from a well-wisher," she sang without confidence. "I'll be calling again to inquire." She scuttled to the entrance and was out in the street before they reached the desk.

Miss Brady wrinkled her nose. "On the level, what did she want?"

"Nothing," Miss Plummer said. She tried to stop with that but she couldn't. She had to go on. They ought to know how the neighbors felt. "She was just talking. She talks too much, she's a terrible talker, they all are around here. You can't shut her up once she starts. Sometimes I think we ought to get a new doctor, she's too familiar with Dr. Kloppel, no respect. They both talk too much and to each other." Her voice rose and wavered.

Miss Small patted her hand. "I'll relieve you when we come back, Ethel. This has been hard on you, I know, but you mustn't give way. She was gossiping, wasn't she?"

"Yes, Miss Small. She didn't really say anything, though, just hinted. It's upsetting when a woman like Mrs. Cashman, who's always lived in the neighborhood, and owning her own home, too——"

"What did she say?"

"She thinks it's odd about Lillian. Same room, she said. You know." Miss Plummer couldn't raise her eyes. "Same room as Ruth Miller, she meant."

Miss Small sighed. "Ridiculous. The next time she comes you send for me or Miss Brady. And stop fretting.

Lillian's all right, everything's all right. . . . Where's Kitty?"

"She went to the kitchen for coffee. She says she has a nervous chill."

Miss Small's smile showed that she believed in the chill as much as Miss Plummer did.

"New doctor, new switchboard girl! When she comes back, you go up to your room and lie down. I know how little sleep you've had."

Miss Plummer watched them leave, spruce and smart in their fine coats and white gloves. They looked as if they hadn't a care in the world. When Kitty returned she wasted no words. "You're to take over," she said. "Orders. I'm going up for a little rest."

On the second floor she went directly to the two rooms she shared with her sister. They were empty. She sat in her rocker and stared at the walls. I can't do my sewing, she thought unhappily; my hands are too cold. I haven't felt real well for weeks, I'm sickening for something. She led herself step by step to the dark place in her mind, pretending that it held a physical explanation of her trouble. Like the day she went out in the rain without her rubbers and caught cold. Or the day she lost the purse with more than a dollar in it. She counted back the days and nights until she came to the one that was lying in wait. She knew she'd have to meet it sometime.

From that day on, she told herself, I've felt wrong. From the day that girl came here. There was something about her, something in the way she looked. . . . As she rocked, she combed the days and nights for fragments of reassurance and contradiction and found none.

The long-distance telephone call. She'd lost the slip. If she could only remember one word, it might help. And now the ad in the paper. . . . She whispered to the walls that were covered with photographs of her sister's husband. Something dreadful is beginning, she said. I've got to get my thinking done so I'll be ready. I've got a feeling I'll be asked things, that we'll all be asked things. I've got to be ready. That was a Sunday night when she made the call. It was a Saturday when she came, and she went right out again and got in late. I didn't notice much then except that she was the quiet kind. I took her to be homesick. Then on the Sunday she came to the tea with Miss Brady. She was queer then, I saw it. Maybe I mentioned it to somebody, I don't know, but I saw it. Then she made the call around midnight, and hung up. Without a word, she hung up.

Miss Plummer went to the door and looked up and down the hall. I wish Ella would come, she said. I don't feel like myself at all. I'm too cold, it's not natural.

She went back to the rocker and her thoughts. . . . The next thing was the party. She was the one I asked to get the iodine for the chef. I know she was the one. Even though she looked like everybody else, all those flat faces staring at me, I know it was her. She didn't know where Miss Brady's room was, everybody else would know, so it was her all right. And she never did get the iodine.

She stopped rocking. What am I thinking? she asked herself. As sure as I'm sitting here somebody brought me the iodine and bandages. What's got into me all of a sudden? I never thought anything like this before. . . . But she knew there was nothing sudden about it. It had been there all along and she had covered it over with her little jobs of work because it had frightened her. She went back to the night, minute by minute, because she knew she must. . . . I saw her go up the stairs myself, and I waited. But I was busy, and everybody was running around, and I didn't see her come back. But she must have. She had to. Didn't I find the things right on the desk, and don't that prove it? I must be crazy thinking she didn't come back, just because I didn't see her. I must be real crazy.

She went to the door again. The hall was thriftily dark in the daylight. She knew the room to her left was empty, it was Kitty's; but to the right, beyond the fire door, there was someone to talk to.

I can't sleep and I won't take those ugly pills, she

said; they might be habit-forming. I'll run along and see if Agnes is in. It's her hour off.

Agnes was mending the sweater for Clara; there was additional mending on the table beside her chair, stockings, underwear, and something made of unbleached muslin, crumpled and not very clean. Miss Plummer thought vaguely that it had a familiar look.

"I'm at loose ends for a little while," she told Agnes. "Can't seem to settle down to anything, so I told myself I couldn't do better than have a little talk with you, Agnes."

Agnes darned steadily. "Glad to have you," she said. She didn't look up. Her needle wove in and out and she frowned with concentration. "Take the chair by the radiator, Miss Plummer, it's warmer there."

Miss Plummer ignored this. She sat beside Agnes. "What are you doing with the muslin, Agnes?"

Agnes raised her head. "The muslin?" She looked as if she were biting something back. "I don't know what I'm doing with it," she said slowly. "I don't know. I didn't want you to see that, Miss Plummer, I'm still thinking about it myself, but now that you have, I——"

"Agnes——"

"That's one of the doll dresses, Miss Plummer."

"Why so it is! For a minute you frightened me, you looked odd." Miss Plummer fingered the material. "There's a lot of wear in this stuff. What do you want it for?"

"Want it! I don't want it! I wish it was at the bottom of the sea! . . . I found it, Miss Plummer."

"Found? I don't see how you can say that. Every last one of those dresses was locked away, out of sight. My sister did that herself, she was very particular about it."

"I know she was. That's it, that's the trouble, I know she locked them away."

"Maybe," Miss Plummer said, "maybe you'd better tell me what's on your mind."

Agnes put the sweater aside. "I meant to keep this to myself until I could figure it out, but I'm not making any headway. Not in the right direction. At first I thought it was pure accident that the dress got over-looked, accident or carelessness. I thought some girl had spilled something on it and got worried and hid it." Agnes took the dress into her lap and smoothed out the hem. "You see this? Miss Plummer, what would you say this stain was? Look close. Reddish brown, not properly washed out, done in a hurry, like."

"Coffee?"

"Did we have coffee that night?"

"No. . . . Is it fruit punch?"

"That was orange and pineapple. . . . In a corner of the packroom on this floor," Agnes said tonelessly. "Hidden. You could tell it was meant to be hidden on purpose. . . . Who would want to do that?"

"But there isn't anybody on this floor but staff. And staff wouldn't have any reason——"

"That's right. Staff didn't even wear any, except Kitty and Jewel."

"Kitty and Jewel turned theirs in, I saw that myself."

"I know. . . . At first I thought some girl had stained it and was afraid to let on. But these girls aren't the kind to worry about a little thing like that. A little piece of cheap muslin, they'd just laugh."

"Yes," Miss Plummer said. "They wouldn't care about a thing like that." Her hand crept forward. Their two hands touched the puckered stain, their fingers met and gripped for an instant and drew back.

"Hidden," Agnes repeated. She looked at Miss Plummer squarely. "Do you think I should speak to someone?"

"No," Miss Plummer said thinly. "Not yet, not now. You put it away for a little bit, lock it away. We'll see, we'll think about it." It was Miss Plummer's turn to look squarely at Agnes. "Who would you want to speak to, Agnes?"

Agnes averted her head. "I don't know."

When Miss Plummer went back to her room, she found that Mrs. Fister had returned. She was checking accounts at the center table, frowning as she worked. Miss Plummer knew it was the wrong time to talk but she couldn't wait. She said, "Ella, can you spare me a minute?"

"Not now, Ethel, if you please. I've got the butcher here."

Miss Plummer studied the massive figure. Ella was strong and sure of herself, she was never even sick. She always made the family decisions, and she was always right.

"I've got to talk," she said. "I can't wait. Something's bothering me."

Mrs. Fister put down her pencil. "Now what?"

"I think Ruth Miller was killed."

"Do you know what you're saying?"

"Yes, I do. I think she was killed. I think I felt it from the first. Others did, too. Kitty, Jewel, some of the boarders, I could feel it in the way they looked and acted. I want you to think about it. You've got to tell me if I'm right or wrong."

"You're wrong," Mrs. Fister said quietly. "Why do you say such things? Do you want us put out on the street?"

"No, Ella." She saw her sister's measuring look. There was no anger in it, only thoughtfulness. That wasn't like Ella. Not that kind of thoughtfulness. Ella looked as if she didn't know what to say next.

"Why should we be put out, Ella?"

"Scandal is bad for a place like this," Mrs. Fister said. "Trouble comes and the staff changes. There's nothing to be gained by such talk, and I don't want to hear another word."

"You're my own sister, Ella. What I say to you is between us two. I've got to talk, my head's driving me crazy. . . . What about Lillian Harris, Ella?"

"Well, what about her? Likely drunk, and we won't discuss that, either."

"Did anybody say she was? Did Dr. Kloppel say so? If he did, I'd have heard, and I didn't. I'm asking you to think about Lillian Harris too. . . . Ella?"

"What?"

"Did you notice anything out of the way when the chef was hurt? Try to remember, Ella."

"No." Mrs. Fister looked at her curtained windows. She kept her eyes on the windows, away from Miss Plummer's twitching face. Her hands were folded in her lap. "You'd better go on," she said. "You'd better do your talking to me. What do you mean?"

Miss Plummer leaned forward in her chair. She began with the night Ruth Miller came and described the look that might have been fear. She omitted the long-distance call, because she'd lost the slip. That would annoy Ella. She told about the strange woman who'd wanted a room for a niece named Ruth. She repeated Mrs. Cashman's conversation. "Little things," she said. "They don't sound like much, but they stay with me. It's like I'm being asked to think about them."

"If that's all, then stop thinking. In all my life I never heard such nonsense."

"It isn't all." She told about the errand for medical supplies. "I saw her go up the stairs. I told her to try this room first, and if it was locked, Miss Brady's. I saw her go, but I never saw her come back again. I never saw her again that night, and I'd come to know her in spite of that costume. I watched for her to come back, but she didn't come. I got the iodine and bandages all right, they were put on my desk. How did they get there? Not by Ruth Miller's hand. She never came back. I never saw her again, not alive."

"You can't be sure of that. You couldn't tell one from another, nobody could. I don't know why I listen to you." Mrs. Fister's hands opened and closed, but she didn't turn her head.

Miss Plummer went on as if she hadn't heard. "She was the type of girl that would have handed me the things herself, so I'd know she'd done it properly. She was that type. The doctor says she died somewhere around that time. So if she did——"

"Ethel, listen to me. You were busy, I was watching you. You didn't have time to notice who came to the desk or who didn't. She came all right. She put the things where you would find them and went back upstairs to do what she'd planned to do. That's what happened and you can take my word for it."

Miss Plummer brushed a hand across her eyes. "No. I've tried to make myself believe that, but I can't. If she'd planned to kill herself, she'd have done it sooner. She wouldn't have gone to all that trouble dressing up and coming to the party. She'd have made some excuse to April and waited until everybody was down here, having a good time. She wouldn't have run my errand and then gone back to take her life. There's no sense to that. No. Not that girl who was even afraid of our little elevator that goes up and down as safe as you please. Don't ask me to believe that. Don't ask me to believe she'd stand in a high window looking down——"

"What are you stopping for?"

"I'm seeing how she looked in that doll dress. . . . Somebody killed her up there and brought me the iodine so's I wouldn't miss her. And the one that killed her is in the House, safe, and walking around among us. Walking around the lobby and the lounge in broad daylight, walking up and down the halls at night, trying to kill Lillian Harris."

"Ethel!"

"It's true. That awful place on Lillian's head, it's almost the same."

"How do you know it's almost the same?"

"I saw them both, you mustn't forget that. A lot of people saw Ruth Miller, more than saw Lillian. The police made them look. Identification. . . . Ella?"

"I've had about all I can stand. You're making yourself sick, and I haven't the time to take care of you. Go and lie down in your own room."

"Ella, you packed the costumes away, didn't you? The next day?"

"You know I did."

"Are they under lock and key?"

"They are. Linen press. Ethel, I'm losing patience."

"What happened to the one Ruth Miller wore?"

145

"That? What do you think? It was examined by the police and given back. It was burned up."

"Who said to burn it up? That was too soon, I know it was too soon! You should have kept it awhile. Who gave that order?"

"I don't remember. Very likely I decided myself. It was in no condition for anything. You saw her, so you know what I mean. The mask——"

Miss Plummer tried to look into her sister's eyes, but they were resolutely turned away. "I saw the mask when they cut it off," she said slowly. "It was bagged out, like it was filled with——" She swallowed and went on. "You couldn't tell it had ever been white. You couldn't tell the color of the mouth or hair or anything."

"Didn't you hear me say I'd had enough?"

"It was her ring they knew her by, her signet ring with initials on it. Like a little girl's ring, like what you give a little girl on her birthday."

Mrs. Fister got up and walked heavily across the room and back again, coming to stop at Miss Plummer's chair.

"Look at me, Ethel, don't hang your head like a fool. Look at me."

Miss Plummer raised her eyes.

"I want to remind you of something," Mrs. Fister went on. "Everything you have you owe to me. I don't like to say that, but you've put me in the place where I have to. You've never been able to hold a regular position because of your health. Not your fault, but there it is. I'm not complaining about that, I've always looked after you and I always will. When Fister died and there wasn't as much as we expected, did I turn you out? No. I sold my nice little home and found this place for myself, and I got you in here, too. I swallowed my pride. I said I had a sister who would be glad to lend a hand for room and board only. I got you the piecework to do, humbling myself to a man I knew before I met Fister. We're all right now, and we'll stay all right if you'll rid yourself of your notions. That's what they are, notions. I ask you to remember that we're no longer young. You don't understand life as I do, you've never married. I know what's best for us, and you don't. Maybe I can send you away for a little rest, I'll see. Now go to your room and lie down, and don't speak of this again."

Miss Plummer went to her room and closed the door. She wanted to die. Her own sister turning against her, refusing to look at her even, reminding her that she'd never married. That hurt. We're drifting apart, she told herself; we're not close the way we used to be. She won't let me talk to her, she won't help me to think.

She moved from side to side in the big bed, trying to find warmth and rest. The room was cold as it always was in the daytime. She reminded herself that fuel was expensive and had to be saved. . . . It must be awful for poor people. For people who were turned out on the streets.

She sat up and rubbed her hands. They were numb. I'm getting the influenza, she told herself. That's the root of my trouble. They say the influenza is weakening all over.

She stared at the sky outside the window, a dull, despairing sky, and her mind rambled on. It wasn't the kind of sky you looked for so near to Christmas. A Christmas sky should be a nice dove gray with snow-flakes coming down. I'll be sick for Christmas, she whispered in an agony of pity. I won't get out to see the decorations. All the pretty trees and all the lights, and I won't see them. She wept softly, clinging to the fiction of illness until it filled her thoughts and left no room for intrusion. I've been sick for days and didn't realize it, she persisted. It happens like that sometimes. Nervous, jumpy, bad dreams, no real flavor to food. That's the influenza. I'll be in bed for Christmas, and I won't get out to see the sights. I'll be all alone. I won't see anybody or talk to anybody. I'll be alone.

She drugged herself with words and pictures and finally slept, exhausted.

Miss Brady came home at four o'clock and went up

to her room; Miss Small came an hour later with an armful of bundles which she stacked on the desk.

"Anything new?" she asked Kitty. The determined brightness of the last few days had left her voice and a note of exaltation had taken its place.

Kitty heard the new tone and wondered. All set up about something, she decided; had herself a good time while she was out, but search me how. Not Marshall-Gill. Marshall-Gill don't send them home happy. "No, Miss Small," she said. She rearranged the bundles and picked at the colored wrappings. "Santa Claus, Miss Small?"

"Mrs. Santa Claus, Kitty, and I love it!" Miss Small laughed. She removed her hat and coat and flung them on a chair. "Kitty, I'm going to break a rule and discuss one staff member with another. Have you noticed anything queer about Ethel lately?"

"Me?" Here we go, Kitty marveled. She's got something on Ethel. Ethel's on her way out. "I don't know what you mean, Miss Small."

"Yes, you do. She's been talking about Ruth Miller and Lillian, hasn't she? I mean talking too much and in the wrong way."

"No, Miss Small. Not any more than the others."

"What others? Oh dear, I've been afraid of this."

"Oh, everybody. You know how they go on. They'll talk about anything, and this time they're punch drunk. It'll blow over."

"I hope you're right. I'm not too happy about it."

"You should worry," Kitty said easily. She patted the bundles. "Want me to take these up for you, Miss Small? Be glad to."

"Yes, please. My coat and hat, too. Miss Brady's room, not mine. And tell her I said no fair peeping."

She watched while Kitty backed into the elevator and closed the door. "I don't know Kitty as well as I should," she said softly. "But it's hardly worth while now."

The afternoon dragged to its close, and Miss Small turned on the lights in the lounge. She returned to the desk and sat there in deep contentment, watching the street door and waiting for the hardy souls who had triumphed over last night's pills and gone to work as usual. For these she had a bright smile ready and she gave it generously as they straggled in. She was happy for the first time in weeks.

Dear Monny, she thought. Dear, good Monny. She saw Monny raking Mrs. Marshall-Gill with cold eyes, standing with her hands in her pockets, carefully insolent and mistress of the situation. "Miss Small and I are resigning," Monny had said. "The Board will have a formal notice in a day or so."

Mrs. Marshall-Gill had bleated. Like a sheep. She hadn't meant to criticize, she hadn't meant to say what she did, she'd only thought that Miss Brady and Miss Small might have been a wee bit more careful.

Monny had been wonderful. How were they to know Ruth Miller was suicidal? she'd demanded. How were they to know Lillian Harris had vertigo or was cockeyed? Did the Board expect them to read the girls' minds and lock them in with a few moral words?

Mrs. Marshall-Gill had babbled something about references. That had been priceless. Monny had laughed and laughed. "We don't need references," she'd said. "We don't need jobs. But if we did, I'd fight you in the courts and make you look like a fool."

Miss Small had chuckled. It had been too marvelous; she'd sent Monny home by herself and gone shopping alone. She'd wanted to be alone, among strangers, free to plan and think about the happy time ahead. And by great good luck she'd found a perfect present for Monny, not a Woolworth present, either. . . . She looked at the clock. Quarter of six. She could push time ahead, even now, make the happy days come sooner.

"Kitty? Do you suppose the kitchen is ready to serve dinner?"

"Yes, Miss Small. They've sent it up. Fifteen minutes to go."

"Ring the bells, will you? Let's get them in and out early tonight."

"But Miss Small! They'll think something's happened! They'll think——"

"Ring them anyway. It'll break up the whispering."

Kitty stood before the panel and pressed the bells one by one. Those on the second floor were shrill, the others echoed faintly down the stairs. One by one they echoed, steadily growing fainter as Kitty's fingers climbed to the top of the panel.

Two girls came out of the lounge with startled faces, met Miss Small's assuring nod, and went into the dining room. The elevator began to hum. Miss Small relaxed and turned to the desk calendar.

The resignation was set for January first. She flipped the pages; there weren't many; there were so few that she wanted to laugh aloud. Monny had said the time would fly, and it was doing that now. She could hurry time with her own hands. Monny's right about me, too, she admitted. I really am a kid at heart. . . . January first, less than two weeks away. Then a couple of days in a hotel, resting up, getting their hair done, last-minute shopping. Then the great day itself. Whistles blowing, the wind ruffling the Hudson, the gulls, the flags, a band playing.

"Good evening, Miss Small," a man's voice said. "May I see Miss Brady?"

She jumped. A tall man with warm brown eyes stood before her. She thought, Why that's——

"Don't you remember me, Miss Small? My name is East."

So, Miss Small said to herself. She left the enclosure with a firm step. "Come this way, please." In the empty lounge she indicated a chair. "If you'll wait, Mr. East, I'll try to find Miss Brady."

Out in the lobby she commandeered the elevator with a relentless finger on the bell. He watched her through the glass doors. She was tapping her foot and smiling at nothing, and he made a bet with himself. She would not find Miss Brady. She would return, full of pretty apologies, and tell him to come back the next day. He lost. Ten minutes later she followed Miss Brady into the room.

"I thought we'd seen the last of you," Miss Brady said gaily. "Find your doctor?"

"No." His voice matched hers. "But I hear you nearly lost another girl."

"I suppose you mean Lillian Harris. I'd like to know where you picked that up."

"From a new client. I've been retained by Mrs. Marshall-Gill."

Miss Brady was astonished. "Well I'll be! Mind telling me how you got to her?"

"Not at all. She got to me, this afternoon, via Mrs. Sutton."

Miss Brady looked as if she were counting up to ten the long way. "All right," she said. "What do you want?"

"I want to interview some of your people. Not about Harris, about Ruth Miller. The Miller ghost is walking again, but I suppose you know that."

"Because of Lillian Harris?"

"Probably. It's got to stop, you know. Mrs. Marshall-Gill says so and I agree. It's a bad business. Now listen for a minute while I tell my side. There's been a strong difference of opinion about Ruth Miller ever since the beginning. That's how I got into this. And getting into it meant talking to people, to Miss Libby, who knew Ruth at Blackman's, to Dr. Kloppel, to a couple of kids who'd better be nameless. They all contradicted each other. It was a nice challenge and I got interested in spite of myself," he told them briefly, watching their faces. "So you see it all boils down to one thing, which can mean everything or nothing. Your team insists that Ruth Miller wasn't much of a person—to put it mildly, a misfit. If you're right, her suicide is tenable. The other team, that's Mrs. Sutton and one or two others, says she was sound and straight. If they're right, her suicide needs looking into. Now there's only one way to pick the winner, and that's a reconstruction job. We rebuild the girl from the fragments we have, make a timetable of her life here, talk to the people who talked to her, make her live again so we can see her as she really was. I've already begun that with Miss Libby, and one nice thing has turned up. The girl was hired without references. That mortifies Miss Libby, but I'm glad it happened. It's a small thing, but it may have big roots. She also told Miss Libby she had never worked before. Miss Libby says that was a lie. Miss Libby is sure that Ruth Miller had not only worked before but that she had worked in a store. She was too good, too quick, for a greenhorn."

Miss Brady answered his smile with a broad grin of her own. "You're making out a case against your own team," she said. "I'll say this for you, you're honest. Or maybe you're softening me up. Well, we might as well get it over. When do you want to start?"

"Now, if I may. I leave the arrangement to you, but I want to see people individually and alone."

"That means you want me and Miss Small out of the way."

"Right. Better for everybody."

"Then I know one thing, this room is out. I can't have girls weeping and wailing in public."

"Girls don't weep and wail for me."

"They will for Ruth Miller, whether they knew her or not. We'll go to my room."

Miss Small flinched. No, she told herself savagely, no, not there. She gave Miss Brady a long, significant look and was rewarded. Monny's eyes said that she understood. They said it was their room now, intimate and sweet, filled with the little things that belonged to them and no one else; the Christmas packages, the box of candy with the half-eaten bonbons they hadn't liked, the travel folders, the Baedeker that made them laugh every time they read it. It was not a room for inquisitive strangers and hysterical girls.

"I think we'll use Miss Small's room," Miss Brady said. "It's in better order; I admit I live like a pig. And the girls are more at home in Miss Small's. That's where they go when they want to pour out their hearts. Have you any ideas about precedence, alphabetical order and so on, or will you take them as they come?"

"I don't want the whole lot, at least not now. With two days' residence behind her, Ruth Miller couldn't have been pals with more than half a dozen, could she?"

"I don't know. I hardly saw her myself." Miss Brady turned to Miss Small. "Who were the girls she talked to?"

"This is amazing," Miss Small said. "It's the first thing I thought of."

"The first thing you thought of when?" He was beginning to appreciate Miss Small.

"When we found her. I was looking for a reason, I wanted to satisfy myself. I knew we'd be asked questions, and it seemed wise to uncover as much as possible about what had gone before. We—we were scared stiff. It's a great responsibility, the care of so many, but Miss Brady will tell you I wasn't surprised."

Miss Brady nodded. "The girl had something on her mind, Miss Small saw it at once."

"Tell me," Mark said. "All of it. Don't try to sell me on anything, just give me your impression."

Miss Small described Ruth's arrival. "She was all right at first, I can swear to that. I'm used to sizing girls up. But then, suddenly, she changed, right under my eyes. She was terrified, all at once. I thought——"

"What?" he asked.

"It was so sudden," she repeated. "I thought she must have seen someone. That was the only explanation, someone who knew something about her, perhaps. Well, that was none of my business, and I didn't think too much of it then. But after what happened, I made a list of the people who were in the lobby. It was the only thing I could think of to do," she finished lamely. "I'm not pointing a suspicious finger, Mr. East, I simply didn't know what else to do."

"That was very clever," he said. "Those are the people I want. Are they available?"

"Yes. You came at the right time, dinner, you know."

"Good. Tell me more about that night."

"There isn't much. She came in, a little awkward and ill at ease, but the new ones are always like that. That or flippant. Then while we were talking, her manner changed. She was terrified, I'm sure some of the others noticed it, too. And—I think this is very odd—she went out again almost at once. I didn't see her again until the next day at tea, and then only for a few minutes."

"Who were the people in the lobby who might have noticed?"

"Oh, yes. I keep forgetting. That's the important part. Kitty at the switchboard, Jewel at the elevator, Dot Mainwaring, Lillian Harris—they were all near the desk. Of course there were others going in and out of the dining room, but I felt she had seen someone quite close. Her eyes, you know, they weren't too good."

"Fine. Now the tea."

"I don't think that means much. She'd already been —peculiar—and the tea was only a continuation. I don't remember much about the tea myself. I was pretty busy." Miss Small smiled wryly. "Mrs. Marshall-Gill."

He understood and said so with a look. "I can probably get other names from the girls you mentioned," he said. "What about the staff, domestics and so on?"

"I was the only one she saw when she came. At least——"

"Plummer?" Miss Brady suggested.

"I can't possibly answer that," Miss Small confessed. "There were people in the rear of the lobby, of course, but my back was turned. . . . Mr. East, are you convinced that this is not what it seems?"

"You're not too sure yourself, are you?"

Miss Brady intervened crisply. "I'll take that one. The miserable girl killed herself. She was caught in a net of her own devising. And when you find out what it was, if you ever do find out, it will be the usual thing, and you know what I mean. I blame myself in some ways. I could kick myself for taking her in."

"Were you responsible for that?"

"Yes. She came to see me. She looked hangdog and the Smiths begged and I had an extra bed."

"Very neat," Mark said.

"What is?"

"The way you've proved it wasn't you Ruth Miller feared. Because she talked to you and came back for more."

Miss Brady colored.

"Now what about those interviews?" he went on.

Miss Small rose quickly. "I'll see to that. Miss Brady, will you——"

Miss Brady also rose. "Come with me, Mr. East. I'll get you settled."

They crossed the lobby to the elevator through a silent crowd that parted before them.

"I'm only co-operating because I want to leave a clean slate behind me," Miss Brady said. "But before I leave I'm going to write something nasty on it."

"Leave?"

"Resigning. Both of us. Fed up." When they reached the fifth floor, she preceded him down the hall, shouting "Man coming, man coming!"

In the near distance a group of bathrobed figures broke up in confusion and scampered out of sight. Not too fast, either; looking backward over their shoulders. He liked that.

Miss Brady explained. "Those are the gay dogs with dinner dates. Swapping perfume and nail polish. This way."

He followed like a small boy, walking softly. The hall floor was concrete and immaculate, and the bedroom doors had neat brass numbers. He could smell hot, soapy water and furniture polish; he thought he could even smell some of the swapped perfume. It was a pleasant place, half school, half home. He understood why Ruth Miller had called herself privileged.

On the other side of a fire door, Miss Brady stopped. "This is Miss Small's," she said. "Go in and wait. Would you like coffee?"

"No, thanks." Trying to be nice, he thought. Knows she's in a bad spot. When she left, he made a shameless tour of the two rooms, telling himself that a woman's

bric-a-brac said more than words, and chairs and tables could be garrulous. Little Miss Small emerged. No
natural taste, he decided, but a good eye for copying.
Given enough time, more money, and the right example, the arty desk with the bad veneer and the fake
pearl inlay would fall into the lap of the Salvation
Army. Bought it in the first place because she thought
it looked opulent.

One lamp shade in the bedroom was covered with
bluebirds, meticulously feathered, and the bedspread
was machine-made lace over bright blue silk. He remembered that another flock of bluebirds, in colored
glass, had nested on the lapel of Miss Small's well-cut
suit. Shoddy background, he told himself, but fairly
quick to catch on. When she realizes that her friend is
expensively unadorned, she'll chuck the fancywork, too.
In another two years she'll have a foolproof accent and
say damn like a lady.

I'd like, he went on thoughtfully, to see how Miss
Brady lives. There we have unmistakable quality and
the preposterous innocence that too often goes with it.
A twenty-five-cent weekly allowance until she was
eighteen; a careful exposure to the procreative process
when she was old enough to have a dog and properly
call it a bitch; a well-schooled belief that sin is spelled
with the same scarlet A that Hester Prynne wore. . . .
Would a grown-up child like Miss Brady stay on the
tracks when she met a situation that refuted her code
and turned her world upside down? Or would she do
as most children do, turn savage and strike? Turn and
strike. Lie and run. . . . It was worth thinking about.
Rich Miss Brady, poor Miss Brady, who read all the
books and knew all the words and was younger than
Moke and Poke. Resigning because she was fed up.
Tut-tut, he grieved, not fed at all.

Someone rapped smartly on the living-room door,
and he hurried to open it. A girl stood in the hall, stoop-
ing as if she wanted to disguise her height.

"I'm Kitty Brice," she began. "Miss Small said
you——"

He knew her. When he reminded her of their first meeting, she wasn't amused, although she pretended to be. He talked persuasively, apologized for taking her away from her work, condemned his own job ruefully, asked questions and seemed not to need the answers. After a few minutes he was almost sure she was telling the truth, not all of it, but enough.

"I didn't pay much attention that night she came," she said. "She was dopey, so I didn't pay attention. You always hope somebody nice is coming, but they never do. I don't know why they're digging her up like this. Trouble for everybody."

"I know," he sympathized. "But suicides always stir some people up. Like my client, for instance. She doubts the suicide theory. Do you, even a little?"

"No. She was dopey. But——"

"But what, Miss Brice? Come on, you're not going to stand in the way of a guy earning his living!"

"I don't know anything, but some people did talk. You know, whispering. There's always somebody in a place like this that whispers. About anything. And this time they really had something. Like why does a girl jump out of a window when she's only lived in a place two days and didn't get any mail, or phone calls, or anything. It won't do you any good to ask me who said that, because I don't know. I just picked it out of the air. And I don't say I believe it, either."

He nodded. "You know, I can't help wondering why she wasn't missed that night. She was a new girl. I'd have thought the rest of you would watch her, help her have fun. Didn't you see her at all?"

"Get somebody to show you the costumes. You wouldn't know your own mother."

"But there was an identifying mole on Ruth's mask. Didn't you know that?"

"Sure I knew. That was one of those secrets that was too good to keep. Everybody knew. But I don't remember seeing her."

"Did you ever leave the party, Miss Brice?"

"I sure did. I've got drops that I have to take, and I

157

went up to my room and took them. I walked up, I live on second. I didn't go up to seventh at all."

"You're giving me more information than I asked for," he smiled. "That's fine. Were you in costume, too, Miss Brice?"

"Sure. Everybody was, except Heads, maids, and Plummer."

Plummer again. "Plummer?" he asked.

"Ethel Plummer. She works at the desk, too, and she's kind of old. She talked to Miller once or twice, I know that."

"Does Miss Small know?"

"I couldn't say. Maybe not, unless Plummer mentioned it herself."

"I see." He studied her face, noting the bad color, the blue line around the mouth that wasn't entirely hidden by lipstick. 'I've got drops that I have to take.' Heart. "Ever see Ruth Miller before she came here?" he asked carelessly.

"Maybe. I don't know. I shop at Blackman's sometimes, for little things. Same price as other places for little things. She worked on the main floor, so I might have seen her without knowing it."

"So you might, I can understand that. Well, that's all for now, thanks. Is the next one waiting?"

"With tongue hanging out." She grinned. "Dot Mainwaring."

He disliked Miss Mainwaring at once. She was wide-eyed, voluble, and saccharine. The wide eyes said he was a handsome man and she was a young girl and they were alone. She kept him at a distance, prettily, and he felt as if she were crawling into his lap. She is, he told himself, the kind of modest violet that chokes the life out of the poison ivy. He asked as few questions as possible. She didn't seem to notice.

"I saw the poor creature the night she arrived," she informed him. "But I didn't remember it until Miss Small reminded me. I was too disturbed myself at the time." She waited expectantly.

"Disturbed about what?" he asked dutifully.

"My roommate was—well, she was—ill. I had stopped at the desk to get a check for her dinner tray. I didn't mind doing that, and I carried the tray upstairs, too, because nothing is too much trouble when you're helping a fellow being. But Minnie May, that's my roommate, she said she wasn't hungry, and that worried me. I'd always been told that food should be taken when alcohol——"

"I'm not interested in your roommate, Miss Mainwaring."

"Oh, you will be, Mr. East. You must be. Miss Small is looking for her now. I'm purposely bringing her into our little conversation because I think she's important and I want to save you time and trouble. I think it will help you in the end. We all have our little weaknesses, I cheerfully admit to mine, and they play a very large part in our lives and color our actions, I think. And if I can help you understand Minnie May, why then I'll feel as if I'd done something really useful. There's nobody that's perfect, Mr. East, we're all human, but if we listen to reason and look to a Higher Guidance——"

He let her run on, slipping her neatly and wearily into the correct file. This, he mourned, is the self-appointed martyr who confesses other peoples' sins in public, radiates watery sunshine, and grabs the burdens off the neighbors' backs. He wondered what she'd do if she found herself with no immediate martyrdom to play with. Negotiate some? By any means? Maybe. They were a hungry lot, the self-appointed martyrs, sometimes too quick on the trigger and always too smooth on the talk. Quick on the trigger, such as, "Everything went black." Smooth on the talk, such as, "I'm not sorry for what I did. I tried to show her the error of her ways. God spoke to me. I did God's will." They had fun in jail, too, got fan mail, got lawyers hired by a religious sect, and sometimes even got off. They rarely paid the full price. . . . He forced himself to listen.

"And as I say, Minnie May simply will not understand how she's killing herself with that poison. I was so worried about Minnie May that I hardly noticed the other poor creature. If I'd really noticed, I'm sure I'd have seen she was in distress. I'm very sensitive that way. But Minnie May was on my mind. You can forgive me, can't you?"

He smiled bleakly. "I can and will. Miss Mainwaring, did you know Miss Miller before she came here to live? Even casually?"

"Oh no! I have a wonderful memory. Oh no, I'd never seen her before, I'm sure of that. . . . At least, I'm almost sure."

He saw a speculative flicker in the pale eyes. "All right," he said hastily. "That's fine, that's all I wanted."

"But we must be sure, mustn't we? You want me to be sure, don't you? If you want me to think back into the past, why I'm perfectly willing. I don't mind going over to that corner and closing my eyes and thinking back into the past. I might find something."

Here was the framework for some nice carrying-on if he made it seem worth while. He tried not to shudder. "Not here, Miss Mainwaring," he said playfully. "In your own room. And if you remember anything, write me a letter. That will be all, thank you."

"All?" She was distressed. "But Miss Small said to tell you everything!"

"You have," he said. "And thanks again." He rose and crossed the room. "Now who's next?"

She followed him slowly. "I'd do anything for Miss Small, anything. She said I was to tell you anything——"

They had reached the door and he opened it. Miss Mainwaring found herself out in the hall.

"Good evening," he said to the girl who was waiting. "Come in, please. You are——?"

"Jewel Schwab."

8

He was surprised to find that he liked and pitied Jewel on sight; probably, he told himself, because her flat, stupid face was a pleasant change from that of her predecessor. And she was no talker. She leaned against the door and watched him with a sleepy look, her arms folded at her waist as if they were rolled in a kitchen apron. Domestic service, he guessed, and not too far back. She looked hopeless, but he couldn't afford to send her away unheard. There would be no badinage with Jewel. He'd be lucky to get a yes or no.

"Sit down, Jewel. Do you know why I want to see you?"

"Yes, sir."

"Were you a friend of Ruth Miller's?"

"No, sir."

"Mind if I ask you a few questions anyway?"

"No, sir."

"Fine. Jewel, you're a very important person for two reasons. You were the first girl to reach Ruth Miller's body and you also operate the elevator. You see and hear things. Now, on the night of the party did you recognize Ruth when she rode in your car?"

"Yes, sir."

"You did? That's interesting. How did you know it was Ruth?"

"She was with April. You always know April."

"Of course. I forgot about that. You couldn't mistake Ruth when she was with April. But when she left the party and went up to her room, did you recognize her then?"

"I didn't take her up." Jewel looked over his head.

161

He heard the faint note of alarm in her voice. She heard it, too, and tried to cover it up with a tuneless little whistle.

"Jewel," he said reproachfully, "stop kidding me. Of course you took her up, you can't get in trouble for that. What's the matter with you?"

"I didn't take her up. She lived on seventh, and I never went to seventh after the party began. Other floors, but not seventh." Only the big hands, gripping the raw, red elbows, betrayed her nervousness.

"You're sure?"

"Yes, sir." She whistled again, with elaborate indifference, and examined the room with a bored look. It said he was wasting his time as well as hers. "I made three trips, that's all," she went on carelessly. "Miss Small said I didn't have to make any, she said the girls could run the car themselves, she said I was to enjoy myself. But I made three trips anyway. But not Ruth Miller."

"Three, eh? How do you know one of your passengers wasn't Ruth? If they all looked alike, and if she wasn't with April that time."

She looked over his head again. "Because I know where I went. I never went to seventh. The first trip was two girls for fourth. I remember it was fourth because they talked disguised and I had to ask the floor twice. And they wanted me to wait for them and I did. And the next trip was one girl by herself. To sixth. I don't know who she was. I remember it was sixth because I went past the floor and had to go back."

"Easy to walk from sixth to seventh, isn't it?"

"If you want to."

"What about the third trip?"

"Mrs. Marshall-Gill. She wanted fifth, this room here. This one. She always comes to this room here to fix her face. After I took her I came on down and went in the lounge to watch the dancing. I never went near the car again. It was eight-thirty-five when I went in the lounge. It was Carlin's band on the radio right after the news."

The first break, he told himself. She's volunteering the time. Shrewd, or coached, or self-rehearsed.

"Can I go now?" she asked. "I've got my work."

"So have I," he smiled. "This is it. But I won't keep you much longer. Jewel, do you think Ruth took the car up herself?"

"Maybe. Or maybe she walked. I've seen her walk."

"To seventh, when there was an elevator? Hardly. But I wish I knew for certain, because when she went upstairs she died." He let that sink in. "She went upstairs, alone or with someone, and died. Died at nine o'clock. . . . You say you were in the lounge at eight-thirty-five?"

She brushed a hand across her mouth. "Yes, sir."

"In costume, of course?"

"Yes, sir."

"Kitty Brice says your own mothers wouldn't have known you."

"That's right." She studied the pattern on the rug, turning her head from side to side. "That's what everybody says."

He went through his pockets, slowly and deliberately, and she abandoned the rug to watch him. "I'm interested in that girl who rode up to sixth," he said. "Do you think she stayed there?"

"I don't know. I only know I didn't bring her down. People ran the car themselves after I quit."

"What about Mrs. Marshall-Gill?"

"I don't know. Maybe somebody went up and got her." Her eyes were on his hands as they moved from pocket to pocket. "But she got down all right. I saw her myself, over by the elevator, fifteen or twenty minutes later."

"Fifteen or twenty? Are you sure?"

"Carlin's band was still on."

"Considering all the excitement," he said, "I should think the girl who brought Mrs. Marshall-Gill down would brag about it. You know—'There we were on fifth and there Ruth Miller was on seventh.' Because, according to you, Mrs. Marshall-Gill was on the fifth floor when Ruth Miller was preparing to die."

"Nobody said anything like that." She started to whistle again.

It was time to find his notebook and pen, and he did; and he gave a pleased exclamation. The whistling stopped, and he heard her shift from one foot to the other. He ignored her and wrote steadily, sometimes frowning, sometimes looking pleased.

Finally she said, "What are you putting in that book?"

"I'm making a timetable, thanks to you."

"You can't prove nothing by what I said."

After a pause he said, "Prove what?" She didn't answer.

He read what he had written, shook his head with disbelief, and returned the book to his pocket. "I don't believe it," he said softly, "but there it is. In black and white. . . . Jewel, will it upset you too much to tell me how you happened to be the first girl on the scene?"

She made a small sound, like a sigh of relief. He knew why. They had come to a safe place, a safe place for everybody. Ruth Miller had been long dead when Jewel went into the courtyard. The trap had been sprung, the trapper had vanished.

"That's no secret," she said. "Everybody knows what I did, everybody knows it was me. We had our masks off. Everybody knew each other then."

She said she had gone to her room at midnight. Some of the others had stayed downstairs. And she had opened her window and seen Mrs. Cashman and her dog in the court. "They were coming through the gate. I watched because sometimes the dog upsets our garbage. Then I heard her holler, not loud, but surprised. I thought she'd found something that was our property so I went down. I live on second and it didn't take long, and I went right out the front door without speaking to anybody. And when I was half in the court I heard her scream. And then I saw it."

"Who came out next?"

"Everybody. Out the kitchen door, out the front, some looked out the windows. Miss Brady got the doctor and police. They didn't know who it was. Even when they cut the mask off they didn't know. Then they saw her ring."

"That must have been terrible. A terrible shock. I suppose nobody slept that night."

"I suppose so."

"If I'd been in your place, if I'd seen that poor girl lying in the rain, I'd never get over it. I'd feel haunted. . . . Jewel, what went through your head when you first saw her? What did you think had happened?"

"I thought she fell. If you fell from seventh you'd look like that. That's what I thought." She was eager. "That's what you'd think, too."

"No," he said gently. "No I wouldn't. Because I wouldn't know who she was then. I wouldn't know who she was until much later." He saw her nails bite into her palms.

"You're mixing me up," she said thickly. She started to advance, slowly, and then her head snapped back and she stopped. She was listening. He listened too. Someone was coming down the hall with quick, firm steps. She had the door open before he was out of his chair. It was Miss Brady.

"Well," Miss Brady said. "Having your kind of fun?" Jewel sidled away.

"You came too soon," he said dryly. "Who's next?"

"Minnie May Handy, if we can find her. It may take some time."

"I have plenty of time. How about taking me to see Lillian Harris?"

"What for? She can't talk. She's unconscious."

"Even so, I'd like to see her. She's on Miss Small's list. Maybe if I see them all tonight, I won't have to come back again. Mull that over. You'll be rid of me. Isn't that tempting?"

"It's corruption. But you'll walk up. The elevator's too public at the moment."

He followed her up the stairs, smiling at her monotonous chant of "Man coming, man coming." It was superfluous. The halls and stairs were dim, silent, and deserted. No huddled, bathrobed figures, no high chattering voices. Not even a whisper. Somewhere behind him the elevator hummed steadily, stopped, and hummed again. People were going from one place to another, up and down, back and forth, moving against time. He could see them, like a steady stream of ants, pouring in and out, running here and there. But not to the seventh floor. And, like ants, they carried burdens heavier than themselves.

"Of course you know Harris has the room that used to be Ruth Miller's," Miss Brady said. "That's why you want to go there, isn't it?"

"Not particularly. This is routine."

She didn't speak again until they came to the door. "You can't go in," she said. "I'll leave it open and you stand right here. And be good enough to keep your mouth shut. There's a blind girl in there, she's the one I'm worried about. I don't want her to know anything about you. She's lived in this neighborhood all her life and can't possibly have any connection with Ruth Miller."

Her finger was on her lips when she opened the door quietly. That, he saw at once, was a sign to the elderly woman who sat between the two beds. The only light was a night lamp on the bed table.

"It's me, April," Miss Brady said. "I'm not coming in, I only want to know how you are. Have you had your dinner?"

"Yes, Miss Brady. I'm all right."

He saw her then, huddled in a deep chair. She was tiny, fair, and too fragile. She was the one who had held the other girl's head in her lap and caressed the other girl's face.

"Any change, Mrs. Fister?" Miss Brady whispered.

He hardly heard her. Lillian Harris was the still figure on the bed. She was swathed in bandages and covered to the chin. Her face was a waxen oval marked with pale lips and dark, curling lashes, and if she was breathing he couldn't see it. He started forward. The woman at the bedside stood up and shook her head. He stopped where he was.

The woman and Miss Brady spoke to each other in the language of looks. Neither moved, even the childish girl in the chair was motionless, but he could feel and hear a cordon form between him and the bed.

Miss Brady took his arm and they were out in the hall again; the door closed behind them and he heard a key turn on the inside. She dropped his arm, and when she spoke her voice was sharp and unnaturally high. "What were you trying to do in there?"

He was blunt. "She looks dead. Is she?"

She drew away from him. "Dead? Are you crazy? She's unconscious, I told you that before."

"Maybe she was, before. But you didn't go near her this time."

She made a sound in her throat. "Mr. East, I'm going to ask you to leave. At once. You're going too far."

"No," he answered. "No, I'm not. . . . Why wasn't that girl sent to a hospital?"

"Dr. Kloppel didn't think it was necessary. He says she'll come out of it soon. Mrs. Fister knows what to do."

He leaned against the clean, bare wall, under the dim hall light, and waited for sounds in the room behind the locked door. "Who is that woman, that Mrs. Fister?"

"The housekeeper. She's been with us since we opened. We also employ her sister. Miss Plummer."

"Plummer. She keeps cropping up. I'd like to see Miss Plummer."

"That's impossible and I mean it. She has influenza, nobody sees her, not even Miss Small and myself. . . . Suppose we go down and check on Minnie May. There's nothing else up here."

"Not yet. Wait." The packroom door was ajar, giving a glimpse of nondescript luggage; a clean paper tablet hung on the wall beside the phone. There was another door a few feet away, marked "Bath." "Is that the one?" he asked.

"If you mean Harris, yes."

"Can you think of any reason why I can't look it over?"

She raised her hands in a sudden gesture and dropped them to her sides. It was a beating, batlike movement, crude and rudderless, common to people like Kitty Brice and Jewel who were short on vocabulary, but foreign to the Miss Bradys. She collected herself at once.

"You've infected me with something," she laughed, "and I don't like it. But don't think I'm cracking up." She led the way, and he stood by while she turned on the light. "Help yourself," she invited. "It's none of my business how you waste your time and your clients' money. See? No blood. We're very tidy. And don't take all night, please. This is a fairly public place."

Nice recovery, he told himself. "I'll be as quick as I can," he promised.

It was not a large room; one tub in an alcove, one shower, one washbasin over by the window. He stepped into the shower and examined the faucets. "Harris looks to be about five feet six," he said easily. "So the faucets are all wrong for a bump on the head. A full inch too high. If they were lower I could understand what happened. Slip, stagger, wham."

"It was the floor," she said. "It's concrete. If she slipped and struck her head on the floor, that would do it."

"Don't you think it's a little small for that?"

"What is?"

"The floor space. Not much more than a square yard. She'd have to be double-jointed. . . . Why don't you tell me all about it?"

"But there's nothing to tell!" She was heartily careless. "She fell or slipped, and blacked out for a minute. Tried to reach her room, got mixed up, landed over by the window, blacked out again, and struck her head on the washbasin. There was blood around the basin and in the shower."

"Who figured that out for you?"

"We all figured it. And the doctor." She laughed again. "What's the matter, don't you believe it?"

He had walked over to the window and was looking at the basin. "I believe the blood," he said. "But it was funny about the light being off, wasn't it?"

"Ah," she said. "One of those wretched girls told you that!"

"The girls told me nothing. I mean nothing about the light. Mrs. Sutton picked that one up."

"Mrs. Sutton! Well there's a perfectly simple explanation. She could walk around and do things up to a certain point. She turned the light out when she tried to get to her room. Habit. That's medically sound. Read up on concussion."

"Maybe I will." He raised the window, absently, as if it were a thing he did every night in that same room. The cold wind came in, and Miss Brady drew back. He stood there alone, looking down into the courtyard. "Do you mind turning out the light?" he asked. "I want to see how it looks when everything is dark."

He heard her cross the floor; the light went out and she came to stand beside him, shivering.

"Now it's Miller," she said quietly. "Not Harris any more. Miller."

"It's always been Miller," he answered.

The night was filled with far-off sound. The city was remote. He thought it was the cold that made him feel lost. He felt as if he and the shivering woman beside him were the only people in the world. Even the house, above, below, and around them, had no substance. He was shivering himself and his breathing matched hers.

The lamp on the street filled the court with a faint glow; only the corners were dark. A white cat sat immobile on the fence, staring at the house. Its sleek white head was held high, its interest was unmistakable, even at a distance. It looked as if it were watching them, watching and listening. It was a beautiful cat, and oddly contemplative.

He leaned from the window and looked up and down. There were lights on the ground floor but only a few above it. They were bright patches on the dark walls. One of the patches was the window in the room to his left. That window was closed. Ruth's window, once. Lillian's window now. There was another light directly over it, and that window was partly open. The shade was drawn, but there was perhaps an inch of space between it and the sill. Something that looked like a sheet of white tissue paper fluttered on the sill. He and the cat watched. He knew the cat was watching.

And as they watched, the paper was caught in an eddy of wind. It turned on the sill and writhed, it rose and fell as if it were alive, and spiraled down into the court. It straightened out and turned on itself and spiraled to the earth. The white cat screamed and flowed down the fence like milk, and was lost in the shadows.

He sighed.

"What was that?" Miss Brady's voice was like a whip.

"A sheet of tissue paper, I think. It came from the top floor, the room over the one we just left."

"Oh. For a minute I thought——that damned cat, it always sits there! That's my bedroom. Miss Small is wrapping Christmas presents and the place is a mess. She isn't very tidy."

He heard her go over to the door; the light clicked on. "I don't see the point of this darkness," she said. "Unless you're trying to frighten me, and you can't. Are you going to spend the night here?" When he didn't reply, she came back to the window. "What's wrong now?"

"Have you got a music box in your bedroom?"

"Not any more." She was startled. "Why?"

"I thought I heard something that sounded like a music box. It's stopped now."

"I did have one but it disappeared several days ago. Miss Small knew how much I liked it so I suppose she found another to take its place." She laughed softly. "Now I'll have to act surprised, thanks to you. . . . Really, Mr. East, we've got to get out of here. What comes next?"

They were in the hall. "I'm thinking about that," he said.

Words were falling into place in his mind, one after the other, falling into line and sequence, making sentences for a child's primer. The cat sat on the fence. The cat saw the paper. What did the cat see? The cat saw the white paper. The cat saw the white——

"Miss Brady," he said, "I'd like to see Ruth Miller's suitcase."

She was amiable and amused. "I've done that and you know it. There's the packroom, get it out yourself. It's a straw affair, just inside the door. Big letter M in black paint. Looks as if she'd put it on herself."

He found the case. "Unlocked?"

"Yes." She watched, incuriously.

He unfastened the imitation leather straps and threw back the lid. Her sudden gasp was as genuine as his own. Ruth Miller's clothing was a jumbled heap; someone hadn't cared what happened to it. A thin summer dress, faded by too many washings, lay on top. And on top of the dress was an enamel box. He took it up carefully. "Your disappearing property, Miss Brady?"

"Yes."

"Yes," he agreed. "And what is it doing here?"

"I don't know! I can't imagine who or why——I simply can't believe——"

He stood under the light, turning the box in his hands. "Pretty," he said. "Somebody thought as much of it as you did, perhaps even more."

"I don't get it," she said. "I don't understand."

"That's easy. Somebody wanted it, took it, and hid it. To be collected at a later date. Can you think of a safer hiding place than a suicide's suitcase? A suitcase that had already been searched?" While he talked, his thumbnail traced the deep carved lines that bit into the metal base. "Pretty thing," he admired. "Substantial, too. Cloisonné on solid bronze. French. . . . What did you do when you missed it?"

"Nothing. What could I do? That insane ad of yours

had just appeared, and the place was a madhouse. I couldn't face more talk."

"In a way I don't blame you." He held the box to the light again. Blue forget-me-nots and pink bow-knots. "Easy to pawn. Easy to smuggle out of the house in a coat pocket, but that didn't happen. This little gadget said something to somebody. . . . Not an ordinary run-of-the-mill theft, Miss Brady. What did it hold?"

"Only powder. Face powder."

"Powder and tunes, the dear French. I'd like to keep it for a while, do you mind?"

"No, but——"

"I'll give it back. I may even find your thief, quietly and without involving you. What tune does it play? Something about love, love, love?" His fingers found the opening catch.

"Don't!" she said. "They'll hear you in there!"

He knew what she meant. The room with the locked door was less than two yards away. That's where Lillian Harris was, swathed like a mummy because she had hurt her head.

He hesitated, fearful of moving too fast. He couldn't afford to lose the precarious ground he had just gained. But he wanted an audience, any audience, residents, servants, staff. He wanted someone to say, "Get this. You know that detective? Well, he's playing Miss Brady's music box up on the seventh floor. He's a nut." And that would travel from mouth to mouth because it was too good to keep. It was crazy, it was comical, it was a scream. That detective, standing in the seventh-floor hall with Miss Brady, playing Miss Brady's music box.

That would mean something to somebody. That would tell somebody the box was no longer safe.

Miss Brady spoke in a furious undertone. "Listen to that! This place is a parade ground!"

He heard the footsteps then, the sharp clean clack of high heels coming down the hall on the other side of the fire door. That would do it, that was what he wanted. He raised the lid of the box as Moke and Poke

172

rollicked through the door and stopped abruptly. The tinkling notes rang down the hall with gentle, plaintive insistence.

Believe me if all those endearing young charms that I gaze on so fondly today——

"What are you girls doing here?" Miss Brady asked. "You know this is out of bounds while Lillian is sick."

Moke held up a paper bag. "We brought her grapes." Her eyes were on the box, wide and incredulous. He saw Poke's hand reach out and touch Moke's. It looked like a warning.

Thou wouldst still be adored as this moment thou art, let thy loveliness fade as it will—— The little box paid homage, pacified, and promised.

"She can't eat them now," Miss Brady said. "Keep them until tomorrow. And do run along now, there's too much racket here already."

Mark beckoned. "Say, you kids. Look what we found in Ruth's suitcase. What do you think of that?"

"Pretty," Moke said.

"It's Miss Brady's," he went on. "She lost it. And now it turns up in Ruth's luggage."

Moke and Poke looked straight into his eyes and said nothing.

They stood in a circle under the dim light, and three of the four faces were blank. Mark snapped the lid and the music stopped. He picked up the suitcase. "Thanks, Miss Brady, you've been very helpful. I'm taking this temporarily, you'll get it back with the box. . . . Miss Small's room again?"

"Yes. I'll come with you."

"Don't trouble, please. These girls will announce my sex and proximity. . . . Come along, you two."

They left her with one hand raised to the locked door.

Down in Miss Small's room he seated Moke and Poke with a flourish. "Now," he said, "take that look off your faces and eat your nice grapes yourselves. And when you've got your voices back, tell me why this little box knocked you for a loop."

Moke put the grapes on Miss Small's desk. "Leave Angel have them. She likes fruit."

"Leave Angel buy her own," he said. "Come on, I'm waiting. What's wrong with this box?"

Moke wet her lips. "Mr. East, that box is stolen goods."

"I know that. It was stolen from Miss Brady." Gasps followed his statement. "Well, what's wrong with that, except that it isn't nice?"

Four frightened eyes almost prepared him for what was coming, but not quite. "I don't know about Miss Brady," Moke said, "but that box was stolen from Blackman's."

He wanted to shout. What he said was, "Glory be! . . . Moke, are you absolutely certain?"

They were both certain, but only after they had turned the box upside down and satisfied themselves about the marking.

According to Poke, Blackman's had imported twenty-four musical powder boxes for Valentine gifts the year before. Different designs, different tunes, eighteen-fifty each. But, she said, they didn't move so good in the counter display, so the buyer got the window dresser to use one in the accessory window on the Fifth Avenue corner.

"Wait," Mark said. "Was the counter display in Ruth Miller's department?"

"Yes, sir. Not her counter but next to it. But she could wait on anybody in the whole department. It's all toilet goods."

"I get it. Go on."

According to Moke, the window dressing had helped like nobody's business, and the boxes went like hot cakes until there was only one left. The one Mr. East was holding, only it was in the window then. And a very good customer put her name down for it. The very same box, you couldn't make a mistake about it, because there was only one with forget-me-nots and pink bows. And *Believe me if all those endearing.* But it disappeared.

"Out of the window?" He held his breath. If she said yes, then he was wrong.

She said no. "No, sir, off the window dresser's boy's truck. The boy cleared out the window around four o'clock, which is what he did every week. He had to get it ready for the new stuff they put in at night. And he parked his truck in a corner by the window, which he always did too, a darkish little corner next to the employees' elevator. He was in and out of the window, and he didn't notice anybody that he could remember when they asked him about it later. But when he took the truck downstairs and the stock clerks checked their own merchandise, there wasn't any box. Gone."

"That was last February?"

"Yes, sir."

"Why do you remember so much detail, Moke? Blackman's must lose a lot of valuable stuff. It can't be much of a shock when an eighteen-fifty gadget disappears."

"This here one was a shock. The customer that wanted it was a relation of the Blackman family. So everybody got talked to. And the window dresser's boy was sort of new and somebody had to be the goat so he got fired."

There was no one in Hope House who could have been a window dresser's boy a year ago. But perhaps in the neighborhood——

"Too bad about the boy. Ever see him again?"

"No, sir. They wouldn't give him a reference either. Just told him to make out like he never worked at Blackman's and they wouldn't have him arrested. They couldn't prove anything, see, so they just let him go without a reference. That's the way stores do. . . . Mr. East, you never found that box in Ruth's suitcase!"

"Yes, I did."

Poke flared. "I don't believe it! It's a big untruth! She was worried sick about it being gone, she was more upset than the buyer!"

"She was?"

"Certainly she was. Everybody that works in a store

hates things like that. If anybody's hinting that she took it herself——"

"Nobody is, Poke. It wasn't in her suitcase when Miss Brady searched it after she died. It was in Miss Brady's room, where it belonged. It didn't disappear until several days ago."

"Well, where would Miss Brady get it?"

"I didn't ask her. I'm saving that. . . . Ever been in her rooms?"

"No, sir. She don't invite you like Angel."

"Maybe it was a present from an old Blackman girl. Did any of them live here last winter?"

"That would be a dumb thing to do," Moke said. "With me and Poke living here too. No, sir, we never had any other Blackman people, only Poke and me and Ruth."

"Dumb?" Poke repeated. "You mean insane. To give away stolen goods is the act of an insane person. I think Miss Brady found it in a pawnshop."

"You both have something there," Mark agreed. "Now run through that suitcase for me and see if everything looks all right. I want to think." They dropped to their knees, and he watched their careful hands as they smoothed and folded and brought order to chaos.

It was indeed a dumb thing to give away stolen goods, but he knew a precedent for it. Miss Lizzie Borden, happily acquitted of a couple of murders and heady with success, had helped herself to a silver picture frame and given it to a friend. And there was something in the pawnshop theory, too. Miss Brady looked as if she would enjoy a pawnshop purchase from beginning to end. Work it that way, he told himself, line it up and what have you got?

Somebody steals a music box from a department store and pawns it. Somebody else sees it and buys it and puts it on her dressing table, presumably in full view. A third person enters the scene and dies violently, and a fourth person nearly dies. And in between the death and the near death, the box disappears. To turn up later in the dead person's luggage. The dead person had been a clerk in the store from which the box was stolen. The half-dead——check on the half-dead.

Something to work with, but ragged. Fuzzy, not clean. Something essential left out and something extraneous added. Find the something extraneous, remove it, and ten to one the resulting gap would turn into a mouth that spelt the answer. M-u-r-d-e-r.

Moke tapped his knee respectfully. He dragged his thoughts back from their dark journey.

"The blue suit," Moke said. "The new one. It isn't here."

"The one she wore to tea?"

"Yes, sir. And she didn't have it on that day—you know, that day. Somebody swiped it. . . . This place is getting me! I'm gonna move!"

Poke said quietly, "Where to?" They sat back on their heels and looked at each other.

"I'd say this was a pretty good place to live in," Mark observed. "Nice rooms, good food, cheap, all that. I don't see how you could do better. Easy enough to do worse."

"We know," Poke said.

"I suppose all the girls feel the same way," he went on. "Even those who work here, like Kitty and Jewel. There may be things they don't like, even things they don't understand, but it's better to turn the other way and say nothing. Better than going back to hall bedrooms, dirt, eating out of paper bags, hiding from the landlady when the cash is low. . . . They don't bother you here when you're late with your board money, do they?"

"Right," Poke said.

"I know I'm right. And if I were one of the Hope House kids, I'd do almost anything to keep Hope House a going concern. . . . Now that's all for tonight. If people ask you what I wanted, tell them you checked Ruth's clothing. And tell them about Miss Brady's box turning up in the suitcase. But don't, don't, don't give the box's history. Got that?"

"Yes, sir."

He led them to the door. "Minnie May's coming to call, and I want you out of here before then."

Someone came down the hall even as he spoke. But it wasn't Minnie May. It was Miss Small. She looked beaten, and she had been crying.

"Finished?" she asked when they were alone.

"Temporarily. You're having a bad time, and I haven't been making it any easier. I'm sorry. Want me to get out of here?"

"Don't apologize and please stay as long as you like. I came to tell you that I've finally located Minnie May Handy, she'll be along any minute. I'd forgotten about her until Miss Brady reminded me that she and Ruth were very friendly at the tea."

"Did Miss Brady tell you about this?" He held up the box.

Miss Small's eyes filled. "Yes. She's terribly upset. She was so fond of it, she adored it, and when it disappeared we didn't know what to think. We can't imagine how or why——there's no explanation. Mr. East, does this make any sense to you?"

"None at all."

"I'm almost relieved to hear you say that. I thought I was being unusually stupid. I've thought and thought, and all I get is the most dreadful feeling of defeat. I'm afraid we've made a sad mistake somewhere, and we'll never forgive ourselves. Are you really going to straighten us out?"

"I'm going to have a try."

She went on, unhappily. "You know, Miss Brady and I are leaving Hope House, and we simply can't have this hanging over our heads. First poor Ruth, then Lillian, then this kleptomaniac——"

"Miss Small," he began, "has it ever occurred to you that perhaps all three of these apparently unrelated incidents are——"

Someone struck the door a smart blow. He hid his disappointment. "Miss Handy?"

"I'm afraid so, and I'm afraid it's very inopportune, but we thought you ought to——"

"Quite right. Have her in and stick around yourself. According to Miss Mainwaring, Miss Handy gets too much out of life."

Miss Small smiled wanly. "Come in," she called.

Minnie May was pale and assured, and she was dressed for an evening of dancing and light wines. Her manner said she wanted to get on with it.

"Miss Handy," he began.

Minnie May took it up. "I know what you want, and it won't take a minute. I don't know a thing. Sure I talked to the girl at the tea, because she looked lonely and dumb. She hardly opened her mouth, and when she did she asked things like how long people had lived here and where they were from, things like that. She had a snoopy disposition. You see, I know what you asked the other girls, so I'm all set. No use wasting my time. I never saw the girl before. I didn't see her when she came, or if I did I don't remember. I wasn't myself that night. The other time I saw her was at the party, and I danced with her."

He pounced. "You danced with her? Are you sure?"

"Twice. And I'm sure. I was cutting up, but I knew what I was doing. I always know. I was carrying on, taking the place. Miss Small was sore and spoke to me about it. Didn't you, Miss Small?"

"I did," Miss Small said briefly. "Go on, Minnie May."

"So I danced with her twice, and you can't make anything out of that."

"I don't intend to," Mark said. "I think it was a friendly thing to do. Do you happen to remember what time it was when you danced?"

"Who watches clocks at parties?"

"True. But I hoped you might remember because of some incident. The music, what other people were doing, if the party was going strong or just starting. Try it that way."

Minnie May became affable at once. "Oh, that. What a mind you've got. Well, the first time was early, I'd say eightish. Right, Miss Small?"

179

"If you say so," Miss Small said doubtfully.

"So. Eightish. And Miss Small shook a fist at me. I calmed down, I'm no fool, and talked to some of the kids. Deaf-and-dumb style for a laugh, and I had some punch and hung around the desk watching Plummer have kittens."

"You say that was the first time?" Mark asked.

"Sure. And let me do this my way. If you ask me too many questions you'll mix me up, and if you mix me up we're sunk. So I watched Plummer. She was going crazy because the chef had cut himself as usual, and she wanted stuff to fix him up. She was grabbing kids as they went by and asking them to go upstairs for stuff." Minnie May's eyes glistened. "She grabbed me, but I'm a slippery cuss. Grabbed everybody but Marshall-Gill, didn't she, pal—I mean Miss Small?"

Miss Small wisely ignored the palship. "Hardly grab," she reproved. "But the confusion was dreadful," she said to Mark. "One of the maids was actually covered with blood, but fortunately we were able to keep it from Mrs. Marshall-Gill. I went down to the kitchen at once. It wasn't serious, he'd been drinking. He does that."

"Some fun," Minnie May said. "Best party we ever had. Worst punch. Next time I stick with the chef. Well I had some more punch anyway, fixed it up a little, my own brand, nobody else got any, and I followed Marshall-Gill around. Blah, blah, blah. She wanted to go upstairs to wash her hands. Wash her hands! Ha-ha!"

"Minnie May! Please!"

"Okay, Miss Small, okay. Now let's see. Eight-thirty-ish, maybe, how'm I doing? Then I went outside for some air and stayed maybe half an hour, and when I got back Marshall-Gill was getting out of the elevator. She looked like—she looked green. I think I scared the —I think I scared her. Had my face on backwards. Cut new eyes and a place for my nose." Minnie May was convulsed. "Nobody thinks of things like that but me. I clowned for the crowd. Everybody said I was a living sight." She drew a deep breath. "Say, am I talking too much? Sometimes I do."

"No," Mark said. "But how about getting on to the second time you danced with Ruth Miller?" He saw Miss Small watching him and knew they were thinking the same thing. Eight-thirtyish, plus half an hour for air. The time was creeping up to nine. It may have reached nine. And at nine——

"Okay, but I think this is silly. You got all this stuff from Jewel, practically. Well, I scouted around with my face on backwards and had some more punch and played some records, and then I ran into Miller. We did a two-woman conga. Now wait, wait, I'm coming to it. Scouting around, punch, records, a lot of records, that took time, I guess it was going on ten."

Mark said softly, "Are you sure?"

"Going on ten, close to ten, could have been ten." Minnie May was positive. "I know, because we had the guessing soon after."

"Miss Handy." She heard the challenge in his voice and stared. "Miss Handy, why do you think you danced with Ruth Miller?"

"Why? Why, because I did! I spotted her right off. I saw the kids put that mole on her face, I knew her by that. It didn't do her any good not to talk, and I told her so. I knew her." She intercepted the look he sent Miss Small. "Hey! What are you doing? What are you looking like that for?"

He said, "Both Dr. Kloppel and the police surgeon said Ruth Miller was dead at nine."

Miss Small made a sign of distress. "She may be mistaken. We all lose track of time."

Minnie May stood up. Panic stretched her mouth into an ugly shape and darkened her eyes. "I forgot that. So help me, I forgot that. I heard somebody say nine, but I forgot it. . . . You can't do this! I see what you're doing! You can't do this! I don't care what the doctor says, she was alive at ten. I saw her! I can prove it!"

"How?"

181

"That mole! It was plain as day if you knew where to look. You've only got to ask——"

"That mole is very convenient, but it means absolutely nothing. Everybody knew about it, so everybody could talk about it. What you need is a credible witness, someone who saw you together, and I don't think you're going to find one."

"But everybody saw me! Everybody! And they laughed!"

"You, yes. But nobody saw Ruth Miller. Apparently she vanished shortly after the party began. . . . Did you do your two-woman conga with anyone else?"

"Sure. Three or four." Minnie May's voice was lifeless. "But that's no good, is it? I can't prove which was which. Am I in a spot or something?"

"What does it sound like? Listen. You disappeared at eight-thirty and returned at approximately nine. And at nine—" he dragged it out—"at nine Ruth Miller was dead."

She screamed. "You! You!"

Miss Small took Minnie May's arm and held it fast. "Mr. East! Surely that's enough? Can't we let it ride for a little while? I'm afraid of what may happen if you go on. She can't take much more."

Minnie May tore loose and backed to the door. "You can't do things like this! You're trapping me! You can't do it, it's against the law, you can't!" She fell against the door and beat the panels with impotent hands.

His directions to Miss Small were quiet and to the point. "Go along with her, but don't let her talk to anyone. And don't leave her alone. Ask her roommate to stand by. I hold you personally responsible, I want to see her again tomorrow."

To Minnie May, he said, "If you're telling the truth, Miss Handy, you've nothing to worry about."

He was afraid she hadn't heard him. He watched them leave. He'd see her as soon as possible and tell her she was all right. And she was. She was safer than any girl in the House. . . . He heard her wailing voice as she went down the hall. Everybody would hear, and the story would be public property in five minutes. Doors would open and shut, bathrobed figures would gather in the halls and rooms and whisper far into the night. Minnie May Handy had lied to the detective and he'd caught her. Minnie May had lied about Ruth Miller. Minnie May had lied, lied, lied. And Miss Mainwaring would stand guard over a sinful soul and play the martyr until dawn.

And Minnie May would meet with no accidents. No open windows or slippery showers. She was too precious for that. She was under suspicion, drawing the fire from Ruth Miller's murderer.

Dr. Kloppel said, "It's blood all right. Deep in that bronze carving. Want me to soak it out and type it?"

"No use," Mark answered. "We can't do anything with it. We can't get a sample for comparison, if you know what I mean. It's better where it is. Even if it belongs to Harris instead of Miller, it's better. It says more."

"Fingerprints?"

"None."

Dr. Kloppel wrapped the box in a clean handkerchief and placed it in the center of his table. The old-fashioned chandelier shed a cold white light. The box looked like a little coffin, shrouded and lonely.

"Ugh," Dr. Kloppel said. "So you didn't get anything out of the girls?"

"Not much, except for the Smiths. The others are scared stiff, holding out, or putting on an·act. They look to me as if they'd scratched and clawed themselves up from tenement rooms with six in a bed, and having attained Hope House they mean to keep it. They're not too bright in the head and they're afraid of the law. The law puts furniture on the sidewalk, for one thing. So what would the law do in a case of murder? If one of those kids saw a suspicious move that night, she'd turn the other way."

"Harris isn't like that. She's the one I told you about

before, the one who was interested in windows. She's a bright, intelligent girl."

"And what did that get her? A locked room and a broken head. . . . You know, Dr. Kloppel, I'm willing to bet my own life that Ruth Miller left that party with someone, or at someone's suggestion. That her murder was all set, that someone was watching and waiting to strike. Once I lick that time sequence and know who was where and when, I've got it. I can't figure that ten o'clock dance of Minnie May's, but I bet I can bust it like a bubble when I get my hands on the right pin. . . . Presumably Ruth Miller went to her own room before nine o'clock, and presumably the window she fell from was her own window. But the box, my friend, belongs on the floor above."

"Miss Brady's box, stolen from Blackman's. Miss Brady's box." Dr. Kloppel hated his own words. "You can't accuse that lady of theft. You can't even accuse her of murder. It isn't fitting!"

"But her box did murder once, and tried it a second time. Unless Lillian Harris knocked herself out for a red herring."

"No," Dr. Kloppel said. "You didn't see those heads and I did." He reached out and touched the box gingerly. "It hurt, Mr. East. It was cruel and painful and slow, blow after blow." He withdrew his hand and rubbed it. "What do we do now?"

"We act like honest taxpayers and yell help, murder, police. Who was on the case before?"

"Foy, for about five minutes. He's a very busy man. He looked up at the window, shook his head and crossed himself, and said, 'Pity.'"

"I know Foy. Call him up tonight, after I leave. Tell him you're dissatisfied, the Harris development will cover that. Say you've talked to me. Then he'll call me, and I'll tell him how I got on to it and what I've done. I'll still work from my end, Foy will understand that. Give him the box and the suitcase."

Dr. Kloppel said, "I like Foy as a poker player, but you've got more than he has."

"Dr. K., I'm touched. But Foy has the pretty badge. He can put a dozen men in Hope House and nobody can stop him. He can pat his holster while he asks questions and blow his whistle and get an army." He thought of Minnie May, beating her hands on the door because he needed a goat, of Moke and Poke, telling God knows who about Miss Brady's pretty box. "You might suggest a guard for tonight if Foy doesn't think of it himself. Tell him you'll sleep better if he puts a couple of men in." He drummed the table. "I've got to see Harris, soon, and I'd like to see Miss Plummer." Plummer going crazy because the chef cut himself, Plummer grabbing girls to send for stuff. Stuff where? Upstairs? "Everybody talks about Plummer, but I can't get to her. People keep shunting me off."

"She's in bed, that's why. Got a cold. And you're a young fellow. Miss Plummer is the type that undresses under a nightgown, all by herself. You can come with me in the morning. Harris, too. She'll begin to worry herself back to consciousness in another twenty-four hours, maybe less. Fine, strong girl. Eight-thirty."

"I'll be there if I can get some sleep now. I've got a couple of stops to make on my way home, so I'll be going."

His first stop was at Mrs. Marshall-Gill's. She was delighted. She inquired into his lineage, his qualifications, his personal hopes, and gave him hers. He was tired enough to scream and fatigue was painting ugly pictures in his mind, but he let her run on because he wanted her affectionate regard when the time came for his questions. He managed to slip the first one in when she paused for breath in the middle of a trip to Yellowstone when she was seven.

Yes, indeed, she said, she had gone upstairs quite early in the evening. So warm, so crowded, and a little cold water on the back of the neck was always refreshing. So she had asked Miss Brady if she might use Miss Small's room, Miss Small being engaged elsewhere, and Miss Brady had given grudging consent. An odd woman, Miss Brady, no management, no discipline,

185

and so cold. So she had gone up. And while she was there she had written Miss Small an appreciative little check, so useful for the holidays.

His eyes told her she was a darling. "Not many people are so thoughtful," he said. "Now, Mrs. Marshall-Gill, I think you returned to the party at about nine o'clock, or very near to it. Did you walk down, or ride?"

Mrs. Marshall-Gill said, "Walk? Really, Mr. East!" She added, "That Jewel!"

"Yes?"

"Insubordination. I'm tempted to report the girl at the next Board meeting. I rang and rang. I could have walked down in half the time I waited but the girl is paid to operate the elevator and I was determined that she should. And when she finally condescended——" Mrs. Marshall-Gill faltered.

"Then she did—condescend?"

"Finally. Finally. It was a very odd thing, very odd. I can't truthfully say she was impertinent, simply because she refused to speak to me, but she was positively venomous in manner. I was really disturbed, after all I've done for the House, deficits and so on. And Jewel——" Mrs. Marshall-Gill drew closer to the fire. "Mr. East, I feel uncomfortable even now when I think of it. Venomous, hateful, I can't describe it except to say that she wasn't at all nice. . . . I think she was thinking things about me."

He drew closer to the fire himself. "Go on, Mrs. Marshall-Gill."

"A naughty girl," she said firmly. "I suspect she'd been drinking or smoking in her room, which is forbidden to employees. She went right up again, put me off at the first floor, and went right up again. No apology for keeping me waiting. That's what happens when you coddle these people. Dressed up like one of the boarders, lolling and slouching and probably making faces at me behind that mask. And a beauty spot, too. Impertinence."

He picked his words carefully after that. He didn't want her around his neck, screaming.

"Do you know anything about that beauty spot, Mrs. Marshall-Gill?"

"Know about it? Certainly not. What should I know? Showing off."

Then, "You got in the car at the fifth floor. Do you remember where it went when she took it up again?"

"I remember very well. I watched the little wretch. She lives on second, but she went up to the eighth. That's under the roof. She was going to walk up to the roof and smoke and drink."

He gloated silently. "I suppose you talked to Jewel when she took you up to Miss Small's?"

"Why, yes. Why, how strange! She did talk that time, surly, of course, but she did talk. I daresay she'd quarreled with someone in the meantime. They always quarrel, people like that."

"Was she wearing the beauty spot then?"

"Was she——oh, no. I'd have noticed and commented. No, not then. That's probably one of the things she was doing when I was in Miss Small's. Sewing it on, making herself conspicuous. Upstart."

He reached for his hat.

9

He stood with his back to the fire and looked at the four faces turned to his. He had talked steadily for an hour, sometimes circling the room, sometimes stopping at a window to stare down into the street. They knew he wasn't seeing that street but another.

"That's all for now," he said. "You'll have to wait until tomorrow for the rest."

"Are you waiting for tomorrow yourself?" Roberta asked pointedly.

He said there was nothing else he could do. With Foy in Hope House and Foy's boys patrolling the Hope House halls, nothing could happen. People would keep to their rooms, doors would stay locked in spite of entreaties of bosom pals. Nothing could possibly happen.

"They're beginning to suspect their own shadows," he said. "And that's the way it should be. I ran over there for a few minutes after I left Marshall-Gill, and you could cut the miasmas with a knife. Foy came in as I was leaving. I didn't see a single soul except Foy, two cops, and Kitty Brice. I didn't hear a sound except the lobby clock and Foy clearing his throat. The cops didn't clear theirs. The switchboard was quiet, the elevator was empty, but all the time I could have sworn there were people on the stairs. Those stairs wind up to the top floor, iron railings like a cage. I even went over and looked up. Nobody. But I kept hearing footsteps. Or thinking I did. I got out of there. I'm glad Foy has it."

"Why didn't you bring Minnie May here?" Beulah asked.

"Here—why?"

Beulah smoothed her skirt and plucked at invisible threads. "Oh, just an idea I had. Poor Minnie May, sitting by herself. I hope she doesn't feel too miserable and lonely. I hope she doesn't feel so lonely that she opens her door to one of her friends. Even if she did, I guess we wouldn't know. No, we wouldn't know about that. . . . Poor Minnie May, all by herself, overcome by remorse. I hope she doesn't leave a little note in shaky handwriting that doesn't look like hers but must be because it has her name signed to it. Saying she's sorry and doesn't want to live." She didn't look at him.

He went to the window again and came back. "I told Foy," he said, "I told Foy everything."

Beulah went on, tonelessly. "There's Jewel, too. Maybe Jewel lied to you. You can't prove she didn't. You can't prove anything about seventy people who looked exactly alike. I don't say she lied, but there was that half hour between the time she took Marshall-Gill up and the time she says she didn't take her down. I don't say she met Ruth by appointment, killed her, copied the identifying mole, and reappeared to make a holy show of herself with Minnie May so that at least one person could swear Ruth was alive when she wasn't. I don't say Jewel was behind that mask. I don't even say there was a cross-eyed Indian behind that mask, but there could have been and nobody would know it."

No one spoke. Nick shuffled his feet. "I've been thinking," he said. "I don't have much else to do. What happened to the costumes, Mark?"

"That's in my little book. That's one of the things for tomorrow. That, Plummer, Harris, and the girl named April." His voice was strained. "Tomorrow. I'm counting on tomorrow. . . . There's that blue suit, too. I don't know why it should vanish. She wasn't wearing it when she died. I can't see another girl stealing it, but it's gone."

"The one she spilled tea on?" Beulah asked.

"Yes."

"The answer to that is positively childish. It's at the

cleaner's. It was new, she'd saved for it, so she took it to the cleaner's right away. She didn't plan to die before she could collect it. Don't worry about it, save your strength for important things. Bessy and I will get it for you tomorrow."

He gave her a look full of pity, with ice in it. That made him feel better. "May I remind you once more that this is New York?" he said. "There are about a couple of thousand cleaners——"

"There is exactly one cleaner," she answered, "and he is somewhere between Blackman's and Hope House."

"That's a wide area. You'll waste too much time. You don't know the neighborhood."

Bessy sat up noisily. "Oh yes, Mark, we——"

Beulah snarled, "Hush. . . . She means we'll find it, Mark."

He began a weary diatribe on their prospects and was about to cap it with an axiom when he stopped himself in time. Where Bessy and Beulah were concerned, an axiom was an old saw that didn't cut. With his own eyes he had seen them find needles in haystacks and thread them with camels. So he told them to go ahead. At least he'd know approximately where they were and what they were doing. And if they failed, that would be all right, too. It wasn't important; a cheap blue suit with a spot of tea on it. "Sure, sure, go ahead," he urged.

"We may have a little trouble," Beulah admitted. "No claim ticket."

"Don't give me that! You'll walk down the first street that takes your fancy and find it hanging in the first window. Up front. But remember this. I only want the blue suit that a Miss Miller left with one of New York's million dry cleaners. Leave all other garments for their rightful owners."

"Not funny," she said coldly. "Where'll we bring it?"

"Call me at Kloppel's. . . . By the way, I've still got nothing on that eye doctor."

Bessy sat up again. "We think," she began.

"Hush," Beulah said. "She means we think there isn't one."

"Maybe, maybe," he said. "I can't fit him in. I suspect he doesn't belong. He clutters things up, and we have all the clutter we can handle. Listen, listen to me for the last time. Blackman's, desperate for help, hired Ruth without references. Her background is a blank, except that she couldn't conceal her familiarity with department-store selling. She was working there when a musical powder box was stolen from a window dresser's truck. We know she reacted badly when anything like that happened in the store. But she was definitely in the clear about the box, she was never in the vicinity of the truck. About a year later, with a good record behind her, she moves to Hope House, having arranged with Miss Brady for a room. Happy as a lark about that move, too. Roberta knows that. Then two days later she was three-quarters beaten to death and apparently thrown from a window to finish her life in a rain-soaked courtyard. The stolen box, now the property of Miss Brady, was the weapon, plus a pair of strong arms. What does that say to you, Roberta?"

He singled out Roberta because her face had that look again, the one he didn't like to see. He'd forgotten to pick and choose his words and it was too late to go back. But he could lift her up beside him, he could make her his own age and equal in experience; she was young enough to rise to that. "I want your opinion, Robbie. What does it say to you?"

Roberta was eager. "I think she saw the person who took the box and recognized——no, that's wrong. I forget she wasn't near the truck. Could she have seen the box in Miss Brady's room at Hope House, and——" She waited for his answer, confused and shy, a natural kid again. That was what he wanted.

"Nice work, but you're putting the box in first place because there is an irrevocable tie. I'm not sure it belongs there, I think it's a secondary issue. Try it this way. Suppose the box was stolen by the window dresser's boy after all, or by a charwoman, or a nameless clerk who never was considered and never will be. And suppose it was pawned, and Miss Brady saw it and liked it and bought it. That could be. That doesn't alter anything we already have. Nothing in that to make Ruth Miller die."

"Well, no."

"Quite. Now go back to the night Ruth moved to Hope House. You all know what happened. She came in, at dinner time. Everybody, or nearly everybody, was in the lobby. Milling around, coming and going, and, I imagine, giving the new girl the once-over. She came in smiling. She smiled at Miss Small who was on desk duty; she shook hands, she was happy, she was where she wanted to be. And in two or three minutes, four at most, she was terrified. No explanation, no conversation. She left the place at once, went out into the street alone. Probably to walk, to think, to pull herself together. And she came back, perhaps because she had no other place to go. But the terror was so obvious that Miss Small told Miss Brady about it and they wondered what kind of girl she was.

"Now get this. Ruth hadn't seen the box. She couldn't have known it was there. She had never been upstairs. She had walked from the front door to the desk and that's all. And yet she was frightened almost out of her wits. The box had nothing to do with that. It couldn't have.

"No, the terror was right there in the lobby. And it was so strong that after that first night she didn't leave her room unless she had to, she stayed away from meals, she avoided people whenever she could. You see what I mean? The box had no significance then. It was only significant later, when it was used as a weapon. A hammer would have done the job as well, if a hammer had been handy. . . . There's something we don't know, see? Something about Ruth that we don't know. Her life, from the time she came to Blackman's a year ago, was as dull and open as any life can be. The box came and went in that same year, too, and nothing happened. No, we have to go farther back."

"Back," Roberta repeated. "Back to where?"

"I don't know. Measuring in length of time, I don't know. But in distance, only to Hope House."

Inspector Foy left Hope House at eleven-thirty, hiding his chagrin under a show of manners that did credit to his sixteen-year-old daughter's nagging. He had been given every facility. Bells had been rung, three rings which meant an emergency; bells and voices had shrilled together in the upper halls. Girls who had gone to bed were routed out and herded down to lounge and lobby; girls who were dressed, half dressed, and undressed overflowed both rooms. He had questioned, cajoled, and wondered audibly if he should call the wagon. In the end he had sent them back to bed, richer for the experience. He had learned that bobby pins look good on some and bad on others.

He'd looked in on Lillian Harris, as Mark had done; he'd listened to Minnie May who had alternately screamed and cried. He'd been glad to close Minnie May's door behind him and climb to the roof. The roof was his own idea. But it was flat and empty, except for a pile of deck chairs under tarpaulin, and the side that faced the court was fenced with six-foot wire. Not even a cigarette butt.

Back in the lounge he was given coffee, and after that he departed, leaving two men in charge. One of these, Moran, spent the night in the lobby, occasionally riding up in the elevator to check with his colleague on the seventh floor. The latter was named Bessemer, and he was stationed outside Lillian Harris's door. That had been Mark's suggestion. Every half hour Bessemer opened the door and received a signal from Mrs. Fister. It always told him things were as they should be. Moran had been told to patrol all floors, but the lobby was warm and the halls were not. And there was a good chair in the lobby.

Bessemer liked his job. He had never seen so much night bathing. Over a dozen women trailed in and out of the bathroom at various times, singly and in pairs.

He could hear them talking, even through the closed door. When Moran came up on one of his trips, he told him about it. Moran said it was the same way on second. From his chair in the lobby he could hear them gathering at the head of the stairs, could feel them listening, could see them hanging on the railing when he got up and walked over that way.

"It's a big night in their lives," Moran said unblushingly. "Two men in the house. Give me a whistle down the stairs if you get overpowered."

Bessemer thought he could handle himself. "What do you make of this one?" he asked cautiously. "Were you on it before?"

"I was." Moran lowered his voice. "I was on it, I stood right beside it, I rode to the morgue with the boys. It's an old story to me. Not that I haven't got a heart—I have, big as all outdoors—but I've seen too much in this man's town. I'm giving you the pay-off right there in three little words. This Man's Town. It's no place for a girl alone, a girl alone can't handle herself, a nice girl I mean. Somebody says he loves her, and she finds out too late that he don't—not her way, anyhow. So what? So a big drink of a common household poison, that's what you get in the respectable residential districts. Fancy sleeping pills in the Park Avenue area. Rooming houses, tenements, cheap hotels—nose dive out the window. Like this one here. Open and shut. I saw it right away. So did Foy."

Bessemer objected. "Then why does Foy——"

"Listen. Foy is an old friend of Kloppel's. Kloppel's got the wind up about that girl inside with the broken head. He's not so young any more. So Foy is playing ball for old times' sake. Couple more nights and we'll be through, and thank you very much, officer. Don't complain. Ain't this better than sitting around the station house or picking up drunks?"

The lobby was dim and quiet. Moran dozed with one ear turned to the switchboard. The switchboard was a part of his job, but no one called.

On the second floor, Agnes sat with Miss Plummer,

194

although Miss Plummer tried to say it wasn't necessary. Agnes said she knew it wasn't; she said Miss Plummer looked fine. She said she felt fine herself but for some reason she didn't feel like going to bed. She felt like company, if Miss Plummer didn't mind. And that big chair was as good as a bed any day in case she should get sleepy. And suppose Miss Plummer wanted a drink of water? Well, there she'd be, ready to get it and only too pleased.

Miss Plummer lay with her eyes closed and the blankets up to her chin.

"Miss Mainwaring was out in the hall a while ago," Agnes said. "I happened to be out there myself. It was before I came in here. I went to the top of the stairs to see if that policeman was still in the lobby. . . . You know about the police being here, Miss Plummer?"

Miss Plummer nodded, but she didn't open her eyes.

"She wasn't doing anything, Miss Mainwaring wasn't. Just walking up and down with her hands folded on her breast. It could be that she was praying, she does a good bit of that." Agnes rocked steadily. "She don't belong on this floor. She belongs on fourth."

"Tell my sister," Miss Plummer said.

"I can't go out there again, Miss Plummer! It's way past midnight. I don't like to go down these halls alone, I never did, even before. And I wouldn't go up to seventh for love or money. I'm sorry."

Miss Plummer said nothing, but her hands drew the blankets closer.

"I wouldn't even go back to my own room." Agnes went on. "Two doors away, but I wouldn't go. Clara's in there with her head covered. . . . What does Mrs. Fister think about the policemen?"

"She didn't say."

"Did you know there was one of them outside that door? He's got a camp chair. I don't see why he's there, with Mrs. Fister inside, and April. They ought to move April. She's too young for things like this. But she won't go. I heard Dr. Kloppel try to make her go, but she won't leave Miss Harris. . . . Did you hear something then, Miss Plummer?"

"No, no."

"I thought I did. Like a voice, preaching. Or maybe praying. Up and down, like in a church. It could be Miss Mainwaring. I've heard she sometimes has a vision. She's a holy girl."

Dot Mainwaring crept along the second-floor hall from the elevator to the packroom, hugging the walls. She did that twice, stopping each time to listen at the same door. Someone was coughing inside; Agnes or Clara, she told herself, Agnes or Clara, but I don't know which one. Lying in bed while a soul is in torment, warming her body with sleep. Agnes or Clara, two old women, and I don't know which one.

She made the trip again, stopping at Miss Plummer's door, at Jewel's, at Kitty's. Then she returned to the head of the stairs.

The policeman in the lobby was walking up and down, she could see the top of his head. A dark head with thick black hair. She watched him for a full minute, timing her breathing to his slow, deliberate pace. What will he do if I scream? she wondered. What will he do? The scream was piling up in her throat, strangling, choking. She circled her throat with her hands and knew she could feel the scream growing there. I'm going to have a vision, she told herself, I'm going to see a lady, but I don't know what she'll look like. She'll come from the third floor, down the steps, above the steps, not touching the steps. In blue and white, in white and blue, with one hand beckoning. She'll try to tell me something, and I don't know what it will be. I don't know yet. I'm going to see a lady coming down the stairs and I see her now. She's whispering, whispering, whispering, telling me things. I've got to scream. I've got to tell them what I see. They'll all come running, they'll think I'm dead or dying. They'll take me in their arms and beg and plead, they'll take me in their arms——

She sat on the top step and buried her face in her hands. Be careful, she warned herself, be careful. You're all right now, you're all right. Be quiet and still. Be careful.

Jewel came out of her single room on the second floor and closed the door. She had no definite plan. The room behind her was better than any she had ever owned, but for the past half hour she had taken it apart with her eyes and counted its faults.

It had no extra lamps with pretty shades, no pictures, no pottery bowls; the dark brown scarf on the bureau was the one they had given her when she came. I like nice things, too, she told herself, but I don't know how to pick them out. If I went in a store and paid out my good money, I'd get the wrong thing. I'd get it too dressy or not dressy enough. I wouldn't know. . . . Jewel come here, Jewel go there, Jewel run me up to sixth I'm going to a coffee party, take me down to fifth, wait for whoosis on seventh, take me up to fourth and come right back again. . . . I'd like to know what would happen if I asked any of them to help me make my place look nice. If I asked them what to buy. I could talk myself hoarse, I could be talking to myself. They'd drop dead before they'd help me, they'd give me the big ha-ha. They got to have a laugh and I'm the easiest one.

She heard someone at the front of the hall and moved quietly forward. A girl was huddled on the top step, head on knees, arms limp and trailing. A smile twisted her mouth. Mainwaring, picking the best place for somebody to fall over her. Picking a place where Miss Brady and Miss Small would be certain to see her and say "Come along to bed, dear, and I'll tuck you up and kiss you good night, because you're a fine religious type and we love girls like you." Rats. Ha-ha. Rats.

The smile was still on her face when she touched Dot's shoulder.

Dot raised tearful eyes. "Who—oh Jewel, I'm so frightened!"

"Don't waste that on me," Jewel said. "Go down and try it on the cop." She nudged Dot with her foot, lightly at first and then harder. When she turned to climb the stairs she was humming. Frightened? Rats. Who wasn't in one way or another? She climbed to the fourth floor.

Minnie May's door was unlocked. Minnie May was in bed, alone, and every lamp in the room was lighted. There was a box of candy on the bed and a thermos jug of cocoa on the table. Minnie May had pottery bowls and flowers and a lace bureau scarf. On Dot's side of the room there were more bowls and flowers. Minnie May's negligee was trimmed with pink swansdown, but she was crying.

"Do you care if I come in for a while?" Jewel asked. "Seeing as you're alone."

Minnie May sat up. "Dot walked out on me and she had orders not to leave me by myself." Her voice rose. "That detective said so, but she walked out! She's supposed to watch me and I know what for! She's to watch me on the sly so I can't sneak off and kill somebody else! They're not taking chances. Why don't they put a cop outside my door like Harris?"

"Don't upset yourself," Jewel advised.

"Walked out on me and I know why. So if anybody shows up dead tomorrow, she can run around confessing how it happened. All her fault, all her fault, God have mercy on her poor little soul. Had to go to the bathroom, and Minnie May got out. . . . I wouldn't leave this room if the house burned down."

Jewel sat on the bed. "I'll stay. I'd like to."

"Aren't you afraid? No, you're too dumb. Listen. Down home my grandpa was a good lawyer, so I know what they're doing to me. Making me the goat. They don't know anything else to do, so they're making me the goat. I've seen that happen lots of times down home. If my skin was black I'd be hanging from a tree this minute. . . . Jewel?"

"What?"

"Didn't you see me dancing with Miller? I mean the

second time, around ten. Didn't you know it was Miller and me, Jewel? Didn't they ask you that?"

"Everybody asks me that. I don't know, I can't remember."

"I did, I did! That was the time I had my face on backwards! And it was Miller, I know it! Everybody saw us but nobody says so. Can't remember, can't remember, that's all I get. . . . I don't remember seeing you, either, if it comes to that. But if anybody asked me, I'd say I did. I know how to be a pal."

"Oh, sure you do." Jewel grinned. "What are they going to do to you, did they say?"

"No. No, and that's where they're smart. Why don't they take me to jail? Why don't they lock me up safe? Then I could sue their pants off."

Jewel took a caramel from the box on the bed. It was Schrafft's. Everything Minnie May had was the best. "I guess you didn't have much company tonight," she said pensively.

"Nobody. Only you. Why?"

"I thought I heard them say your door was kept locked. I was surprised it wasn't. I thought they gave that order."

"I don't want it locked. What for?"

"I guess they were afraid somebody might——I don't know."

"Somebody might what? What are you getting at? You mean somebody might come in?"

"Yeah."

"Well what's wrong with that? You're here, aren't you? What's wrong with that?" Minnie May read something in Jewel's eyes. She wasn't sure what it was. It could be one of two things. It could be——

"You don't need to stare at me like that," Jewel said heavily.

They looked carefully away from each other, shifted their bodies slowly, quietly, drew apart. Jewel concentrated on the box of candy and the jug of cocoa.

"Have some cocoa." Minnie May's voice held a tremor. "I'm sorry it's all I've got. There's the candy, too. I don't care for it. You help yourself, take all you want, you're welcome to anything you like."

"Yeah? Thanks."

After a while Minnie May said, "You don't have to stay if you don't want to, Jewel. You must be tired."

"I'm not tired. I'll stay till somebody comes."

Kitty Brice crossed the roof, feeling her way in the dark. She skirted the pile of deck chairs and came to a stop before the wire fence. The mesh was as wide as her hand. She tested its strength with hand and body; it was strong enough to climb on. She left that side of the roof and went to the front, where she leaned over the parapet that faced the street. The street was empty and dark except for the lamps at the corners and the single light by the courtyard gate. It was too late even for Mrs. Cashman and Brother.

She went back to the courtyard side and tested the wire again, gripping the mesh above her head and pulling herself up. For a few seconds she clung there, panting and frowning. When she went downstairs to her room, she was breathing heavily and talking to herself. That cop that went up there, he told the other one he didn't have any luck. No break in the wire, no cigarette butts, no nothing. No signs of a struggle, nothing. I could have told him that myself. I could have told him he was wasting his time. Cops! They make me laugh! . . . But I had to see for myself. I wanted to see.

Miss Brady was sitting cross-legged on the sofa, chain-smoking.

"Look at me," Miss Small said. "Tell me what worries you, and I'll take care of it. I can do that with you, you know. Everybody thinks you're the strong one, but I am. Tell me what worries you."

Miss Brady laughed shortly. "Suppose Lillian dies too?"

"That's morbid, Monny! She's coming along beautifully. Who's been talking to you?"

"Nobody. I'm just thinking again. . . . That cop won't let me in her room."

"He's doing that for your own good, darling. He won't let anybody in. She probably looks dreadful. . . . I feel pretty low myself, it's been a bad night. Too much happening and all of it horrid—that man East, and your little box turning up the way it did, and police tramping all over the place. . . . Monny, you're shivering! Stop it this instant!"

"I wish we were away from here," Miss Brady whispered. "I wish it were all over."

"Soon, soon," Miss Small said softly. "You've done everything you could, Monny, everything. And soon we'll both be free, with no more worries, with nothing but our own lives ahead. Beautiful lives. . . . Monny——"

The night crept on, taking too long to die. Miss Plummer held a lonely wake, watching the window and waiting for the end. When morning came at last, it had a clear white light; snow, soft and clean, dropped gently from a dove-gray sky, the Christmas snow. But it gave her no pleasure.

At eight-thirty Agnes came in, her face twisted in a false, bright smile. She bent over the bed. "The doctor's out in the hall with Miss Brady and the detective. To see you."

"Detective!"

"Hush. He wants to talk to you, it's what we both hoped for, and it's nothing to be afraid of. With the doctor here, it's safe."

"But my sister—Agnes—if my sister——"

"Upstairs all night, having her breakfast now. You know what to do. If you have trouble, if you don't feel free to tell——" The door opened.

"I'll leave you now," Agnes said brightly.

Miss Plummer's eyes found Miss Brady's. Miss Brady looked as if she hadn't slept herself. "Miss Brady," she said, "I'm sick, I really am. I can't really order my thoughts. If I make any mistakes, I hope you'll forgive me." She looked from Miss Brady to the doctor, and then, fearfully, to the detective.

He was smiling down at her, in a nice way, as if he understood how she felt. Almost as if he understood what she wanted to say and knew some of it already. He reminded her of a minister, only ministers never looked like that. It was something in his eyes; it said he knew what the world was like, but he wanted to live in it just the same. East, his name was, East.

"Mr. East," she said, "I want to do my part, but I'll have to ask you to be quick. I haven't got much time." She hoped he wouldn't ask her what she meant, and he didn't.

"I haven't much either," he said gravely. "So suppose we let you decide what you want to tell me. You do want to tell me something, don't you?"

"Yes, sir." She turned heavily in the bed and faced the door. "If you'll stand right here, sir, where I can see you. Mr. East, I have it on my mind that Ruth Miller was murdered."

No one spoke until he said, "Why, Miss Plummer?"

"I have it on my mind, that's all I can say. And I think the one that did it knows how I feel."

"Do you know who did it, Miss Plummer?"

"No." They had left the door open, and the hall was quiet. She could hear the elevator in the distance. If it stopped at her floor, she'd know. "But I am responsible in a way. I sent her to her death."

He sat beside her on the bed. "You say you haven't much time," he said. "Maybe I can guess what you mean. How's this? Nothing will happen to you because you are talking to me. Your job, your life, they'll go on just the same. Miss Brady and Dr. Kloppel are my witnesses. Nothing will happen. Now tell me what you mean when you say you sent Ruth to her death."

She found her hand creeping over the covers to take his. It didn't surprise her when his own closed over hers. Even his next words didn't surprise her.

"It's about the night of the party, isn't it? You sent

Ruth upstairs to get the bandages when the chef was hurt."

Miss Brady said, "Ruth? You sent Ruth?"

She answered painfully. "Yes, Miss Brady. Yes, Mr. East. I know it was Ruth. She spoke to me, I knew her voice, and she said she didn't know where Miss Brady's room——" She stopped and wet her lips.

"Go on, Ethel," Miss Brady said sharply. "What are you stopping for? You sent her to my room. So what? I wasn't there."

"I know," she said humbly. "You were down in the kitchen with Miss Small. I didn't mean anything, Miss Brady, I'm only trying to straighten myself out." She turned to Mark. "Maybe I better start at the beginning, and then you can ask me about the things you don't understand. It was when the chef cut his hand. It was Clara that told us. Clara thought he was dying but Miss Small said more likely he was drunk but we should call the doctor to be on the safe side. In case he tried to sue. And if the doctor wasn't in, to send one of the girls upstairs for iodine and bandages. And she said she'd go down to the kitchen and see for herself. Then Miss Brady came over and said she'd go down, too, and I wasn't to worry. And I didn't worry, not then. But I couldn't get the doctor, we'd forgotten it was his club night, and that upset me. So I tried to find a girl who'd go upstairs for the bandages and I had a dreadful time."

He nodded. "You had trouble finding a girl, didn't you?"

He knew, he understood. "Yes, sir. You wouldn't believe the trouble I had. Nobody wanted to go, and for all I knew the poor man could be dying. I'd just about given up when I got hold of Ruth. She spoke to me, she answered me. I know it was her. And even if I hadn't known for certain, I'd have guessed. Because she walked up. She was the only one who did that. She was afraid of the automatic elevator."

The elevator. She could hear it running now. It had been quiet for perhaps a minute, but now it was running again. She could see the shaft in her mind, see the way it looked from the inside when you were a passenger. She could count the whitewashed bricks that showed through the grille. Not many bricks between the first and second floors. . . . Mr. East put his other hand over hers.

"What time was that, Miss Plummer? Between eight and eight-thirty, wasn't it?"

"Nearer eight-thirty."

"She didn't come back?"

The elevator was stopping. She heard the big metal door slide back with a muffled clang. She couldn't hear the little safety door, but she could see it in her mind, folding into itself without a sound. She had less than a minute. "I never saw her again, never, never. Somebody brought me the iodine and bandages, but I don't know who, I don't, I don't. I found them on the desk a long time later, but I didn't see who put them there. She didn't, I know that, she didn't. I never saw her again. She was dead. Murdered."

Footsteps, coming down the hall, coming to the door. She closed her eyes and waited.

Dr. Kloppel was the first to speak, and his voice was mild and natural. "Good morning," he said. "It looks like a white Christmas, doesn't it? You know Mr. East? Mr. East, Mrs. Fister."

Ella didn't answer. She heard Mr. East say, "How do you do, Mrs. Fister. I wonder if you'll get me a glass of water?" She heard the rattle of the glass in the coaster as he took it from the bed table, heard Ella's heavy tread crossing the room, going back to the door, going down the hall without a word. Heard Miss Brady say, "I'm leaving, you don't need me now."

When she was sure they were alone, she put out her hand, blindly. "Agnes," she whispered. "Agnes. Room 206. Talk to Agnes, she knows."

Ella returned, still silent, but she couldn't mistake that tread.

Mr. East said, "Mrs. Fister, the doctor and I think Miss Plummer needs complete rest and quiet. No callers. Not even you, although that may sound harsh.

It might be a good idea to lock the door and give us the key. We'll be dropping in again before we go. After we see Agnes and Miss Harris."

Ella said, "I'll go along with you. It's customary."

Mr. East said, "Thank you, but this is police work."

The key turned in the lock and Miss Plummer was alone. She opened her eyes then. There was nothing she could do. She watched the snow.

Agnes was expecting them. Mark knew that before they reached her door. He had stopped at the hall telephone to call Foy's man on the seventh floor. A new man, Jones, had relieved Bessemer. He told Jones that no one was to enter Miss Harris's room and added that "no one" meant anything in human form regardless of how it dressed and talked. When he turned from the phone he saw the door of 206 standing open. Agnes was waiting.

She nodded to Dr. Kloppel and quietly took Mark's measure. He took hers. What he saw was a thin, bent woman with deep lines around her eyes and mouth. They looked like laughter lines of long standing, the kind that begin at the age of one and deepen through the years. He imagined the last few days had given them little to do.

"Well, Agnes?" he said.

"Come in, sir. You too, doctor. . . . So she lost her nerve." She closed the door.

"Was that it?" Mark asked.

"Yes, sir. It's no good in me trying to explain, it has to do with too many things. And aside from that, nobody likes to be the one to point the finger. But I've always been a bold piece. I want to talk. And since you were the one to bring this thing to light, I want to talk to you. Foy had his chance, and what did he do? . . . Are you in as big a hurry as I am?"

"Yes. I want to see Lillian Harris as soon as possible."

Something like affection showed in her eyes. "You're a cute one. Now you come over here, both of you." She led them to her bureau. "This is what Miss Plummer wanted to tell you. One of the things." She gave him the costume, neatly folded. "Shake it out, show it to the doctor. He knows what it is, he's seen one like it before."

He felt as if he had seen one, too, even seen the one he held in his hand. He knew the fringed lashes, the yellow curls, the twisted, pouting lips; the long, full sleeves, the clumsy skirt that would almost touch the floor. He folded the mask and put it in his pocket with a casual air, because he also knew the small, brown mole.

"I've been wondering what happened to the costumes," he said.

"Locked up in the linen closet. The very next day. Every girl who wore one turned it in and was checked off. All except the one that was burned. You know which one. . . . I'd like to call your attention to that hem."

"You don't have to. I saw it."

She sat down abruptly. "I'm so relieved I could scream," she said. She was almost crying. "Mr. East, we've had a terrible time here and a terrible night that's just passed. We can't have another. If we do, I don't know what may happen to—to one of us."

"To any one of you in particular, Agnes?"

"Maybe Miss Harris, I don't know. Maybe—that's what's killing us by inches! We don't know, we can't be sure. There isn't a single one I'd trust, not one. Everybody has a look, an awful look. You walk down the halls at night, and you meet somebody who turns away. Somebody you've known and respected for years. Maybe she's scared too, but maybe she's—the one!"

He gave the costume to Dr. Kloppel. "Can you get this out of the house for me?"

Dr. Kloppel hesitated. "Foy?"

"Foy had his chance," Agnes said. "You can bring it back when you've done with it, and I can find it all over again. For Foy."

Dr. Kloppel opened his large, old-fashioned bag and turned his back. Then, "Nobody saw me do that," he said. "Where did you find it in the first place, Agnes?"

She told them, with curiously few digressions and

none of the odd hazards that usually beset her class. Her heart kept out of her throat, her hair stayed flat on her head, and she was not laid low by a feather. "And what's more, I know who it belonged to, I figured it out. I know why it wasn't missed."

It had been handed out to Miss Edith Campbell, she said, a third-floor single. Put on her bed the same as the rest, the morning of the party. But Miss Campbell's father had been taken sick and she'd been sent for, so she'd gone across the river to Bogota that afternoon. Not many knew she'd gone, she was a quiet girl that kept to herself. But somebody knew, and knew she wouldn't be back until the next day, if then. And her room was unlocked. Easy enough to steal Miss Campbell's costume, easy enough to change from one to another in case of blood. Easy enough to lock yourself in a bathroom. "Maybe the second-floor bathroom," Agnes elaborated, "then hide the extra one in the packroom, where it wouldn't be found till spring, and walk down one flight as calm as you please."

She paused, but it was clearly for breath, not other people's conversation. "And there's something else, too. I talked it over with Miss Plummer last night, and we fixed the time. The time is right. It fits."

The something else was a summing up of Miss Plummer's story, with two additions. The first was that Agnes had taken Mrs. Marshall-Gill a cup of punch, and shortly after that she'd seen Mrs. Marshall-Gill enter the elevator. In answer to his question, she swore by the calendar of saints that Jewel had operated the car. She said there was something about Jewel that you couldn't mistake; it was the way she held herself—slouched, like. But between taking the punch to Mrs. Marshall-Gill and seeing her go upstairs, she'd noticed something queer.

She was watching the rag dollies having their fun, over by the desk, and she'd laughed to see them. That is, she'd laughed until she saw how mean they acted when Miss Plummer begged for someone to run her errand. Nasty girls, every one, ungrateful as they come, shaking their heads and cackling like geese. She'd tried to guess which ones they were, because she meant to give them what-for in the morning. And that was when she'd seen the peculiar one.

"Peculiar?" Mark repeated.

"Not in looks," Agnes said, "unless you count bunchiness. Peculiar in actions. She was kind of following one rag dolly around, I saw her. She was like somebody rounding up a stray sheep—herding, like. I couldn't take my eyes off her. She got the other dolly up to the desk, right under Miss Plummer's nose, as slick as you please. Almost threw her, she did. Just like she'd been planning all along. Then she went away herself, mingled, and there was no telling her from the others. I looked to see where she went, and that's how I saw Mrs. Marshall-Gill get in the elevator. But when I turned back to my punch bowl I noticed a dolly on the stair landing, going up. It looked like her, the bunchy one."

He kept the excitement out of his voice. "The other doll, the one she pushed, that one was Ruth Miller, wasn't it?"

"I said you were a cute one," Agnes agreed soberly.

She followed them to the door when they left, her eyes on Dr. Kloppel's bag. "That's the one he brings the babies in," she said crossly and absently. "And I'll thank him to forget my niece's address."

When they had started down the hall, they heard her speak again. She sounded as if she were whispering behind a cupped hand. She said, "Be careful."

They continued in silence until they reached the elevator and the stairs. "We'll walk," Mark said briefly. They started up.

"I'd like to talk to you about that mask," Dr. Kloppel said.

"Not now," Mark said. He set the pace, moving slowly, frequently looking back. When they came to the fourth-floor landing he leaned over the railing. The empty flights curved steeply down between cream walls and wrought-iron balustrade, broken at intervals by small, bare landings, ending in a patch of red that was the lobby carpet. He looked up into the same monotonous pattern of stair and railing, ending in an iron door. The roof.

On the next landing he flattened himself against the far wall. "Go up to the sixth," he said, "lean over the railing and look down. See how much of me is visible. Assuming, of course, that I have the protective coloration of unbleached muslin."

The result was what he expected. "I can see you," Dr. Kloppel said, "because I know you're there and because your clothes are dark. Otherwise, no." He added, "She had poor vision, too. Even if she did look back, the peculiar dolly would blend with the walls."

"Yes. That's the way it was. I can see it too well, and I wish I couldn't. The Miller girl, on what might be called an errand of mercy and was certainly one of courtesy, climbing straight to her destruction. The other one behind her, keeping out of sight and moving up, up, up. . . . This place is too quiet, isn't it?"

"All at work. They'll be home shortly after noon, most of them. Saturday half holiday. . . . Can you explain Minnie May's story?"

"That's the mask story. Later."

"Motive?"

"So-so. I can guess a few things about the private life of the girl we're looking for, but guessing gets me nowhere. I need facts, and there aren't any. I can't pick her out of the crowd unless she panics and pulls a sloppy job, and she probably won't. I could use a miracle, a little sign-pointing by what I'm sure Agnes would call the Hand of Heaven."

They came to the door of the room that had once been Ruth Miller's. Jones was glad to see them. He had come on duty at seven, he said, and there was no one inside but the sick girl and the blind girl who was taking care of her. The blind girl had put a breakfast tray in the hall and said good morning as plain as you please. His outraged voice denied the blind all right to the power of speech.

"Foy been here?" Mark asked.

"He telephoned, sir. You're to have access."

"Thanks."

The door opened before they knocked. April turned her head from one to the other, accurately. "Dr. Kloppel," she said. "And Mr. East. Come in."

Dr. Kloppel said, "You look all right, April, but I'd feel better if you were somewhere else."

"Oh, no," she answered quickly. "This is where I belong. Even my boss said so. He said I was to stay with Lillian, he knows I've had experience." She turned to Mark. "Two of my family were killed, so I'm not afraid of anything. And Lillian would rather have me than Mrs. Fister." She crossed the room and sat on her own bed and the high, sweet voice went on. "Lillian's better today, Dr. Kloppel. I think she's better."

Dr. Kloppel saturated a wad of cotton. "Well, we mustn't hope for too much." He frowned at the quiet figure on the other bed before he touched the cotton gently to the closed eyes.

"What are you doing, Dr. Kloppel?"

"Bathing her face, that's all. With something nice and cool."

"I've done that," April said. "I've done it with cold water." She looked as if she were listening. "Dr. Kloppel, is the other one really Mr. East? You didn't tell me, and he hasn't said anything."

Mark answered. "We haven't any manners, April. Of course I'm Mr. East. I wish you'd tell me if there's anything I can do for you, anything I can get."

Relief flooded her face. "No, thank you. Kitty told me about you. She said not to worry about you."

"Had you worried?"

"A little."

"What about now?"

"No, not now." She bent over the other bed and put her own face beside the one on the pillow. She whispered, "It's all right, Lillian, it's all right." A small laugh bubbled in her throat. "Scare the doctor, Lillian, scare him like you did me last night."

Lillian opened her eyes and gave them a fugitive

smile. Dr. Kloppel's quick intake of breath made April laugh again.

The doctor's capable old hands moved at once to the girl's temples and wrist as if he trusted only what he could touch and count. Mark watched. There was a bruise under the bandage, ugly, swelling.

"If you can talk," he said softly, "I'd like to hear what you have to say. . . . How long have you been conscious?"

"Since last night. Late last night."

"Anybody know?"

Her smile was wry and painful. "Am I crazy? No. Not even Fister. . . . I've been wondering when you'd get around to me, I've been ready for days. Since the day your ad was in the paper. I called you up then, but you were away."

"Do you know anything about that doctor?"

"No, it wasn't that. I don't know anything about that. I only wanted to talk to you."

"What about?"

"After Ruth Miller died, some of the kids began to act funny, and I thought it would be smart to find out why. They didn't tell me anything, I don't think they knew anything, but they had the creeps. So did I. So when you came into the picture I thought I'd better get my story in as soon as possible."

He nodded. "Right. Let's get on with it."

There was no time for sympathy, sympathy ate minutes. No time for coddling in the traditional bedside manner, no time for anything but give and take. Kloppel's frown said plainly that he didn't approve, but Kloppel didn't know about time. He and Miss Plummer knew about it, and perhaps they were the only ones who did, he and Miss Plummer and one other. It was too soon to tell about Lillian Harris. But he forced himself to slow down, for Kloppel's sake. "Tell it your way," he said.

Her eyes clouded. "I thought I heard music last night. I was still groggy but I thought I heard a music box. And if I did——"

"You heard it. I was out in the hall, outside this door. I found the box, and I know what it was used for. Does that fit in with what you know?"

"It fits something," she said. "You know she was murdered, don't you?"

"Do you know?"

"Maybe we'd better get together. Blow by blow description. . . . I was working on a night job when they had the party and I took time off. But the party was too young for me, so I went up to my room for a cigarette. You can check with Jewel, she took me up and I think she knew who I was. I lived on sixth then, in the room under this one. When I got there I wrote some letters and had a smoke. But I turned out my light for that and sat on the window ledge with the window open. That was when I heard the music the first time. I knew it was a box of some kind, but I didn't know whose. And everybody was supposed to be having fun downstairs. It didn't make sense. I got curious. So I leaned out and looked up and down, trying to place it. I placed it right off. There was an open window above mine, on the eighth floor. Miss Brady's bedroom. There was a light on, too—dim, but on. That was one for the book. Light, music, open window, and Miss Brady was supposed to be——"

"Wait. Where are the medical supplies kept? First aid and all that?"

"Two places. Fister's on second and Brady's."

"Good. Did you see Miss Plummer send a girl up for supplies?"

"I didn't see it happen, but she was trying to rope one in when I left." Her eyes narrowed. "Say, is that how?"

"Wait. Another question, this time on the foolish side. When you were looking out of your window did you see a white cat in the courtyard?"

She answered evenly. "Not so foolish. He was on the fence. I'd never noticed him before, but he comes every night now."

"He's curious, too."

They both laughed, each looking straight at the other, each waiting for the other to stop first. It was as if the white cat had given them a sudden release and timed the duration. When they spoke again, even April knew they had left one road and were starting down another. Their voices were the same, but she burrowed into the pillows of her own bed, putting space between herself and them. Dr. Kloppel, because he could see as well as hear, leaned forward.

"All right so far," Mark said. "Go on."

"Where was I? Brady's room. Music."

"Brady's room," he repeated.

"And Brady at the party—or else. . . . I decided to have a look, so I went out to the stairs and walked up. The fire door on the eighth was propped open, and I could see to the end of the hall. A girl was backing out of Brady's room and locking it. There was an open door right beside me, so I ducked in and closed it part way. It was dark in there, I could watch her without being seen. She came up the hall, walking fast and not making a sound. She was wearing sneakers." She waited for his reaction.

"Anything familiar about her? Posture, anything?"

"No. Except that she didn't look—right. She was the same as all of us, same dress, same mask, but there was something else. She didn't look—right. Then I heard the elevator ringing and remembered that I'd heard it before, when I was walking up. The girl was hearing it, too, and she muttered something and moved faster, almost ran. I thought she was a thief and I was afraid she'd get away. She'd passed the room where I was so I stepped out and started after her. But the minute I did that, I knew it was a boner. She heard me and turned her head. She stopped where she was, turned her head and looked straight through me, straight through the costume, down to me, inside. She didn't say a word, she held her head on one side as if she were taking me apart, memorizing me, making sure she'd know me again. I ducked back and closed the door and waited to die. There was something terrible about that look, it came through her mask and mine, and I knew her eyes were telling me she'd kill me then and there if she only dared. So I stayed where I was, with the door locked, until she had time to get away. Then I went down to my own room and locked myself in there, too. I didn't go near the window again, I wish I had. . . . I might have been in time."

He walked to the window and looked out. The snow had covered the courtyard and was beginning to ridge the fence. There was nothing on that clean white surface, not even the four small prints of an animal. He went back to the bed, whistling under his breath. "No," he said. "That night or the next, it would have been the same. That night or the next or the one before. No one would have been in time." He said it again, to himself, before he went on. "Did you go back to the party?"

"Not for a long time. I was afraid. I was afraid to show up in that costume. I thought there might be something about it that marked me from the others, something in the way I looked that was different and would give me away. So I stayed in my room until I knew they'd unmasked and then I went down wearing my regular clothes. No sneakers on anybody, of course. I looked. Everybody happy and having fun. No cracks about the way I was dressed. Not a single person asked me where I'd been or gave me a funny look. Nobody tried to keep out of my way. That's all. . . . Except that she knew who I was, all right." She touched her head with cautious fingers and winced. "She waited a long time, but she finally landed."

"Are you too tired to tell me about that?"

"There's nothing to tell. I don't know what happened. I was having a shower, late, and somebody turned the light off. I thought it was April, acting up, so I said, 'Cut it out, kid'. . . I didn't hear her that time either, I guess she wore the sneakers again, but I know that's who it was. Something hit me on the side of the head and the next thing I knew I was in this bed. When I heard the music I thought I was dreaming, and then I heard Fister and April talking. That's how I knew

I'd been out for some time. So I stayed out until Fister went down for some food and then I told April I was all right."

"Who would know you were in the shower?"

"Nobody, unless I was being watched. I'm sure I was being watched. I went all over the house that night, just as I'd been doing every night, sticking my neck out, asking dumb questions that wouldn't sound dumb to the right person. I even carried the paper with your ad. I wanted to smoke her out, I thought I could spot her. I didn't. But she knew me, all right. I worried her, I was getting too close, and she decided she'd had enough. I know she meant to kill me, and I think she thought she had. Or maybe somebody came down the hall and she had to run before she could check. And maybe she was afraid to come back because she didn't belong on that floor and couldn't think of a good lie in case she was seen. I've been wondering why she picked that night in particular and I think it was because you were away. She knew you were suspicious, but you were away. She felt safe. . . . Could that be it?"

"How would she know I was away? It wasn't public knowledge. Ever think of that?"

"No, but I'm thinking now. I didn't tell a soul. I called you from April's drugstore and the place was practically empty. I mean the only people there were strangers."

He got up. "See how confusing it is? We'll forget it for a while and go on to something you can be sure about. This is the old routine, everybody's had it but you. Did you know Ruth Miller before she came here?"

"No."

"Did you see her at the party or talk to her?"

"No."

"But you did see her come in that first night?"

"Yes. I was in the lobby then."

"How did she look?"

"All right at first. Then—not so good."

"What does that mean? Ill at ease? Sick? Frightened?"

"Frightened."

"April?"

April sat up, hugging a pillow and looking as if she wanted to hide.

"April, can you add to Lillian's story or change it in any way?"

"Oh, no, sir!"

10

Bessy and Beulah began the day at six o'clock with a call for lemon juice in hot water. They bathed, dressed, and toyed with breakfast. They studied the weather reports and tested the staying power of the snow by raising the windows and letting it into the house. At nine they embarked, disdaining advice and all offers of assistance.

They would find Ruth Miller's suit in fifteen minutes, they said; and after that they'd shop all day. No, they did not want a box lunch, a suggestion that came out of the corner of Roberta's mouth; they did not want name tags pinned to their coat sleeves by Nick. They did not want the company of Mrs. Hawks who followed them to the elevator explaining that she had time on her hands, that she knew the proposed itinerary like the palms of the same, and that this was not her first experience with sudden death. Some years before, she told them, when traveling in the Balkans with the ducal family, she had crossed a public square ten minutes before an assassination failed to come off. They left Mrs. Hawks looking snubbed, which was a good omen for the day.

They taxied to Blackman's, dismissed the cab, and struck out in opposite directions. They had put half a block between them before they discovered the error. Then arm in arm, and somewhat shaken, they went down the adjacent crosstown street.

It was obviously the wrong one. There were no cleaners. The windows were filled with boxes of feathers, artificial flowers, and bolts of ribbon and straw braid. But they were pretty windows, so the time wasn't wasted. After that they returned to Fifth Avenue and took the next street. Boxes of buttons, bolts of tape and binding, buckles, zippers, hooks and eyes. Not pretty, but interesting because of the quantity.

It was ten-thirty when they finally found a block that looked promising. They didn't know it, but Hope House was less than five minutes away. Several nights before, Beulah had limped and shivered along that same shabby stretch of houses and small shops, but the daylight and falling snow had changed its face.

A very young child, with an accent and a diverting scab between nose and lip, recommended a cleaner and dyer named Tom. He also recommended Tom as a grandfather and said he was a nice man. He led them to a shop a few doors away.

Tom and his grandson were an affectionate pair, alike in feature, speech, and temporary blemish. Yes, Tom said, he had Miss Miller's suit and they were welcome. Hanging in the back room for a long time, under a sheet, and he was making ready to ask if anybody knew where the lady was.

Beulah told him the lady was sick. He said he wasn't surprised. She was a sickly looking lady, and he was making ready to wonder what had happened to her. He brought out the suit and held it up, shaking his head. In spite of cleaning and pressing and only a few hours' wear, it had begun to sag and fall into twisted folds.

"Botch tailoring," he said sadly.

"Did Miss Miller say anything to you about not feeling well?" Beulah asked.

No, he said, but it was written on her. Her hands had no strength to them, she was always dropping everything on the floor. She was always looking into the street while talking and turning her head if somebody went by, and no color in her face and no flesh on her bones. A fever, he thought.

Beulah said he was right. Miss Miller had a kind of fever and she'd gone away.

To the country, Tom hoped. She had a suitcase, she carried the suit in it. She liked the suit good, you could see in the way she gave it to him. It was a botch, it was trash, but who was he to say so? And she wanted he should keep it for a couple weeks, until she came back. And she paid in advance so he would know for sure that she was coming, and he was to keep it safe away from the dust. He was to take care.

"Paid?" Beulah's voice cracked. She repaired it with a long, loud cough. "She forgot to tell me she paid. I wish she——wrap it up, will you? And many thanks."

There was a slip of paper pinned to one curling lapel, a crumpled slip with a line of penciled figures. Tom's hieroglyphics, she thought. A bulge of currency in the sweater pocket of Tom's grandson completed the business, and she went out into the snowy street followed by a silent Bessy.

"Don't talk to me," she snapped. "I don't feel like it."

"Neither do I," Bessy said.

The mask, the costume, and the music box were on Dr. Kloppel's table. Mark pointed to the mole. "So," he said, "that's the key. If that isn't Ruth Miller's mask, it's a copy."

"Copy?"

"The girl who killed Ruth needed a mask with a mole. She needed to show her ugly, hidden self to the public and give the impression that Ruth still walked the earth. She had the mask she swiped from Miss Campbell's room, but it was what you might call unadorned. So she removed Ruth's mask and substituted Miss Campbell's, or she marked Miss Campbell's to look like Ruth's. This mask rode down in the elevator with Mrs. Marshall-Gill when Ruth was dead. It danced with Minnie May, too, unless Minnie May is lying."

"But Mr. East! If she took the original away from the poor girl, it would be——I mean it wasn't a very neat——"

"Listen. If this is the original, it isn't stained because she got hold of it first. Get me, first. And that would be easy, too easy. Ruth Miller at bay, like a little cottontail facing a man with a gun. No trick at all. Simply snatch it, do the grisly job, substitute the other when she was half-conscious. Go on downstairs and parade around. A beautiful alibi, for self and victim. I don't know why I haven't heard it. Why hasn't somebody given me a wide-eyed stare and said, 'Oh, I'm sure I saw her, Mr. East. I'm sure I saw her at nine-thirty or ten. The mole, you know. I think I even called so-and-so's attention to her.' Why hasn't somebody given me that?"

"Maybe because it wasn't needed. You've got a smart girl there. She wouldn't overdo it, she'd wait until you pressed her and then she'd try to remember. If you didn't press her, she'd keep her mouth shut. Very wise."

"Yes. . . . And now I'm beginning to worry about the staff. Maids and Fister."

Dr. Kloppel said, "Ridiculous. Impossible."

"Why?" Mark asked. "Sell it to me and then I can throw it away."

"I'll sell it to myself at the same time." The doctor stroked the leaves of his rubber plant as if it were the only reliable thing in the world. "First, Mrs. Fister. She's too big for those costumes. Forget Mrs. Fister. Second, the maids you haven't seen are Clara, Pauline, and Mollie. They've been with the place since it opened, and they all have some connection with somebody, like being cousin to a cook who works for one of the Board. The chef and his helpers, two neighborhood women, never show themselves abovestairs; I doubt if they know one girl from another. And you can forget the Miller girl's rooming house, too, in case your thoughts are turning in that direction. Foy covered it and found nothing. . . . Foy called me up this morning and told me about his Hope House interviews. He sounded like monastery material."

"Let that plant alone. You'll have the leaves off. . . . There weren't any scratches on the window sill in Ruth Miller's room, either."

"You're backtracking on something you already know," the doctor complained. "Ruth Miller went out of Miss Brady's window, Lillian Harris says so."

"She doesn't say so, she suggests it. She puts a light

in Brady's room and a suspicious, not to say evil, character in Brady's doorway and hall. Plummer puts Ruth Miller on the second floor and possibly the eighth at approximately the same time. I admit it fits. . . . I used to wonder why Ruth Miller wasn't missed. I don't now. She was new and friendless, but Lillian Harris was neither; and Harris disappeared for nearly two hours without causing a ripple. Even when her disappearance coincided with a murder, even when the cops took over, did anybody squeal?"

"You mustn't forget it was pretty hard to tell those girls apart."

"I'm beginning to think it wasn't as hard as they say. Didn't Miss Mainwaring win a prize for spotting her heavily disguised playmates? Now why didn't I think of that before? How many did she guess and who were they? Do you know?"

"I do not. Maybe somebody over there can help you."

"Hah! I can see that! No, I'll go up to Blackman's and talk to Moke and Poke. I want them to look the mask over, too. They ought to be able to identify their own sewing. . . . This much we've got to believe. Lillian Harris was upstairs when Ruth Miller was. She saw the cat and she heard the music, and she couldn't have made that up. The cat saw the body leave the window and heard the music, too. I know he did. He gave me an unmistakable playback. So that being as certain as anything can be, we'd better concede that Lillian Harris met the murderer in the eighth-floor hall."

They were both quiet then, each of them seeing what the cat saw, what Lillian Harris saw, what the other, nameless one saw and was probably still seeing late at night when the hours went by too slowly.

Dr. Kloppel, one arm relaxed on the table, his eyes on the falling snow beyond his windows, absently raised the lid of the music box. *Thou wouldst still be adored as this moment thou art,* the box sang sweetly. They flung themselves forward and closed it.

Dr. Kloppel fumbled for a cigarette, broke it, and found another.

"All that stuff goes to Foy this afternoon," Mark said too casually. "I'll take it down there after I see the kids at Blackman's." He turned and twisted in his chair and went on with a sudden, repressed fury. "Somebody lied to me! Not a good, big lie that I could see coming a mile away, but a mousey little stinker that merged with the landscape. Some smart girl fed me a smooth little whopper that got by because it was the natural, normal thing for her to say. Such as, 'I went into the lounge to see if the fire needed more wood.' That's the kind of thing I mean, that's what a woman like Plummer could give me if she wanted to hide her actual whereabouts, and I'd swallow it whole. She might have been walling up a body in the cellar, but I'd have a picture of the old girl messing up the wood basket, because that's her type. That's how I've been reasoning, and that's where I've gone wrong. I've put too much time on the outstanding deviations from routine when what I really want is the small piece of extraneous matter that some bright girl slipped into the machinery. It's so small and so simple that I don't know what it is or who did it. But somebody looked me straight in the eye, folded her hands in her lap, and told me she was breathing, Mr. East, just breathing. And she's my girl."

"Getting mad now, aren't you?" Dr. Kloppel said with satisfaction. "In people like you it's a good sign. . . . Some of those girls gave pretty detailed accounts of themselves, didn't they?"

"Some. Miss Kitty Brice gave me absolutely nothing and made no bones about it, and Miss Mainwaring, self-appointed handmaiden to the Lord, also gave nothing, but with flourishes. Jewel, not much; Minnie May and Harris, a lot. But excessive detail isn't necessarily false, if that's what you mean. Innocent people often stampede themselves into remembering. . . . I've wasted too much time trying to prove somebody was upstairs when she said she wasn't. I've got to prove somebody wasn't downstairs when she said she was."

Dr. Kloppel said, "Upstairs, downstairs, wasn't, was. You need a drink." He went to a bookcase with opaque glass doors and selected a bottle. "No ice, it dilutes. And don't look at the clock. I know what time it is, but I've got those things in my stomach that young ladies call butterflies." The scotch gurgled into two scrolled and posied shaving mugs marked SON and PAPA. "Papa's was his," Dr. Kloppel said gently. "Many's the time I've stood on a hassock and watched that man throw the soap around and sing 'Bright Her Smiles.'" He pushed SON across the table and kept PAPA for himself. "Do you feel as bad as I do?"

"Worse. I got into this when it was cold, and I wasn't convinced, either. I didn't see how Brady and Small could make a mistake. Girls are their business, I figured they knew what they were talking about. But so help me, I did have a queasy feeling."

"You're entitled to the queasy feeling, but no more. You've been on this case less than a week and look what you've done. Then look at Foy."

"I haven't got time to look at Foy. I haven't got time to take those girls aside one by one and beat a life story out of each and double check. That would do it. And Foy hasn't got the time, either. Foy and I ought to take turns at twenty-four-hour duty in that place, but if we do, I'm afraid we'll be opening another window. If you get what I mean. . . . I don't like my girl."

"Do you mind telling a practically superannuated stork just how much you know about your girl?"

"My girl is the kind who couldn't take it when she was five years old and some other kid in the block was prettier than she was. When she was ten, she couldn't take it when some other kid got better marks in school or had more spending money. She can't take anything now, anything that makes her feel inferior, imposed upon, or gets in her way. Anybody who does that, even unconsciously, is asking to be a dead duck. My girl will gamble on the impossible and bring it off, because she runs around with people who've been taught that nice girls don't do bad things. Nice girls do anything and

223

everything, as your stork trade must have taught you. My girl gambled on Ruth Miller. Ruth Miller was a threat, still unclassified, but a threat just the same. So out she went. And for several weeks it looked like success. Then I came in, then Foy came back. That must have burned her up, but it hasn't finished her, not by a long shot. Look at Lillian Harris. One of these nights I'm going to wake up screaming because my girl is walking in my sleep. Walking and talking, telling me that if she's caught she'll blow the place up and herself with it. She's capable of it, too. If she can't have what she wants, then nobody else can. Life is cheap. See?"

Dr. Kloppel shuddered. "I hope your trouble is an overactive thyroid."

"Yah! You know what I'd do if I could? I can't, of course, but this is it and it would work. I'd hire me a nice, brave girl from a theatrical agency, dress her in this costume, take her over to Hope House at three A.M., and send her up and down those halls with a faint obbligato of powder-box music."

The doorbell rang, a series of sharp, clear rings. He jumped. Dr. Kloppel gave him a disapproving look and went to answer it, mumbling to himself. When he returned he had Bessy and Beulah.

"I thought I told you to phone," Mark said coldly.

"Wait," Beulah advised. She advanced to the table, holding a paper garment bag at arm's length. At the sight of the smiling mask, she dropped the bag. "Is that what they wore?" she quavered.

"You sound like me," Bessy said happily. "It's ugly, isn't it? Pretty, but ugly. Think of a whole houseful, running up- and downstairs, peeping at you out of doors. . . . I wish I hadn't thought of that."

Mark said, "Amen. Dr. Kloppel, these are my friends. And I suppose this bag holds the suit?" He drew it out, carefully.

Dr. Kloppel carried the mugs over to the bookcase. He refilled them with his back to the room and added two glasses of sherry to the tray.

"Oh, thank you," Bessy said before he turned around.

"We didn't phone," Beulah said, "because the place was near Hope House where I said it would be all along. So we simply came. Tom the Cleaner and Dyer. A European peasant of some sort, and a grandson with the same accent and so on. We had no trouble at all. I get along with peasants."

"What's this?" He fingered the slip of paper pinned to the lapel. It was an oblong of pale pink with a serrated edge, and had obviously been torn from a pad. It was familiar in an indeterminate way, and he decided he had seen something like it on Roberta's desk. Fancy business for the peasant. America the Beautiful. He frowned at the penciled scrawl. The peasant's code for Ruth Miller, electric blue, two piece. Wiggle, wiggle, 2 dash 8277. He hung the suit on the back of a chair. "So that's that. Anything in the pockets?"

"What do you think I am!"

"You heard me. Anything in the pockets?"

"No. . . . Tom says it was written on her that she was sick. I told him she was, it seemed the nicest thing to say with a child present. I knew at once that he didn't read newspapers or listen to gossip. And I don't think he does much work for Hope House. The clothes in the shop had a hard-working-housewife look. So when he didn't say anything, I knew he didn't know anything."

"Too bad. Didn't he ask for a claim check?"

"No. He's very unsophisticated. She was carrying a suitcase and she didn't give him an address. She said she was going away."

"Going away. She meant running away. . . . No, she wouldn't give an address. Anything else?"

"Her hands shook, she dropped things on the floor, and she kept looking back at the street. He thought she had a fever. Mark, she paid for it in advance. She said she might not be able to call for it for a long time and asked him to take good care of it."

He lowered his face to the mug and drank slowly. "Good work," he said. "Finish your sherry and get along home. That's a nice job you did."

"What are you going to do with the suit now that you've got it?"

"Look at it. I don't know. Just look at it. Maybe it will say something to me."

Bessy put her empty glass on the table with a reluctant sigh that got her nothing. When she realized that, she became crisp. "Why don't we go, Beulah? We have shopping to do."

"In this weather?" Mark asked. "You're crazy. Go home and sit by the fire. I'll see you later." He took them to the front door, saw them flounder against the wind, and closed his eyes and the door simultaneously. "Together," he said to the doctor, "they have about ten thousand a year and nobody to spend it on, but they'll walk to the shopping center because gentlemen will pity them and offer strong arms. I'm going down to Foy's." He made a bundle of Ruth Miller's relics, all but one. "I'll leave the suit here," he said. "Bad weather out."

"Following instructions?" Dr. Kloppel observed softly. "Taking care?"

Mark slammed the door and walked toward Hope House because he felt like looking at it. The snow was thick on the sidewalk, and his footsteps made no more sound than sneakers on a concrete floor. He plodded steadily around the corner and turned. A truck was drawn up before the neat, brick building and two men were unloading Christmas greens. A tall spruce, branches of hemlock, two wooden crates of holly.

The front door opened and a figure appeared on the top step. He slowed down, although it wasn't necessary. She didn't look in his direction, she was telling the men with large gestures that their entrance was through the courtyard gate. It was Kitty Brice, and even from a distance he could see that she looked ill. Her face was gray-blue and she stood as if she were bent under a burden.

Joy to the world, he quoted to himself. Peace on earth, good will to men. Make way for the cops who've got to kill a girl they don't know because that's what she did to a girl they don't know either.

He found a cab and rode up to Blackman's, where he used the employees' entrance. In a few minutes he was in the toilet-goods stockroom.

Moke and Poke said the mask was Ruth's. They knew it at once. When they had finished making the mole, they'd knotted the thread on the wrong side because they didn't have scissors; no girl in her right mind ruins her teeth biting thread. They showed him the knot. Even if somebody had copied it, it wouldn't have that kind of knot. It was theirs, and hers.

He returned it to his bundle while they stood stiffly at attention, their eyes round with curiosity. But they didn't speak until they were spoken to.

"By the way," he said, "what about that prize for guessing? How many names did you get?"

Moke said she got seventeen, and Poke got twenty-nine because she was studious.

"And Miss Mainwaring, the winner?"

"She got thirty-four. She's a one!"

"She certainly is. But so are you; I don't know how you did it. People keep telling me that everybody was unrecognizable."

"Oh, that was in the beginning. When it got near the time for unmasking, a lot of people gave themselves away. It was fun doing that. You know, laughing natural instead of like a hyena."

To prove that he did know, he laughed like a hyena himself. They joined him. When that was over, he said, "Do you remember any of the names you got?"

"Yes, sir. We all got the same ones, except Mainwaring. Her extras were people we didn't know so well no matter how they laughed. The clucks."

"Did you get anybody I know, including the clucks?"

Moke looked wanly sinister. "I'm right behind you. Sure. Everybody you know. But you can't detect nothing from that."

"Who says I can't? Suppose somebody went upstairs for a while and came down just before the unmasking?

227

Somebody you didn't guess until the last minute, because you hadn't seen her for an hour or so?"

Poke answered with dignity. "I'm right behind you, too. The only ones we guessed at the last minute were people who wouldn't know Ruth Miller if they fell over her. Take my word for it, that's indubitable."

For a few seconds he was more disappointed than he would admit, even to himself. But then, without warning, a door slowly opened in the back of his mind, a door that had been closed and camouflaged. He could almost see a face peering through, like the picture Bessy had drawn. It made him whistle and kept his mouth open after the whistle had stopped. Moke and Poke watched him fearfully. He didn't see them, he was seeing someone else. His girl. . . . She had staggered her appearances, dressing for the part each time. She had gone upstairs as herself, done her work, and returned wearing Ruth's mask. Then upstairs again, then down as herself once more. If she used the second floor as a base, she could do it half a dozen times. She wouldn't be missed, not gone long enough at a stretch. She had broken it up, spread it out; there one minute, not there the next. No wonder the kids had guessed all the ones he knew. Her name was probably on every list, the early ones and the late. No wonder, as Moke said, he couldn't detect nothing from that. . . . The unholy devil.

"You haven't seen me today," he warned. "I'm always saying that to you two, but it's only temporary. Pretty soon now I'm going to flaunt you in the eyes of the world." Then he was gone.

After leaving Dr. Kloppel's, Bessy and Beulah returned to the only location they were sure of, the Fifth Avenue entrance to Blackman's. They planted themselves in the center of the teeming sidewalk while they discussed their next move. They were oblivious to everything but their own words. Because they were among strangers, they considered themselves alone; and because they were alone, they shouted.

Hadn't they found the suit? Hadn't they shared Mark's confidence with that wonderful old man? Unmarried, settled, still earning, and broad-minded about his bookcase? Next time it wouldn't be sherry. Now all they had to do was find the eye doctor.

"But Mark says to forget about him," Bessy objected.

"I only want him for our record," Beulah said. "Also it would give us an added interest in the end."

"The end," Bessy repeated with pleasure. Her sweet voice rose happily. "The end. That's Ossining. They'll give her anything she wants for her last dinner. Chicken, I suspect. And the lights grow dim when they turn the juice on."

A substantial matron with two children, blocked in her efforts to reach Blackman's entrance, gave Bessy one long look and left the neighborhood.

In a short time they were alone, like two treacherous rocks in the middle of a stream before which even the waters divide. Only a small and very thin Santa Claus stood fast. He rang his begging bell without a pause, but he put one gnarled and dirty hand over his money kettle.

"Chicken," Beulah said reflectively. "I'm hungry. I didn't eat all the breakfast I wanted. Let's go to that place for something, and then we can try the man the girl told us about."

Bessy knew what she meant. They turned and walked rapidly in the wrong direction, reversed, and started out again.

The girl at the orange-drink stand knew them at once, but it was the lunch hour and she had little time for talk. As soon as she could, she left her griddle and urn and came over. "Was it him?" she asked.

They confessed that they hadn't found out. "My friend," Beulah said, "began to feel nervous, so we went home. But we're going there after we've had something to eat."

"The hamburger's good today," the girl said. "Gee, I hope it's him."

They ate two of everything as before, and also as before they promised to report.

This time the dark, uncarpeted stairs looked cleaner, and the upper hall, when they reached it, was furnished with a strip of worn linoleum and a bamboo table holding a lamp. A door at the rear said, "Dr. John Thomas Eagan. Walk In."

There was no secretary, no starched office nurse. The small, white-painted room held another bamboo table, a lamp, and three chairs. A second door, half open, led to an inner office. They heard a sound like feet coming to the floor from a height, presumably the height of a desk. "Doctor?" Beulah called.

He stood in the door of the inner office, a young man in a clean white coat, with dark skin and hair. Beulah remembered him. He'd been scowling before, but now he was smiling. She stepped back and took Bessy's arm.

"I'm afraid I've made a mistake," she said. "I was looking for a doctor who treated my niece's eyes but I don't think——"

"Sit down," he suggested. "I may be able to help you." He brought the chairs forward. "What is your niece's name?"

"But she——I'm quite sure I've come to the wrong place. I was passing by, and for a minute I thought—— I'm sorry, but I'm sure I'm wasting your time."

They saw him look them over, saw his smile widen. "It's a bad day," he said smoothly. "Why don't you rest a bit before you start out again?"

"We," Bessy began. "We——"

"You're looking for your niece's doctor, I got that. And it's very interesting, because I don't have many nieces. How did you happen to find this office? Not many people come here unless they know about it beforehand. . . . Who is your niece?"

"Ruth Miller," Bessy said in a high voice. "She was murdered."

"Please sit down," he said.

The contents of Mark's bundle, neatly arranged on

Foy's desk, brought respectful and hearty laughs from the men who put their heads inside the door when they heard music. They were the ones who didn't know. After they'd been told, they creaked down the bare corridors as if they were walking in a mausoleum.

"You're a good guy," Foy said to Mark. "If everybody in your profession was like you, we'd have better luck all around. Most of your pals are glory hogs but you give what you've got. I appreciate it. Now how in hell can I break this?"

"I don't know, but it's got to be quick."

"Even I know that." Foy took another cigar. "As long as that Harris girl is alive, she's a menace to somebody. She knows too much, saw and heard too much. Do you think she told you everything?"

"All she could."

"That's a good man outside her door. Jones. Jones knows how to keep his head. He won't let anybody in there that hasn't the right."

"And who's to say who has the right?"

Foy slumped.

Mark went on. "It wouldn't change the outcome if the blind youngster heard somebody enter. A crack on the head, a pillow on the face, and she'd be quiet. Then Harris, same as Miller, plus a suicide note to clear up the tag ends. A farewell confession. I didn't figure that one out myself, I got it from a respectable woman. It's respectable female reasoning, and as we're dealing with allegedly respectable females, it's probably accurate. . . . I'm going back to Hope House when I leave here, and hang around. I want to watch the girls. I may offer to help them trim their Christmas tree, but whatever the excuse, I'm staying. Also, I'm going down to the kitchen and beg a cup of coffee from the help. Want to see what they look like."

"You're holding something out!" Foy accused him eagerly.

"Nope. You've got it all. This will be an ordinary casing of the joint. If this were London, I'd be a grimy individual in work clothes with a bit of paper identifying me as the waterworks come to look at the geyser. Here I'll be myself, a nice young man with a job too big for him, and may I have a cup of coffee, please. I want to look for things like back stairs."

"Why?"

"Because I never have." That was the truth, but not all of it. "And exits. To the courtyard, for instance. And does the elevator run to the basement or not. Things like that."

"I'll put a man in the courtyard right away," Foy said firmly.

"Not yet, please. Maybe later. She won't make a break for it now. She knows we haven't spotted her. She knows a break will give her away, and she also knows we can find her. That's what I'm afraid of, finding her, the wrong way. She'd gamble on a break if she thought she was caught, and we'd find her in the river."

"East," Foy said thoughtfully, "you know what could happen if you had a piece of rubber hose in your pocket that somebody put there by mistake when you weren't looking? It could slip out of your hand. We'd both feel bad about it, too, and I'd give you loud and prominent hell."

"Shame, shame, and you the father of a young girl!"

"Yeah. Sixteen. Seventeen next July. I saw girls that age in that place." Foy treated himself to a picture of Miss Maureen Foy as she had looked that morning at breakfast. A little bit of heaven, that's what, a wild Irish rose; eyes of Killarney, voice of a dove, fair as the clouds that kiss the hills above Kildooey. . . . He dragged his thoughts back to the business at hand and looked with loathing at the crinkled, rosebud mouth that smiled up from the desk.

"I don't know why we can't lock somebody up," he snapped. "I don't like to be diddled by a girl!"

"But this is no ordinary diddling, and no ordinary girl. She looks and acts average, and that's why she has us by the throat. This one is as smart as anything that ever went through your hands. She did her stuff like a mathematician. In the end, when we take her aside for a little heart-to-heart, we'll probably find that her schedule ran something like this. She got hold of the extra costume, because she knew all about it. She hid it—my guess is the second-floor bathroom or packroom; easy to get at. She was lucky about the chef's accident, that gave her a break; but she could have worked without it. She could have followed Ruth to her room after the party. A blind witness, and a disguise to boot, in case she was seen in the halls. No involuntary exclamation from anybody, no name cried out in terror. Oh, she'd have worked it. . . . She saw her big chance in the chef's accident, and gambled. There was a lot of confusion then, and the whole thing ate up a lot of time. She eased Miller into position under Plummer's eyes when the other girls turned Plummer down. She'd had Miller spotted from the first, probably because Miller appeared with April who was too easy to identify. The blind have a posture all their own. Even if Miller had stayed away from the party, she was marked for death. In one way or another, sooner or later. But the gamble worked. . . . She went upstairs and waited, and I think she locked Fister's door for added safety. Too close to the first floor. So Miller, poor little devil, had to go on up to Brady's. And in Brady's we had the business. Knockout with music box, trade masks. Then a quick look-see down the hall, another safety measure. But the elevator was ringing then, and that might bring trouble. So she took the elevator over, she didn't dare not to, and ferried Mrs. Marshall-Gill to the main floor. She returned at once to eighth, Marshall-Gill watched the indicator. Back in Brady's she finished her job, and I don't have to tell you what that was, went down to Miller's room and opened the window. Getting set for the suicide angle, see?" He gave his theory of the changed masks, the series of appearances as Ruth Miller and herself. "I've gone over that routine until I'm sick of it," he said. "It's clear, it fits with what I've been told. So what? So that's all it is. A piece of reasoning that fits." He got up and fought with the sleeves of his overcoat. "Bye-bye for now."

"Can you think of anything you'd like me to do?" Foy asked unhappily.

"Not right now. Call you later. Maybe something will happen to me."

"In the Hope House kitchen?"

"Could be."

Jewel was clumsily working the switchboard when he arrived. She did her best not to see him. The lobby was empty but the lounge was crowded. He saw that much through the glass doors.

"I'll wait," he said carelessly to Jewel. She nodded.

He watched her awkward fingers and stolid shoulders. Behind him the lounge door opened and closed, but no one came out. Presently Jewel left the board and stood before him.

"New job?" he asked genially. "Or is Kitty sick?"

"Sick. She went upstairs for her medicine." She waited for him to go on. He was waiting, too, wondering if a few minutes with Jewel would net him more than an immediate trip to the kitchen, when a call came in. She left him with alacrity.

As soon as she spoke, he knew the call was important. Her speech was painfully correct and she tried not to look at him, but in spite of herself her eyes kept returning to his face.

"Yes, sir; yes, sir," she said. "I'll tell him, he's here. I'll tell him right away, sir. At once."

He said, "Me?"

She returned to the desk. "That was the office of Inspector Foy. Inspector Foy wants you right away over at Dr. Kloppel's. He's on his way there now, he left in a hurry in a car, they said he could be there already."

"Thank you," he said. "That sounds hot, doesn't it?"

"I wouldn't know," she answered.

There were four people sitting around Dr. Kloppel's table when he arrived, Kloppel, Foy, Bessy, and Beulah. In the center of the table, ringed with mugs, sherry glasses, and a stein of beer, was the blue suit.

"You're going to love me more than ever," Beulah screamed. "Ruth Miller came from the Middle West!"

The only answer he could think of was, "Who says so all of a sudden?" He looked at Foy.

"The ladies," Foy said, "have done the da——have had a fine piece of luck. They found that doc you advertised for. The good doc called me at once, and it's all straight. Your story, ladies." His smiling bow placed their forebears in the South of Ireland.

Beulah's recital was almost too leisurely to be borne; it included every step of the previous search, Bessy's non-co-operation, the weather at all times, the pangs of hunger, and the new friend who sold orange drink. "His name—I mean the doctor—is Eagan. John Thomas Eagan. And he reads the *Herald Tribune,* that's why he didn't know you were looking for him. And he didn't see the suicide notice, either. When I mentioned Ruth Miller's name, he remembered her at once. I don't think he has many patients, it's a poor-looking office. A girl cousin of his roomed at the same place as Ruth for a little while and that's how she happened to come to him. Then the cousin moved back to Boston. That's why the Inspector didn't have any luck when he tried there. Run-down house in the West Sixties."

"Middle West, Middle West," Mark chanted through clenched teeth.

"Haven't you ever heard of self-control? . . . She went to Dr. Eagan last spring and he told her to come back in six months. She didn't. He says he often thought about her because she was nice. Finally he phoned the rooming house, and she was gone. Must have just missed her. I think he liked her, too. He said he'd kept hoping she'd show up, because her eyes were really bad, and he was afraid she was staying away on account of money. When I told him she was murdered, I thought he'd drop."

"How much did he know about her personally? How much did the cousin know? Where can we find the cousin, I want to talk to her. Where does the Middle West come in?"

"Am I a fool? I did as much as you can do and more. I saved you time. The cousin doesn't know a thing. He

235

wrote to her and asked. And he doesn't know a thing himself, either, except that he has an idea. He fools around with accents."

"What!"

"Accents. He collects them as a hobby. Coming from Boston, as he did, he had an accent himself, but he got rid of it because it made him mad when people looked at him and said, 'Beans.' It made him accent-conscious. That's how he noticed Ruth's. He said it was Middle West and probably Chicago."

"Chicago," Mark repeated. "Population one hundred. Advertise? Radio?" He turned to Foy.

Foy was staring at the blue suit. "Who wrote on that?" he asked.

"Who wrote on what?"

"That." Foy pointed to the paper on the lapel. "What's it mean?"

"How should I know. Cleaner's ticket."

"On Hope House paper?"

"Hope House!"

"Telephone pad. One on every floor, hanging beside the phone." He saw Mark's face and added hastily, and in time, "Ladies present!"

Mark smoothed the paper, held it to the light, read the penciled scrawl a half dozen times. Then he left, hatless and coatless and without explanation. They heard the front door slam.

Bessy said, "Have we done something wrong or right?"

"Right." Beulah's voice was pitying. "If we were wrong, he'd be the first to tell us. Loud."

He was back in less than five minutes. "It was in the coat pocket," he said. "Crumpled up as if it had been put there in a hurry. The cleaner calls everything in a pocket personal property, so he saved it. Pinned it to the coat himself. Didn't think it was worth mentioning, because he was sure Miller would know what it was." There was a lift in his voice. "Can any of you bright people identify it?"

"Wiggle, wiggle," Bessy began.

He interrupted with bitter triumph. "It's a telephone number. Foy knew it was telephone-pad paper. He sat here and looked at it, but it didn't say anything to him. I myself saw those pads hanging by the phones, and all they said to me was Roberta's desk. But Tom the Cleaner and Dyer knew what it was right away. The knife Beulah uses for cutting miasmas wouldn't make a dent in the peasant's accent, but he looked me straight in the eye and said it was a telephone number in a beeg city like New York or Worcester, Mass. Because it had five leedle figures. I allowed him Worcester, Mass. because it is clearly close to his heart. If I had a shield I'd turn it in and shoot myself with my service gun. . . . New York is beeg, Chicago is beeg, where do we start?"

"East, West, home's best," Bessy said.

"And nearest," he agreed politely. "Bird in hand. But what does the wiggle stand for?" .

Foy studied the slip of paper. "That could be something beginning with a W. That could be a W, an M, or an N. I can have the number called on every local exchange, but it may take awhile."

"Worth it if it takes the rest of the day. How long?"

"Half an hour, hour, I don't know. Thing to do is get all the locations lined up. Then check each one. We can get anything, apartment houses, hotels, stores, theaters, railway stations, bus lines. Can get a car barn. And we can't afford to pass up one."

"Do it. You can start it rolling from here, can't you? I want us both to stick in this neighborhood. Get all the 2-8277 phones first, have them call you back on that. Meanwhile I'll run over to Hope House and see if it clicks there. It may be one of their regulars. You know, drugstore, ice cream, cigarettes. I'll be back before you're ready for me."

He left Foy murmuring instructions into the doctor's phone and Bessy and Beulah loudly admiring the doctor's bookcase. The doctor, poor fool, Mark noted, looked happy.

Kitty Brice was back at the switchboard and Jewel was nowhere in sight.

Kitty denied all knowledge of the number. Yes, she kept a list of local calls until they were paid for, which was at the end of each week. Long-distance calls were kept on a special record, in the desk. When the monthly bill came in from the telephone company, the girls were billed and the record was filed away. She checked three months' bills while he looked over her shoulder. There was no 2-8277. When he asked if Ruth Miller had made many calls, she shook her head.

"Not when I was on duty," she said. "Maybe late at night when Miss Plummer ran the board. You'd have to ask Miss Plummer."

He nodded. Then, "You don't look well, Miss Brice."

"Who does?" she answered.

He was thinking of that when Miss Plummer finally admitted him to her room after asking him to wait until she got back in bed. Her face was ashen.

"What is it?" she whispered. "Why did you come back?"

Sympathy would break her down and make her useless. He knew that. He took an easy, matter-of-fact tone. "Miss Plummer, did Ruth Miller ever use the phone when you were on duty?"

She looked as if he had struck her. "How did you know?"

"I don't know. I'm asking you. If I could be sure, it might help me."

"Yes, she did. I forgot to tell you." She corrected herself painfully. "No, I can't truly say I forgot, it was more like being afraid to say anything. You see I lost the slip I wrote the number on. That didn't worry me so much at first, because there wasn't any question of a bill. The call wasn't completed. But later, after she was dead, it worried me something terrible. I was afraid it might be important and I'd get in trouble with the Board for losing it. Or with the—the police." She told him how the call had come through, how she had been surprised to hear Ruth Miller's voice, because it was late, close to midnight.

"The Sunday night, it was," she said. "The night of

the tea, the night before she died. And she was breathing hard, like she'd been running, and she begged me to put it through quick. A person-to-person call, long distance, and she didn't know the number, only the name. It was to a gentleman, a prominent gentleman she said. She said I wouldn't have any trouble finding him because he was prominent."

"Chicago?"

"Mr. East!" She was hearing a sorcerer who could raise the dead and bring back lost voices. "How did you know? How did you know that? Nobody knew but the poor girl and myself. Unless there was another person on the line, unless there was another person listening in. That must be it. Mr. East, I was so confused, I don't often have a call like that, and to this day I can't remember anything about it, no name, no number, nothing. If she hadn't hung up, I'd have remembered, because I'd have had the record then. It would have been what you call completed, and I'd have had it down on paper and filed away. But she hung up just when I was ready to put her on; I think she was crying, or something like that. I could hear her breathing like she was standing beside me. I never had a chance to talk to her about it again, either. I wanted to talk to her about it. . . . Wait a minute, Mr. East! Law, Craw——"

"What is it, Miss Plummer?"

"The name. It seems to be speaking to me. Law——" Tears filled her eyes, too easily.

"Forget it now, Miss Plummer. Ignore it. That's the way we make our minds behave. It'll come back to you. . . . Do you have many Chicago girls living in the house?"

"Do we have——" She reached for the glass of water, and he had to help her.

"Take it easy," he said. "Don't tell me if it upsets you. I can probably find what I want in the house records."

"We don't keep records like that." She looked away when she spoke, across the over-furnished little room, out of the window and beyond. She sounded as if she were talking to someone miles away, or even thinking

239

out loud. He knew she was preparing to meet the self-accusation that would come later, she was getting ready to answer her own reproachful finger. When the end came, she wanted to be able to say, "He must have guessed. I didn't tell him anything. Maybe I mumbled something, I do that when I'm sick. Half the time I just lie there talking to myself. Why, I was so sick I hardly knew he was in the room. He must have guessed." She sighed.

"No records like what?" he asked softly.

"Not of the places people come from. Or what they did before. That's to help people start a new life."

"I see. But do you happen, quite by accident, to know of anybody from Chicago, or near Chicago?"

She answered in her own way. "I think the Board might know if anybody does. When we opened the House, everybody was interviewed by one or more of the Board, to see if they were worthy. Then somebody, I don't know who, said it wasn't fair to do that. Un-American, they said. So it was stopped. Now they only ask you where you work and who should be notified in case of—sickness."

"Good enough. On second thought, I may not need that information after all, but if I do, there's always Mrs. Marshall-Gill! Chatty old girl, Mrs. M-G. . . . You're beginning to feel better already, aren't you? You look better. Like to watch the snow, don't you? So do I. Lazy-looking stuff. Drifting down as if it hadn't any place to go and didn't care. Nice and soft and lazy. . . . That name you want to remember is Law, Craw, Law. . . ."

"Crawford," Miss Plummer said quietly. "Crawford or Lawford. You brought it back to me."

"Don't stop," he said, and his voice was as quiet as hers. "Try."

She shook her head. "I can't, sir. I have tried, and that's all. If I have to die for it, I can't say more."

He gave up. He had more than he'd hoped for. "You've been good," he said, "and I thank you. I've got one more question but it doesn't amount to much. I don't suppose you know anything about a musical powder box in Miss Brady's room?"

"No, sir. . . . Mr. East, I'd like to go back to sleep. I'm afraid I'll have to work tonight. I've got to get some rest, I've got to. My sister says——"

"Maybe you won't have to work," he said easily. "I'll see what I can do about it. You know, don't you, that I can be reached at Dr. Kloppel's if you want anything?"

"Yes, sir."

He heard her pad across the room after he closed the door. The key turned.

When he reached the doctor's, Bessy and Beulah had left. "I sent the ladies home," Foy said virtuously. "They were anxious to do all they could, but I told them this wasn't woman's work, not now. You've got something new, haven't you?"

"What about the New York calls?"

"Too soon. Why?"

"Because it's Chicago we want. At least I think so. Doctor, SON needs a little attention. . . . Listen, I've got a name, or part of a name, or something that sounds like a name. Chicago resident."

Foy exploded. "Name! Part of! Something that sounds like!"

"All right. I have some syllables, then, Lawford or Crawford, that may be the name of a man Ruth Miller called. My source of information isn't too strong in the head, but I don't want to throw this away because of that. Do you think Chicago could track down Lawfords and Crawfords with one hand and check the 2-8277 phones with the other? Lawford or Crawford is supposed to be a man of prominence."

Foy was doubtful. "But we'll be wrong if we drop New York entirely. From what you tell me about your source's head——"

"Doctor," Mark said, "how reliable is Miss Plummer?"

"Well, she tries."

"That's enough. We'll try, too. Foy?"

The only sound for the next few minutes was Foy's

low voice apologizing to Chicago. He was interrupted once, when an empty beer bottle rolled across the table and crashed to the tiled hearth as Dr. Kloppel's hospitality tangled with his curiosity. Mark pushed the old man gently into a chair.

Foy hung up. "They'll do what they can, but they say it's a paper chase. Can't you dig up a little more?"

"One thing at a time, wash this up first. Did they know a big shot with a name like Lawford or Crawford?"

"They didn't say so. Sometimes a man is so big that people don't think of him."

"Right. But he needn't be big at that. A man of prominence in Ruth Miller's world could be anything, a civil-service employee or a minor city official, a nice guy in a clean white shirt who finished high school and took courses at night to improve himself. Respected in his neighborhood, which may have been hers, too. A giant among men, to a girl with her back to the wall. Apparently he was the one person she could turn to, the only one who could help her, who knew how she felt and could tell her what to do." His voice rose. "What made her hang up?" He told them what Miss Plummer had said. "That call was a life line and she dropped it. Why? Because somebody came down the hall while she was at the phone? Somebody going to the bath or looking for conversation? Never. Ruth Miller wouldn't throw away her only chance for an interruption like that. Not with help so close at hand that she had already jotted down the precious number that she must have overheard. She was stopped by the thing she was afraid of. . . . I wonder where her roommate was? That phone's directly outside the door."

Dr. Kloppel coughed eagerly. "What night would that have been?"

"Sunday night, the day of the tea."

"That night April had an upset stomach, and I prescribed over the phone to Mrs. Fister. Mrs. Fister moved April down to her own room. That would leave Miss Miller alone in that end of the hall."

"And that," Mark said, "is why we haven't heard about this business until now. Only Plummer and one other person knew about Ruth's call, and the other was the girl who couldn't afford to tell us. She knew we'd try to trace the call, knew we might even succeed. If Ruth's prominent friend could help Ruth, he could also point to Ruth's murderer."

Foy said, "That guy could be a former employer."

"That's what I'm crossing my fingers for. An employer, preferably in a department store or a shop. Maybe a floorwalker. Miss Libby thinks there's a tie-up with a store or a shop. Miller claimed inexperience, but she knew too much about selling. Libby thinks——"

The phone rang. It was the first New York call, from Headquarters. Four exchanges had been cleared, and a squad was covering the locations.

They sat on; talking, silent, talking, watching the clock. New York reported at intervals, but there were no leads. Nothing looked hopeful enough to warrant Foy's presence. Did the Inspector want a typed report sent up to him? Foy said no. He didn't know how long he'd be where he was. He'd tell them if and when he moved on.

It was three-thirty when the first Chicago call came through. The crew that was checking the telephone numbers had five promising addresses. One was a packing house that employed hundreds of women, three were apartment houses, one was a private residence in an exclusive suburb.

"So what?" Mark said into Foy's disengaged ear. "So what are we supposed to do, clap hands because they can count? Tell them to get inside those places. Packing house! That's good for hours, and look at the time now. Tell them to put the packing house at the end of the list and go after the apartments and private house. And what are they doing about Lawford-Crawford?"

When Foy hung up, he said the Lawford-Crawford crew hadn't been heard from. "That's a slow and thankless job," he reminded Mark. "You ought to know. A man's name is his own business, and he can slam the door in your face if he wants to."

Once more they sat in silence, watching the clock, poised for the next soft whir of the telephone. Dr. Kloppel drew the curtains as the winter afternoon moved on to dusk.

It was a few minutes after four when Agnes came to the door, looking as near to bursting as a lean woman can. She said she had a note for Dr. Kloppel from Miss Handy. Would the doctor read it right away, please, and give her an answer? Miss Handy said it was life and death.

She saw Mark before she finished her little speech and grinned broadly. "There now," she said, "I might have known you'd be Johnny-on-the-spot. Miss Handy was wondering where you'd gone to. That girl! Locked herself in and won't talk to nobody. Know how she got this note to me? Hollered out the window to Macy's truck. Taking precautions, she says. Precautions! Miss Mainwaring's going to have to sleep on somebody's floor tonight unless you can talk Miss Handy into putting the furniture back where it belongs so we can get the door open. Miss Handy says she'll scream the place down if anybody so much as knocks. Well, you can read it for yourself." She had clearly done the same.

It was a short note, not as incoherent as first glance suggested.

DR. KLOPPEL, I kept the sleeping pills you gave me and everybody the other night. I didn't take mine and Mainwaring didn't take hers and we put them in the bureau drawer. And Liz Hull and Kate Warriner didn't take theirs either, so Mainwaring traded two piqué dickies for theirs because she said it was dangerous for people to take them and she was collecting all she could find to save people from danger. This noon I took a nap, I didn't go to work because I didn't sleep all night, and when I woke up and went to get a handkerchief the pills were gone. Mine and Mainwaring's and Liz's and Kate's and God knows how many more. I had the door locked, but there's such things as passkeys if you know where to look, and everybody does. So is that a fatal dose? I mean that's pills for four people at least, and if one person got them all in say a cup of coffee would it be fatal and kill? Could you taste it? Please reply at once. This is important.

MINNIE MAY HANDY.

P.S. Still alive and going to stay that way.

They gave the note to Foy.

"Who takes care of this girl's food?" Dr. Kloppel asked Agnes.

"Anybody, sir." Agnes began to look worried. "Anybody that wants to be obliging can get a tray from the dining room and take it up."

"That won't do. We'll have to think of something else. I don't like this; I never had a thing like this happen before. Saving pills—I don't like it at all!"

"Agnes," Mark said, "can't you fix a tray yourself without letting the whole world know what you're doing?"

"I can!"

"Then that's the answer. Boiled eggs, crackers, fruit. Shell on the eggs, skin on the fruit, crackers in a sealed package. Got that?"

"I have indeed!"

"And tell Miss Handy you talked to me. Tell her to keep on with the furniture routine and don't worry about Miss Mainwaring. And you might see that Miss Handy has a pitcher of water that you draw from the tap yourself. All right?"

No spoken reply was needed. Agnes left the room with a backward look and forward stance that said she was about to cross the ice in advance of bloodhounds and single-fingered plug a broken dike.

"What would four doses do?" Foy asked.

"In her case, I don't know." Dr. Kloppel squirmed. "At best, it could be pretty bad. At worst——those women! How do we know it's only four? There could

245

be dozens, collected and swapped for a——what's a dickey?"

"False front," Mark supplied. "You know, if anything happens it's squarely on my head. I made that girl the goat because she was tailored for it. I wanted to draw fire. Now I don't know what I've drawn. I'm going to spend the night over there. That stuff is the same as poison."

Dr. Kloppel groaned and raised haggard eyes. "Poison! Heaven help me. They've got cyanide over there. Brady wanted it a couple of months ago, and I got it for her!"

Mark said, "What!"

"Cyanide." Dr. Kloppel shrunk in his chair. "A straightforward request and she signed for it. There could be some left. I can't remember what she told me, but she signed for it. It was all out in the open, nothing furtive, nothing suspicious. . . . Please don't look at me like that."

Foy snarled. "All out in the open. Up on a shelf with the first-aid kit. Standing next to the aspirin and the court plaster, labeled and all!"

"I don't know, I don't know, but it was all straightforward. She hasn't mentioned it since—since this business started. And she's a smart, intelligent woman; if there was any left, she'd throw it away or tell me about it. She's intelligent, she wouldn't keep it around."

Mark took pity. "Calm down, even if it's still there it won't be used. It wasn't used on Ruth, and you know why. It needs a special setup, the victim has to be willing or unsuspicious, and nobody in that house is either. Not now. And it's too dangerous, it works too quick, no time for a getaway. No, I don't think it'll be used. If it's been there all this time and——"

The phone rang.

Chicago had canvassed the first apartment house, a small one in a lower-middle-class neighborhood. No Lawfords or Crawfords. No Millers. Some of the tenants were new, and the janitor had lost track of those who had moved. The latter were the kind who slipped away in the night, leaving broken bedsprings behind them. A second squad was working on the other houses and would report shortly. More exchanges had been cleared. The car sent out to the suburbs hadn't phoned in. It was a long way out, in a snooty section, and the boys were probably fighting off butlers.

After that the calls came five minutes apart. Lawfords and Crawfords were cropping up in office buildings, markets, poolrooms and factories. Dr. Kloppel's bookcase began to look like Mother Hubbard's cupboard. Then, at a quarter of six, the car that went to the suburbs paid off.

The suburban house belonged to Norman Crawford, president of Bassett and Wright, one of Chicago's largest department stores. Crawford wasn't home, but they knew where he was and were getting to him fast. It would be a matter of minutes, they were keeping an open wire.

Foy sat with the receiver to his ear.

"At times like this," Mark said softly, "I wouldn't take a million for my job. Sometimes I get as sick as a dog, and I'll be a lot sicker than that before this night is over, but I wouldn't take a million. Ruth Miller is gone. Now we're working for a window dresser's boy who got fired to save somebody's face. . . . Not two million."

Foy said, "Hello. All set here, get on with it."

The other two crowded him. They heard respect creep into his voice and saw it straighten his shoulders. He sat as if he were standing at attention.

Chicago talked, first in a hearty growl, then in a steady, flowing stream. Foy said little beyond, "Yes, sir, you have it correct, sir," but he clung to the phone as Ruth Miller must have done. He had nothing to fear, nothing to hide from, but his mobile Irish face told the watchers that Ruth was living and dying again in Norman Crawford's story. The story took seven minutes to tell, and Foy interrupted only twice, toward the end. He said, "I've got everything but the name, sir," and after that he said, "I'll be damned."

The receiver rattled into place on the hook.

Dr. Kloppel went back to his shabby chair and listened. He knew they had to talk as they did, this was their job; but he had seen her lying in the rain, had lifted her broken body. He picked up the mug marked PAPA. It was empty, but he made no effort to refill it. He held it to his breast with both hands as if it had the power to strain the evil that was entering his heart. If he held the mug in his hands they could not turn into fists.

11

Mark knew she was Clara because her sweater was clearly a hand-me-down, mended with too bright thread and fitting too well in the wrong places. She was eating bread pudding at one end of a long wooden table, and two other women were chopping soup vegetables at the other end. Just as clearly, these were the neighborhood women who worked in the kitchen by the day and returned to their homes at night. One of them was already wearing her hat, eloquently, and both were watching the clock. It was exactly seven.

The chef sat by the gas stove, dividing his attention between a pot of soup stock and a newspaper. The dinner rush had abated, the time was right for talk.

They hadn't noticed his entrance, and when he spoke to them, standing in the door that opened on the courtyard, they turned astonished faces.

"I'm East," he explained. "Mark East. I've been wanting to talk to you people, but this is the first chance I've had."

The woman who was wearing a hat silently laid down her chopping knife and made a bolt for the door, nearly knocking him down. He said, "Just a minute, please. Who are you?"

She dragged a worn coat from a wooden peg in the wall beside the door. "I've got a baby at home," she shrilled. "I've got no time for talking. I'm late, I got a baby at home, and I'm going there."

"What's your name?" he asked.

"Trimble, Mary Trimble, I don't know nothing, you can ask the others, I got to get home."

He let her go, holding the court door open and

watching her run through the snow, pulling on the coat as she ran. The other woman looked undecided. "You may go, too," he said. "It's Clara I want to see, Clara and—Alexander, isn't it?"

The chef nodded. "Go," he said to the woman. "Come early in the morning to finish." He gave Mark the kind of shrug that is reserved for equals. "Rabbits. . . . You want to examine my hand?"

"Later," Mark said. He turned to Clara.

Clara ate steadily, her mild eyes unclouded and undisturbed. If she has a mind, he thought, it doesn't function in the presence of food. He moved the bowl of pudding out of reach and laughed. "One thing at a time, Clara." Alexander laughed, too, and joined them at the table. Clara smiled helplessly.

"Is better you examine my hand now," Alexander said. "Later is no good." There was a red scar across his wrist, and he displayed it with loud modesty and a running comment on the capacity of Poles for bleeding and living. Mark encouraged him, tossing in names like Sklodowska, Kosciusko, and Pulaski. Alexander returned the compliment by pouring coffee, not the Hope House stock but his own special reserve. It was worth more than the time it consumed.

"Who looked after you that night?" Mark asked.

"Not her," Alexander said of the listening Clara. "She run out on me. No nationality, all mixed up, little of this, little of that, all bad. But the ladies of the House were okay, and what you just saw, the day workers, not so bad. The day workers got children of their own, and a man is like a little child when he is hurt, isn't it so? Miss Brady, no children, was very tender. Like a mother. Miss Plummer, no children, no wits, arrives when the worst is over, but is all kindness. Many come and go. I am always a novelty, everywhere I work I am always a novelty."

"What did they fix you up with?"

"A tight dressing. Gauze and iodine. No doctor, no stitches, I mend like a dream. It was all to the good, I

have too much blood, too hot, it is okay to lose some."
He winked.

Mark responded in kind. "When did this dressing arrive, and who put it on? Can you remember?"

"Me? Remember? I remember kindness, soft hands of ladies, and screaming." He glared at Clara.

Clara had been listening with a child's intentness. Now she interrupted happily. "I remember," she said. "But he don't, he can't. He kept his eyes shut, he was fit to be sick to his stomach when he saw his blood. On top of all that prune brandy. Mrs. Fister put the bandage on. Miss Plummer brought it down, we had to wait some time for it, and he drank his prune brandy with his eyes shut. Mrs. Fister is the same as a district nurse, she knows what to do. Around ten o'clock it was."

When he asked her how she could be sure of the time, it was the same old story built around the unmasking. She had been in and out of the kitchen all evening, taking her turn at guarding the punch, making sandwiches, washing the little glass cups. She had carried up a tray of clean cups a few minutes before the unmasking began. And a few minutes before that the bandage had arrived. She and Mollie and Pauline had taken turns at the kitchen work so they'd all have a chance to watch the party. She and Mollie and Pauline had seen some of everything that went on because they had taken turns. That's how she knew. Ten o'clock, as near as anybody could tell.

When he asked where Mollie and Pauline were, she said they were waiting on table in the dining room, with Agnes. Some of the young ladies ate later than others.

No, she said, the elevator didn't run down to the basement. It was stairs, stairs to the serving pantry where the dumb-waiter and steam tables were.

Did she know Miss Miller? Well, no, she didn't. Her mild eyes regretted that. But Agnes had just reminded her, not an hour ago, that Miss Miller was supposed to be the one who did that crazy dance with Miss Handy. Miss Handy had done the crazy dance lots of times, but Agnes said Miss Miller's was the craziest.

Had she seen that dance, the craziest one? Had she! She'd split her sides. It was better than movies. She'd left the punch bowl and the clean little cups that were always getting used up, and walked to the front of the lobby. Four or five times she'd done that, to watch the young ladies. Singing as well as dancing, and playing that game where you march around chairs to music and fight over the last one. Something going on every minute, but Miss Handy put on the best show, Miss Handy and that poor Miss Miller. She'd clean forgotten it wasn't her place to be in the front of the lobby, and she'd been spoken to sharply on account of it. But it was worth it. She sighed happily in recollection. "All that fun, all that laughing, why anybody would want to die! I'll never understand if I live to be a hundred."

"Who spoke to you sharply?" he asked.

"Who would you expect? Heads. Near-Heads. Miss Brady, Mrs. Fister. Came to me afterwards and said my place was with the bowl." Clara sighed again, this time not happily. It was, she said, a small, mean thing to do. Especially Mrs. Fister. Considering how she herself was one of the oldest workers in the place, two days older than Mrs. F., and had always done what she was asked, even to getting up in the middle of the night to help with a sick girl. And pleasure was something everybody was entitled to, no matter how old or what you did for a living. She'd complained to Miss Plummer about it; well, maybe not complain exactly, but she had mentioned that her feelings were hurt. And Miss Plummer had mentioned it to Miss Small, she must have, because the next day Miss Small apologized for Mrs. Fister and Miss Brady and told her to overlook the whole thing. And Miss Small had given her a little brooch. "I cried like a baby," Clara confessed. "I never had a brooch before. I was due for a raise, and I thought I'd hurt my chances, so when I got the little brooch I cried."

"Did you get the raise?" Alexander asked.

"No," Clara admitted.

"Hah!" Alexander said.

Mark led her back, step by step, over the ground she had sketchily covered. Her four or five deflections from the bowl had taken her into disputed area, both in time and place. He gave her no theories of his own to play with and mangle, no names to tempt or confuse, no hours to recall. He guided her skillfully through the accident in the kitchen, through her turns at guarding the punch; he charted her little excursions to the front of the lobby and the doors of the lounge, where the fun was. When her mind had been brought to focus, she recaptured the night as it had literally and inexorably moved to its end.

She made the elevator hum from floor to floor, he could hear the doors clang. She gave the simulated pearls to Miss Mainwaring, and even reproduced Miss Brady's presentation speech. She put people where they were, not where they claimed to be, and she did it like the legendary child who told the world the king was wearing no clothes.

Clara didn't know how or why Ruth Miller had been killed, but she told him who had done it. He knew that already, but he needed Clara's soft say-so. If the State came up against a tough defense lawyer, Clara was the girl to make him sweat.

During the leisurely recital, which had the open impact of a game of "Authors," Alexander moved from table to dumb-waiter, drinking his superior coffee and removing stacked dishes. He complained softly throughout and he might have been talking to himself. When Mark leaned back in his chair and lit a cigarette, Alexander reached out for attention.

"Cop in the courtyard," he said briskly.

Clara screamed at once.

"That's the Inspector," Mark said. "He's waiting for me." He got up. "Thanks for everything, and you might tell Agnes I was here. And ask her to pass the word along to Miss Handy." He remembered the bread pudding when he had one foot in the courtyard, and he turned back and restored it to its former position.

He and Foy leaned against the fence and looked up

at the Hope House walls. They were alone. It was too early for the white cat.

"So that's the way it was," Foy said. "Well, we figured it about right. . . . That her window up there?"

"Sure. . . . You're going to love Clara on the witness stand. No matter what she says or does or wears, she's going to be every juror's Aunt Hattie, the one who made the cookies. Clara, like the Aga Khan, is worth her considerable weight in gold."

"Time to talk about the witness stand when you've got somebody to prosecute! What are we waiting for?"

"What have you done?"

"Bessemer's back on the seventh floor. In a little while Moran takes over the lobby, he may be there now. I told him to walk in, sit down, and say nothing. Soboloff takes over here, as soon as we leave. He's outside the gate, waiting and watching the front door. One man to each of the floors and the roof." Foy looked up again. "I hate that roof! She could get up there by way of the fire escape, even with the snow. With the bathroom lights out, Soboloff could miss her. And she knows where the switch is. If she tried that, and failed——" He swore bitterly. "I don't want another body with its face smashed in! I want a living, breathing body with a face that I can talk to. I want to look it in the eye and hear it talk back. . . . Can they get her off on insanity?"

"You heard Crawford," Mark said slowly. "Plenty sane. But she may change her mind about that if it looks like a better buy. I don't know what she'll do, but we've got her on premeditation. I'm freezing. What's next?"

"I've been thinking. I want to go in there now but some of the kids are still eating dinner. When I was in the lobby, checking the week-end book, I saw them. And there's another bunch of them hanging up Christmas greens. Ugh! Go in there yourself, and you'll see what I mean. I don't want to take her out in front of everybody. It'll be a messy business no matter what. Suppose she carries on."

"You'll have to go easy." Mark looked at the kitchen windows, barred but uncovered. Clara was still at the table and Alexander had returned to his paper and the stove. Steam rose from the pot of soup stock. The lounge windows showed moving figures, indistinct behind the straight net curtains. Even as he watched, someone drew a curtain aside and hung a wreath. It had a brave, red bow. "There'll be more in there soon," he said. "That's where they're setting up the tree. You'll have to wait, Foy. You can't take her out with that kind of an audience. You'd start a panic. No matter how you work it, you'll have to go through the lobby. The elevator doesn't run to the basement. Wait until they're bedded down for the night, you can afford to lose that much time."

"Can I, now? And maybe you can tell me what's to stop her walking out the front door this minute?"

"What excuse?"

"Say she was going to the theater. Out to mail a letter. Figure that one."

"If she tries it, let her go. You can close in on the corner, all quiet and orderly. But as long as she stays in the House, you've got to let her do as she likes until you have a clear and unmolested field. You don't know how she's going to take it, and some of those girls are no more than kids." He was thinking of Moke and Poke. "Let them miss her tomorrow, let them wonder for a while."

"Come to think of it," Foy said slowly, "I wish she would walk out."

"I know how you can start her thinking that way. Lock the front and back doors, make a show of it, and spread the word that nobody goes out, nobody. Not even to the corner for a magazine. When the late workers and the diners-out show up, let them in, chase them upstairs, and lock up all over again. Tell them nothing, they'll do a better job of talking than you can. You'll know almost at once if she's taken the bait. She'll get to one of your men with the most convincing tale on record, then—Open Sesame. . . . Do they all know what she looks like?"

"They do now."

"Then you've nothing to worry about. Tell them to let her get away with it. Where will you be?"

"Down the street in a parked car that doesn't say 'Police.' If nothing happens, I'll come back here around midnight."

"You're all set, you can't fail. Either way you win. Smooth sailing!"

"Smooth sailing!" Foy repeated. "How many people in there are going to be asleep at midnight? None!"

"None," Mark agreed, "but every innocent little head will be smothering under a blanket. You won't see a soul. Take the elevator up and bring her down in it. All steel construction, like a little cage, and handy if she cuts up. . . . And you might ask your boys to keep an eye peeled for Plummer. She seems to think they'll ask her to work tonight. You can't have that. If she shows up, send her back to bed. And don't count on our friend to open her door to you like a lady. The passkeys are in the top left drawer of the lobby desk. I saw them this afternoon while chatting with Miss Brice on the subject of long-distance calls."

"Think of everything, don't you? Do this, do that. Just what do you expect to be doing yourself?"

"I'm through. I'm going up to the Suttons', turn in my report, get my check, and proceed to spend as much of it as possible. Accompanied by friends from the country. I may let the Suttons help me. I may need help. Maybe you can join us later. Maybe, with luck, I'll be flat on my face by midnight."

Foy eyed him curiously. "Do you always act like this?"

"A couple of times, no. A couple of times I haven't cared. . . . Come on. I'll give the place a last look, and then I'm off."

They left the court, nodding to the silent Sobeloff who stood like a snowman against the outer wall.

Moran, on duty at the front door, gave them a smart salute, but he looked beaten.

Mrs. Fister was in charge of the desk, a black serge monolith with a white face and stubby white hands. The hands were busy with pretty work, weaving sprigs of holly into an evergreen garland. The top of the desk was a litter of berries, leaves, and small packages wrapped in colored paper.

"All set for Christmas!" Foy said too heartily. "Those your presents?"

"I'm always remembered very nicely," she said. "Some of our girls leave tomorrow for the holidays, that's why I have these now." She looked from Foy to Mark, calmly. "Did you gentlemen wish something?"

"The passkeys," Foy said.

She bent to the drawer without hesitation and handed them over. Foy was confused. He could understand opposition, but not co-operation. When she blandly offered to unlock whatever he wanted unlocked, he turned brusque. No one was to leave the building, he said. She was to post that order and see that it was obeyed. Later on an officer would be stationed on each floor. Nothing to be alarmed about, it was routine only. Routine until the case was closed. He said it again, chopping off words until routine was the only one left.

Her mouth curled at the corners. "I understood the first time, Inspector," she said. "But it's to be hoped your men will be quiet. We don't care to have the girls disturbed, not for anything. Now or later." She nodded in the direction of the lounge. "We don't care to have them disturbed."

He knew what she meant. The lounge doors were ajar. Someone was playing the piano while four thin, serious voices struggled with "The First Noel." It was a valiant performance, easy to visualize and hard to listen to. The Inspector's thoughts returned again to Miss Maureen Foy. Miss Foy could sing "The First Noel" in convent French. Learned it when she was six. She'd sung it two nights before, cute as a bug, in her grandmother's parlor in Brooklyn, wearing a skimpy little skirt and a skimpy little sweater and no lipstick to please the old lady. Those kids in there——

"Okay," he said.

Mrs. Fister continued, addressing Mark. "They'll keep that up until ten or after. Some of them are trimming the tree. I'm sure the Board would appreciate your leaving things as they are for a while. I can't speak for myself, not being in the position, but I'm sure the Board would want them to finish."

He nodded. "But I have nothing to do with that, Mrs. Fister. I'm through here, the Inspector's in charge." He clapped a hand on Foy's shoulder and went away.

Moran let him out. Before the door closed behind him, he heard the chatter of the late diners as they straggled from the dining room; the pianist in the lounge struck a false chord, the singers broke down and squealed, and he left the House with the sound of laughter following.

Later, much later, he told the Suttons and Bessy and Beulah that he'd been walking. That was true. But when they asked him where, he couldn't remember his route. Not all of it. He'd walked along the river for a while, he remembered the docks. He remembered the wooden sheds, roofed with snow, the clean, cold smell of the water, the ferry boats that moved from shore to shore like toys drawn by a child with a steady hand. Had Roberta ever cut windows in a cardboard shoebox, pasted them over with colored tissue paper, fastened a lighted candle inside and a long cord outside, and pulled the resulting wonder up and down the sidewalk at night? He knew she hadn't even before she told him so. Kids with money didn't have toys like that. . . . He'd stopped at the library and read the newspapers. What newspapers? Any papers. Papers, that's all. And he'd walked by Blackman's, dark from top to bottom except for one window with strong lights behind its draped and tufted silk curtain. Window dresser at work. He'd stopped at other places, street corners, little parks with snowed-in benches, dog wagons. He didn't get to Roberta's until long after midnight.

He walked and thought and talked to himself. He turned the thoughts into pictures, real and imaginary. Foy, parked in the snowy street, waiting. Soboloff in the snowy courtyard, close to the wall for shelter, waiting. Another man on the snowy roof, watching the fire escape, watching the roof door, waiting. A man on each floor, pacing the dim halls, listening, waiting. Moran in the warm lobby, looking through the lounge doors to the corner where the Christmas tree twinkled in the light of the fire. Those were the real pictures.

The figure that vanished up the stairs was both real and imaginary. Real because he knew who she was and what she had done, even though he hadn't seen her. Up the stairs from the first floor to the second, turning the key in Mrs. Fister's door, retrieving the extra costume from the packroom, returning to the lobby to stalk Ruth Miller, to put Ruth Miller within reach of Miss Plummer's arm. Always hurrying, always looking over her shoulder, always prepared to meet inquisitive eyes. Always prepared.

What had she thought about when she followed Ruth to that eighth-floor room? Nothing new, nothing that she hadn't thought for years.

He saw her as she must have looked five years before when she first came face to face with the girl she would later kill. Norman Crawford said they'd brought her to his office, calm and undisturbed in spite of the evidence, ready to talk herself out of it. She'd taken small things, glittering things, gilt compacts, novelty jewelry, little boxes set with semiprecious stones. She'd told them they were purchases, that she'd been collecting them one by one, that she'd been looking for a clerk. She had no charge account, there was no money, no checkbook in the handsome, capacious handbag. Only the small, glittering things, the little boxes. She'd liked little boxes.

Then they'd confronted her with Ruth Miller, who had seen the last, quick movement at the counter. Ruth

Miller, standing with her back to the light for her own protection. The detectives had told her where to stand. They knew their stuff. And they'd told her not to speak. Protection, but it hadn't been enough.

Norman Crawford said he would never forget it. The other one had broken loose, screamed, fought, tried to reach the girl who had identified her. Crawford said: "We sent Miss Miller away, we had to. She went to pieces, I nearly did myself. I still quake when I think of it. Demoralizing, horrible. . . . The other girl got the usual sentence, plus medical care." Crawford repeated the psychiatrist's report. It was hideously accurate. And he'd asked what he could do, his voice showing plainly that he knew the answer. Nothing.

Ruth Miller in the Hope House lobby, clinging to her suitcase, wrinkling her eyes, peering at the new faces, seeing an old, familiar one. No wonder she had tried to keep Roberta from investigating the shoplifter at Blackman's. Roberta had given him that story in parentheses, but he'd known it was important. And when Libby had described the short-change episode, he'd known that was important, too. So had Libby. . . . A good saleswoman, one of the best, who said she had never worked before.

Libby was nobody's fool. She knew the value of past performance in estimating future behavior. Her work had taught her that. She knew that past performance could be overlaid with fancy trappings, including promises sworn on the Bible, but given a duplicate set of the old circumstances, wham, it broke through. Good or bad, it broke through the veneer.

No experience in selling, never worked before. Easy to understand that now. Timid Ruth Miller, quiet, shy Ruth Miller, doing the only job she knew and trying to forget what it had once done to her.

Miss Brady's room. The open window, a light, a stolen music box. Had Ruth opened the box herself? Before it killed her, had she listened to its music, identified it beyond doubt, relived the past that was already walking in her footsteps? Had she heard the past walk-

260

ing across Miss Brady's Persian rugs? No, because it walked in rubber sneakers.

He walked on, thinking, talking to himself. It was ten-thirty. He didn't want to know the time, but the clock on the Metropolitan tower told him with a bright face and emphasized it with chimes. After a few blocks he called a cab and returned to the place he thought he had left for good.

Miss Small looked at the traveling clock on her desk, looked at the silent telephone, and began to pace the floor. It was half past ten. The phone had been silent since nine-thirty, when Kitty Brice had called from the lobby. Kitty had sounded miles away because she was whispering.

She'd wanted to know if anyone had told Miss Small about the policemen. She'd tried to tell Miss Brady, but Miss Brady wasn't in her room or else she wouldn't answer her phone. Somebody ought to be told. There were policemen on every floor, and the one in the lobby wouldn't let anybody out. Two girls had a date for the second show, their names were in the late book, but he wouldn't let them out. Crossed their names off and sent them upstairs.

"We had more trouble, too," Kitty had said. "I think you ought to know. Dot Mainwaring had about fifteen sleeping pills; she was counting them in the bathroom and Jewel caught her at it. Jewel took them away. Down the drain now, she says. I don't know."

Miss Small had told her not to worry.

"I'm sick," Kitty had said. "Miss Small, I'm sick. I want to go to the doctor, but the cop won't let me out either. And Mrs. Fister and Jewel quit, so I'm all alone."

Miss Small had told her to go to bed. That was the first she had heard about the policemen, it was the first time Monny had failed to consult her. She thought it over, wondering.

She was still thinking about it an hour later. Was Monny trying to keep things from her? Monny had been strained at lunch, and she hadn't even come down to dinner. And she hadn't phoned. . . . Miss Small sat at her desk and put her aching head in her hands. If this thing came between her and Monny, if it broke their lives and happiness, canceled out the years ahead and the planning—— She whispered fiercely to herself. "It can't, it can't, not when we have so much!"

She reached for the phone, let her hand fall, and reached again. When the other voice answered, her own was almost too choked to reply.

"You didn't call me," she said. "I'm worried about you. Are you all right?"

Miss Brady admitted to a headache.

"Is it too bad for company?" Miss Small asked. "I mean, would you like me to come up?"

"Not tonight."

Miss Small replaced the receiver and looked at her surroundings. She hardly saw them, even though the carefully chosen lamps were bright, and the English chintz was gay and arresting. She was blind to everything but an absent face and filled with a pain that was like a drug. She knew she was living, but there was no life anywhere. No floor beneath her feet, no walls between her and the world. No world. She looked down into her lap and stroked the material of her skirt without feeling it. She dug into the rough tweed and rubbed a fluff of wool into a little ball that she rolled between her fingers. She knew how the little ball of wool ought to feel, but she felt nothing. She lifted the ornate inkwell, heavy with bronze and marble, and set it down again, hard on the polished wood. But she couldn't hear it. The only thing she could hear was a congress of wind gathering on the rim of the world, small winds meeting in an ordained place, falling into line, whispering to each other, joining their soft, gray arms for added strength. Growing, swelling, darkening, ready for the signal to descend. . . .

Miss Brady moved about her room in a litter of Christmas wrappings, picking up odds and ends of colored paper and string, sometimes raising the lid of a cardboard box of tree ornaments. A few of the boxes were brown and dusty, crumbling at the edges. They were the old ones, her own, the ones she had brought from home. After a while she raised the lid of the smallest box; it had been carefully tied with knotted tinsel cord, ragged and tarnished. The box held the angel for the top of the Christmas tree.

The dingy pink face was the face of a friend. It was the oldest thing she owned. She couldn't remember a Christmas when she hadn't looked first to the highest branch to see if it were there. Now the silver stars in the flaxen hair were almost black, and the gauzy wings hung limp and dejected. Last year she had darned them with silk thread, an awkward task for her fingers, and wired them to the body with tiny hairpins. But they hadn't held.

She didn't touch the angel but looked down at it, standing with her hands gripped behind her back. Then she put it aside with the other boxes.

There was one light burning in her bedroom and the bed was turned down, ready and waiting. The room was cold. But in spite of the cold she raised the window as far as it would go and looked out. There were lights in Miss Small's windows. There were other lights along the walls, above and below. A white cat sat on the courtyard fence, almost invisible against the snow. But she saw him easily because she knew he was there. In the corner by the street gate a large man stood in the shadows.

She left the window open when she went back to the other room.

A sedan was parked down the street, but there was no one in it. There were two sets of footprints leading away, and it was easy to see where they went. They hadn't been made too long ago, because the falling snow was filling the deep depressions. Mark followed them.

The courtyard was empty, too, and footprints told the same story there. Not too long ago.

The kitchen was empty and warm. Unlocked. That

didn't matter now. The night light showed the scrubbed wooden table, a large earthen bowl of cooked prunes, a stack of blue willow saucers.

He crossed the floor and listened before he started up the stairs.

When he entered the lobby, Moran was sitting at the switchboard, talking softly and urgently into the mouthpiece. Moran jumped when he heard the footsteps, but when he saw who it was he grinned feebly. His eyes and shoulders apologized for his nerves, and he jerked his head upward. He went on talking into the phone.

The hours between had brought few changes to the lobby. The desk was still littered with berries and leaves and scraps of tinsel ribbon. But the gift packages were gone, and the evergreen garland, trimmed with holly, now framed the elevator door.

He went into the lounge. Embers of fire, smell of spruce, music on the open piano. The tree reached to the ceiling.

He walked up the stairs while Moran talked on.

Miss Brady didn't answer his knock. He gave her a minute before he opened the door and went in. She was clearing out her desk, tearing sheets of paper and dropping the fragments to the floor. He took a near-by chair and waited for her to speak. Soon she did, without looking at him.

"I thought you were through," she said.

"I was. I am. I quit when Foy took over."

"Then what, exactly, do you want?"

"I want to know if I can do anything for you."

"Nothing. Where's Foy now?"

"Somewhere around. . . . I'm sorry, Miss Brady."

"You had your job, I had mine. . . . What are you waiting for?"

The door to the hall was open. He'd left it that way because he was waiting for the hum of the elevator and the warning sound of footsteps. As Miss Plummer had once waited for the elevator and counted the bricks between the floors, as Ruth Miller had waited for Mrs.

Fister's return. But he didn't know they had done that, too.

He answered her quietly. "I'm leaving in a few minutes. As you say, it was my job; and now it's over." He underscored the last words, not too much, but enough. She understood.

"You asked if you could do anything," she said. "I've changed my mind. Could you—— I'm thinking about the girls. Will they—see?"

"No," he said. "Foy feels as you do. He's going to wait until everything is quiet." He added, "He expects your co-operation."

"He'll get it." The paper fragments were thick on the rug. Letters, circulars—— She destroyed them all, methodically. "Some of the girls are young, too young. . . . Demoralizing."

Foy had felt the same way. Norman Crawford had used the same word. Demoralizing. He said, "I heard someone else use that word this afternoon."

"This afternoon? Is that when you found out?"

"Well, yes. We were on our way to sewing it up, but somebody clinched it for us."

"You were in the kitchen, I know that. Talking to Clara. Is that what clinched it, that and Plummer?"

He said, "Yes. But I'm thinking of something that may be news to you. This afternoon we got the background. We got a story, a name, and a psychiatrist's report. It's an old report, but it's as good today as it ever was. I'm telling you this because I like things neat, tied up and labeled, and you're entitled to the play-by-play."

He told her about the telephone number, and repeated Norman Crawford's conversation as Foy had repeated it to him. "So you see how it adds up," he said. "The girl who killed Ruth Miller was born wanting things. She was ambitious, devious, lazy. A psychiatrist said that five years ago when she was up for shoplifting. Ambitious, devious, lazy, although she did take jobs when they were worth her while. She could fit herself into any sort of job if her particular pot of gold was at

265

the end of it. Nobody ever checked on her, she was too good for that. She could charm the birds out of the trees if she wanted the birds; she could be, and act, anything. She was a superb actress. She still is."

"Yes," Miss Brady said.

"And there's another thing about her that worries Foy. She's a bad loser. If she can't have what she wants, nobody can."

"Foy's wrong."

A car backfired in the street below, and they both jumped. Eight floors down, and they heard it.

"You've got a window open in that other room," he said sharply. "Close it."

"I will," she said.

He got up and went to the door. He'd said enough. "I'm going now. Would you rather—I mean do you want to go down with me?"

"No."

He shut the door behind him.

When he had gone, Miss Brady looked at herself in the mirror and rouged her face carefully. Then she too went down the hall, making as little noise as possible. No need to let the whole world hear me, she thought, although I don't care now. I don't care.

Miss Small was still at her desk when Miss Brady walked in. All Miss Brady said was, "Changed my mind. Couldn't sleep after all."

Miss Small said, "I know. I couldn't either. . . . Monny, I'm frightened. The place is crawling with policemen!"

"Ugly devils, aren't they? All shoulders and feet. Tramp, tramp, tramp, the boys are marching. . . . If you can't sleep, why don't you take something? I'm going to."

If Miss Small heard, she gave no sign of it. "It's a dreadful night. Monny, what's going on? What's going to happen? You've got to tell me."

"Maybe East and Foy are going to earn their money."

Miss Small drew back, but her eyes followed every move of Miss Brady's hands. Miss Brady was lighting a cigarette. "Have you talked to them, Monny? They must have said something. Did they ask your permission to take over like this?"

"Take over?"

"Yes. They canceled all late leaves, wouldn't let anybody out. Not even poor Kitty, and she wanted to see the doctor. Not Kloppel, some other man she goes to. Did you tell them they could do that?"

"Tell them! I'm locked in myself! . . . Want to see something?" Miss Brady crossed to the window and drew the curtains aside. "Look down by the gate. A cop. There's one on every floor, I know because I walked down. A rat couldn't get out of here now. Not even a mouse." She laughed. "There's a cat on the fence, too. See him? The cat would get the mouse, the cops would get the rat, but who would gnaw the rope? Nobody." Miss Brady's voice was flamboyantly careless. "I was building up to Mother Goose but it won't work." She dropped the curtain, and they returned to their chairs.

Miss Small's voice, in contrast to Miss Brady's, was like a whisper. "What are they looking for, Monny?"

"Who said they were looking for anything?"

"They must be. Maybe something of Ruth Miller's. Did she leave anything?"

"I think they found everything she left. When they confiscated her suitcase. Unless there was something at Blackman's that I didn't know about. . . . They went down to the kitchen, too."

"Kitchen! Monny, you're raving. What kitchen?"

"Ours."

"But that's fantastic! Ruth Miller wasn't near the kitchen, I don't think she even knew where it was. I don't understand it. I don't know why they——"

"Maybe we'll know why tomorrow. Maybe sooner. But East went down there early this evening. I didn't see him, didn't know he was in the place, but the grapevine, the good old creeping, crawling grapevine, passed the word along. Clara told Mollie, Mollie told Pauline, Pauline told Agnes. Agnes brought my dinner up at eight and told me."

"Monny! You're so mysterious and funny! Told you what?"

"About East. East asked the chef about his hand, all tender and compassionate. He asked Clara, too, all about herself in conjunction with the hand and the party. He made a great fuss over Clara. Clara told Mollie, Mollie told Pauline, et cetera, et cetera, that Mr. East acted like he'd won a sweepstake."

"But why, Monny, why? Monny, you look dreadful, don't look like that!"

Miss Brady examined the room as Miss Small had done before, not seeing it. "Don't ask me why," she said. "Don't ask me why about anything. I was down in the kitchen myself that night. I saw blood and tears, that's all. That's all I saw. . . . Got anything to drink?"

Miss Small sighed. "Brandy," she said. She reached into the desk and hunted out the bottle. "It isn't very good brandy, but it's all I can offer. I'm sorry. Will it be all right?"

"Sure."

"I'll wash out the glasses." Miss Small went into the tiny bathroom and returned. "Anything new on Lillian Harris, Monny?"

"She's all right."

"That's good. . . . Here, Monny. Don't spill."

Miss Brady raised her glass with a flourish that called for applause. It was one of the old gestures. Miss Small promptly laughed.

"Clown!" Miss Small said.

"Sure. . . . But you're holding back. Aren't you going to join me, as the etiquette books don't say?"

"I'm not holding back," Miss Small said. "Not me. . . . But you know I hate this stuff. I always have. I really do hate it, Monny."

"I know. Me too."

They touched their glasses, held them high and smiled. "After this, beddy-bye," Miss Small said.

There was a shout, the world rocked, and Miss Brady fell to the floor. Her mouth was bleeding where a hand had struck her. Foy's hand. Foy's. His square hands were on her shoulders, gripping, not hurting, lifting her up. He was lifting her up and talking to someone across the room. He was talking to East. She was surrounded by men who looked like Foy and East; a wall of men, crowding, pressing close.

She put her hands to her head; she had hurt her head. I fell, she said to herself, I remember falling. He struck me, he struck the glass out of my hand and I fell.

"Why did you do that?" she asked vaguely.

Foy's answer came from a distance, although he was standing beside her.

"Because there was cyanide in your drink," he said. Cyanide. Cyanide. Now where——?

"Easy does it, Miss Brady. Easy now. It's all over."

"Cyanide," she repeated fretfully. "I had some once." The room was filled with the sound of tramping feet. . . . Tramp, tramp, tramp, the boys are marching. . . . "I had some, I had some once. But I threw it away. I gave it to——"

She raised her eyes and looked at Foy and East. East turned away.

The night came back like thunder, the hour, the minutes, the last words. "It's all I can offer. I really do hate it, Monny. I always have." The beloved voice. Returning like an echo.

Then East's voice, living, close beside her. "I tried to tell you."

She couldn't see his face, her eyes were blind with remembering. He had tried to tell her what the end would be. He had said, "If she can't have what she wants, nobody can."

"Oh no," she cried. "Not to me!"

Little by little he told Roberta.

Foy had watched the door himself, waiting for the house to grow quiet. But when he saw Brady go in, he began to worry. He thought of all the things that could happen, a tip-off, suicide, poison, and he moved in closer. He heard them talking. Talk, just talk. And then they had laughed. Together. He hadn't liked the sound of that, so he'd signaled to the nearest man on duty, and the signal had traveled up and down the stairs from floor to floor. After that it had been a near thing. In time, he had heard the clink of glasses. In time, he had reached Brady. But only Brady.

Roberta shivered. "Bad."

He went on, quoting fragments of his first interview with Plummer. "Miss Plummer unconsciously gave us the answer when she told Brady that Small went down to the kitchen when the chef was hurt. That didn't say anything to me, I'd heard it before, from Small herself, when I was interviewing Minnie May. But it said a lot to Brady. I saw how she looked at Plummer. She looked like somebody getting a preview of hell. You see, she knew Small hadn't gone. She'd been there herself, the whole time, so she knew. . . . A few hours later everything broke and Norman Crawford and Clara mopped it up."

"Mark, has anyone said anything about suspecting her?"

"Not in words. But when Foy and I left, we met Kitty Brice in the lobby and she didn't look crushed. . . . It was a made-to-order job from the start. When Small went to Hope House as a boarder, she couldn't face the character investigation they required. So she turned on the charm and the grave, sweet talk about private rights and the un-American way. Brady was enchanted. Right off the bat she gave our girl a job, and the reference rule was tossed out. Our girl climbed up and up. When Ruth Miller came on the scene, she was pretty close to the top of her world, and she wasn't climbing down. So Ruth had to go. Ruth's fear was too obvious, the story was bound to come out eventually."

Roberta said gently, "Poor Ruth."

Mark saw the woman he had left only a short time before, slumped in a chair, looking at the drift of torn paper on the floor. Letters, notes, travel folders——

He answered Roberta, but to himself. He said, Poor Monny.

For a complete list of books available from Penguin in the United States, write to Dept. DG, Penguin Books, 299 Murray Hill Parkway, East Rutherford, New Jersey 07073.

For a complete list of books available from Penguin in Canada, write to Penguin Books Canada Limited, 2801 John Street, Markham, Ontario L3R 1B4.

If you live in the British Isles, write to Dept. EP, Penguin Books Ltd, Harmondsworth, Middlesex.